Sato Family,

Born in Fukushima, Japan, Kunio Yamagishi graduated from Hosei University, Tokyo, and immigrated to Canada. He worked at the Consulate General of Japan in Toronto, also in Toronto, Tokyo, and New York's Wall Street as an investment banker.

His publications include short stories, magazine articles, and academic translation work.

Happy reading!

Kunio Yamag

Dedication

To: the Issei and Nisei,

Yoshiko Yamagishi, and

Kyuji Yamagishi

Kunio Yamagishi

THE RETURN OF A
SHADOW

AUSTIN MACAULEY PUBLISHERS™

LONDON • CAMBRIDGE • NEW YORK • SHARJAH

Front cover photo: Yoichi Haruta
Back cover photo: courtesy of Cumberland Museum

A CIP catalogue record for this title is available from the British Library.

ISBN 9781786937155 (Paperback)
ISBN 9781786937162 (E-Book)
www.austinmacauley.com

First Published (2018)
Austin Macauley Publishers Ltd.
25 Canada Square
Canary Wharf
London
E14 5LQ

Acknowledgements

If an era has a spirit, for good or ill, it is to elucidate its characters per se, and I thought that it was my part to put it down in writing as a story. I wrote this humble work in the hope of dedicating it to the Issei and old Nisei, who experienced the internment camps and relocation, as a paean and eulogy. They went through the series of heartrending and deplorable incidents, yet overcame those adversities and rose again.

My interviews include Takeo Nakano, Takaaki Kitamura, Dr. Michiko (Midge) Ayukawa and Masao Aida, who all were interned in Canada during World War II.

Maya Koizumi had a number of interviews with the internee Issei and Nisei and let me use her unreleased tapes for this story. Those interviewees were: Sigeru Sakamoto, Koichiro Okihiro, Tokiichi Tanaka, Saitaro Hama, Bunichi Takahashi, Nobuyuki Ichikawa, Betty Kobayashi, Hideo Kokubo, Junji Ito, Tatsuhiko Sonoda, and many others.

Dr. Lynne van Luven, former Associate Dean of the Faculty of Fine Arts, University of Victoria, gave me a useful guidance as to how to write fiction.

Dr. Toyomasa Fuse, Lois Fuse, Joy Kogawa and Nancy MacDonald gave me constant support and encouragement, as did all members of the Comox Valley Writers' Society.

R. Adam Robinson did an initial edit of my story.

Walter Stephenson, Hayley Knight, Kristen Jolly, Larch Gallagher, Matthew Smith and others at Austin Macauley Publishers Ltd. helped me finalize this book.

Lastly but not least, my wife, Margot, who assisted me in critiquing and editing of this novel.

I would sincerely like to give thanks to all of the persons mentioned above.

Kunio Yamagishi

Contents

Prologue

His name was Eizo Osada. I was never acquainted with Eizo personally; only saw him talking with my colleagues over the protective glass wall at the Japanese Consulate General in Toronto. No doubt everyone has some experience meeting someone who leaves him or her with an unforgettable impression even if it was a brief glimpse. It was that sort of encounter. Eizo was modestly attired with a black hat and black overcoat, and two deep wrinkles ran between his eyebrows; a shadowy figure amplified by his solitary and dispirited demeanor. He appeared to be a man haunted by a nightmare, or as if he had perpetrated an unforgivable crime in the past and was tormented by his guilty conscience. His image was etched in my head like a shadowgraph, and as a natural consequence I asked one of my colleagues who he was and what his story was. The colleague told me that Eizo Osada had gone through the internment camp in Canada during the Second World War and was returning to Japan to reunite with his family but great uncertainty lay ahead of him. Eizo's letters to his wife had been unanswered for more than twenty years.

Several decades later, I attended the ninetieth birthday celebration of another Nikkei and unexpectedly heard the story of Eizo Osada from the party's host, who had been in the same internment camp as Eizo. By then, Eizo had passed away, and the tale of his life deeply impressed me. I felt it was more than a strange coincidence and decided to follow his path, dredge up his history and reconstruct the extraordinary life of the man. According to the party's host, Eizo's dream to reunite with his family after his four decades of solitary life in Canada had been shattered like a sand castle flattened by a single wave. I set about documenting his life in the manner of a disciple to an ascetic Buddhist monk, painstakingly tracing the road his master had suffered.

My research took me many places. However, the insights of Martin Sato, whom Eizo wished had been his own son, were treasured. Martin was a soft spoken and sedate grey-haired high-school chemistry teacher, now retired, who lived in North York, Toronto. His candid talk about the latter half of Eizo's life dispelled any previous concern I might have had that he would not be willing to share the full story of Eizo with me. "It was one dark spot in Canadian history for sure," Martin said. "I'll tell you Eizo-san's story so that you can tell your readers that we should never let an incident like the unjust, deplorable treatment of the Nikkei happen again." And he started telling me this story.

Soon after the meeting, feeling obliged to witness Eizo's tombstone in Cumberland, I flew to Victoria and took Route One north from the British Columbia capital. Alongside the car, the rippled surface of Georgia Strait glittered like the silver scales of a huge fish, reminding me of Eizo's fragile life.

I arrived in Cumberland; a once-thriving coal mining town and one of the many Japanese settlements that are now all but gone from Western Canada. The curator of the Cumberland Museum took me to the Japanese cemetery, a secluded place surrounded by mature firs. The cemetery had been vandalized after the Nikkei were interned and the tombstones scattered. Since then, the headstones had been

12

gathered together to form a sort of cairn. Several metres away, Eizo's tombstone, still gleaming, stood alone under the shade of the trees. It was slightly less than one metre high, slim and made of granite, in contrast to the rest of the old moss-covered tombstones. The way the tombstone lay was symbolical of his solitary life. I instinctively prayed for his soul to rest in peace.

We then went to the site of Japanese town, Number 1 Mine, called Jap-Town, where there was nothing but a field of scattered trees, shrubs and few shards of Japanese dishware in the dirt. Witnessing that, my heart was choked with images of the thirty-one families from the town that were forcibly uprooted and shipped first to the Hastings Park detention centre in Vancouver, and then on to one of the internments camps in the interior of British Columbia after the Pacific War broke out. Some Japanese Canadians were given only a few hours' notice to pack their belongings and evacuate to the detention centre. At the centre of Number 1 Mine town stood an old cherry tree with its branches now hanging half-dead. I imagined the community at its peak; Japanese miners and their families holding *hanami,* flower-viewing parties, sharing a picnic lunch and *saké* under the branches of a young cherry tree. I pictured Eizo, too, being there, enjoying those warm spring days. Of that, though, there was no sign.

No longer were Eizo's experiences mere points in history; I felt as if he were imploring me to tell his story. I have written the following story to shed light on the shadow of Eizo's life; to bring a voice to the old memories before they, too, are swept away by the winds of time.

Glossary

Nikkei – People of Japanese origin
Issei – The first-generation Japanese
Nisei – The second-generation Japanese
Sansei – The third-generation Japanese
Tabi – Japanese style socks to wear with kimono
Geta – Wooden clogs
Nappa – Chinese cabbage
Irasshaimase! – Welcome!
Noren – A shop curtain
Monpe – Women's work clothes
Okyaku-san! – Mr.! or Ms.!
Anime – Animation cartoon
Tokonoma – An alcove
Ikebana – Flower arrangement
Hanafuda – A Japanese version of the card game trump
Onigiri – A rice ball
Inochi no sentaku – Recreation of one's life
Kunimono – People from the same prefecture
Nomiya – Bar
Dōhō – Compatriot
Goshin'ei – The photo of the Emperor
Tenno – Emperor
Naginata – A sword with a long handle
Katsudon – Pork cutlet on a bowl of ric

Part I — Canada

1
December 1977, Toronto

Stepping out of an elevator on the twenty-third floor of a downtown skyscraper, Eizo Osada looked uncertainly right and left and saw the sign for the Consulate General of Japan on a black steel door. He approached the imposing door, making sure his hat was still on, and pushed the buzzer mounted on the wall. Buried in worries, he tried to sort out his story rationally, but it was a daunting task. He sought the clues to solve the matter of his family's break in contact, but never found the right answer to it. The answers he thought of were contradictory to each other.

A few moments later, a uniformed Caucasian guard with a gun on his belt admitted him to the Consulate.

Inside, a glass wall screened off the reception counter and several civil servants were working behind the partition. A Japanese female clerk in her mid-twenties, with well-combed bobbed hair, stood up and came forward. Seeing her approaching, Eizo took his hat off and put it on the counter.

"Hello, how may I help you?" she greeted him in English.

How am I going to explain to her? Eizo faltered, despite the fact that he had been considering his situation carefully for a long time. He thought his life was too intricate to tell in a few words, but tried to explain his seventy years of struggle—mostly in a foreign land—in a way she could understand. His tongue twisted. Taking the simplest route, he gave his name to the clerk.

"Ah, Osada-san," the clerk switched to Japanese.

"Well," he said, patting on the chest of his overcoat to make sure his passport was in the inside pocket. "I want to go home."

"To Japan, you mean?" she asked over the glass.

"Yes, that's right. My supervisor, Donald McCord, called your office last week."

"Yes, McCord-san phoned us regarding your situation."

"I'm grateful." Muttering, he put his hand into the pocket and removed a paper bag, from which he withdrew a black-covered passport, as if handling a piece of fragile porcelain.

"Let me see," she said.

He slid the document under the glass.

"This was issued before the Second World War by the Government of the Empire of Japan," she said, inspecting the worn-out passport. "What do you want to do with this?"

"To go home, I need to renew my passport. Isn't that right?"

"Yes, that's right. To renew your passport, you need your family registration paperwork."

"But … sorry, I don't have it with me." Eizo grimaced and watched the clerk, who was turning the pages of his passport. She said nothing.

"… In the past year, I've written twice to Kino—that's my wife's name—asking her to send the paperwork, but she hasn't sent it to me. My son …" He hesitated. He had told the clerk more than he had intended, knowing it was entirely his family's problem, yet trying to make his case. Eizo had hoped to get a new passport issued with a family registration document Kino would send, and reunite with her and their three sons in Japan. If Kino had been too frail to go to the

18

town office and get the paperwork, at least his eldest son, Isoshichi, could have sent it to him. He had heard nothing from either her or his son. He blushed for shame and just managed to stand straight.

The clerk was silent, waiting.

"Actually, I waited for about a half year and then asked them to send the documentation again, but nothing came." Shivers gripped him. He involuntarily straightened his back against the anxiety again.

The clerk still stared at his passport, without blinking.

"I've no idea what my family is thinking," he said, forcing a smile, but troubled with the terrifying thought that his wife and sons might have already abandoned him. *No, no* ... He denied the thought and clung to his dream that his family was still waiting for his return to live happily together, as they had before. But another suspicion crept into his mind. *Is their silence a message of their refusal for my homecoming? Although called husband and father, I was that in name only. Who the hell leaves one's family for forty-three years, without seeing them, even once?* He felt like he was standing on the edge of an abyss, and his smile was all that was saving him from falling.

"How many sons do you have?" the receptionist asked, looking up from the passport. Eizo thought she sounded hopeful, which made him feel slightly better.

"Three. Although I say sons, my eldest is fifty years old now. My second and third are over forty. Everyone is on their own. My eldest son's name is Isoshichi."

Eizo had named his first son Isoshichi, meaning 'Fifty-seven', hoping that his son would one day exceed Isoroku Yamamoto, a star commander in the Japanese Imperial Navy, whose first name meant 'Fifty-six'. At the time, he had had no idea that Yamamoto would later become a Japanese

Naval Marshal General and lead the attack on Pearl Harbor, the event that had changed Eizo's life forever. But according to Kino, Isoshichi had not become a star commander; but worked at the local Agricultural Co-operative Association delivering fertilizer and other goods to the townspeople.

"What about your wife?" the clerk asked, "Does she know you want to return home?"

"My wife? Of course, well … I think so. It's been twenty-three years since she last wrote to me. But I kept writing to her." Once he had cleared the first hurdle, keeping his problems to himself, the second one was easier to jump across, and now he began revealing more of his family circumstances.

In the letter, Kino wrote that the reconstruction of Japan after the war had been extremely slow, work was hard to find, and she had asked him to stay in Canada and continue sending money to her and their three sons. Though the letter disheartened him, he accepted its contents. Eizo did not know that letter would be her last. Afterwards, Isoshichi's wife, Fumi, had sent him the family news several times. According to Fumi, Kino was fine but sometimes forgot important things. Fumi's last letter had arrived ten years ago.

"Did your wife not say anything about the registration?" the clerk asked.

"Kino? No … I think my wife would be too old to go to the town office herself. If I weren't in the concentration camp, my situation would've been much different …"

"I'm sorry to hear that," she said. "But we'll need your family registration before we're able to issue you a new passport. Moreover …"

"Does that mean I can't go back home?" Eizo cut in.

"No, but one issue needs to be cleared up."

"What is it?" Eizo asked anxiously, bending forward.

"According to McCord-san, you have acquired Canadian citizenship, and therefore your nationality is now Canadian. Is that correct?"

"Yes. Is something wrong with that?"

"In that case, even if you have your family registration, in accordance with Japanese law, you cannot also retain Japanese citizenship."

"What do you mean? Why?"

"Japanese law stipulates that one automatically loses one's Japanese nationality if one becomes a citizen of another country."

"Well ... then, I'm no longer Japanese?" Eizo felt something collapse inside him. It was far beyond his imagination that he had been separated not only from his family but also from his beloved native country. He simply gazed at her, hoping she would correct him with, 'It was my mistake, Osada-san.' Instead she said nothing. He recalled that Donald McCord had used an expression that sounded like 'lost your nationality' last week, but he had failed to understand because of his poor English. Once again, he wished he had made better progress at the English night school.

"So, I can't switch my old passport to a new one?" He put his hand to his forehead and stroked it several times with his fingers.

"No, you cannot."

"So, I'm not Japanese by law, even if my wife and sons live in Japan?" He felt the hollow inside him expanding rapidly, as if rippling out in waves.

"Just a moment, please," the clerk said, leaving her seat and taking his passport with her.

If my family doesn't accept me upon my return to Japan, I might have to come back to Canada. No, I could build a shack on my property not far away from their house, watching for a chance that they'd change their minds one day. Ah, hell! That'd be pathetic!

Without any thread of connection, Eizo's thoughts drifted back to the snowy night the previous year when Gus, a young Greek immigrant co-worker at the Hi-Lite Soft Drink Company, had driven him around Rosedale, a high-class residential neighbourhood in Toronto, to view the Christmas decorations. Lights on the trees and houses cast colourful tints on yards covered with snow. It was an ethereal beauty. Near the end of their circuit, Eizo had noticed a small boy sitting in a window. Under a warm interior light and a decorated Christmas tree, the boy watched the street, leaning his forehead close to the glass. Eizo imagined he was waiting for his father to come home, and asked Gus to stop so that he could look at the boy for a while. When he had left Japan, his second son, Tamotsu, was around this boy's age. Eizo could not contain his tears. When the boy walked away from the window, Gus started the car without a word. Eizo thought of how long he had stayed in Canada without seeing his family. *How many times have I told you not to dwell on those days?*

"Hello Osada-san, I'm Arai." The man with a round, boyish face, spoke to him from behind the glass. "I heard about your situation from McCord-san. You want to go back to Japan?"

"Yes." Eizo felt a surge of optimism, as if turning a new page. Some new developments might occur.

"I understand that you have acquired Canadian citizenship," Arai said, making doubly sure before saying anything meaningful.

"Yes, I took it some time ago."

"What she said to you is right," Arai said looking at the female clerk first and then at Eizo. "By acquiring Canadian citizenship, you lost your Japanese nationality."

Eizo stared blankly at Arai, waiting for him to say something more positive.

"Didn't McCord-san explain it to you?"

Eizo apparently had not understood the legal ramifications that Donald had described in English. "Well, then, even if I had a copy of my family registration, it wouldn't have made any difference."

"That's correct," Arai said.

Eizo was at his wit's end. *Why does everything go in the wrong direction? But, no, things are not that simple.*

Whether his family had known the legal ramification or not, the fact that they had neglected his request was his family's response without question. Now finally he saw the devastating truth that was hidden beneath the silence of his family. Although he was clouded by suspicion about his family's silence from time to time—however deep it was— it had remained only a doubt, since his judgement was biased by his deep love towards them. Until now he could not believe they could be so cruel. An obscure black spot of doubt had taken definite shape. His right cheek cramped.

If my family had difficult times during my absence from Japan, then I had a much more difficult time in Canada. Who do they think has been working overseus all this time enduring the treatment the Nikkei received and still managed to send money home? I wanted to be with them all this time. That was the only dream I carried with me.

"Well, anyway," said Arai, "you're a Canadian by law, so we can't issue a Japanese passport to you. If you're going back to Japan, you can go on a Canadian passport. If you decided to stay there with your family for good, then you can make an application for naturalization while you're there. It seems a bit complicated, but that's the way you must go about it."

"If I go to Japan on a Canadian passport, how long can I stay there?" asked Eizo.

"You can stay for three months without a visa."

"A visa for Japan?" Eizo was dumbfounded, scratching his forehead. "But I'm Japanese."

"Sorry to say this, but you are not, at least legally speaking," Arai said. "Also, if you're going to stay longer than that, you'll need to apply to the Japanese authorities to extend your stay. Under your circumstances," he continued, "an extension would probably not be a problem. But there's also another way. If you're going to visit your immediate family, you can stay a little longer, but you'll need a letter from your family. But, of course, in your case …"

Eizo tried to say something, but he could not find the right words.

"After arriving in Japan, you'll also have to register as an alien at the nearest municipal office," said Arai.

"Eh, register as an alien?" Eizo could not conceal his bewilderment and disbelief.

"Yes, unfortunately that's the case. If you go with a foreign passport, this is what is required."

"… I see. I think I've got it. I was wondering, no, I don't know …" Eizo said. The habit of talking to himself was getting worse as he got older. He struggled to avoid the embarrassment of having Arai respond to his internal dialogue. Living in solitude for so long, Eizo had become his own best friend, as there was no one else to make him laugh or cry or sigh or whistle and sing or feel anger or sadness or happiness or joy. Many times he had felt the urge to say

'Hello' to total strangers on the streets and, now he would be a foreigner when he went home.

Six months after Kino's last letter, twenty-three years ago, he had lent his savings to a man who worked beside him at the soft drink company and who suffered from acute renal failure. His co-worker had said his doctor had told him that the disease was curable, and he promised to pay the money back within two years. Kino's response for his returning home was negative anyway, and, judging from his experience in Canada, the prospect of obtaining a new job in Japan at his age without any notable skill looked bleak. Since he had no immediate possibility of returning to Japan, he decided to lend the money to help his friend, but two and a half years later, the borrower had passed away without repaying the loan.

Eizo had to put off his plan to return home, and started saving money again by leading an extremely frugal life. He had also reached the age at which he had to worry about his retirement. So Eizo kept saving what he could and sending money to his family twice a year, while time slipped by. A year slid into two years, two into three, and finally into twenty-three years. When he looked back at those past years, there was only a dull waft of futility, distress and remorse.

"Would you mind waiting for a moment?" Arai said and left.

Eizo felt a little uneasy talking to the young clerk about his situation. "When I didn't receive the support I expected from my family, I felt terribly upset."

"I should think so," the clerk sympathized, furrowing her brow. "How is Mrs. Osada? Is she well?"

"Kino?" Eizo asked, "I think she is fine, but ..." He was ashamed to admit that he did not know.

25

"You have three sons. You don't have to worry, do you?" the clerk said, forcing a smile only on her mouth.

"Of my three sons, the second one has a very gentle temperament and he wouldn't kill an insect. His name is Tamotsu; surely he'll look after me when I get back home."

When his sons were young, Isoshichi was the most mischievous. He used to snatch insects from Tamotsu and trample them under his feet making his brother cry. Once, he caught a snake and skinned the poor creature and on another occasion had pumped air into a frog's stomach, using a bicycle pump. He had enjoyed doing those things. Sometimes, Isoshichi was so absorbed in plotting something that he even forgot to eat. His younger brother was never strong enough to challenge him. Eizo thought fondly of Tamotsu. He did not really know much about his third son, Kozo, who had been only two years old when he left for Canada. According to a letter from Kino, he was a quiet and highly sensitive child, easily frightened by even the smallest sound in the night. Eizo was worried if Kozo was bullied by Isoshichi, and suspicious that his absence from his family was the sole cause of Kozo's sensitivity and personality. He used to blame himself for his third son's cowardliness.

"I'm sorry to keep you waiting." Arai returned to the front with an expression that told Eizo he did not bear any good news. "I checked again, but it's just as I said."

The protective glass wall seemed suddenly to be thick and domineering over Eizo. "I see. It's troublesome."

"Pardon me?" Arai said.

"No, nothing. I talked to myself. When you get old, you develop odd habits that you're not even aware of."

"… And since you have acquired Canadian citizenship, you have to renounce your Japanese citizenship."

"Renounce my Japanese citizenship?" said Eizo.

26

"Yes, as I explained, you lost your Japanese citizenship." Arai's face turned into a worried look, but he continued, "you need to sign a form formally renouncing your Japanese citizenship."

"… That doesn't hinder me from returning and living in Japan, though, does it?" Eizo managed to ask one more question. Japanese citizenship had been his last bulwark to protect himself from the cold reality of society.

"No, it doesn't."

"I see," Eizo said blankly.

"Osada-san, do you have any other questions?" Arai meant to show kindness.

"No, I don't think so."

Taking his reading glasses from his pocket, Eizo helplessly followed the procedure of officially renouncing his Japanese citizenship. He tucked his glasses into the pocket again and gave the signed paper back to the clerk, who was holding his passport. She took a final look at his worn-out black document in her hand. His business at the Consulate General was done. He put his hat on. Then, another male civil servant came into the visa section and stopped briefly. Eizo noticed the man looking at him in a deeply impressive manner, but then saw him walk by, behind Arai and the clerk.

"When are you going back to Japan?" Arai asked Eizo.

"Probably next spring. I've many things to do before I leave."

"McCord-san seems to be a very kind man."

"Yes, he is. I'm lucky to know him. I'm ashamed to admit it, but English is difficult to learn. He's very patient to listen to me."

"Actually, I found it pretty hard to learn English too— the spelling of words, those irregular verbs and tons of idiomatic expressions!" Arai laughed, showing his slightly irregular teeth.

"Is that right? Even for young people like you?"

"If I have to speak proper English, it's not that easy. First, I have to think what I'm going to say. It's not like speaking Japanese. If I speak English as it's taught in a Japanese school, Canadians don't understand me. If I make a mess of the pronunciation and say something in a hodgepodge-way, people usually understand. Bizarre, isn't it?" Arai smiled, blinking his eyes a couple of times.

Eizo thanked them and left the Consulate General feeling that a part of his heart had been torn out.

2
Birth of a Shadow

As Eizo pushed the heavy revolving door of the building and stepped outside, he was hit hard by the cold again and inundated with the noise from King Street. He could not yet fully grasp what had happened to him at the Consulate General and looked up at the white building towering above him in front.

The weather had changed and clouds, the colour of old cotton, were hanging onto the top of the high-rise buildings. People with overcoats were moving along fast; a steady stream of cars and trucks rushed past. Union Station was a couple of blocks away, but he did not feel like walking outside.

There's no need to hurry. I heard from the clerk that there was an underground passage.

Following other people and descending to the underground level by escalator, he heard a loud version of 'Away In A Manger' echoing down the corridor. It was a Salvation Army band; a female and four male musicians in dark blue uniforms were making an ear-splitting sound with a trumpet, trombone, tuba and baritone horn. Eizo hesitated, but stopped in front of them, drew a five-dollar bill from his wallet carefully, smoothed it down and slipped it into the donation kettle.

"Thank you very much. Have a nice day!" said the young woman, still ringing her sleigh bell.

"Thank you," Eizo said, hesitantly smiling back. He left the spot quickly as though ashamed, but his mood lightened a little. He was thankful to have been recognised as a good citizen, as opposed to an 'enemy alien', which Japanese were branded during the previous world war.

In the underground mall many items were on sale for Christmas. As he had to buy souvenirs for his family, he kept looking around for something suitable, but nothing caught his eye. To begin with, he had no clue what would be appropriate for Kino and his sons. His wife would soon be seventy years old and his three sons were no longer at an age where they would enjoy knick-knacks. Nor did Eizo know exactly how many grandchildren he had. *Darn it!* He knew that his eldest son and daughter-in-law, Isoshichi and Fumi, had a baby boy, but that news from Kino came twenty-three years ago. After that, according to a letter written by Fumi, they had another son.

Ta! You don't know how many grandchildren you have. Shame on you! His shadow reproached him. *How could you have let things slip this far? You should've done something before it became this bad.*

Eizo shrugged his shoulders, a habit he had acquired while living in Canada. After the release from the concentration camp, he had hidden himself under the veil of a hesitant smile and a bewildered polite mask, as if nothing dreadful had happened in the wartime, suppressing his true nature and thoughts in an effort to avoid conflict with *hakujin*, white, society. *What rights do we have against the white society? They always win and we have to lump it.* He had never thought of the act of complaining or protesting about how the Nikkei were treated before, during and after

30

the war. To him, it was altogether a shame to tell those stories to the persons of other ethnic groups. *Be a shadow. Wear a mask of an ambiguous smile and hide yourself behind it. Then, everybody thinks that you're a model citizen. That's a wise man's advice for you. That means not to tell anyone how you feel and reveal any weakness,* the shadow warned him.

However, loneliness was his arch enemy. Having been a shadow from the society created another deeper shadow within himself. It was a creation due to an extremely long, solitary life he had spent in the huge, inhumane city. The shadow acted as a friend to talk to when he felt lonely, consult with when in trouble, and comfort when in despair: a faithful and indispensable companion who gave advice when he made mistakes and rebuked him for his thoughtlessness. It was created out of necessity. It was his other self and his salvation. To his surprise, the shadow even smiled back at him. This illusive, yet persistent part of Eizo, never twisted his arm against his will.

Sometimes Eizo had nightmares about the freezing nights in the concentration camp when he did not have enough blankets and lay all through the cold night worrying about his family living halfway around the world and what the next day would bring. Other times, dreams of the endless flow of empty bottles at the soft drink factory made him sit up sweating in bed. At those times, the shadow consoled him, touching his heart gently and soothing his mind tenderly.

Unable to find gifts for his family, Eizo got into Union Station located at the end of the underground corridor and took the next train that slid into the platform. It was at around eleven thirty in the morning and the subway was not crowded. He took a seat nearby the door, placed both hands

31

on his lap demurely but was still troubled by his family's disregard for his request. That worry did not leave him alone, coming back to his mind like waves breaking on the shore. In front of him was an elderly *hakujin* woman with a long neck like a crane's and next to her was seated a young man, reading a newspaper. Eizo took off his hat and saw that the sweatband was wet. He drew his handkerchief from his pocket and wiped his forehead. *Is this a cold sweat, or am I sweating due to my walk?* He did not and could not know.

Soon the train decelerated—he was now able to count the pillars at the centre of the tunnel—and finally stopped in between the stations. The interior lights flicked. The conductor made a short announcement through the PA system, which Eizo could not understand well. Eizo's anxiety lifted its head up and the moments of darkness pulled him back into his old memories.

In December 1941, right after the bombing of Pearl Harbor by the Japanese Imperial Navy, some Nikkei were scared of physical attacks by the *hakujin.* Eizo happened to be in Vancouver when the bombing was carried out and was extremely careful not to bring the *hakujin*'s hatred on himself. As the initial shock passed, he was seized with the terror of how serious the matter was. Canada and Japan, where his family lived, were at war. He had left the inn where he had stayed as if fleeing, deeply ashamed of the way the Japanese had bombed Hawaii. To him, it was a sly attack.

When walking down a street near the area called 'Little Tokyo', he noticed a young white man, over six feet tall, broad-shouldered and in a stained dark green parka. The fellow kept staring at Eizo as he walked closer. A couple of steps before they passed each other, the man shouted "Jap! Son of a bitch!" and raising his arm above his shoulder, swung at him. The fellow's bulky parka slowed the blow and

Eizo was able to dodge his fist by a hair. Taken aback by the unanticipated agility of Eizo, the man yelled "Shit!" at him and walked off. Overwhelmed by the man's force, Eizo scurried away, shaken, wary of his surroundings. He thought the eyes of Canadians contained the colour of censure and detestation against the Japanese.

Some old Issei, first generation Japanese, started having nightmares about the Vancouver incident of 1907 in which roughly a thousand white men out of eight thousand demonstrators demanded the exclusion of Orientals from British Columbia, and, led by the Asiatic Exclusion League, turned into a mob, rioting and smashing the glass store windows in Little Tokyo. Might such a time occur again? Eizo knew one young Nisei woman who used such extreme caution as to remove any black hair from the white bathroom sinks—no matter if the hair was hers or not—hoping not to inflame the *hakujin* hatred towards the Japanese.

Eizo involuntarily shook his head to throw off the image. Then realizing he was in the subway, holding his hat and handkerchief in each hand, he looked around to see if other passengers had noticed his strange pose and behaviour. The elderly white woman with the crane-like neck watched him, but looked away without changing her expression. The young man seated next to her kept reading a newspaper. No one in the car paid attention to him. Noticing he had unconsciously reacted in the old servile way, he regretted his act of looking around at the passengers. Eizo's experiences during the war were haunting and left ugly scars on his mind. Though Canadians' attitudes towards his people had changed, he still felt intimidated and his nervous smile revealed his uneasy emotion towards the *hakujin* society.

The train started slowly moving again. Taking an advantage of still being downtown, he decided to get off at the Eaton's Department Store which he thought was a good place to look for souvenirs. It was a lunch time and the mall was crowded with all ages, some holding shopping bags with 'Merry Christmas' in slanted, fancy letters. A giant balloon Santa Claus waved its hand to shoppers from the skylight. With yuletide music in the background, Eizo strolled through the department store. He did not like to think that the cost of the gift would determine how his family would receive him, but the presents should at least symbolize his thoughts towards his wife, sons and daughters-in-law. He wandered around to the handbag corner with a vague idea that he could give Kino a purse, perhaps something exquisite. Something made of alligator skin …

Are you crazy? His shadow picked at his shoulder again.

It seemed an ill-matched item since Kino had been farming all of her life in a small town, aged to the point she would not want anything fancy and probably never attended a party. There had never been a party in his hometown before he left Japan.

But, if I don't buy it now, she would never ever have a gorgeous handbag!

He walked up to the sales counter and, oblivious to the other customers, motioned to the sales clerk. "Uh …"

"Just one moment please, sir. It'll be your turn soon," said the clerk without looking at him, irritation evident in her voice.

Eizo shrank back, realizing his mistake, and started looking at handbags in the showcases. One item caught his eye, and he wanted to touch it with his hands. Beside him, several well-dressed women also bent over the counters. He bided his time listening to the Christmas music throughout the store. After a while another female sales clerk approached him.

34

"How can I help you?"

"Eh … I want a handbag, a party handbag, please," he said.

"One of these small evening bags? These are quite popular," the sales clerk said with a smile any saleswoman would show to her customers. "May I ask the age of the special lady?"

"About sevente …"

"Excuse me? Seventy?" exclaimed the clerk. Not missing a beat she deliberately opened her mouth a little bigger, pushed her face closer, and asked, "Or seventeen?"

"Uh, seven zero." Eizo could not hear the music anymore.

"Ah, seventy. All right," said the clerk. "Did you have one in mind?"

"That … please." Eizo pointed to one.

"The one with the alligator skin?" She removed the bag from the display and handed it to him. "How do you like that? Do you think your special lady will be happy with that evening bag?"

Eizo stroked the surface of the bag and had a pleasant feel. It was gleaming, sleek, firm, cold, rough yet delicate—a distinct feel of alligator skin. He suddenly felt elated as many women probably would. He turned the bag over but did not know if it would be appropriate for Kino who might be bent with hard field labour. He wavered.

"We don't carry many alligator evening bags." She saw him hesitating and said, "I'll see if we have any others."

While the sales clerk was gone, Eizo, holding the purse in his hands, looked at the other white, gold and silver evening bags on display. A tall woman wearing a thick application of makeup caught his attention. She was about Kino's age, wore a black fur coat and hat with a net veil that

35

partially covered her face; she was inspecting the golden evening bag. Eizo imagined that the woman lived a luxurious life. An enormous mansion, gorgeous limousines with chauffeurs, expensive wines, gracious dances, and sunny holidays. He had seen a similar looking woman in a Hollywood movie. The actress had worn a beautiful party dress and carried an alligator skin handbag. The elderly lady he was looking at probably wore fancy dresses and attended parties every day.

Poor Kino! I don't know if I ever made you happy.

"Sir, I've two evening bags of alligator skin."

Eizo was snapped back to reality by the clerk's voice. One bag was made of white leather bordered with alligator skin and the other was entirely made of alligator skin.

"This is a wonderful and elegant evening bag. It is first class. Look at this design," said the sales clerk.

Instead, he looked at the price tag. It was over three hundred dollars which was more than he had expected. He thought that Kino, being a woman, would appreciate the splendid evening bag but worried that she might be enraged; blame him for leaving her until she had become a withered, hunched-over old woman still working the fields, only to mock her with the unsuitable gift this late in her life.

Eizo cautiously took the brown evening bag into his hands and caressed it. Another euphoria enveloped him. He caught a glimpse of the lady with the black fur coat and veil. She was about to finish her payment for the golden purse, her eyes sparkling with joy behind the black veil. *She bought that purse!*

"I'll take this," said Eizo.

"Certainly, an excellent choice, sir. I'm sure the lady you give it to will be delighted."

Eizo carefully counted out twenty-dollar bills onto the counter and smoothed down the corner of the last bill. The clerk flashed her diplomatic smile once again and went to the cash register. Feeling more confident, he went to the cosmetic department, bought Chanel No. 5 for his sons' wives and asked a sales clerk to put them in small individual bags. He still had to buy gifts for his sons and grandchildren but was already tired; it could wait for another day. He went to a restaurant in the store and, after a late lunch, headed for home. On the way, he thought about looking at the alligator purse once he arrived at his apartment, and hoped that the gift would appease any negative thoughts Kino might have of him.

3
Kino's Last Letter

Eizo's cramped apartment was located in an old brick building and had been his home for nearly eighteen years. The walls had cracks running through them, the windows were held in by rotting wooden frames and paint was partially peeled off, but it was his and he was used to it. He had seen neither young residents nor children in the building, except one family with a small girl, whom Eizo knew little of. The girl hid herself behind her mother whenever she saw Eizo.

Having unlocked the entrance glass door with an effort, he checked his mailbox located at a corner of the hall near the staircase. It was the type of mailbox where a mailman was able to open all residents' boxes with a master key where faded typed names were displayed on some.   *Empty!*

Anxious for some words from home, he had fallen into the habit of checking the mailbox when he returned from work. A surge of fatigue caught up with him; his family and the whole world had forgotten him—perhaps a long time ago.

He dragged himself up the narrow stairway—he could not see any colour on the faded carpet anymore—, arrived at his room and inserted the key. The lock was old and difficult to open, unless he pulled the door toward him while turning the key. He had asked the apartment owner to fix the problem several times, but Tim only repeated that Eizo had to know how to handle it. 'If you treat the lock gently, like you treat a woman, it will open by itself, you know. Otherwise it will be stubborn, you know.' Tim always said this with a suggestive smile and a wink at the end of each sentence. Eizo never had much to say in reply. He was afraid Tim was going to suggest that he didn't know how to handle a woman.

The room was dark, which he did not like, but that was offset by the cheap rent. Eizo turned the entrance light on and looked into the mirror hung on the entrance wall; his shadow looked back at him.

"I'm home, safe and sound." He felt the fatigue run through his body again.

Welcome back. His shadow replied.

He took his shoes off. The familiar scene greeted him. The kitchen and living room in one, piled jackets on a chair, the faded curtains, the sofa stained and worn and the ancient black and white television covered in a thick layer of dust. Old Japanese weeklies were scattered about, and most depressing of all was the telephone that rarely rang. There was a scratched desk against the wall near the window decorated with a family photo as if to greet him. Eizo and his family had their picture taken by the professional photographer in Minokamo City, the nearest city to his hometown, prior to his voyage to Canada. The picture was badly faded and had yellowed over the years.

"I'm exhausted." Eizo took off his overcoat, sat heavily on the sofa and lit a cigarette. All was quiet, except for the occasional car horn and children shouting somewhere outside. Though there was no wind, the smoke of his cigarette rose in the air as if it were some sort of creature without a spine. He took his time finishing it. The fatigue in his legs did not go away easily, but smoking calmed him as he reflected on the day's events. Visiting the Japanese Consulate General did not solve any of his problems, but at least it played a part in putting them in order. In any case, he would have to face the fact that he was no longer legally Japanese and he tried to take some meaning from the experience.

Eizo was about to light another cigarette, but remembered imposing a limit on himself of three cigarettes a day to save as much money as possible. Instead, he reached into the shopping bag and removed the evening bag with his clumsy hands. The alligator skin gleamed dully and no longer seemed to breathe as it did in the showcase. Suddenly, the tall woman in the black hat and veil in the department store came across his mind. She was like a gorgeous lily in full bloom just before it perishes. Her dreadful beauty lured men into acting absurdly and irrationally towards her. To partake in that momentary exquisiteness—even though men had been aware that it was a vice—was to leave the man having no choice but to follow her. The beauty of that flower would have brought the evening bag to life. He sighed with the thought.

Kino, you must have aged toiling the earth and raising three children alone.

He carefully put the purse down on the carpet, went to the desk and picked up the family photo and came back to the sofa. In the picture Eizo wore a suit and sat stiffly in the chair with tight lips, staring intensely at the camera. Kino sat beside him in a formal Japanese *kimono* with a pair of white *tabi* and *geta,* wooden clogs, on her feet. Kozo, who had just turned two, was on his mother's lap. Kino's face was young and fresh. Behind them Isoshichi and Tamotsu stood as though afraid of the camera.

Kino, I bought you an evening bag because I want you to be happy. I hope it doesn't cause you pain instead.

Eizo placed the picture on the sofa, leaned forward and held his head with both his hands placed on his thighs. What he knew of Kino was only the memory of her; there was nothing there to predict her reaction about his return. She might have changed into someone he no longer recognized or did not want to recognize. He caught his breath and suddenly broke down crying.

Kino, I'm sorry.

His shadow was there ready to console him.

Eizo, trying to stop himself from crying, put the evening bag back into the box and stowed it away in a colourful shopping bag imprinted with Christmas salutations. A lump remained in his throat and his eyes clouded. And yet, as the hot tears trickled down his face, his soul began to feel cleansed. Strange black spots appeared on his trousers where the tears fell.

There is no use doing this! His shadow prodded him not to dwell in remorse anymore.

Eizo stood up, hung up his overcoat, and changed his clothes. Then, like most nights, he felt an urge to read Kino's last letter once more. He gave in to his weakness and fetched the shoe box he kept important documents in and pulled out the partially-torn yellow envelope. His name and address were scratched in wavy English letters as if an earthworm had crawled across the face of the envelope. On the other side, Kino's name and address were written in Japanese. Eizo carefully plucked the letter out with trembling hands. The ink had faded and the sepia pages had lost their crispness. He traced Kino's inept handwriting line by line with his gnarled and tobacco stained fingers, tenderly, as though he was touching her hands.

November 28, 1954

Eizo-sama,

How are you faring over there? Isoshichi, Tamotsu, Kozo and I are all well.

The season where the red dragonflies fly high in the evening sky has come and gone. I am very busy in the fields. I have been tilling the mulberry fields. We could really use a second set of hands. But we did not have a good rice harvest this year.

Recently, there was a big uproar here because ashes have drifted in from the Bikini Atoll where America carried out a hydrogen bomb experiment. The ashes of the bomb also fell onto the crew of a tuna fishing vessel called the Fukuryu-maru No. 5. The crew suffered from atomic bomb syndrome and Kuboyama-san, their radio operator, became very ill and later died. It was big news in Japan. People here are really worried because the rain contains fallout from the blast like the Black Rain of Hiroshima. We have been told not to go out and not to get wet.

They say that the war in Korea boosted the Japanese economy, but that really only applies to larger cities. The price of goods has gone up so much and life for people has not been easy because of it. People are leaving for the cities looking for work. Even Genjiro-san and Shinsuke-san have left.

Murata-san came back from Canada and now is short of money. He had to leave again to work as a labourer. He said that he could make much more money in Canada than here. Everybody is having a hard time finding enough work. Even young people are finding it difficult to get work and many lay about unemployed. The only thing that the Pacific War brought us is lost factories and industries from the American bombing. No matter what we say there's not much we can do about it now. The reconstruction of Japan has been extremely slow, slower than a snail's pace. If you came home you would end up unemployed as well. We need money. It is best that you keep working in Canada and send us as much as you can. That would be the best way for us to continue to manage.

Isoshichi is doing well and is still working at the Agricultural Co-operative Association delivering fertilizer and other goods. Our grandson, Shoichi, is starting to get his front teeth now. Tamotsu is still working as a mechanic in Tokyo. He has been able to save a little money and is going to high school in the evenings. I have regretted not being able to afford to send him to high school. He sends me small amounts of money sometimes saying that this is pocket money. I am always moved to tears reading his letters.

Kozo is attending university in Tokyo and is now a fourth year student and trying to find a job. I hope he can find good employment. Times have changed, but it is still rare for a person from around here to go to a university. We are very proud of him.

I'm sorry for returning to the subject of our finances again, but we need money badly. As you know, the earnings Fumi and I make from the rice fields, sericulture, and Isoshichi's salary are not enough to provide for us as well as the cost of sending Kozo to university.

There is no job for you in Japan even if you come back now. Please stay in Canada and keep sending us money, as you have been doing. I ask you to do so from the bottom of my heart, since this is the best way for our family. All of us are depending on you and the money you send. Please do not worry about our health. We are doing well.

Take care of yourself,

Kino

Finishing the letter, Eizo lost himself in thought.

There was a time when Eizo had desperately searched for a clue in the letter that might indicate why his wife quit writing. He had read the letter over and over in a futile effort that simply led him back into the world of vain thought.

Kozo was already in his fourth year of university at the time Kino wrote her last letter and should have graduated the following year. According to Fumi's letter, Kozo graduated university the following year. Why then did Kino insist that they needed more money?

Thinking about it now, it was obviously a self-contradictory story. But, when he received the letter he never doubted or questioned its contents. This letter and the unpaid loan to his co-worker put his plan to return home off accordingly.

If not for this letter from Kino, I would have long since returned to Japan and been living happily with them. And although the time has now come to go back, they refuse to answer me.

Eizo felt exasperated and disappointed with how his family had treated him, but could not blame them completely. Apart from the time the Nikkei were detained at the concentration camps, he had been free to make his own

44

decisions. The Government of Canada had even questioned him in the camps about whether or not he would repatriate to Japan after the war. He had several opportunities to return to his family and it was he who had made the decision to stay.

Don't think like that! Don't blame yourself to that point!

It was getting fairly dark outside. Eizo could not hear the calls of children playing outside anymore and realized that the living room was dark. He stood up and turned the light on. The room was picked out by the unpitying brightness and seemed to reflect the state of his mind—messy, pathetic and lonely. Above all else, the soundless world inside the room isolated him from the world outside. He could not alter his past, but could he create a new future? However, his shadow comforted and contained him and left his future paralyzed in a monochrome of uncertainty. He was falling into a void.

Please, shadow, help me!

Eizo could barely move his body into the kitchen. The counter was bare and he did not own many utensils; he did not need them with his limited cooking repertoire. He skilfully sliced beef, onion and *nappa* and prepared a Japanese dish with rice. It was disappointingly tasteless, not at all what he had expected, but he forced himself to eat, as he abhorred waste. Most of the time, he could not name the dishes. They were his own nameless creations.

Later, Eizo felt like having a drink. He had once come close to becoming an alcoholic as he had kept liquor at home where the temptation was too strong to resist. It had been a struggle for him to return to the semblance of a normal life. After that, he had decided not to keep alcohol in the apartment and now whenever he felt like a drink, he made a habit of going out to a bar.

Still, in order not to spend money, the best way he found to restrain the need for alcohol was to stick to the television like a parasite. A fool who is not destined to change reality would rather avoid it than suffer the pain that comes from confronting it. At least life gave him that small bit of wisdom.

Although he wanted a drink, he did not feel like going out tonight. After listening to the idiot box blare its one-sided message and conversing with his shadow, he was soon exhausted and crawled into bed grateful the day had finally come to an end.

He slept the sleep of the dead.

4
Mr Donald McCord

The next morning Eizo went to work by bus under a murky winter sky. The Hi-Lite Soft Drink Company was located in a suburb far from the centre of Toronto. In the summer time, the neighbourhood surrounding the factory was a vivid array of green grass and colourful flowers but, as the winter came, nature painted the dead yellow grass a snowy white against the grey sky on the cold canvas of reality. Emerging from the bus, he instinctively pulled up his collar against the harshness of the winter chill.

The factory was busy with commuting workers and trucks transporting the bottled products and the materials. In the locker room Eizo changed into his uniform with the company logo and went to his assigned position. His job was to ensure the washing equipment for recycled bottles was working correctly and the flow of bottles was uninterrupted. Empty bottles passed through an endless cycle. Although another employee worked within several metres from him, the noise created by screaming bottles and biting machines isolated Eizo. Work like his was limited to those with neither trade skills nor English fluency; he had been doing this job for more than twenty years.

Four years after Eizo started working at the factory, he experienced a strange mental fatigue, an odd numbness in his hands and feet and an aching stomach. He was losing his appetite; his uniform and clothes hung loosely and his overcoat looked like he had borrowed it from a much larger man. He went for a medical examination, but the doctor could not find anything physically wrong, diagnosing him with depression and prescribed anti-depressants and exercise. It was then, three years later, after coming off medication that Eizo began to indulge in alcohol to numb the pain of his loneliness.

"Eizo." Someone called from behind loudly.

Eizo turned and faced Donald McCord who had been his supervisor for the past six years. Donald reminded him of a football player, with a thick neck, big hands and chest and nimble movements—despite his size—with sharp eyes. He knew Eizo's family situation well, sympathized and had befriended him.

"You went to the Japanese Consulate General yesterday, didn't you?" Donald asked, raising his voice so as not to be beaten by the barking sounds of the machinery and the screech of empty bottles.

"Yes, I did."

"How did it go?"

Momentarily, Eizo did not know how to answer him.

"Did you get a new passport?"

"No," Eizo answered bluntly.

"No? You didn't get it?" Donald's eyes widened as if he had digested something indigestible and his eyebrows shot up. "Wait." He disappeared around the machinery and soon came back with someone to watch the machines, then took Eizo down to the cafeteria. It was an early hour and only a handful of other workers were there. Eizo could hear the cooks banging pots, cutting vegetables, scraping cauldrons and shouting to each other. He sat down at one of the tables near the entrance while Donald went to the serving counter and came back with two cups of coffee.

"You didn't get your Japanese passport yesterday … eh?"

"That's right … I'm not a Japanese, no more!"

Eizo explained what had happened at the Consulate General. Donald listened carefully, frowning from time to time as he tried to understand Eizo's broken English.

"So, you'll have to go to Japan carrying a Canadian passport."

"That's right."

"That's not too bad, is it, huh?" Donald suggested. "When you applied for Canadian citizenship, didn't you think that one day you'd be going to Japan as a Canadian?"

Eizo was unsure how to answer the question. The main reason he became a Canadian after he moved to Ontario from the concentration camp in British Columbia was as a precaution against further imprisonment. Of course, even Japanese who were born in Canada—Canadian citizens who had never been to Japan—had also been put into the concentration camps as 'enemy aliens'. So applying for Canadian citizenship was, in itself, neither an answer to nor a precaution against discrimination, but after the war Eizo was like a drowning man clutching at straws. Psychologically, he had needed something, actually anything to hang on to.

"If I go back to Japan, I have to make alien legislation."

"What do you have to make?" Donald asked, not catching what Eizo said.

"Alien legislation …" Eizo strived to pronounce the words.

"Eh … alien registration?"

"Yes. Yes."

49

"You are an alien in Japan and an alien in Canada too. Who on earth are you anyway? A shadow?"

"Me? A shadow?" Eizo flinched. But it appeared that Donald had not meant anything else by it.

"Seriously though, even if you're a foreigner in Japan, you shouldn't have a problem living there?"

"No, no problem."

"Well then, your problem now is what move your family will make next," Donald said slowly so that Eizo could understand him. "Has your family written anything to you lately?"

"No, they haven't. I don't … expect a lot from them."

"Why are they being so cold-hearted?" Donald spoke as though he were talking to himself.

"As I said before, I want to stop working for the company this year end."

"That's okay, there're only a few weeks left anyway. When are you going to Japan?"

"I want to go back next spring. In Japan, in spring, you can see cherry blossoms."

"Cherry blossoms?" Donald laughed, turning his face upwards. "That's good! I'm glad you're thinking of cherry blossoms. I hope your hard work for the sake of your family wasn't wasted. You've been such a dedicated worker. Don't worry; I think everything will be all right."

Despite Donald's optimism, Eizo was serious and knew his words were meant to encourage him. For him, Japan had become an imagined dream. He had not witnessed all the changes the country went through during and after the war. His only news source was the local television station, which did not cover much, and the old weekly magazines. Japanese grocery stores sold those a few months old for next to a penny. He saw some photos of the country, but those photos were fragmented and did not show the whole picture. The more real his homecoming became, the more difficult it was to imagine his birth country. The thought of arriving in Japan and being confronted with the difference between his imaginary country and the real one was like a blanket of anxiety wrapped tightly around him.

"Eizo, we are planning a farewell party for you one week from today. What do you think about going to one of the Japanese restaurants downtown?"

"Oh, that's good. Very good, sir. Thank you, thank you very much." Eizo said gratefully. He appreciated the fact that his co-workers wanted to have a party in honour of his departure. Times had certainly changed.

"Super! That settles it." Donald smiled.

Since it would be a party for him, Eizo thought he should at least say a few words. He had never made a speech in front of other people in English. What would he say?

"If you hear from your family, let me know, okay?"

"Yes, I will."

"When are you going to get a Canadian passport?"

"Maybe next year."

"Do you have any holiday time left? If you do, why don't you take one day off and apply for your passport?"

"Yes, thank you very much," Eizo replied vaguely. Since it would be almost four months before he departed for Japan, he did not think it was necessary to rush things.

The two stood up and left the cafeteria. A few minutes later, Eizo was back at his post watching empty bottles move slowly into the washer, his ears filled with their ceaseless screeching.

5
A Red Butterfly

On his way home from work, Eizo stopped at a corner store located near the bus stop to buy a pack of cigarettes. While walking toward his apartment, he had to restrain his temptation to smoke and kept fingering the package in his pocket instead. As he entered his apartment building, he hurriedly lit a cigarette. Again, he checked his mailbox.

Nothing!

The wound he had received at the Consulate General yesterday began to ache afresh.

The piquant smell of grilled meat hung in the air in the hallway but the stairwell echoed his solitary footsteps as he climbed to the second floor. Holding the tobacco in his mouth, he opened the stubborn lock, exchanged glances with his family in the photo with eyes full of sorrow, affection and reproach to himself, then hung up his overcoat and sat down to finish his cigarette. The smoke swirled around him. He let the cigarette burn.

You should eat!

Not wanting to fight against his shadow, Eizo hobbled into the kitchen to check what he had. There were pork and carrots in the fridge and potatoes and onions in the cupboard.

How about we make curry rice?

It would take a couple of hours to finish making the curry, but that would better fill the emptiness that followed a quicker meal. After setting dinner to cook, Eizo changed out of his regular clothes, turned on the television and switched channels through the few local choices. Most were a little beyond his grasp, so he preferred game shows, westerns that characterize good versus bad clearly, and children's shows over programs with complicated plots, such as murder mysteries and detective movies.

Supper ready, Eizo sat at the table and began eating. The cackle of television laughter in the background let him know that he still lived on this planet, that civilization was intact and people still laughed at idiotic things. Someone like Eizo who had forgotten how to laugh was suspicious as to what other people found humorous. "Ho, ho, ho," he sarcastically mimicked the laughter while munching, and then the curry caught in his throat. He dashed to the kitchen, quickly opened the fridge, grabbed the milk and chugged the white liquid, letting it run down his neck onto his clothes and the floor. A few moments after gulping, he took a tentative breath. *Fuckin' stupid!* The shadow scolded him. But, feeling slightly better now, he started cleaning up the floor, only to be overcome by how alone he was, that he could choke and no one knew or cared. *Too bad ... You'd take care of yourself!* The shadow suddenly changed his tune. Unable to take any more of the laughter, Eizo snapped the television off and the silence flooded his small apartment.

Eizo's thoughts drifted back to the evening bag he bought for Kino and then to Kino herself. He thought about her face when she was young and the picture she had sent to him after the war. She, surrounded by their three sons who had grown taller, sturdier, and more unrecognizable, stood in the front yard in farm clothes and squinted into the sunlight in the picture. Because of her squinting, he could not tell how she really looked, but sensed that she was in the prime of womanhood. Then he envisioned Kino's face in deep disappointment as she received the gift that he had bought. He remembered the beautiful lady with the veil in the department store; that glorious flower who longed to bloom to the very last moment of her life.

Kino!

The silence was so dominating that he could even hear a dead pine needle falling to the ground. It was the silence he most feared, hated and cursed. Then he thought he heard someone's cackle of laughter from somewhere outside. Eizo needed to have human contact. He could not bother a friend by visiting at this late hour but, defeated by the stifling feelings, decided to set out to find human companionship. There should be another world somewhere out there where he could put his worries and solitude behind. Although it was slightly after nine, the buses and subway were still running, and there was plenty of time before the bars closed.

This is the last time you should go out like this in Canada. Remember!

The shadow tried to throw a shield around him.

Eizo stood up to change his clothes before going out.

This is the last time. Remember!

His shadow constantly followed him to make sure of its message.

*

Eizo did not see anybody as he went down the stairs and exited the apartment building. The air outside was cold and cut into his face. He looked up and saw the sky, black with menacing clouds and walked to the empty bus stop. To avoid the chill of the wind, he stood inside the plastic booth; the lights of the cars shot past like arrows. He was tempted to smoke and took a cigarette out of a package but thought better of it and put it back. A young couple came into the booth with their hands around each other's waists and started kissing, ignoring Eizo. Every time a car passed, the caressing couple were silhouetted against the headlights.

When the bus finally arrived, Eizo yielded to the couple, and moved to the middle of the bus where the seats were arranged lengthwise along the windows. The young couple took their seats in the rear and exchanged light kisses again as if not wanting to waste a minute. There were only a few other passengers.

Having transferred to the subway, he encouragingly found more people aboard. Many of them wore the colour of fatigue or relief on their faces towards the end of the day and passengers' motions at stations were sluggish as if they had consumed all of their energy. This time the subway did not remind him of his past incidents. Via Bloor-Yonge, he got off the train at Woodbine Station and watched the taillights of the subway cars moving away. After that, empty footsteps echoed plaintively inside the station. As he passed through the wicket and walked up to the landing, a flower girl called out for him to buy a rose.

"A rose? No, no thank you." He kept climbing up the steps and exited the station. The bar was only a few minutes away.

Despite the neon light that illuminated the front, the bar was clearly run-down. Eizo shuffled up to the entrance and pulled the iron ring which served as a handle on the rough wooden door. There were about a dozen customers inside, either seated at the counter or at tables nearby. Three young women, all heavily made-up, were talking with a group of men. Two of the women wore low-cut pink and purple tee shirts and jersey skirts so tight and short they looked like pigeon bands on scrawny legs. The other woman looked top-heavy in a shabby fur jacket and tight black slacks. The men hunched their broad denim shoulders over the table full of beer. They were all smoking and laughing loudly. The smoke curled white over the heads of the customers.

Eizo sat down near a corner so that he could watch television.

"What would you like?" the waiter, who had a slightly disfigured face with a broken nose, like some boxers have, asked. He looked like a bouncer, unfriendly and tough.

"A beer, please," Eizo replied, looking down and away.

Two men came into the bar and sat near the counter. One of them pulled out a pack of cigarettes, and offered one to his partner before pulling out his own and lighting up.

"Here you are," the waiter said putting a pint on the table.

Eizo left his change as a tip on the waiter's tray. As he sipped, the alcohol spread a sense of euphoria throughout his body. Wagon wheels, horseshoes, and other equestrian equipment decorated the walls, which were covered with roughly sawn boards. The wooden floor, originally oiled, was now dirty and worn. Near the entrance hung an oil lamp with a small electric light that flickered like a flame. Through the stale boozy air, something with a twang played in the background.

A woman stood up and left with the man she was seated with.

Eizo took a long time to finish his beer, drinking it in thimblefuls, ignored by the other patrons. Across the bar in another corner there was a fellow, obviously drunk, who sat half-leaning with his eyes transfixed on his beer glass. He had a pitiful expression, as though he was considering how to drown himself in the beer. The door opened and the flower girl from the subway station came in. Eizo was a little taken aback. He did not think she was old enough to be in a bar. Holding the flower basket in her left arm, she strode around the counter, looking into the customers' faces, trying to sell flowers. She went to each table, but no one was interested. One man waved her away like a pestering dog. Then she approached Eizo.

"Would you like to buy a rose?" the girl said flatly. She seemed not to have remembered that she had asked him once before at the station. Her lips parted, but it was a distorted smile that Eizo recognized, set to conceal the fatigue and poverty. Sympathy for the flower girl hit him hard. *You know the hardship, don't you?* the shadow said.

"How much?" Eizo asked.

"Five dollars, sir."

That was more than he expected, though not a large amount of money. He pulled out his wallet and handed her the money.

"Thank you very much," she said with a shy smile playing about her mouth, picking a pink rose from the bunch.

"I don't want a flower."

"You don't want a flower?" She threw the question back at him.

The thought of returning alone to his apartment with a pink rose made him feel ill. It would simply add to his misery. "No, I don't want it."

"Really?" The girl looked at Eizo incredulously. "It's good to be kind to others. Not many people can do it. Thank you." Her mask fell away to flash a gentle smile and expose her vulnerability.

Eizo was happy that he had this rare glimpse into another's soul. His heart quickened. "That's okay."

"Well, then, enjoy your evening, sir." She smiled again, a tired smile, then left.

Just before the exit the girl turned and came back to Eizo's table. He became uptight. *Did I do something wrong?* She put the flower basket down, picked up a carnation, and cut its stem short. "Excuse me," she said, and inserted the stem of the carnation into the hole of his lapel. "Oh, you look handsome!" the flower girl said in a singsong voice.

"Thank you very much," Eizo mumbled with mixed emotion.

"Good bye," she said heading for the exit again.

A faint and hollow scent emanated from the carnation in contrast with the season. Without knowing why Eizo felt better. Perhaps that had been what he was looking for, the sentimentality brought on by casual contact with others. Or, perhaps it was just having the unfamiliar girl put a carnation in his lapel. In the end though, he thought it was all a little pathetic. Yet, from another perspective, what he did for the flower girl was insignificant, but it gave her a moment of joy. What was certain, though, was that the existence of the flower girl let him forget his solitude for a few moments and brought him a little closer to the world he thought he wanted to be with.

You don't have to be pathetic. That was what you were looking for after all, wasn't it?

The woman with the fur jacket draped over her shoulders, put out her cigarette and slowly approached Eizo's table. His eyes were drawn to the big red dahlias on the black slacks that clung to her thighs. At Eizo's table she gently placed a hand on the back of an empty chair and began stroking it with her white, delicate fingers.

Eizo stiffened and quickly averted his eyes.

"Can I sit down?" the woman asked, her voice low and mellow.

"Ah, yes, yes," Eizo stammered, straightened his back and pulled his beer glass towards him.

Without saying a word, the woman unhurriedly sank into the seat and rearranged her fur jacket, watching him carefully as she crossed her legs. Eizo could not meet her eyes but he knew she was slyly observing her effect on him. The scent of her pungent perfume coated him like syrup.

"You have a carnation. It's beautiful. Can I have it?" The woman asked as though she were talking to a small boy.

"Yes, that's right, yes," He obediently took the flower out of his lapel and gave it to her, its scent fading.

"Oh, thanks. You're a gentleman, aren't you?"

Her bloused, cheerfully coloured sleeves appeared from under her jacket like unfurling petals. Reaching to take the carnation, she brushed his hand. He knew it was intentionally done. The warmth of her skin was intense, as though something was burning just beneath the surface. Eizo flushed from the heat of her touch, while enjoying the unexpected sensation. She brought the flower to her delicate nose and closed her eyes as she softly inhaled. Her breasts swelled under her blouse, and then suddenly, wildly, she exhaled.

"I love dahlias, but I like carnations too. I love their purity." Saying so, she closed her eyes and again inhaled the flower's perfume, her breasts moving upward.

Eizo stared, enraptured with her almond eyes enhanced by a thick hue of blue under her perfect eyebrows.

"Do you know that flower girl?" she asked, brushing her dark hair softly back onto the shoulders of her jacket.

"No."

"Hmm," she said, sounding careless, yet assessing him carefully. "Flowers are beautiful. Sometimes, I want to be a flower."

Eizo did not know how to respond.

She put the carnation down on the table offhand as if it had not existed, opened her handbag, drew a cigarette out and placed it between her painted red lips and waited for him to light it. Eizo put his hand into his pocket with indecent haste. She looked at him through her eyelashes and then bent over to the flare of the match.

"Thank you," she said glancing at him, while exhaling smoke through her nostrils. "Are you married, or single?"

"Yes," he said.

"No, I'm asking you if you're married."

"Yes, married," he murmured.

"Then, what are you doing here all alone?"

"My wife's not here."

"Did you say your wife was not here? Where is she?"

"She is … in Japan."

"Aren't you a little lonely in Canada all by yourself?"

"Yes, but I'm okay."

"What does that mean?"

Eizo did not want to get into the details of his life.

The woman took a drag on her cigarette and lazily exhaled through pursed lips. "What do you do when you're lonely?"

"I come here, drink and watch TV."

"This isn't a place to watch TV," she laughed.

"Yes, but …"

"Do you have children?"

"I have three sons."

"What? Tree sons? What's that? … Oh, three … three sons. Aren't you lucky? Are they in Japan too?"

60

"Yes."

"Do you miss your wife?" she continued.

"Yes, very much."

The woman cackled at Eizo's answer. She suddenly pressed close to him and murmured in his ear, "Do you want to sleep with me?"

Eizo had known the question would come sooner or later. While waiting for his reply she puffed the cigarette from the side of her mouth, eyes still fixed on him. Eizo was nervous. He thought about his age and the fact that he had already lost his sexual capability some time ago. Going with her to a motel nearby would certainly create disaster and punish him in the end. His mouth went dry. He could not decide whether to submit to temptation or not.

Why are you hesitating? What did you come here for?

The shadow was relentless.

If he turned her down Eizo knew the world he just grabbed would immediately crash to pieces and he would ruthlessly be tossed back out into the cold. The woman sensed that the time he had to decide had come and did not wait long. "Thirty dollars. Do you want to or not? Hurry up."

"Ye … yes."

"Good man, good man." the woman said, touching his arm.

He unconsciously glanced around the bar, but no one was paying attention, aside from the drunk at the other corner of the bar who had cast an unfocussed eye on them.

"Near Christmas business tends to be slow. Men suddenly become holy, family men."

Instead of answering Eizo nodded his head several times.

Her expression shifted and she suddenly looked tired. "Do you know the Cupid Motel?"

61

"Yes."

Eizo had stayed at the Cupid Motel several times before; it was old and was reputed to have questionable guests and therefore the price was cheap.

"Take a room under the name of Todd and wait for me."

"Tod?"

"Yes, Todd, T-o-d-d. All right?"

"Yes." He stood up and began to button his overcoat.

"See you later," she said, looking straight ahead exhaling smoke through her nostrils. "Oh, remember this, nice guys always finish first, you know," she added, seemingly uncaring whether he was listening or not, or whether he understood her or not.

Eizo stepped out into the street. The air had become considerably colder. He walked to the Cupid Motel and took the room reserved for Todd as directed. The man at reception had a Pompadour hairstyle, was unshaven, wore a sweat-stained muscle shirt and kept looking at Eizo through his hazy cigarette smoke. When Eizo paid the room fee, the man handed him the key, telling him the room number without comment.

Eizo made his way up to the second floor. The room was bare except for an old television set and a bed covered with a cheap quilt. He sat on the bed sinking deep into the mattress. Despite the expected rendezvous, he did not feel elated and sighed.

This is the last time!

He would never do this kind of secret tryst again, although, ironically, he was attracted to the grimy old room. The motel was part of Eizo's clandestine life.

If Kino asks me how I managed without a woman, how will I answer? I wonder how Kino got on alone tending a farm the size of a postage stamp and raising three kids, all

*the while denying her inner desires. Poor Kino! If I had died,
she would have been able to approach another man. But
Fumi said Kino was getting on just fine.*

Eizo heard footsteps come down the hall and then the
knock. He jumped up and rushed to open the door. The
woman stood a step away from him holding the collar of her
jacket close to her face. Then she swept into the room
without saying a word. Eizo felt her body heat as she brushed
past him. The heady fragrance that followed overwhelmed
him. He had not felt like this in over two years now. As he
closed the door, he thought the room suddenly changed its
colour to red. He could not really believe that his partner
would be the woman now standing in front of him.

Without expression the woman quickly surveyed the
room then shrugged off her jacket and carefully put it on a
hanger. As she moved, the sleeves of her blouse fluttered
about like a butterfly's wings. The set of her face gave him
the impression of a tired-out insect caught in a spider's web.

"I want the money," the weary butterfly said, as she gave
him a sidelong glance.

He opened his wallet and handed her the money.

"Thanks," she muttered, tucking the bills into her
handbag. The woman looked at the bed, her face blank and
slowly began unbuttoning her blouse one button at a time as
much as to say, 'Here we go again. Sucker!'

Eizo was conscious of his heart hammering in his chest
and the pulse in his fingertips, his blood driven by the
combination of alcohol and the intoxicating closeness of his
female companion. She finished unbuttoning her blouse and
let it fall from her shoulders as though metamorphosing into
a new creature. Eizo became totally absorbed as she
undressed in front of him.

"What are you doing? Aren't you taking off your clothes?"

"Ah, oh, yes." His hands sprang to the buttons of his jacket. As he took off his suit and threw it on the chair, he stared at the woman. It was not without some trepidation that he prepared to lie with her.

The woman hung up her blouse and began unzipping her slacks. The zipper parted like it was being torn. Eizo was beside himself with the intense desire to know more of her secrets, to feel alive again through an exchange of body heat. She slipped off her slacks revealing well-proportioned legs in dark black stockings, her body stark against the background of the white wall. What a showy flower her figure was!

"Are you undressed yet?" she asked without looking.

"No."

"Hurry up, otherwise you'll run out of time."

Chastened, he hastily began pulling off his pants and socks. Halfway through, poised on one foot, he lost his balance and fell onto the corner of the bed. "Oh!" Eizo groaned, reaching out with one hand for support.

"What happened?" asked the woman giving him a suspicious look.

"No, nothing."

"Are you okay? Don't give me any trouble. I'm not calling the ambulance or the police, okay? You understand?"

"Yes, I understand."

Eizo sat heavily onto the chair and finished pulling off his pants and socks. His legs, thin and withered, stuck out in front of him. Eizo, who usually did not look at his wizened body, was struck by what he considered his undeniable ugliness. He got into the bed quickly so that the woman could not see his wasted figure.

"Oh my, you're quick," the woman said rolling down her pantyhose.

Her hair hung softly on her shoulders and across her breasts, though she kept her brassiere on. The lines of her well-carved waist curved out into her bounteous hips and dropped to her marvellously shaped legs. Her lace lingerie did more to reveal than conceal. His eyes followed the line from her shoulders to a constricted waist, her two white buttocks, her thighs, legs, and ankles, the symmetrical beauty of her legs gracefully supporting her body. Under her stockings the woman's supple, white skin waited unprotected. Eizo felt his stomach drop.

She slipped out of her panties in one smooth movement, her skin shining as she moved. She turned unhesitatingly to Eizo. The scene overpowered his world of illusion. The walls, curtains, bed, quilt, chair, television set and ceiling— everything was washed down by the glaring truth in one sweep.

The woman slipped into bed, her perfume settling over him like a blanket. He was acutely aware of her eyes on him, her warm breath against his face, and her body pressed close to him. As their eyes met, she turned her face away and stared up at the ceiling.

Inside the cut of her brassiere he could see the milky-whiteness of her breasts. In contrast to her emotionless eyes, her breasts rose and fell like waves on a sea. Like all the times before, he believed a woman's breath on his skin and her warmth against his would be wonderful beyond words, a resemblance of love's touch. She lay beside him waiting for his next move. But, as he already knew, his body had failed him. He did not know what to do next. Lying on her back, resolved herself for what was coming, she glanced at him with a look that said he had better start soon. Without being ready physically and psychologically for the next act, he pressed closer and drew his legs up toward hers. Her legs were warm, but her eyes were cold as she continued to stare at a point on the ceiling. A couple of minutes passed.

"Pardon me," he said to the woman.

In his mind, she was an integral part of his world now, but anxiety grew within him as she became aware of his impotency. His hatred of the inevitability of aging tangled with the strange euphoria in their shared warmth.

"You can't do it, can you?" she asked, as she turned her face towards him.

He felt as if the world was watching him with guarded eyes and he was not ready for this warmth to slip away just yet. To be able to touch another person's skin made him feel alive again, gave some meaning to his existence.

"Come on!" she said impatiently. "Are you impotent or what?"

Her rebuking eyes were fixed on him. He wanted to abandon his embrace as much as he wanted to hold on to this reality.

"Can you, uh, stay with me ... little longer like this?"

The woman pushed his upper body away with both her hands and looked into his eyes. He feared the world he had just acquired would tear apart if she pulled her warm body away. He half expected her to burst into a volley of profanities and leave.

"Maybe you drank too much," the woman said, unexpectedly coming to his rescue.

"Yes..." He clung to it.

"Okay, two minutes. That's all."

He held her carefully and tenderly but soon the woman jerked from his arms and got out of the bed without saying anything.

"I'm sorry."

"Never mind," she said and walked to the closet.

Eizo felt battered. He was stunned by how his time with the woman ended so abruptly. She began to put on her clothes; he expected her to leave quickly. He hazily watched her dress.

His consciousness shifted and the figures of two women he had kept company with long ago stole upon him. The two women were Japanese-Canadians. He had met one of them soon after being released from the concentration camp, but then lost contact during the time he moved around looking for a place to settle. Susan Tominaga had been a good companion and easy to talk to during hard times. Later, he got to know another woman, but when she learned he had a family in Japan, she refused to see him anymore. His relationship with them had always been limited to companionship, never sex.

He believed that he had loved his wife and three sons and that thought had given him the strength to endure difficult times. But, the distance between his family and himself was obvious. Loyalty to his wife and sons held him prisoner in another kind of camp; he could neither join them nor leave them. Such conflicting feelings kept a delicate balance within him. His freedom warped, Eizo wretchedly surrendered to the cost of being held and touched by women who worked at the Cupid Motel. He drifted back to the room. The woman came out of the washroom, her hair was brushed and her lips repainted. She put on her jacket and cast a glance at him without expression, took a cigarette out and lit it. He saw that she had already transformed back into a butterfly, her milk-white, supple skin was again covered in the black slacks with dahlia patterns. She was ready to leave him behind, old and unable to fly.

"Are you still here?" she asked, more to fill the silence than to say anything meaningful.

"Yes, I am."

As she blew smoke through her red lips she set her face, turned the doorknob, and disappeared. It was as though nothing had happened between them.

Eizo felt hollow, without muscle, bones and organs. As he lay in the bed he looked at his wrinkled arms. They were frail and his skin was dry like old parchment.

What have you done? Why do you do things to make yourself more miserable? The shadow loomed in the background.

Leave me alone. Besides, you agreed to come with me.

He wanted to drive the shadow away before it started.

Yes, I did agree, if that satisfies you. But I didn't mean to come this far to make you feel more miserable. You should've been satisfied with the flower girl.

"Bloody idiot!" He spit out the self-reproving words at the wall.

Eventually Eizo got out of bed and put his clothes back on, feeling the weight of loneliness all over his body. He pulled on his overcoat and, as he closed the door, glanced back inside the room. Memories from these kinds of rooms offered no consolation now. He turned away and walked through the dimly lit passageway. The man at the reception pretended not to notice him as he returned the key to the counter. Eizo stepped out into the night as his body and soul shrank in the cold.

6
Sickness of Mt Fuji

Snow had been falling since morning on the day of Eizo's farewell party and was still falling by lunch. Snowploughs with blue lights flashing passed in front of the factory, through an endless stark white world. The traffic in front of the factory was dilatory. Eizo sat at a table in the corner of the cafeteria and started his lunch.

"Hey, Eizo, I'm coming to your farewell party tonight," called Jeff. He was a short, overweight, round-faced guy with a little goatee who worked close to Eizo's division. His nickname was 'Butt'.

"Thank you," Eizo said looking up at him.

"Whose farewell party is it?" asked a young woman sitting across from Butt.

Jeff explained and then turned back to Eizo. "I hear we're going to a Japanese restaurant downtown. What on earth do you guys eat? I've never had Japanese before," he laughed, wiping the both ends of his mouth with his hand.

The younger workers beside Jeff, all in the same work coveralls and caps, said that they had had Chinese food, but had never tried Japanese. Another worker piped in saying that Japanese restaurants served raw fish.

"Yuk, raw fish? Do we have to eat raw fish tonight?" A worker named Greg grimaced.

"Eizo, is that true? You guys eat raw fish? If that's the case, I'm not going," Jeff said. The gang around him burst into laughter.

"Raw fish? That's gross!"

"Tell me Eizo, are we really going to have frigging raw fish?" Jeff asked, with a glum expression on his face.

"Jeff, I don't know … what they have on the menu."

Hearing this, his companions returned to their own world and did not bother Eizo anymore. Although it was only for a few minutes, Eizo was glad that his workmates had shown interest in his farewell party. Donald mentioned earlier that almost twenty of the crew from his division were planning to attend. Eizo had not associated with them much on a daily basis and had thought that at most five workers would show up. In the worst case he even thought that it might be only Donald and himself. The prospect of twenty of his colleagues in attendance was a joyful surprise.

"Eizo-san!" Kitani called, striding up and greeting Eizo in Japanese. "So, you're finally going to quit the company."

He sat down opposite to Eizo. He was about thirty-five and married with two children. He had been an elevator engineer at another company and was among the first to be laid off when business slowed; Kitani thought it was because of his poor English. Now that he was a truck driver at the soft drink factory, he had forced himself to approach his Canadian co-workers in order to polish his English, and had distanced himself from the immigrant workers.

"I'm well up in years. It's time to quit," Eizo said in Japanese.

"Excuse me Eizo-san, can I ask how old you are?" Kitani leaned forward, pulling on the seams of the beige company uniform. He was a thin man topped by a company ball-cap with a logo.

"I'm seventy."

"Seventy … really? You say you've been working here for more than twenty years?"

"That's right."

"You've endured very well, Eizo-san. I don't think I could bear staying here that long." Kitani might have made a compliment to Eizo.

"You've a skill and an engineering degree. So you won't need to put up with it as long as I have. Everything will be all right for you, when the time comes."

"Hopefully, things will go that way. But right now isn't the time. Sometimes I find a suitable job opening and call the company the same day. But they always say the position has been filled. Of course, it's a downright lie. I know it's because of my English," Kitani said glumly. "It's discrimination, you know. They don't even check out someone's qualifications if their English isn't perfect."

Eizo let him talk.

"When you can't find a job, it's like drowning in the sea where no one is coming to rescue you." Kitani continued his rant, "A friend of mine sent about a hundred job applications out by mail and you know what? All the replies were refusal letters."

"No, that's not easy."

"Hell no! You get really bummed out. You hear the same old hackneyed phrases. Refusal after refusal. When you've seen so many of those letters, you begin thinking you won't find a good job anymore, anywhere."

"Your trade is kind of particular. Elevator engineer is a pretty specialized field."

"Yeah, but listen. Even when I had just come to Canada, I had a hard time finding a job."

"Not just you. Everyone has a hard time at first."

"Well, I suppose. When I went to interviews, most of the employers asked if I had any experience in Canada. I had only just arrived—there's no way I could've had Canadian experience. Can you imagine? They were just making an ass of me. That's the way they treat new immigrants," the truck driver continued. "A friend of mine couldn't find a job in his field and was hard up. So he went to a restaurant to get a temporary job as a dishwasher. Surprise, surprise, Eizo-san? He was asked whether he had Canadian experience or not. He was mad, upset. Anywhere you go dishes are always the same shape. Why would you need Canadian experience to wash dishes? Stupid!"

"Well, possibly, the employer saw that your friend would only be temporary. I have nothing to boast about myself. I had neither skills nor an especially good command of English. So when I got this job, I was in seventh heaven. That's why I stayed with the company for such a long time. There were hard times for me, as well."

Eizo paused and, after swallowing his saliva, continued, "Right after the war, Canadian people in general still hated the Nikkei and there were a lot of employers who didn't hire us. We were enemies, you know. But I found a job with a farmer, a hard job at a very low wage. We Japanese had difficult times. But Jewish people were different. After we moved east, they had no problem hiring us."

"Jewish people?"

"Yeah, Jewish people. Many of them knew the hardships of discrimination. They understood what it was like and willingly offered us jobs. Of course, I think they knew we were low paid, hardworking people."

"Oh."

"In any case, we owe them a great deal."

Eizo felt the experiences of new immigrants could not be compared to the hardships the prewar Nikkei had suffered. Among the Japanese, some new immigrants thought poorly of the prewar immigrants because they, generally speaking, were neither well educated nor highly skilled. On the other hand, the prewar immigrants themselves thought that *hakujin* society in Canada had a high regard for the hardworking and diligent Nikkei. The Issei and Nisei criticized the new Japanese immigrants for taking advantage of the reputation they had built up with their sweat and tears. Those newcomers were an arrogant lot. However, Eizo kept these thoughts to himself.

"Well, I can't help but be impatient. If you stay away from your field for more than three years, employers don't consider you a specialist anymore. So, I can't fritter away my time," Kitani said.

It seemed to Eizo that this young chap only cared about his situation.

"Kitani-san, how long have you been working at this factory?"

"Nearly a year and a half."

"Then, you don't need to get flustered yet. Besides, you're still young."

"Eizo-san, you say so, but there isn't that much time. The past year and a half is short when you look back at it. The next year and a half will go by in a flash, too. I have to do something before that."

Eizo knew Kitani was right. As proof, he himself had a hard time grasping that forty-three years in Canada had passed by in a twinkling; time that he could not recover but wanted to recover at any cost, if possible.

The two ate their lunch in silence.

"Kitani-san, are you going to live in Canada for good?" Finally, Eizo spoke.

"Well … when we came to Canada, we intended to live here for good. We had huge hope for Canada. But I guess every immigrant is forced to re-evaluate his situation at some point."

"Yes, you're right about that."

"I went back to Japan before I started working here. When seeing how everyone at home seemed so strung-out trying to achieve a comfortable life; trying hard to beat rivals and fight for a position, I was strongly inclined to stay in Canada for good. I wouldn't live in that rat race. You see some people in cities literally running."

"Is Japan such a busy place now?"

"Eizo-san, you only know the old Japan. Everything has changed … everything. I think people were, like it or not, forced to change themselves too. I'll tell you what I saw on the commuter train in the suburb of Tokyo. It was around eight o'clock in the morning. Even though it was a rush hour, there still was a space to move your body around in the car. Then I saw a middle-aged man standing in the aisle muttering, 'Life is good-for-nothing, you know, life is good-for-nothing.' He wasn't drunk, no, no, he was very sober. He was on his way to work wearing a fine suit, an ironed shirt, necktie, nice shoes, just like any other businessman. When I heard him say those words, I was deeply disturbed. I couldn't believe what I was seeing. Other passengers pretended not to notice him or looked the other way. I had to look away too, but felt miserable. If that was a life in Japan, then no, I wouldn't live there."

Eizo pictured the scene Kitani had described. He felt the man on the train must have worked hard all his life and as he reached middle-age, found there was nothing waiting for him. *No, that wouldn't be my case!* Eizo imagined what it would take for the man to say those words in public. The thought drained him.

"I think as Japanese we force each other to assimilate too much. If someone is different they feel insecure and society doesn't tolerate their uniqueness. Our society kills originality, you know. *Deru kugi wa utareru*: the nail that sticks up gets hammered down. I will take no part in that. On the whole, we as a people have little sense of self. If a drop of poison were dripped into Japan from outside, it'll kill all the Japanese. Of course, I'm talking about this in terms of their mentality. We can evaluate ourselves only from the point of view of how others see us. It's kind of sad really."

Eizo felt like he was listening to Kitani through cotton wool; this was the society he would soon return to. For him, no matter what others might say, Japan was the country where he was born and raised and returning to reunite with his family—that had been his dream for decades. He pictured his young days with nostalgia and was ready to accept Japan as it was. He was preoccupied with his desire to go back to his country.

The cafeteria was noisy, filled with the conversation and a roar of laughter of workers who had finished their lunch and men playing on the foosball and pinball machines. The yells of the young workers "Goal! Goal!" came from the corner at the foosball machines, then the players slapped each other's palms in the air in high fives. Jeff's group was still at the table, both men and women sipping half-cold coffee, some giggling.

Kitani briefly looked up at the industrial clock. There was still time before the afternoon shift started. He continued, "Compared to that, the Canadians are true to their creed. Whatever others say, they try to live their life the way

75

they want, you know. I think life here has a kind of serenity and affluence to it."

Eizo was a little confused that this co-worker from Japan used the word 'serenity' to describe his life in Canada, since he had just said explicitly that he felt pressured to find a job outside of his field. But Kitani's point of view was no doubt going to be different than his own.

"After I was laid off, it was a while before I could find a job. As I said I went back to Japan. I would've stayed there if I could've found a good job but …" The truck driver didn't finish the sentence. He paused for a while and then continued, "Anyway, you'll be really surprised when you go back. You'll be a total stranger."

"A total stranger?"

"I bet you will. Things are changing rapidly over there. I didn't go back for three years and I could hardly recognize some areas. I assure you that you'll be shocked." The man in uniform spoke half-seriously and half-jokingly.

Behind his bitter and bewildered smile Eizo could not help but feel anxious at Kitani's words. "How were your old friends? Were they satisfied living in Japan?" he asked.

"Well, more or less, I guess. Or probably, there is no choice. I met one of my former colleagues in Tokyo and couldn't believe how much he'd changed."

"It might be you who has changed."

Stunned, Kitani looked as if Eizo had just singled out his vulnerable point.

"That may be true," he said hesitantly. "I live in Canada, so I might have changed. But, my former colleagues in Tokyo have changed much more."

"In what way? Tell me about that."

"They've become accustomed to the company they work for and they've begun showing differences in their business results and rankings as well. Many of them are at a turning point in their careers, so now they are desperately competing against each other for their future positions—positions where only a few can succeed."

"Hum."

"One day when I was in Tokyo, I called a friend for a drink. I thought we would have a million things to talk about. Do you know what he said? He said he was too busy and couldn't make it. Nice guy, eh?"

"He must've been busy."

"Yah, I know. But, I had come a long way, over the Pacific Ocean from Canada, and he could've adjusted his schedule a little for me. Anyway, we met four days later, but he only spent a couple of hours with me. When we parted he said, 'Well then, work hard in Canada, so long,' and went back to work. A pity. And he didn't even write to me after that."

"Is that so?"

"I felt kind of out of place. Some of my other friends from university were the same. They only talked about their jobs and had little sense of anything else. I definitely felt as if we were worlds apart."

Worlds apart!

How fitting thought Eizo. That expression applied to him very well. Substantially more so than Kitani's case.

"But, mind you Eizo-san, hard work and high technology, that's the only way Japan, with few natural resources, can survive. I guess I'm lucky to be alive and live in Canada."

"I was brought up in the days of 'Don't waste even a grain of rice', you see. It seems to be a totally different era from yours."

77

"'Don't waste even a grain of rice'. I've heard those words somewhere before, but ..." The Japanese man opposite Eizo mumbled and lifted his cup and shifted in his chair.

"Look at you, I envy you!" Eizo waved his right arm.

"Why?" Kitani asked, perplexed.

"Why? You're young and have your future ahead of you."

Kitani seemed a little embarrassed, but couldn't help smiling.

"Yes, I envy you young guys. You have a good command of English and are able to return to Japan as often as you please. Perhaps none of you have suffered from the 'Sickness of Mt Fuji'."

"What's that? It sounds strange."

"Haven't you ever heard of it?"

"Never."

"Probably it is hard for new emigrants from Japan to understand. In the old days, once you left Japan, it was your whole life's work to go back. For the people like me, who left their families behind, we often had to live alone for a long time. And, of course, we were faced with the added difficulties of communicating in English and navigating through foreign customs and culture. That was a hard job, anyway to us. Probably you young people today don't feel that way. People frequently became depressed and some even had mental breakdowns."

"Is that what you call the Sickness of Mt Fuji?"

"Well, in short, yes. People who became mentally ill couldn't be cured while they were in Canada. Their hearts were broken. Finally, they had to leave Canada for Japan. Strangely enough, as soon as they reached Japan and saw Mt

Fuji, they were cured, the depression gone!" Eizo again waved his right arm, without knowing it.

"Oh. Nowadays we call it 'culture shock'. But you didn't get the Sickness of Mt Fuji, eh Eizo-san?"

"I thought I might, but managed not to."

"You're strong."

A fly buzzed around them, then landed and climbed up Eizo's plate. He watched as it unsteadily took to the air again, circled several times, and landed on Kitani's sleeve.

"A fly at this time of the year? Shoo! Go away!" The truck driver lifted his hand and was about to swat the small creature.

"Oh, no, Kitani-san, don't kill it!"

Surprised, Kitani looked at Eizo.

"It was born into this world and has a short, precious life. Let it be. Let it live a little longer." Eizo's watery eyes appealed for the fly's life.

"Precious? Eizo-san, it's only a fly, you know."

"Even if you don't kill it, it'll die soon. Let it live till that time."

Kitani moved his arm without saying anything. The fly took to the air again and flew lazily away.

The truck driver looked Eizo over again. He knew that some old generation Japanese, who practiced the Buddhism of their ancestors, would tell an insect that had flown into the house, 'Come back the day before yesterday!' and then release the poor existence without killing it: an idea of reincarnation, transmigration of the soul and pity. But what he witnessed now was something different—pity from a dying man for a dying creature. The old man appeared weaker than usual and for a few moments, he could not even look at Eizo. Kitani forced a smile and said, "When are you going home?"

79

"Around the beginning of April, next year."

"You haven't seen your family for a long time. You can finally all get together."

"Well, yes," Eizo responded after a pause. His eyes drifted in the air, losing their concentration. He had not told Kitani about the strained relationship with his family.

"Today's your farewell party," Kitani said in a more formal tone. "Unfortunately it's at the same time as the New Japanese Canadian Association's meeting. I'm terribly sorry I can't go to your party."

"Don't worry."

Kitani looked up at the clock. "Lunch is almost up. I'd better go. See you later."

He stood up and shook hands with Eizo.

"Well then, see you later," Eizo said.

"*Sayonara.*"

Kitani turned his back and walked toward the exit.

"I like the word '*Sayonara*'. It sounds so exotic," offered Jeanette, one of Eizo's co-workers.

"Is that right? Thank you." With little else to say Eizo left the table with the lunch tray in his hands.

"Hey, this way here," someone in a white chef's uniform and cap shouted in the kitchen, waving his hand over the sink.

"Okay, I'll be there." A man with his thick arms wrapped around a cauldron shouted back.

Eizo recognised one of the older dishwashers in the kitchen, a fellow from Hungary, and waved to him. He was stocky, double-chinned yet had his watchful movements, doubting eyes and tightly-shut mouth, and seemed to be a man who had thousands of stories to tell. But since their work hours differed, the two never exchanged more than a few simple greetings in the cafeteria.

Perhaps he too had been repressed by the authorities and fled to Canada. Who knows what he has gone through?

As he left the cafeteria, the laughter of the other workers, mostly in their twenties, echoed behind him.

7
Farewell Party

After work, those who planned to attend Eizo's farewell party carpooled to the Japanese restaurant in town. As Eizo was leaving the factory, Donald asked him if he needed a lift. Eizo had planned to go with Gus and was reluctant to ride with Donald, since their conversation was often stalled with 'Pardon me?' and they misunderstood each other frequently. It was not that Donald was inconsiderate to others—he was rather opposite to it—, but immigrants' life and their usage of language was beyond his understanding and his time was totally taken up with his work and family. On the other hand, Eizo worked close to Gus at the factory, and could be frank with him. Even in their broken English, the two men still managed to understand one another, using imagination and shared experiences to fill in the gaps.

The snow had become powdery in the evening air and was thick on the Firebird. As Gus turned the key, the engine roared to life and some snow fell from the roof of the car. While the car warmed, he brushed the snow off the windows.

"Do you have another?" Eizo pointed at the brush.

"No, I have only one. Thanks, Eizo. Get in the car."

"All right."

"Okay, let's go." Sliding into the driver's seat Gus was ready to go. He was a handsome young fellow with a cleanly shaved face, straight nose, thick eyebrows and dark complexion. He fastened his seatbelt, dropped the vehicle into gear and spun the wheels out of the snowploughed parking lot, slithering on the icy roads.

The snow glimmered in the reflection of the city lights against the dark sky and despite the dirty piles thrown by the ploughs along his side, it was an exquisite winter scene. Eizo remembered many similar scenes in the concentration camp that always glowed heartlessly in the winter. Those nights, he would gaze beyond the camp in despair, thinking of his family in the enemy country and his fate, and wonder when and how he would ever be released. The nights in the camp were dead and long and felt endless, endless like reaching out his hand to a vanishing star. At one point, he believed the Nikkei would be impounded in the camp for good.

Gus turned the radio on, startling Eizo back to the present. The station was playing classic guitar.

"Good music, eh? Greek people like Lauta music a lot, you know."

"Lauta?"

"A lauta is like a guitar. It plays melancholic music, you know."

"Melancholic music?"

"Yeah, melancholic music, kinda like sad music. And people dance to it." Gus began moving his upper body and snapping his fingers, both hands off the steering wheel.

"Oh, Gus, *abunai*, danger! Danger!"

"Ho, ho, ho. Eizo, not to worry."

On the way to the restaurant, Gus asked Eizo when he would leave Canada and how his preparations were coming along. Eizo could see that Gus only half listened to his answer, tapping his fingers on the steering wheel and looking at other cars and passengers on the road, but when he asked a question about Gus's girlfriend, he perked up.

"You know I went to West Germany last summer," Gus said.

"Yes, I know."

"I visited my girlfriend there."

"How was she?"

"Ah, Beatrix was fine. Her family runs a small auto parts factory and business is doing very well."

"That's good."

"I got to know her in English school. We dated many times but a couple of years later she went back to Germany. When I visited her, she came to the station to pick me up with a Mercedes-Benz and dressed in gorgeous one piece. Oh, she was beautiful. Other people were speaking German in the train, so when I met Beatrix and spoke English with her, I thought I had met an angel." Gas stopped tapping his fingers on the steering wheel and concentrated on his talk. "I love Beatrix. I think she loves me too, but I'm not sure. And there's a problem. Beatrix doesn't want to come back to Canada."

"Why not?"

"She didn't say why. Beatrix has an older brother. He's looking after the business with his father. She's helping with sales and she likes it. I asked her to come back to Canada and live with me. She said it's impossible."

"She said 'No' to you?"

"She didn't say 'No', but it was no to me. She has tons of money and she doesn't want to give up her rich life style … I think so."

"Why did she come to Canada in the first place?"

"Probably, she was dreaming of something but became sober and realistic now, or she wanted to learn English to use it for business. She didn't say which."

"Do you want to marry her?"

"Well, you know, I don't think so."

"Don't give up Gus! It's not good to give up."

Eizo's high-pitched voice surprised Gus and he glanced at his passenger. "Don't worry about me. I'm okay. Maybe I should go back to Greece next year and marry a Greek girl," Gus said, giving a hollow, sad laugh, and tapping his fingers on the steering wheel again. Eizo watched the bravado of the young and envied that.

The road conditions caused the traffic to back up, making them later than they had hoped. At the entrance of the restaurant, they were greeted by waitresses dressed in *kimono*, calling '*Irasshaimase*', and the traditional Japanese décor of bamboo and rice paper screens. They saw almost everyone else was already there. Besides that, perhaps because of the snow, the guests were arriving sporadically.

"Hey, Eizo! Tonight's guest of honour," Greg called out and the others echoed his welcome.

Eizo smiled back at them but soon was urged to sit at the head of the table, which he declined by waving his hand hesitantly. The table was arranged with paper-wrapped chopsticks, and cups for tea and napkins. Several of Eizo's co-workers laughed as they practised using the chopsticks.

"Gosh, this darn stuff! They aren't easy to handle."

Eizo now realized that he did not know many of his co-workers' names and felt ashamed. Before long Donald and the rest of the party arrived. One of the waitresses came to serve them.

"Eizo, what would you like to drink?" Donald asked.

"How about *saké*?" the waitress recommended.

"Oh, *saké*. That's good. How about *saké*, Eizo?"

"*Saké* is good," Eizo said.

"I don't know what to eat at all," someone said.

"Eizo can help us. He should know what's good. I've had *tempura* and *sukiyaki* before," said Donald.

"Is there any raw fish on the menu?" asked Jeff as he winked at Eizo.

"*Sukiyaki* is good," Eizo said quickly before Jeff got him into trouble.

Looking around at the table while everyone studied their menus, Eizo felt the irony of his fate. During the Second World War many Canadians their parents' age had shown him open hostility and hatred and it was their government that had interned the Nikkei. Today, the children of that generation came to dine with him and bid him farewell. *Never mind about the past. Just enjoy your farewell party.* The shadow nudged him.

Saké was served with anticipation around the table, as each poured for one another. Then Donald called everyone to attention.

"Good evening everyone. I'd like to say a few words. First of all, thank you for coming to Eizo Osada's farewell party today."

"You're welcome," Jeff said in low voice.

"At the end of this year Eizo will retire. As you might know, he has worked for our company for more than twenty years. His contributions to the company have been great. Today, we are gathered to toast Eizo's happiness and health as he gets ready to return to Japan. Cheers!"

"Cheers!"

Taking Donald's lead, everybody raised their cups and toasted Eizo. The men sitting beside Eizo reached over to clink their *saké* cups against his. Their sentiment caused a hot lump to rise inside his throat.

"Wao! *Saké* is sweet." someone exclaimed.

"Be careful. *Saké* is strong. It will have an effect on you later," Donald warned. "There's a rule in our company that we must honour a person who has worked continuously for twenty-five years. You know that?"

"Eizo's been a good worker. Give him a decoration. A big one." It was Jeff again, making everyone laugh.

"Hold your horses, Jeff."

"Yes, sir!"

"Regrettably, Eizo's a little shy for that. Even so, we all know he has worked with devotion and I'd like to express my sincere gratitude. Congratulations, Eizo. Now, as a memento of distinguished service, we'd like to make a presentation." Donald pulled a box from a vinyl bag and presented it to Eizo, shaking his hand.

Everyone clapped and some added, "Hooray!"

"Thank you very much, Mr. McCord, uh, everybody." Eizo began uncertainly, looking for the words he had previously thought to say. "I worked for the company for a long time and everybody was very kind. I won't forget that even after I go back to Japan. Thank you, thank you very much. Thank you." He concluded his speech quickly and bowed several times, taking a tissue out of his pocket and blowing his nose. Everyone cheered and clapped again.

"Well done, Eizo." Donald said.

"Eizo, why don't you open the box now?" Jeff suggested.

Eizo put the tissue paper into his pocket and began opening the gift box with clumsy fingers. Inside was a silver cookie plate.

"Your name and our division are engraved on the back of the plate," Donald said.

Eizo did not understand the word 'engraved' and got muddled. The co-worker seated next to him turned the plate for him and pointed to the engravings.

"Oh, wonderful! Thank you very much." Eizo exclaimed, truly appreciative.

"Eizo has a wife and three children in Japan. Of course, although I say children, they are grown-up. He has worked for more than forty years in Canada and has been sending money to his family during that time," Donald said, enlightening everyone about Eizo's circumstances.

"For more than forty years, alone in Canada?" one of his co-workers said, plainly surprised. With the turnover at the factory over the years, it wasn't unthinkable that most workers were unaware of Eizo's situation.

"In the last forty years you went back to Japan sometimes to see your family though, didn't you?" Jeanette asked.

"No," Eizo said in a low voice.

"Not even once?"

"No."

"Holy cow!"

The jovial atmosphere cooled at once.

"Eizo had particular reasons not to be able to go home," Donald interjected, defending him from his co-workers.

The female workers had grim faces and exchanged glances among themselves. Eizo was at a loss for words, sat quietly and waited to see how things turned out. An awkward silence dominated the party.

"When you see your wife, you can go on a honeymoon again. That'll be great, eh Eizo?" Jeff jumped in to break the ice.

Suddenly everyone burst into laughter.

"I know a similar case. The father and his son worked in Canada for a long time and saved money to go home. When he finally returned, he built a new house and bought a new car. He had a honeymoon, too," Gus said.

"Super," Greg added, "And they came to Niagara Falls for a honeymoon, right Gus? Ho, ho, ho."

The celebratory mood reappeared as if the curtain for a new play had just opened.

"I don't know about that. But his son stayed in Canada. He's Canadian and likes it here," Gus answered.

"Eizo, are you going to build a new house and buy a new car too?" someone asked, trying to be funny. Nobody laughed.

Apart from buying a new car, it seemed quite probable that he would build a small house near his family's home, if his wife and sons had turned away from him. *Oh, shoot!* He was praying that would not be required.

"I'm not that rich." Eizo waved his right hand.

Everyone laughed. The laughter was refreshing, particularly since the conversation had drifted towards more difficult issues for Eizo to appreciate. He could not grasp the flow of the conversation among the young Canadian workers and felt left out in spite of being the reason for the gathering. An hour later, everyone was satiated and absorbed in conversation. It was as though he no longer existed. Eizo quietly drank his *saké* until the bottle was empty and sat absentmindedly, toying with his cup. Contrary to his expectation, the food had been popular and his co-workers' appetite was a surprise. When the sliced, raw fish arrived Jeff tried to speak to him, but the waitress interrupted to explain how to eat the delicacy. The group devoured the *sashimi* that most had been afraid to even touch at first.

"Eizo, what do you call this sliced raw fish in Japanese?" Jeff asked, picking up the last sliced piece on the plate with his shaky fingers.

"It's called *sashimi*."

"*Sa-shi-mi*. It's pretty good. What do you call this frigging green stuff?"

"*Wasabi*."

"Darn, it burns my nose. But it tastes good. I'm going to bring my girlfriend and let her try it," Jeff said, pinching his nose.

Final tea was served and then it was time to go. Everyone shook Eizo's hand and said a few parting words. His departure from Canada became suddenly and abruptly real.

"Don't worry, Eizo. Everything will go well for you and fit into its place." Donald put his lumber like arm around Eizo's shoulder and gave him a tight squeeze.

"I hope so," murmured Eizo.

"I'm sure it'll work out. By the way, it was a very good farewell party. I think everyone had a good time."

"Thank you very much, sir … Mr. McCord," Eizo said appreciatively, nodding.

It was half-past nine. Some of the guests had already left. Eizo stared vacantly at the co-workers' backs as they walked out to their cars and felt a little sad. *All good things come to pass quickly.*

"Eizo, do you need a ride?" Gus asked, breaking Eizo out of his reverie.

"Yes, thank you."

The two put on their overcoats and exited the restaurant.

It had stopped snowing. Christmas lights decorated the downtown stores. Though busy with last minute shoppers, some stores were trying to close up business for the day. As they settled into the Firebird, Eizo realized he had mixed feelings about leaving Canada. Despite his detention in the concentration camp during the war, time in Canada had filled a major part of his life and leaving from here would no doubt make him feel as if his heart would break. Then, the scene where he was being taken to the Hastings Park Detention Centre by ship came out of the blue in his mind. When the ship was about to dock in Vancouver, one police officer from the wharf yelled at one of the Japanese evacuees that he could not take a big black cello case to the detention centre. The father was carrying the cello for his daughter, despite the fact that they were imposed a limit on the amount of belongings they were allowed to carry.

One of the people watching the ship docking yelled at the father that he would buy that cello for a dollar. As soon as the father heard the man say that, he flew into a fury realizing that the man was trying to take advantage of his weakness and decided rather to discard it than sell it for a dollar. He dashed to the starboard of the bow and hurled the cello into the sea with all of his strength and so that it caused a loud splash … Eizo shook his head to emerge from the nasty memory and looked outside of the car. *I told you not to recall those memories. You never listen to me!* The sidewalks were cleared but still the snow was piled on the roadside. They were approaching to Bloor Street.

"Maybe, the Christmas lights are pretty tonight. Do you want to drive around and look at them again?" Gus asked.

"Yes, I want to. Thank you. But I want to go alone."

"Alone? Okay, it's up to you. Do you want me to drop you off there?"

"Yes, please."

"No problem."

As they passed Rosedale, it was covered in snow, that muffled the noise of the Firebird and turning to the right, Gus slowed to let Eizo out. He tried once more to insist on driving Eizo around in the car, but he politely declined.

As Eizo expected, the sparkling red and green lights were brightly reflected on the snow but for some reason the Christmas scene had lost the appeal it had had the first time that he saw it. Some houses were not decorated at all. He remembered someone saying that a big building downtown that had traditionally lit up the word 'Noel' by turning some rooms' lights on and some off, had stopped doing so. Even the bus companies had ceased sightseeing tours to see the Christmas lights in high-class residential areas. It was all to save energy and Eizo reflected on how change was inevitable.

Enveloped in his thick black overcoat, Eizo slowly made his way down the sidewalk in his rubber boots. Although most of the snow had been shovelled away, he lost his footing on the ice a couple of times. He carefully stepped forward, balancing his body by swinging both hands. The air was biting, crisp and brittle as if it could fracture into pieces. Even with lined leather gloves, Eizo still had to rub his hands together for warmth.

Occasionally a large passenger car would rumble past. The houses seemed huddled, most of the curtains were pulled.

Ha. Inside those houses, there are families living together. The father might've bought cakes on the way home from work to share the joyful time with his family. You did it once when you came home from work in Osaka. Remember how your wife and kids were happy to see you and share the cookies you'd brought as a souvenir? Isn't that a normal family life for you? Something is wrong. Look, they even haven't sent the document you requested.

Shadow, I don't need your blame for that now. You know my situation very well and you are supposed to stand on my side. An hour ago, I was at my sayonara party and was feeling good, after a sort. You've ruined everything now. I know to the marrow of my bones how abnormal my life has been here in Canada. I came here to recall my family. Don't give me another blow, please. I'm already daunted. Leave me alone!

No, you are not. You neglected everything for too long, far too long.

Eizo stopped at a corner and looked up at the sky. He saw a few stars shining through a parting in the clouds. Was this an omen? Although not a Christian, Eizo suddenly felt as though God was watching over him and his family, that they would soon achieve happiness together. The starlight was telling him this. He took off his gloves and hat, closed his eyes, and hands clasped, prayed:

"Dear Lord, may my family pardon me for my long absence and accept me. May my family and sons and I be happy together again. I pray for their continued good health and that Kino does not desert me."

Eizo finished his prayer with a sense of peace. His mind was now clear. He stopped walking in front of a house. Strings of colourful lights outlined every peak and window, white-light reindeers and candy canes glittered through the snow, a big snowman stood in the yard and a thick holly wreath hung on the colonial front door.

Stay calm. This is the last year in Canada for you. Leave your experiences behind—no matter how dreadful those have been—and go home to your family. There will be a way for you.

With one final look, Eizo turned and started back home.

Stay calm ... stay calm. Everything will work out for you in the end.

Occasionally, a soft breath of air would stir the powdery snow from the branches of the trees and it would dance down splendidly under the light of the street lamps.

8
Cold, Ugly Skeletons

Friday, December 30th arrived: Eizo's last day at the company. He was not ready to face it.

After breakfast, a bowl of cereal and milk, he shuffled over to the television, but abandoned the idea in favour of a quiet morning. He went into the washroom, stood in front of the sink, and looked in the mirror. An old man looked back, the years written all over his face. He rubbed two deep wrinkles between his eyebrows with his fingers and tried to say something to his shadow, but the words would not come. He sighed. One thing was sure; he was retiring today. Tomorrow he would no longer contribute to the working world and would only watch the younger generations from a distance. He would still be a part of society, but only from the sidelines. A touch of pathos floated across his mind. Under usual circumstances, one's retirement would mark the turning point of their life, but for him there was an important challenge ahead of him which he had to deal with: his reunion with the family. He finished shaving and left for work.

"It's your last day, eh, Eizo!" Greg called.

Others in the factory had become aware of his retirement and the people that Eizo ran into expressed their congratulations. Some raised their hands to salute him.

Soon after he started his shift, Donald came to see him.

"You need not work today if you don't want to. You've worked long enough."

"No, sir. I'll work today."

Donald's eyebrows jerked up. "You know the word *no*? I thought you only knew *yes*. That's good!" he said chuckling. "Okay, if you want to work till the end, you go ahead. You can work as much as you want."

"I've worked, uh, till today. And I want to work till the end." Eizo raised his voice so as not to be drowned out by the noise of the machinery and the screech of the bottles.

"Okay, it's up to you."

"Oh, thank you very much."

Eizo appreciated his kindness. He knew Donald didn't care whether he worked until the end of his shift or not, but it was important to him. If he did not work the last day that he was paid, it would be a stain on his pride. He had to bring his working life to a satisfactory conclusion.

"Anything from your family?" Donald asked.

"No. Nothing."

"Don't worry. You've been of great value to them."

"I hope so."

"You hope so? Don't be so timid. Even if your family doesn't accept you back, just stay on in your house. It is your house," Donald said half-smiling.

"Yes … Uh, I'll try."

"Good. You need a positive attitude to achieve things, you know." Donald paused. "Let me know if there's anything I can do for you."

"Yes, thank you very much, uh, for everything," Eizo said and bowed to Donald.

"You did your best. I know you'll do the same in the future," Donald replied, with an awkward bow in return. "Eizo, good luck! I pray for your happiness. Okay, good-bye." Donald shook Eizo's knobbly hand and grabbed his upper arm with the other.

"Good-bye, sir."

*

At twelve o'clock the factory shut down for New Year. Even while the machines were slowing down to stop operating, shouts of joy were heard here and there. Some of the workers ran towards the change rooms jumping with joy. Eizo did not move and watched the machinery slow down. He stayed there for some time watching the procession of empty bottles halt their parade into the washer.

It is over. It is finally over.

Now he could walk away from this factory with a whistle and not look back. But, Eizo was frozen in place and stared blankly at the machinery that lay on the factory floor like cold, ugly skeletons. He recalled the summer of 1953, when he began working at this factory. In those days, people still remembered the Second World War as a recent event and the Nikkei were still subject to criticism on the attack at Pearl Harbor. Eizo, a citizen of a former enemy country, knew how fortunate he was to have landed this job. However, after the initial euphoria evaporated, he settled into a long, monotonous spiritual battle against the relentless machines. Knowing that his wife and sons relied on him for those wages saved him.

Eizo reached out and plucked a bottle from the conveyor just before it was carried into the washers. At first he thought about bringing the empty bottle home as a souvenir. He had never won an award. The empty bottle would be a fitting symbol of his long working life, maybe making it easier to rationalize his life through the solid shape of the bottle, rather than fading memories and sentiments. He wondered whether he should take the bottle home, but decided not to—after all, his memory at the factory would not necessarily be the one he wanted to recall often after returning to Japan—and put it back on the conveyor, reluctantly.

"Eizo, you don't have to work anymore," Gus said as reached out and shook Eizo's hands enthusiastically.

"Gus, you're still here?"

"No, I looked for you and thought you're still here and came back to say good-bye and good luck to you." Gus said in one breath. He had already changed from his work uniform to a coat and trousers.

"Oh, thank you, Gus."

"Don't mention it. From tomorrow, you can sleep in till the lunch time every day," he laughed.

"No, I don't."

"You don't? But, you have no work to do."

Eizo could not help but laugh.

"There is a story about a guy who I know. He retired from his job, but he still got up early every morning. While he is living, he wants to see everything, every incident. He doesn't want to miss anything. When you retire, you are going to be like that, hah?"

"I don't know, Gus. Maybe."

"Yes, you're going to be. Well, Eizo, take care. Good-bye and good luck!" Gus hugged Eizo.

Eizo was nearly choked with emotion. He managed to tap Gus's back several times. The young man's shoulders were thick.

"Goodbye, Gus. Thank you!"

After releasing Eizo, Gus turned and left. His retreating figure did not project any sadness at their parting; rather his steps seemed to be quite blithe. Eizo realized this was possibly the last time he would see him in his life. He appreciated Gus's presence, but at the same time he was afraid to imagine that he would soon forget Gus in the activities of a new environment. He tried to deny that repulsive idea.

The machinery was silent, dead, mutely waiting for its new caretaker without any sentiment for the old. With some bitterness Eizo took in that he would simply be replaced with another worker. After touching the machine again, he went to the change room, stuffed his work uniform into a bag, and left the factory.

Once on the street, he stopped and looked back. All that sat before him was a large, featureless building shrouded in an ominous silence. It was dull, cold and noisy with the cars and trucks passing nearby. The twenty odd years of struggling with inner and outer torments condensed into emptiness.

9
Banzai! Banzai! Banzai!

Like turning a page of a calendar, the first of January 1978 arrived. Although Eizo had not set the alarm, he woke up at the same time as for work. Today he planned to visit friends, the tradition at New Years, and say his goodbyes to them.

Many Japanese Canadian families living in Toronto celebrated the New Year with a feast. They prepared various dishes over several days, making almost fifty portions for visitors expected on New Year's Day. This custom had been broken while they were interned, but was revived after a number of Japanese moved to Ontario at the end of the war and found it a little easier to make a living.

The Nikkei also evolved, created new customs, conversational styles, and ways to celebrate the festivities apart from those practiced in Japan. Their culture had its own complexities and was the result of mixed practices from the many regions of Japan, and, of course, those of European origin. For example, Christmas was celebrated in much the same way Canadians celebrated it, while celebrating the New Year followed the Japanese tradition of a feast. These customs, though, were not necessarily the same as those found in Shinto, where the masses visited shrines throughout Japan on New Year's Day.

In everyday conversation, the Nikkei, particularly the Nisei, often started sentences in English and finished the same sentence in Japanese or vice versa. They used both languages frequently in conversation. This could be traced back to the necessity of communicating with their Japanese-speaking parents and later interacting with the English-speaking world.

Eizo made his first stop at his friend's home, Senkichi Sato, whom he had first met in the forced labour camp. Five years older than Eizo, Senkichi was a retired stonemason now living on a pension. He had one son named Martin, a chemistry teacher at a local high school, who was married with two children. Since the war, Senkichi had struggled to forget his detention in the camps and the hardship that followed.

Once out of the camps, Eizo had often called upon Senkichi to find solace in his counsel and escape out of his solitary misery. In those days, Eizo's life was unstable, moving from job to job; his mind had not yet been emancipated from those unhappy years. He was living alone and could not help but bring up memories of the camps and news of their friends; he did not want to talk much about his family either. Senkichi, however, was reluctant to reopen old wounds. He had his family and needed to live for tomorrow, not for yesterday. When Senkichi finally secured a job as a stonemason, life stabilized and he became increasingly unwilling to talk about his bitter past.

Senkichi's son, Martin, was growing up, and as the dark shadows of the concentration camps faded from the Satos' faces, Eizo was increasingly reminded of his own unnatural family situation. The war was over. There was no longer any reason for him to stay in Canada, but Kino had sent her last and final letter when it was time to return to Japan. Around that time Senkichi's and Eizo's relationship began to slide. Eizo continued talking about the past, not understanding that this was painful for Senkichi whose family had once lived in a dingy barrack in the concentration camp and fought for the use of the kitchen along with other families. Nor could he bear listening to Senkichi talk about his family when Eizo could not be near his own. It was inevitable that Eizo's visits to Senkichi's became infrequent.

When Martin had grown and become a teacher, Senkichi and his wife often spoke proudly about their son's friendships and future plans. This always made Eizo feel uneasy and disconnected. He had known Martin since he was a child, watched him grow, get a job, get married, have children and do well in the *hakujin* society. These were pleasant things for Eizo, too, but Martin was a constant reminder of the wife and three sons that he had left behind.

When Eizo got off the bus it was almost ten o'clock. The morning air was brisk. Senkichi's house stood just off the main road.

"Oh, Osada-san. *Shin-nen omedeto gozaimasu*, A Happy New Year!" greeted Matsu, Senkichi's wife, as Eizo rang the doorbell. She called everyone out of the backrooms. Senkichi responded in a cheery voice and appeared from around the corner. He was a heavier and shorter man than Eizo, medium height and slightly bent, a large well shaved face with a wrinkled forehead. Martin and his two daughters joined the chorus of New Year's greetings.

"Martin, your daughters have grown so much since I last saw them," Eizo noted.

"Yes, they have, haven't they? You know Anne is fifteen and Lisa is thirteen now. Both are teenagers," Martin said proudly, smiling at his daughters. "No wonder I'm turning a little grey." He was a little taller than his father, thin, had glasses with thoughtful eyes behind them and wore a cardigan and dark trousers. His hair was neatly cut.

After the exchange of greeting, Anne and Lisa disappeared to another room.

At that moment, Martin's wife, Heather, came from the living room and managed to greet Eizo in Japanese. She was third generation Japanese Canadian and could speak very little of her grandparents' language. She seemed to feel ashamed of not being capable of speaking Japanese fluently.

"Osada-san, would you have *saké*?" Senkichi offered when they got into the living room.

"Oh, that would be nice. Yes, please."

"Matsu, *saké* please."

Matsu, dressed up in a sober one-piece, her dyed black hair bundled in a tight bun, went into the kitchen with Heather, leaving the three men behind in the living room. An *ukiyoe* print was on the wall behind Eizo and on the other wall an old Japanese scroll of countryside scenery hung above the western style lamps on the side tables.

"So, what's new?" Senkichi asked Eizo.

"I quit my job the day before yesterday."

"Oh, you did! You've joined our retirement club at last."

"I get full membership now, like you."

"So, you must be planning to go home soon, Eizo-san?" Martin said.

"Yes, I'm going back," Eizo said emphatically.

"The time has finally come," Senkichi said lightly, but distress seemed written on his face. The three men became quiet.

"Now you can go home to your family. That's good, that's very good," Senkichi said finally, breaking the silence.

Eizo was momentarily puzzled by Senkichi's words and did not know how to respond. Senkichi, of course, knew about Eizo's family situation very well and could not expect him to say much about it at this stage.

"Well, I don't know if we'll end up together or not, but, well, it'll be nice going back to my old home anyway," Eizo said with a forced smile.

"Eizo-san, it'll be all right. You don't have to worry," Martin said, leaning forward on the couch.

"Thank you, Martin. Anyhow, I'll go back and see how things are." On a visit to Senkichi's family about eleven months earlier, Eizo had mentioned the issue surrounding his family registration.

"You aren't very good at hiding your worry," Senkichi said. "I mean I'm sure everything will be all right. Everybody'll be waiting for you."

I heard the same words somewhere before.

He and Martin remained quiet.

" … Have you received any correspondence lately from your family?" Senkichi asked.

"Unfortunately, no." Eizo started talking about his visit to the Consulate General when Matsu re-entered the room.

"I'm sorry to have kept you waiting," Matsu apologised as she set the rustic *saké* decanter and matching cups on the table.

"Matsu, Osada-san retired a couple of days ago and is planning to head home."

"Is that right? When you came over last time, you mentioned the possibility of retiring."

"And there has been no contact from Japan," Senkichi added.

"I'm sorry to hear that. Well, please have *saké* while it's hot."

Matsu poured for each of the men and Martin poured for her. They toasted the New Year.

"Osada-san was just mentioning some problems returning to Japan."

Eizo continued where he'd left off, relating the situation around the loss of his Japanese citizenship, the necessity to register as an alien, and the need to apply for naturalization in Japan.

"An alien registration for you? But, you were born and raised in Japan. That's ridiculous, isn't it? You've immediate family there," Matsu said, astounded.

"Well, that's the law and there's nothing anyone can do about it. I don't think the government makes those kinds of laws randomly, but it's sad nonetheless," Senkichi said.

"When you return to Japan and are naturalized, then you can live there, right? Why not go to Japan on your Canadian passport?" Martin interjected.

"Martin, you don't understand how the Issei feel. There's a deep attachment to the country we were born in," said Senkichi.

"I know that, Dad." Martin cut him short. "What I was trying to say was, even with a Canadian passport, you could stay in Japan legally and do a lot of things."

"That's enough," Matsu interrupted. "No more arguing, please. It's New Year's Day and it's supposed to be a happy day."

"By the way, have you called home?" Senkichi asked Eizo.

"No, I haven't. I don't know if they have a phone or not."

"I'm sure they do. Nowadays everyone has a phone. I'll ask the operator," Martin offered.

"Good idea, Martin. Give it a try," said his father.

"What time would it be right now in Japan?" Martin asked.

"It doesn't matter. The Osadas will talk for the first time in forty years. It shouldn't matter whether it's day or night in

Japan. Call them! Wake them up! Aren't I right, Matsu?" Senkichi said supportively.

"I think it'll be okay," said Matsu.

"No, wait a minute, please. Please wait," Eizo cut in.

The Sato family paused, puzzled with Eizo's hesitation.

"I'd rather not call right now, Martin. What would happen if they say 'No' to me? I'll be going home soon enough. I'll talk to them face to face. So, please, no."

The family was at a loss for words.

What are you afraid of? Frightened by the shadow of the past and what you haven't done for your family?

What an irony it was to compare how courageous a young volunteer firefighter Eizo was in Japan to this spineless state of mind now! When he thought about the fear of his family's rejection, he could not contain his anxiety and desperation and felt beaten down. Once in his hometown in Japan, he was about to go home as he was tilling the last ridge of field. It was late autumn and the air was dry. He suddenly heard the fire-bell begin ringing fast which was telling him the site was close. He threw the hoe down and ran to the shed where the hand fire pump was stored, out of breath.

When he reached there, other volunteers had already pulled the pump out and were on the point of dashing to the scene. As they ran, they saw the black mass of towering smoke and an acrid reek greeted their noses. When they arrived, a farmer's house was engulfed in the fiendish orange blaze, flaring tongues of fire licking through every corner of the house vertically and laterally, its sparks flying high in the evening sky, sucking up the air from the ground and fueling the flame. The sharp snapping sounds of burning resin, splitting lumber and the inaccessible heat of the fire overwhelmed the firefighters. The farmer's family were standing stock still and forced to watch the blaze ravage their house.

The firefighters extended a hose to the river nearby, Eizo holding the hose against the inferno. They pumped the water, the fire fizzed but its red tongue was moving as if swallowing them. Eizo, holding the hose for dear life, fought tenaciously, and never once thought of his exposure to danger. The fire engines came from the nearest city but he was still occupied with the firefighting work until it died down.

In addition, he had enough courage to cross the Pacific Ocean to Canada to work as a lumberjack, a job that required mental endurance and physical strength.

Where were those days? From where does this timidity come? He felt weak. It was inexcusable to have let things go for this long. The longer he dragged out his stay in Canada, the worse the situation became. It was too late to place the call to them; too much time had gone and wasted away.

"Osada-san might want to call later, you know. So, why not just ask the operator the phone number, Martin?" Matsu suggested after a short silence.

"That's a good idea, eh, Osada-san?" Senkichi said.

Eizo pondered the idea for a moment. "Okay, ask for the number, please."

Martin fetched a pen and a piece of paper and asked Eizo to write his address in Japan in Romanized letters. Martin then went into the next room and made the call.

"When I saw Martin for the first time in the camp, he was this small." Eizo spoke in a hardly audible voice, indicating how small Martin had been with his stretched hand. "He reminded me so much of Tamotsu."

"I know. Well, you did your best, Osada-san," Matsu said, dabbing her eye with her fingers.

After a while Martin came back into the living room. "I've got it, Eizo-san." He handed the paper over to Eizo.

A series of numbers unfamiliar to Eizo were written under his address. If he dialled these numbers he could speak with his family immediately. He suddenly felt closer to Kino and Tamotsu. The phone number took on new meaning and tempted him to make the call. But again Eizo wavered. He knew he should call. Kino could not ignore him.

What are you afraid of?

He felt his chest tighten. If anyone in the room had continued to press Eizo to contact his family he probably would have made the call. He lifted his face from the paper. Three faces stared back at him, waiting. He saw the solidarity in the Satos' eyes, nurtured by the bond of a lifetime spent together as a family. A sudden chill ran up Eizo's spine.

Look at their faces. This is a family that knows each other perfectly well. Even though I have worked all my life to support my family, one phone call cannot atone for leaving them alone for so long. It could never be enough. I can't call them now. If I call Kino and if ... if she tells me not to come back, what on earth will I do then?

"At least if you have your family's phone number, you can get hold of them any time," Matsu suggested, taking the pressure off Eizo.

"Mmm. You can call them whenever you need to," Senkichi agreed.

"Thank you for the phone number, Martin," Eizo said.

"Osada-san, you seem to be troubled," Matsu said, like a consoling mother, trying to understand Eizo's predicament.

"I think you're taking this a little too seriously," Senkichi said gently.

Eizo knew they were just trying to comfort and support him. It was the best they could do under the circumstances.

"I wish the war never occurred. After the attack on Pearl Harbor, we had so many sleepless nights with worry about what was going to happen to us," Matsu recalled, looking at Senkichi.

Martin listened quietly, sitting with Eizo at the other end of the sofa. Matsu, alone in the love seat, looked at Senkichi beside her in an armchair.

"Those days were the worst. In the camp we had no hope for the future. We couldn't go back to anything because there wasn't anything left to us. We were on the brink of a cliff. Or, we were already in hell. So, we had to only go forward. I could never go through that again," Matsu added.

"I remember the first winter in the camp," Eizo inserted, "even the weather got to us."

"Martin often cried because it was so cold, you know. The inside walls of the barracks were white with frost. I had to keep Martin in my arms to warm him. I cried so many times I can't remember …" Matsu said with great difficulty, unable to finish.

Everyone's eyes were wet with tears. Martin stood up beside his mother and held her as if holding his crying daughter.

"There is one scene that I can never forget. Martin and I were on the train at a station in Vancouver, about to evacuate to the internment camp. There were RCMP officers here and there to keep watch on the crowd and another RCMP officer was standing at the end of our car. You were already in the internment camp," Matsu said, looking at Senkichi, wiping her tears again. "In front of us were an elderly man and a young mother holding a baby, oh, about two weeks old. The baby was crying. The young mother offered milk but the baby kept refusing it. It was a wretched scene! Outside along the train, there were many Japanese people who had come to see us off. 'Be patient,' I heard someone call. 'We'll be all right,' others called to the evacuees on the train. People were leaning out the windows, holding each other's hands, and some kids were yelling and shouting and it was chaos.

After a while, the mother said, 'Excuse me,' to me, the timid elderly man beside her was her father, and started changing a cotton diaper, laying the baby boy on the wicker seat. Probably the baby felt relieved and began peeing. Strangely enough, I was moved. For me, it was the breath of life. Yes, a breath of life! Looking at the baby peeing, I thought I had to live … for Martin and you. It uplifted my broken spirit. I'm funny, am I not? That baby taught me how important it is to live.

Then, the train jerked and started moving slowly. Somebody somewhere shouted *banzai!* And then everybody jumped in echoing *banzai! banzai! banzai!* raising their arms up in the air, over and over. I thought you say *banzai* only three times. But they kept on shouting *banzai, banzai.* Everything I saw was so dusty and red, just like looking through red glasses. We were off to the internment camp for the crime that we had never committed …"

"Hey, that's enough. Let's stop talking about those times," Senkichi cut it.

Eizo and Senkichi had slipped into silence, occupied with their own thoughts. Matsu wept silently, but the tears seemed to have cleansed her spirit. She recovered her composure and smile. "Well, we've Martin and he's made us proud. We're lucky."

"I know all about your hardships and I've learned a lot from you about life," Martin said to his parents.

Eizo sighed.

He thought about his sons. He was not sure that they knew anything about his experiences in Canada. He wondered how much Kino had told them. Looking at Martin, Eizo tried to imagine his third son, Kozo, showing affection for him the way Martin did for his father.

Impossible. I am a complete stranger to Kozo. In time, perhaps.

The doorbell rang. Eizo could hear the exchange of New Year's greetings. A group of four or five teenage girls passed by the open living room door and followed Anne, Martin's older daughter, into the dining room, all chatting and laughing noisily. Eizo noted the girls all were white except Anne.

"Oh, look at this! Wow, what a lot of food!"

"They're Anne's school friends," Martin explained.

After a while Matsu invited Eizo into the dining room to partake in the elaborate spread. Anne's friends were already enjoying the food. The table was covered with dishes of both North American and Japanese origin. Eizo feasted his eyes on lobster, shrimp, baked salmon, and a simmered dish of smoked herring and burdock root. There were also pickled foods, meats, *sashimi*, *sushi*, herring roe, salad and so many other dishes that Eizo could not help but feel delight. Senkichi and Martin followed them into the kitchen and started dishing up.

Then the adults returned to the living room and sat down.

"We've had some violence recently," Martin started. "There are a few students who have assaulted teachers and vandalized school property."

"That doesn't sound good. You weren't attacked, were you?" Eizo asked, while still preoccupied with his own family.

"No, I wasn't. I've been all right so far."

111

"That's good."

"At another school a student set a fire to one of the buildings."

"That's awful!"

"In the sixties a lot of students were anti-establishment, challenging the old values, you know, but today's young people draw attention through violence. Still, it's pretty rare. I sometimes wonder about those who make too much of freedom," Martin said sighing.

"Nonsense! Freedom and peace must be fought for and cherished," Senkichi directed to Martin. "You were too small to understand what it was like inside the camps, where our liberties and freedom were stripped away. You don't appreciate what you've lost until it's taken from you."

"Dad, I'm not forgetting the camps, for goodness sake," Martin said irritably to his father. "Anyway, one thing for sure is that they're looking for something, but they can't get it in today's society, I think. As a result, they get frustrated and vent by damaging property."

"I can't believe this type of thing is happening. It would be inexcusable if someone gets killed," the father grumbled. "Today's youth are indulging themselves too much. They should be severely penalised for their crimes."

"Dad, even if you sentence them to harsh punishment, that won't solve anything. Discipline isn't the fundamental remedy for the problem. I know from my teaching experiences that you can't motivate students by flatly pressing something on them, but you have to help motivate them, draw out something from the inside of themselves. You can say the same thing about crime. You have to search out the cause of the crime and remove the root of it."

"There're always some bad apples in society. And you have to remove those bad apples before they get …"

"Dad, those apples are not necessarily bad in nature," Martin argued, cutting him off.

Eizo listened silently but was worried about how his three sons had grown up. According to Fumi, in his daughter-in-law's last letter, everyone was supposedly fine at home. Eizo, of course, had taken her writing at face value and assumed that everything was all right. But was that really the case?

I wonder if Fumi considered my position too much to make it seem all was normal so that I wouldn't worry about them. Am I negligent for not fully realizing that till now? Am I to blame for anything that's happened to us?

"No, that's not so. Nowadays, if a person kills someone, depending upon the situation, they will go to prison for only four or five years. A second-degree murder or whatever ... sentences have been too lenient. That doesn't teach them anything and does nothing to set an example for others who might follow their footsteps." Senkichi maintained his position.

The discussion descended into argument. Eizo was not listening anymore. Matsu stepped in to interrupt the father and son.

As they sipped *saké* together, talk eventually shifted to more neutral topics, such as which liquor store sold *saké*, how much the Sato family had donated to the Japanese Church they belonged to, what Christmas presents the Satos' granddaughters got this past Christmas, and so on. During the course of the conversation Eizo became increasingly restless and kept fidgeting with the paper in his pocket. He looked at his wristwatch and realized that he still intended to visit a couple more people.

"By the way, could you do me a favour?" Eizo finally brought up what he wanted to ask Senkichi.

"Of course, if it's within our means."

"It's not a big thing. Just in case, I'd like to apply to a seniors' residence here."

"Seniors' residence here? In Canada?"

"Yes, here. Of course, I called the Nipponia Home, but they said they didn't have any vacancies and there's a long waiting list. I thought, since a resident can carry on with their affairs in Japanese there, it would be better for me. Anyway, I hoped you could let me use your address for any correspondence that might come with regard to my application."

"Of course, you don't have to ask. Plumb nonsense to ask me such a thing! Oh yes, please go ahead. But … Osada-san, why are you going through with this?" Senkichi asked, making more creases in his forehead.

"It's only a precaution."

"Precaution? Against what? Do you think your family won't take you back? I think you worry too much," Matsu said, but she could not hide her doubt.

Eizo was trying to keep his tears in check and deliberately said in cheerful voice, "That's why I said, 'Just in case.' Besides, it's not clear whether or not I can reacquire my Japanese citizenship and I may have to return to Canada."

"Eizo-san, when you go to apply for your passport, I'll come with you," Martin said.

"Ah, good idea Martin. Take Osada-san in your car and help him fill out the application."

"Thank you, Martin. But, I can go alone."

"That's okay, Eizo-san, it's no problem."

The doorbell rang again. Matsu went out to the entrance and a young male voice carried though the house.

"It's Saeki-san."

"Ah, okay," Senkichi replied as he stood up.

"Eizo-san, don't worry, I'll take you," Martin insisted.

"Thank you for your offer, Martin. I'll probably ask you to come with me."

"Okay, good."

"Have your parents been to church lately?"

"Yes, they have. They go every Sunday, rain or shine. You know that. But, these days, I take them to the church."

Eizo knew that, after their release from the concentration camp and relocation to Ontario, Senkichi and Matsu became Christian converts. Christian missionaries in Canada had devoted themselves to the education of the young Nisei and Sansei, the third generation Japanese Canadians, and had counselled about the various issues for the Nikkei in the camps. The Satos had been deeply moved by their ethical and moral values, kindness, good deeds and unswerving religious faith. Many Nikkei had converted to Christianity for similar reasons. Although Eizo had attended at a Bible study group in the camp, he did not become a Christian.

Anne came into the living room. "Excuse me, Eizo-san," she said and then turned to Martin. "Dad, we're going out to see a movie, okay?"

"A movie? Are they open today?"

"Of course, some of them."

"Okay, but if you're going to be late, make sure you call."

"I know, Dad. Bye-bye." Anne spoke in such a way as to suggest that her father was nagging, bending her fingers several times in good-bye. Their entire conversation was in English.

Just as Anne left the room, two men entered followed by Senkichi. Both were about thirty and dressed in dark business suits as if the two talked and arranged it before they came.

"Hello, Martin. Happy New Year! Long time no see!" one man said with a loud, gravelly voice, thrusting his hand to Martin.

"Oh, Mr. Saeki. Happy New Year! Good to see you again."

"I would like to introduce a friend of mine. This is Mr. Tajima," Saeki said in somewhat exaggerated English, his jaw sticking out.

Tajima sheepishly exchanged greetings with Martin. Martin suspected Tajima might be a new single immigrant who was taking advantage of the food offered at New Year's. Martin introduced Saeki and Tajima to Eizo.

"How are you, Mr. Osada?" said Saeki, again flamboyantly.

"Ah, I'm fine, thank you. Nice to meet you," Eizo answered in Japanese.

"It's Japanese," Saeki laughed, as though he had encountered something strange. Taking a seat, Saeki continued to speak in English, prompting Eizo to take his leave.

Senkichi and Matsu came into the living room.

Instead of sitting down, Eizo said to them, "Well, it's the time for me to leave. Thank you very much. I enjoyed it."

"Do you have to leave now? Then, take care. We'll see you before you leave to Japan." Senkichi said. The couple saw Eizo off at the front door.

*

An hour later, Eizo called at the Akiyamas, his former landlord from the Cumberland days after the outbreak of the

Pacific War. Akiyama came from the same prefecture and, after his logging camp was closed because of the outbreak of the war, Eizo temporarily stayed at his home. Again, he had *saké* and a little food and spoke about his retirement, but this began to have a draining effect on him. The day was supposed to be filled with the joy and the brilliancy of New Year, but Eizo felt lonely and strangely irritated as he watched the families he visited interact. The lightness of spirit that he had felt that morning was gone; a mix of envy, frustration, lonesomeness and self-pity had replaced it. He had no outlet for all these pent-up emotions, which seemed determined to embitter his last days in Canada.

10
Don't Cry, Matsu!

Several days after New Year's, when Martin had some spare time from his teaching schedule, he and Eizo went to the passport office in downtown Toronto to apply for a Canadian passport. Later in Martin's car on the way home, Eizo fantasized that the man he was sitting beside was his son. Eizo hoped it would be like this when he met his own sons again, but when he tried to imagine driving with them through the dusty country roads in Japan, he could not. He was only able to conjure up the children they were the last time that he saw them.

The thought prompted him to offer Martin lunch for his trouble.

"Thank you Eizo-san, but I have to go back to the school. I haven't finished work."

"Oh, that's right. I'm sorry, I'd forgotten all about that," said Eizo apologetically. "I'd appreciate it if you could drop me off at Bloor Street, then?" Before the car reached the subway station Eizo tried again. "Do you have time for a coffee?"

"No, I'm sorry. I appreciate your offer. Maybe next time," Martin said.

"Right, sorry about that. You've been a great help. Thank you."

"You're welcome. Oh, about the seniors' housing, I'll make some calls and look into it. I'll call you later."

"I'd appreciate that, Martin," Eizo said as he slowly pushed himself out of the car, age getting the better of him. Martin waved as he pulled away. Alone on the crowded street, Eizo waved back.

A few days later, Eizo's phone rang. It was Martin on the line. He related to Eizo the results of his search. "If you call City Hall a social worker will come out to interview you, help you with the application, and explain the options open to you. I also asked whether or not you could apply before you leave for a temporary stay outside Canada, I mean … in Japan. They said there would be no problem provided that you qualify," Martin explained.

"You've been a big help Martin," Eizo said gratefully. "May I impose on you to make an appointment for me?"

"Oh, sure, Eizo-san."

Where would I be without you, Martin?

*

Eizo started to sort out his belongings in preparation for his departure. He kept many things 'just in case' but never used them; an excess in frugality so he could send more money home to his family. Flattened carton boxes, wires and plastic sheets he found on the streets, old nails and things like that; most of what he had would just get tossed. The Issei were more or less that type of people. He smiled sourly.

When the Issei tried to get work right after the war they were typically faced with wage discrimination and made only enough to get by on. To build any amount of wealth they had to either practice extreme economy or create their own businesses. Being thrifty meant they could not buy the

119

clothes they wanted, nor live where they would have preferred. To save even more, some resorted to picking through the trash, circumstances not unlike those of the Great Depression.

Eizo pulled out the bundle of Kino's letters and spent a couple of days going through them. As he had done many times before, he searched for messages that may have been hidden in Kino's last letter; read it line by line, but he could not find any clue as to why she had suddenly stopped writing. What Eizo found instead was an aftertaste of sweetness and bitterness and put his head between his hands. Then he reminisced about the happy times with his family. Strangely, those happy days were always associated with a piercing cobalt blue sky without any clouds. Under the scorching sun, Isoshichi and Tamotsu ran around half-naked in the front yard of his house, shouting and laughing, while Kozo with a finger in his mouth watched them run endlessly. Eizo, as a father, enjoyed looking at them chase after each other.

Instead of living in an extended family household Eizo's parents had let him and his wife establish a branch family to tend his portion of the family rice fields. Those fields, however, were not enough to support his family alone so he always had to find other sources of income. From time to time he went away for work. This did not seem to bother his children; they simply ran around laughing and enjoying themselves as though there was no tomorrow.

Fumi's letters were mixed in amongst Kino's. There were also the telegrams that told Eizo of the deaths of his father, mother, and older brother. Eizo remembered how Martin had helped each time he had to telegraph condolences to everyone back home. Regrettably, Eizo could not attend any of the funerals. The trip would have taken more than a half a month, first to cross the continent to Vancouver by train, and then to cross the Pacific Ocean to Yokohama by boat. The cost of air travel, to his thinking, was out of the question. He later learned that his father, although remembered as a healthy man, had died of a stroke. Although Eizo was sad, it was always heartening to know that his immediate family hadn't forgotten him. While it was customary to keep up the appearance of unity in front of the community, Eizo had felt that these telegrams were an undeniable sign that his family still cared about and remembered him.

He planned to send those letters with his belongings to Japan. The final letter from Kino, however, he decided to carry with him.

*

Several weeks later a social worker, a woman in her late-thirties, came to Senkichi's home to interview Eizo for the retirement home. Martin also attended the meeting. The social worker appeared a little irritable, but listened carefully to Eizo's situation.

"If you decide to stay in Japan for good, please contact me immediately so I can cancel your application. And, before you go I suggest that you visit one or two seniors' complexes. Here are the addresses," she said tersely.

"Martin, can you ask her if it is possible to transfer to a complex where there are other Japanese if spaces become available?" asked Eizo hopefully.

"Yes, that can probably be accommodated should that occur," she said, packing her things to leave.

A week later Eizo and Martin visited a seniors' housing complex, a modern high-rise in a quiet suburb. The property backed onto a small wood with a stream burbling through it. A pleasant Caucasian woman guided them around the facilities. They stopped at the sitting room where about twenty people were seated around tables or chatting by the windows where the weak rays of the winter sun shone through. Eizo felt a faint aura of resentment. He surmised the residents had a hard time grasping meaning in their lives, and unable to do so, embraced all they had left, sour remorse. The atmosphere bore no resemblance to the young people he had worked with at the factory, alive and full of energy. He suddenly realized that he was old.

The seniors sitting beside the window were almost all Caucasians.

"Are there many Asians in this building?" Martin asked.

"No, not many. But, there are several people of different cultural backgrounds."

"Are there any Japanese?"

"I don't remember exactly, but I don't think so," she said softly.

"Okay," Eizo mumbled.

The manager was puzzled with Eizo's response, but said nothing. The three entered the elevator and stood silently until they reached an empty third floor apartment.

Eizo walked around; everything was tidy, much better than the place he was leaving.

There was a balcony where he imagined himself watching the changing seasons and enjoying the cool breeze off the stream.

"As a tenant you need to provide your own furniture, is that right?" asked Martin.

"Yes, that's right. You're responsible for anything that you need to make yourself feel at home," she replied.

"Do they do their own shopping?" Martin asked, firing off more questions.

"Yes, they do. Essentially, this is an apartment for seniors who can take care of themselves. There're other types of facilities."

"What happens in the event of an emergency?"

"Here, we have adopted a system," the manager explained, walking over to the front door and returning with a sign similar to a hotel 'Do Not Disturb'. "Tenants are expected to remove this sign at ten o'clock every morning. If the sign is still there at ten, then we assume something's wrong and take action accordingly."

"You can't sleep in," Martin said half-jokingly.

"If you want to sleep in, you can take the sign away and go to bed again," the woman said, seriously.

Eizo and Martin thanked her and left.

Settling into the car Martin said, "It seems to be a good apartment, eh? The facilities are in good order. Life here wouldn't be so bad, Eizo-san."

Eizo glanced at Martin.

Martin is not my real son!

Eizo felt empty and betrayed; his affection towards Martin was a one-sided illusion. He knew Martin spoke kindly to encourage; however, Eizo could not help feeling betrayed and, therefore, miserable.

*

That week, Eizo began the arrangements for flying back to Japan. At first he considered stopping in British Columbia to visit the old site of the concentration camp where he had spent roughly five years with bitter feelings and memories which he would rather avoid.

123

Would such a visit reopen old wounds? Then, why do I have to go there?

The compulsion to visit the once-detested place puzzled him. The barracks had all been demolished and there was no longer any trace of those times. A winter venture into the snowy areas off the Coastal Mountains only to warm up old memories was reckless.

Better to go straight back to Japan!

He reserved a hotel room near Haneda International Airport in Tokyo, expecting the trip to be long and exhausting as he had never flown anywhere before.

As the day to depart drew near, Eizo found that his feelings toward his memories were changing in an unfamiliar and confusing way. For him, the hard experiences of the concentration camp and his relocation to eastern Canada had become a little like history, no longer real, yet connected in the sense that his life would not exist without them. He was trying to turn the pages of his personal history one by one, but those pages were flying by wildly and would eventually fade into eternity. He felt dizzy and confused.

*

By the middle of March he finished cleaning his apartment and had sent several boxes to his address in Japan. At the same time, he mailed a letter to Kino letting her know the date and flight number of his arrival. He expected the letter to arrive in Japan about ten days before his departure. That would give his family enough time to prepare to come to Haneda International Airport to see him, if they wished so.

He closed his bank account and went downtown to finish buying gifts for his sons and grandchildren. Of course, he did not know exactly how many grandchildren he had, but he bought enough to cover all of them. His preparations were almost complete. When his belongings were finally gone the apartment echoed coldly. This coldness and his anxiety about returning to his wife prevented him from going forward psychologically; his shadow still lurked in the dark corners. Eizo was impatient during those final few days. His shadow needled him with worry.

Maybe the letter won't arrive on time.

I wonder if you should send a telegram as well.

Or, you'd better call them. What an idiot you're!

Don't call them, just go!

Caving in to his shadow, Eizo asked Martin to help him to send a telegram. Martin suggested to Eizo that he call his family as well, but Eizo declined again.

There's no turning back now. They'll see me whether they want to or not. Kino had three sons with me and they're of my blood. It might be difficult at first, but someday the ice will thaw and we'll grow to understand each other again. We can live together.

He clung to this glimmer of hope despite his hovering shadow.

*

Eizo spent his last night at Senkichi's home. The family were to drive and see him off at the airport. An early departure necessitated Eizo's stay, not that anyone regretted this last opportunity to be together. After dinner, they sat in the living room and talked about the old days, steering clear of the concentration camps. They spoke about earlier times, the trials and tribulations of those first Japanese settlers; some stories moving them to laughter.

Matsu related a story about one woman who wrote a letter home to her friends in rural Japan telling them about the wonderful conveniences that could be found in Canada. Barely containing her mirth, Matsu explained how the woman was enthralled by the beautiful porcelain washing machine that was fixed to the floor with a tank that filled while the washing was done in the tub it was attached to. She was happy that it had a lid, but didn't understand the purpose of the horseshoe shaped devise between the lid and the tub which moved up and down.

Everyone had a hard time holding it together when they realized that the washing machine was none other than the toilet. Once the woman in Matsu's story found out her washing machine's true function she never spoke of it again. And she likely never used it again for laundry.

Senkichi told them a story about the male Issei's habit of making water outdoors and how the young Nisei mimicked their behaviour. One day, the *hakujin* male students joined the Japanese male students in chorus line-up urinating along the hedge. Of course, that incident was brought up at a PTA meeting, stirring quite a controversy.

The four laughed at these cultural misadventures.

Pleased with this success, Senkichi told another story that some Issei parents gave their school children lunches called *Bottera*, a fried paste of flour mixed with water and a bit of salt, in order to save money. The Nisei school children were embarrassed in front of *hakujin* students and hid themselves in the bushes nearby the school to eat it. This time Senkichi's listeners did not laugh, but rather became sad.

At around ten o'clock, Martin, citing their early morning departure, took his leave. Eizo sought to maintain a calm external composure. His eyes, though, were moist when he saw Martin off at the door.

Early the next morning, Martin came to pick them up. They headed for the Toronto International Airport with Senkichi and Matsu sitting quietly in the back. Eizo sat up front and watched the familiar landscape go by for the last time. In a few hours he would finally be on his way home.

Eizo felt a natural inclination to look back in the direction of his old apartment despite the fact that it was not visible from the car.

We're on our way at last!

Unaware, he slipped back into old memories.

What were the camps to my life? What did the relocation here mean? Did any of it mean anything to me?

Even now, when Eizo looked over the last forty years for answers, there was no response. The past remained silent and kept its face hidden.

They arrived at Toronto International and made their way to the check-in counter. Despite the early morning, the terminal was crowded.

"Where's your passport and a plane ticket?" asked Martin, prompting Eizo to prepare for his turn in the queue.

Eizo, however, was in such a state that he had to fumble through all of his pockets and the words coming out from his mouth were unintelligible. "Ah, I had them here in my bag, or somewhere, or but ..." He finally found them in his pocket. As he made his way through the check-in, the four proceeded to the departure gate through a cacophony of scratchy announcements and the distant metallic screech of jet engines. Suddenly, a woman's sobbing cut through the din. Eizo looked around

"Don't cry, Matsu!" Senkichi rebuked in a low voice.

Matsu could not control herself. Martin held her gently and Matsu slowly regained her composure. Eizo took Senkichi's hand and thanked him for all that he had done for him.

"Not to worry, not to worry," Senkichi murmured, momentarily lost for words.

Eizo said his good-bye to Matsu who was able, by this time, to hold her emotions in check. He took Martin's hand. Martin suddenly embraced him and softly patted Eizo on the shoulder. He had not expected such a display from Martin and was moved to tears. He pictured Martin as one of his own sons in Japan.

Eizo's face crumpled with a surge of new emotion as he, holding his carry-on with one hand, reluctantly proceeded through the security gate. Looking back for the last time he gave a deep bow to his friends, and then turned and made his way to the departure gate.

*

After take-off, Eizo peered out the window. Cloud concealed the view at first. He sat back and closed his eyes. After some time the clouds broke and the vast, brown prairie spotted with snow opened up under the wing. The flat land stretched out in ominous stillness, reflecting his state of mind. Several hours later, they crossed the Rocky Mountains, the sheer peaks encased in snow and ice. It was a magnificent sight, but Eizo knew that it was also a display of nature's harsh reality.

Eizo tried to pinpoint the location of the old road construction camps, but to no avail. It was here that he had been forced into road building, with little more than a pick and a shovel. He continued to stare at the awe-inspiring splendour below until his eyes began to burn. For years Eizo had searched for meaning in the time he had spent incarcerated here. He felt the Rockies were forever a part of him and, like the mountains, a part of him remained buried under the snow. Even now he searched for an answer, but the frozen landscape was mute. Although to other internees the experience was already history, Eizo still felt raw.

After transferring planes at Vancouver International, Eizo finally headed for Japan and home. Forty-three years earlier he had arrived in Vancouver by ship during the summer and was met by Murata, an acquaintance from his hometown, who had taken Eizo to a logging camp on Vancouver Island. Then, he was young and full of hope. Now he was old, worn out, and filled with worry.

He leaned forward and looked out the window at the islands scattered along Vancouver Island in the blue sea. After his long voyage to Canada, he was received with a half-hearted welcome by his arrogant boss at a logging camp on Vancouver Island, which was carved only on his mind as a distant memory. The mountains on the mainland were deep green or blue, depending upon how distant those were, and silent. Somehow they reflected everything he had gone through in this vast country. The clouds closed around the land as if his story here would remain secreted away, forever.

Canada.

Sayonara!

Part II—Japan

11
April 1978, Japan

After crossing the International Date Line, the 747 cruised through the slowly brightening sky to Japan. The passengers began to wake from their slumber to the sounds of the flight crew preparing breakfast. Eizo was no longer sure how long he had been flying because he had already adjusted his watch to Japan time. In a few more hours he would land on Japanese soil, the decades' long journey finally coming to an end. Everything would have changed: his family, the people, the landscape, the town and local customs.

What about their love and thoughts towards me?

Eizo felt cramped in his seat, but could do nothing except look outside the window. Despite the dry air in the plane, he felt his palms were moist. Another half an hour, he could see a silver cloud stretch endlessly beneath the wing, as endless as the questions that were streaming through his mind. It was implausible for him to see such brightness with the sun rays reflecting on the cloud, as opposed to the murkiness beneath it. He could not help relating even such an insignificant sight with what might be happening in regard to his family situation; the other side of darkness could be totally fine, therefore, his family situation would be, too. He was consumed with, or almost afraid of, his envisioned scene of their family reunion at the airport. He had to close his eyes for a while and then the recollection of his first boat trip across the Pacific Ocean forty-three years ago, full of the seasickness from the rough voyage, occurred to him. He remembered the pain of separation and seeing the images of Kino and his sons constantly flash through his mind. When a large cargo ship had passed in the opposite direction, he had been seized with an impulse to jump overboard and swim to the other ship so he could return to his family.

Now Eizo began to think about the telegram he had sent to Kino, telling her of his impending arrival.

Kino would be too old to come to the airport, but someone should come to meet me. That would be a good sign. Maybe the whole family will come and even the grandchildren might be there to welcome me.

His chest tightened painfully, as his shadow appeared and teased him with doubt.

If all my family comes to the airport, then it'll have been worth going through that hell during the war.

Eizo looked at his wristwatch again.

How much longer to Haneda International Airport? What if they reject me? I'll have to leave Japan in a few months or maybe half a year. Alone.

Almost drained of strength, Eizo pushed those shadow thoughts away. Quiet until now, people around him livened up at the news they would be landing within half an hour. According to the captain's announcement, the weather in Tokyo would be cloudy.

At last, I'm coming home.

Feeling the plane sink he gripped the shoulder strap of his carry-on as if he might have to make an emergency exit from the aircraft. He looked out the window but could still only see silver clouds: land was not yet visible. The 'Fasten Seat Belt' sign came on.

As the plane lowered its flight angle Eizo could hear the engines drop and felt the strange effects of gravity pulling on his body. Dark clouds filled the window as the plane dropped further and droplets of water began to streak horizontally along the glass. Finally, they dropped out of the dark clouds and Eizo could see the ocean spread out below him as if the bottom of the world had fallen out. Forward of the wing he saw the blue land of the Japanese coastline. A pleasant shock coursed through his body as Eizo suddenly realized he was almost home. He had dreamt of this for such a long time.

Will my family be at the airport and glad to see me? Am I ready to meet with them and what shall I say? ... What shall I say?

His stomach cramped and did a roll. Now he could see the farmland and small houses and buildings below but not the Haneda International Airport. The plane flew over the land for a while and Tokyo, with its sheer vast number of buildings, came into sight. Soon the wake of several ships as they plied the waters in Tokyo Bay became visible. Eizo felt as if the plane was dragging him to a destination he didn't feel ready to face. He stretched his hands in front of him and saw them tremble, like bamboo leaves that rustle in the breeze.

Calm down!

His legs were shaking; his mouth was dry.

The plane abruptly landed on the runway as if it had alighted on the sea. The scenery passed fast and the engines roared as the thrust reversers were engaged. This was not the homecoming Eizo expected. It was anticlimactic, mechanical at best. His vision of events and how they would unfold clashed with travel's mundane occurrences. While the plane taxied to the terminal, he tried to take in everything

135

through the window as though he were trying to catch up on forty-three years of his absence.

You're finally in Japan. Are you happy now?

I don't know. Look at this scene. This is not Japan I've been dreaming of. It looks so foreign and I am afraid to see my family.

You have to have guts to face reality. Everything will be all right.

I knew you'd say that. Sometimes you're no use.

The plane stopped and the passengers scrambled for their luggage in the overhead compartments and after an interminable wait for the doors to open slowly began moving toward the exit. Eizo peeked out at the terminal.

Is my family waiting for me? Eizo could not refrain from talking to the shadow again.

Of course, they are. Don't be afraid. You did your part in Canada and have nothing to be ashamed of.

Nothing to be ashamed of and don't be afraid? Why then am I shaking?

The shadow did not answer his question. Eizo was hardly able to move forward.

How will I know them? How will they know me? I didn't prearrange anything with them. I should've asked them to bring a big sign with my name written on it or something. Stupid me!

His legs dragged, he felt light-headed and his eyes were bloodshot with worry. His heart pounded in equal parts: anticipation and dread.

Is anyone here?

*

136

After proceeding through Baggage Reclaim, Immigration and Customs, Eizo immediately started searching for Kino, despite the fact that this was a restricted area. He did not know what his sons would look like, but thought that he should be able to recognize an older Kino. Finally, he was allowed to proceed through the exit and had to shuffle along behind an Asian businessman and a Caucasian couple.

"Daddy!"

A girl of about seven dashed out from the crowd and grabbed on to the arm of the businessman. She clung to his arm, jumped and skipped with joy. A woman, apparently his wife, took an attaché case from him and the happy family moved out of the Arrivals area, exchanging words and smiles.

Eizo strained, trying to see Kino in the throng.

Maybe she's aged a lot and looks different.

He worked his way through the crowd examining faces as he went. Everybody was looking at the exit and nobody paid attention to him. Eizo could find neither Kino nor a man whom he imagined might be one of his middle-aged sons. His strength began to give out.

He felt dizzy and staggered as he realized four decades of effort culminating at this moment. *Was every effort and perseverance I made in Canada for my family a waste?* He did not want to think so but the absence of family on his arrival was telling him so expressively. The world around him swiftly lost colour and sound, the crowd swirling around him meaninglessly.

What an idiotic expectation I had ... I ... I even thought there might be grandchildren here to see me. What a fool I am!

Reality hit Eizo full in the face. He groaned.

They didn't want me to come back. That's why they didn't send the family registration. Of course, it was as plain a day. Why didn't I see it?

He needed to sit down, completely exhausted. Slowly and carefully he pulled out of the crowd, dragging his suitcase behind him. *I should rest first.* Then he recalled he had a room reserved at a hotel nearby. He wanted to settle in his room and think about what to do from here. But he did not have the strength to make his way there.

I came back to be with my family and can't just go back to Canada now!

He barely avoided running into the people in the lobby as he made his way to the chairs. He plunked himself down.

As soon as Eizo sat, he heard a voice above him.

"Excuse me, are you Mr. Osada?"

His head jerked up. A man of about fifty-five was observing Eizo's reaction. He wore a construction company uniform with dried mud on his pants and brown leather shoes. His hair was short, forehead wide and tapered to a narrow chin, thin and tall like Eizo. He was trembling as if he were a leaf fanned by the wind.

Eizo flinched at the seriousness of the fellow's looks.

He resembles ... he might be Tamotsu! He looks too old to be Tamotsu, but the characteristics of his face are Tamotsu's. Must be!

Unsure if this was Tamotsu or his eldest son, Isoshichi, Eizo ventured, "Ta ... mo ... tsu?"

"That's right, I'm Tamotsu."

Eizo was stunned.

"Well ..." Tamotsu tried to say something, his mouth working, but nothing came out.

Tamotsu looked older than his years; the two men almost appeared to be brothers. He was only four when Eizo had left

138

Japan. The father reached out slowly, took Tamotsu's hand, shook it and then leaned forward and embraced him. There was no reaction from Tamotsu. Eizo released him. He saw the face of the man wavering between timidity and self-consciousness.

Is Tamotsu just following Japanese custom or does he resent me for being away so long? Maybe he doesn't want me here.

Tamotsu tried again to say something but hesitated. Captured by an uneasy premonition, Eizo wondered if some unfortunate incident occurred at home while he was traveling, or if Tamotsu was about to reproach him.

"I'm glad to ... see you. You look fine ... You've had a long trip ... you must be very tired," Tamotsu at last said.

Eizo smiled spiritlessly. He did not know if what Tamotsu had said made him happy or not. He was irresolute but decided to take it as a happy welcome.

"Ah, I'm fine. I'm glad you're fine too, Tamotsu. Good, good. How's everyone? Kino, Isoshichi, Kozo?"

Suddenly Tamotsu's expression darkened. "Yes," he said, and after some hesitation, "yes, everyone's fine," he added without looking at him.

"That's good. I've been worried about all of you for a long time. The letters from your mother stopped and I wasn't sure what had happened. I was quite anxious and nervous." He was about to ask where everyone else was, but held back, not wanting to embarrass his son who had come to welcome him.

"We're in the way here. We'd better move. We can talk in the car," suggested Tamotsu.

Eizo had been concerned that Tamotsu would confront him about his long absence, but his son had said nothing about it.

139

"Where are we going?"

"My home. Well, I say my home, but it's actually a company residence."

"Of course," Eizo said quickly and remembering he added, "by the way, I have to cancel my hotel reservation."

"Hotel reservation?"

"Yes, I thought it would be a long trip so I reserved a hotel room to rest in before carrying on. But, now I don't think I need it."

"What's the name of the hotel? Let me cancel the reservation."

Eizo waited while Tamotsu got the number of the hotel and went to use a public telephone. He moved his suitcase to a corner where he would be out of the way from other people. He had recovered somewhat after meeting Tamotsu, glad that someone had come to see him. The family wasn't rejecting him in spite of everything that had happened or not happened.

"All the telephones are occupied. I'll try calling from home later," Tamotsu said, walking up to his father.

Eizo looked at Tamotsu with adoring eyes but for the most part with amazement at how that little weakling boy had grown into a man—actually, a man of nearly fifty. Still, he could not help but sense Tamotsu was uncertain about this reunion.

Maybe this is just how he is. Perhaps we just need some time to break the ice.

"I see. Thank you for taking care of that," said Eizo.

In response Tamotsu just looked down and away. Eizo moved to pick up his suitcase, but Tamotsu reached out first.

"I'll carry it for you," the son said, lifting it easily.

"Thank you."

"No, it's okay. This way please."

Tamotsu moved toward the exit. Eizo noticed that Tamotsu did not bother to call anybody to say that Eizo had arrived, although he had mentioned that all telephones were in use. Eizo felt his euphoria deflate and anxiety sneak in. As they exited the building, the shriek of jet engines and accelerating vehicles assaulted Eizo's ears. The warm weather, the smell of the ocean, car exhaust, and rank sewage combined to make him feel slightly nauseous.

"Please wait here. I'll pull the car around," Tamotsu said.

Eizo saw a line-up of people close by waiting for a taxi. "If you parked your car nearby, I'll come with you," he said, not wanting to wait.

"All right, it's over there," Tamotsu said, pointing. He led his father silently, walking a few steps ahead, to a car with 'Fushimi Construction Co. Ltd.' on the doors. A yellow helmet was on the rear seat and a filthy khaki jumper was rumpled on the front seat.

"Do you work for a construction company?"

"Yes," Tamotsu answered tersely, opening the door of the car, throwing his khaki jumper to the back seat and brushing away the dust for his father.

"Thank you very much." Eizo suddenly realized he had spoken in English; he quickly switched to Japanese. "I think I've been in Canada too long." He looked at Tamotsu for some reaction as he placed Eizo's suitcase in the trunk.

"That's okay," Tamotsu finally replied.

"Now I'm back in Japan and speaking with you, I feel every Japanese word reaching into my heart. It makes me very happy. I've not felt like this for a long, long time."

Tamotsu did not say anything but sat in the driver's seat and turned on the ignition key. Looking at the sombre profile and silence of his grown-up son, he felt an unknown inner trepidation rising.

As they were leaving the airport, Eizo looked back, saw the big signs of 羽田国際空港, Haneda International Airport, both in Japanese and English. Despite his anxiety caused by Tamotsu's dismal silence, he was struck by the fact that he was actually home and that his long absence was at length behind him. There was finally something to look forward to.

12
How Is Your Mother?

"I'm happy to hear everyone is doing well," Eizo said, breaking the silence in the car.

Tamotsu kept driving, not responding.

"How is your mother? Is she doing all right?" Eizo did not miss the tenseness that suddenly ran through Tamotsu's face.

"Yes … well, ah, Mom is fine," Tamotsu stumbled through his words and he shifted uncomfortably in his seat.

Eizo noticed that Tamotsu was acting strangely and was irritated at his attitude. But, having just met after four decades, Eizo did not feel in a position to expect more from him.

It's natural that I'm worried about my wife. Even if I ask the same question twice or three times, don't I deserve some sort of proper response?

"Is she sick?"

"Well … that … Mom is okay physically."

Of course Kino was a strong woman. She worked the fields and carried heavy loads even when she was pregnant. Kino is healthy, that's a relief. I ought not to want more than that.

"That's good. Your older brother is looking after your mother?"

"Yes, Mom is with Isoshichi."

143

"How are Isoshichi and Kozo's families doing? Are they well?"

"Yes, they are."

"How about you? Your wife and children are well?"

"Yes, we're doing okay." Tamotsu answered looking over at Eizo. He neither smiled nor showed any emotion, but his eyes glistened. Some emotion was at work.

"Children! How many do you have?"

"My children?"

"Yes, yours."

"We have two."

"How old are they now?"

"Both are in high school. The elder one is a boy in his last year and his younger sister has just entered high school."

Eizo tried to imagine his teenaged grandchildren. He was not sure he could call it love, but a feeling of affection for them was already putting out buds. With the sudden understanding that he had two grandchildren, he felt as though a miracle had just occurred.

"And how about Kozo's children?"

"He has a daughter, Chiaki. She is the same age as our daughter, Mayumi."

"Oh," Eizo said.

"He had another daughter younger than Chiaki, but …"

"You say Kozo *had* one more girl."

"Yes …"

"Well then, what happened?"

"She was unwell and passed away when she was little. It was very unfortunate," Tamotsu said with a sigh.

"Died … She died … Kozo's child?" Eizo was about to shout, but he restrained himself.

Why did they not tell me such an important thing? I'm her grandfather and ought to know. What was Kozo, or anyone else, thinking about such a grave matter?

"That was more than ten years ago," reflected Tamotsu.

"Why did no one tell me …?"

Tamotsu glanced over at his father's tone, but turned his attention back to the road.

"I don't know. I really don't know," Eizo repeated, as though it was mantra for the dead. He raised his right hand to rub the two deep wrinkles between his eyebrows and then hit his thigh a couple of times. They were already on an elevated expressway.

At the very least I would've been able to send a telegram of consolation to Kozo, if I had known.

Father and son kept silent for a while. The traffic trickled along and Tamotsu was driving his car very close to his next. Beyond the car window, the city was a mass of concrete structures and smaller buildings crowded into every conceivable space available. Tall red Tokyo Tower was visible in the haze.

"How was your life in Canada?" Tamotsu asked his father, without looking at him.

Tamotsu's tone had softened, but the question was so abrupt that Eizo was caught off guard.

"Yes, uh, a lot of things happened. I intended to come home much earlier, but so many things happened, one after the other, you know … It became impossible. I thought I would tell everyone about Canada all at once." Eizo did not want to have such a long story interrupted and even if his family could understand, they may have many questions that would take time to discuss.

"You must have a lot to talk about, so, that might be better," agreed Tamotsu.

145

The conversation ceased as abruptly as it had begun. The traffic was still slow and in some places had completely stopped. Eizo was thinking of his deceased grandchild while he stared out at downtown Tokyo.

Why did Kino not tell Kozo or Isoshichi to tell me? Or did my sons not follow Kino's request? I wonder if Kino also asked them to send a copy of the family registration. Perhaps they didn't do that either. And, Isoshichi and Kozo did not come to the airport to see me. Anyway, that doesn't necessarily mean that they reject me. What was Kino thinking all this time? Damn it! I had forgotten all about Murata-san. I could have written him a letter and asked what was going on with my family. Good heavens! What's wrong with me? Ah, but how could Murata-san know anything? He's not really known that well by the family and couldn't have helped anyway.

"Is Murata-san well?" Eizo asked.

"Murata-san … who?"

"Oh, uh, the Murata-san who suggested I go to Canada, the one that lived in front of the elementary school of our town."

"Oh, that Murata-san. I don't know how he's doing. I live in Tokyo. When it comes to our town, I really don't know very much."

"Oh. Didn't you hear anything about Canada from Murata-san?" Eizo asked, surprised.

"I don't really remember …"

Almost without realizing it, Eizo began talking about Canada. "Before and after the war, I mean the Second World War, Japanese immigrants worked hard in Canada and were poorly paid. But when you converted the Canadian wage into Japanese yen, it was much better than anything you could make in Japan. After the war, the foreign exchange rate was fixed at 360 yen against one US Dollar right up to seven or eight years ago, so it was very favourable for me to send money from Canada. Today, a dollar is worth only a little over 200 yen. When I send the same amount of money, nowadays, you get only a half of what you used to get. Not so good to send money from Canada. It was time to come back home."

"Is that why you came back?" Tamotsu looked at him suspiciously.

"Oh no, no! I came back to see and live with Kino and you guys. As you probably know, I worked over there only to send money home despite the hardships. Many Japanese wanted to make a quick buck to send home to their families or to start their own businesses, so they gambled in the logging camps."

Tamotsu kept quiet.

"Luckily enough, I didn't gamble. I knew someone who lost big and made his wife and children quite upset. They had worked hard for nearly half a year, eating very poorly to scratch a meagre amount into savings only for the husband to lose it gambling in a single night. I couldn't do that. You were all too important to take such stupid risks," Eizo said looking at Tamotsu.

Tamotsu kept his eyes on the road, his expression stiff. They drove through the heart of Tokyo amidst the maze. There was no space between the structures. Eizo glimpsed some areas dense with trees, but these were rare. There were buildings after buildings and houses after houses, old and new mixed. He looked at Tamotsu again and could not see any sign of excitement in his face. For someone who was seeing his father for the first time in forty-some odd years his son was eerily quiet.

Is this usual for Tamotsu?

147

Eizo wondered if this was the same Tamotsu he knew as a little boy, the child who cried for an insect crushed by his elder brother and when his father left for Canada. He suddenly felt exhausted.

No, for Tamotsu I must seem like a mysterious old man who has appeared out of the blue claiming to be his father. I suppose he has the right to be doubtful of me.

He put his head against the headrest, closed his eyes, and tried to breathe deeply.

"You must be tired. Why don't you take a nap," he heard his son say.

"How long does it take to get to your home from here?"

"Judging from this traffic, it might take another hour or even more," Tamotsu answered.

"An hour. Well then, I might as well rest a little."

"Please do. When we arrive, I'll wake you."

"Thank you," this time he said in Japanese. "It's been a long day. I didn't sleep very well on the plane."

"By the time we arrive home, Akiko, that's my wife, will have a meal and bath ready for you."

"Akiko-san. I remember Fumi-san mentioned your wife's name once in a letter. She's preparing a meal for me?"

This's what it's like being a member of family. I'd totally forgotten about it. This's not Martin beside me. It's not Senkichi's grandchildren whom I'm going to see soon.

Eizo was amazed at how quickly the images of Martin's family were fading since he had met Tamotsu. It was a little less than a day ago that he had left them in Toronto. Now they were far away, not only in physical distance, but in time and memory.

*

"Where are we now?" Eizo asked. They were already off the expressway. He thought that he had taken only a short nap.

"We are on the Kōshū Highway. We'll be home in another ten minutes."

Car dealers, machine shops, vegetable stores, beauty salons, dry cleaners, barbers, gas stations, restaurants with *noren*s, bicycle shops, clothing stores and a myriad of other establishments lined the road. People both walking and cycling crowded the sidewalks. Black exhaust fumes from a heavy truck in front of them blew inside their car. They turned at a large intersection.

"We're almost there," Tamotsu said.

Eizo began to prepare himself. He straightened his back, took a few deep breaths and wiped his forehead with his handkerchief.

"Are the kids already home?" Eizo asked, intentionally avoiding the use of the word 'grandchildren'. He thought it would be presumptuous to use that word in front of Tamotsu.

"I think so."

They stopped in the parking lot of a four-storey concrete apartment building: Fushimi Construction Co. Ltd. Residence.

"Here we are."

Eizo got out of the car. He felt his heart beating and his chest contracting with the anticipation of seeing his daughter-in-law and, moreover, grandchildren. As he looked up, he saw a young girl looking down at him from the corner apartment on the second floor. When their eyes met she disappeared inside. He sensed intuitively she was his granddaughter. "What floor are you on?" he asked, unable to wait.

"We live on the second floor."

Tamotsu, occupied with Eizo's luggage, motioned with his head in the direction where the girl had disappeared.

That was my grandchild.

Eizo felt a stab in his chest. But he did not want that emotion to be noticed by his son. The appearance of the granddaughter even from that distance was hard to comprehend.

They came to the building manager's office. Tamotsu mentioned his father's visit to the manager and Eizo bowed slightly to him. Then they proceeded through the clean, bright entranceway and climbed the stairs to the second floor. The door of Tamotsu's apartment was open.

"*Tadaima!* I'm home," Tamotsu called.

"*Okaeri nasai!* Welcome back," a woman's voice resonated from inside.

Eizo was able to see the part of the living room. The table had tea and cookies freshly laid out waiting for them.

What a difference from my life in the apartment in Toronto. I only had myself in the mirror and that old family photo to welcome me. This is no doubt family life.

Eizo was blissfully ignorant of his shadow's absence from this happy event as he entered the apartment.

"Welcome to our home. I'm Akiko. How do you do? Please come in."

Eizo responded in kind.

Akiko was a stocky woman with large facial features for someone Japanese. She looked Eizo over as if assessing him from the top to toe and Eizo shrank back slightly. Two children came into the room to meet their grandfather.

"Hi, I'm Noboru."

"Hello, I'm Mayumi."

The sudden appearance of his grandchildren, though he had glimpsed Mayumi a few minutes before, shocked him to

150

the core. No longer was this event a mere hope or wish. It was real, very real. Noboru wore a black school uniform and had large eyes and a nose like Akiko. Mayumi wore a navy blue and white sailor blouse, a girl's school uniform, her hair bobbed and had rosy cheeks and long legs.

How and from where did these two appear into my world? Are they really my grandchildren?

It was as though they were too dazzling to watch, glittering in the morning sun, youth radiating from them. His senses were wiped out for a moment.

"Both of you are grown up," Eizo said, barely holding himself up.

"I think they took after me. Only their bodies are growing big," Akiko laughed, humorously acknowledging Eizo's comments.

"It's a small place, but please come in and make yourself at home," Akiko urged.

Eizo took off his shoes and went into the living room. It was bright and cheery, and despite its small size, beckoning him to enter. *Tatami* mats were laid and the window had a curtain of flowers. Cushions were set around the low table where they sat. This was typical of most Japanese homes where the *chabudai,* the low table, in the living room served as the centre for family life. A television sat by the window. A wooden cabinet with ornaments and family pictures were against a wall. The kitchen was adjacent to the living room allowing Akiko to put out a meal or serve guests easily.

Eizo sat down on one of the cushions.

"How long was your flight?" Akiko asked.

"Probably, fourteen or fifteen hours."

"That long! I didn't realize Toronto was so far away. No wonder it took so long to come to Japan. You must be very tired. Did you sleep in the plane?"

151

"No, I couldn't sleep very well." Eizo appreciated Akiko's consideration.

"How was the weather? Was the plane crowded?" Akiko shot questions out as rapidly as Eizo was able to answer them. It appeared that she was monopolizing the conversation, although she was probably compensating for Tamotsu's glum silence. Tamotsu suddenly remembered to cancel his father's hotel reservation, closed the sliding door and went into the kitchen. Although Eizo would have wished for the two children to stay in the living room, they disappeared into their rooms.

Tamotsu made another call. "Ah, it's me. That's right. We just arrived."

Eizo, no longer paying attention to Akiko's questions, overheard Tamotsu talking on the phone in a low voice.

"Yes, he seems to be fine. It was a long trip and he looks pretty tired. Uh, I did not ask him yet, but probably. Okay, see you later. Bye."

Who did he call and what did 'probably' mean?

Tamotsu started dialling again.

"Hello, ah Michiyo-san? This is Tamotsu. We're home now. That's right. Okay. Talk to you soon, bye."

Again, the conversation had been short.

Michiyo must be Kozo's wife.

Tamotsu came back into the living room and sat down.

"I'd like to make a call home and talk with Kino," Eizo said.

To this Tamotsu sat up rigid, and then collecting himself said, "Ah, I talked to Isoshichi and they know you've already arrived safely."

"Oh, you should've told me you were going to call Isoshichi before you made the call." Eizo was displeased, but quickly hid his expression.

Tamotsu did not say anything.

"I'd like to call anyway. I want to tell her myself that I'm back. May I use a phone?" Eizo struggled to stand up.

"Ah… ah, Mom is not at home right now."

"She's not at home? Is she in the hospital? You said …"

"Isoshichi said that Mom went for a walk," Tamotsu interrupted.

"A walk? Went for a walk?"

Akiko, who had been very chatty, was now quietly watching.

"Did Isoshichi say that?" Eizo asked.

"Yes, he did."

If Eizo called, he would only end up talking to his eldest son. When Isoshichi was young, he was a nasty, or mischievous kid at best. He did not expect that Isoshichi would have changed much.

Is Tamotsu playing some game? I still need to call Kino and tell her I'm in Japan.

"Excuse me, but can you dial for me?" Eizo did not give in this time.

Tamotsu hesitated, but then stood up and dialled. He handed the phone to his father, now standing beside him.

"Hello, Isoshichi? It's me, your father. I arrived in Japan. I'm at Tamotsu's home." Eizo stopped when he noticed that the listener was quiet. "Isoshichi? I know I've made your life difficult for a long time. I'm sorry for that, but … anyway I need to speak to your mother. Is she there? What? Went for a walk? Okay, well then, when she comes back, please tell her to call me at Tamotsu's. Are you well? That's good. I'll be coming by the bullet train. I'll be leaving Tokyo Station at ten, tomorrow morning, and transfer to the branch line at Nagoya Station. I'm looking forward to seeing you guys … okay, see you soon, bye."

Eizo was deeply disappointed. Isoshichi's voice was very flat, formal and aloof. He had even faltered in welcoming his father home. As Eizo hung up the telephone, he again felt the strength sucked from his body, hope drain away like water soaked up by sand.

Kino knew when I would be back. Or, maybe she no longer wanted to wait for my call.

"Are you okay?" Tamotsu asked, standing just off to the side of Eizo.

"I'm all right. Your mother seems to have gone out for a walk. What can I say? When you're old, a long trip makes you more tired than usual." Eizo sat down on his cushion. "By the way, is Kozo well?"

"Yes, he's fine. He's away on a business trip."

"Ah, no wonder he could not come to the airport. Where does he live?"

"Kozo lives in Koganei City, which is about a twenty minute drive from here."

"What does he do?"

"He works for the Matsunaga Electric Company. He's the sales director for the home appliance department."

"Matsunaga Electric, a big company. That's good." Eizo was glad that the money he had sent home to his family had not been wasted. "Well, Akiko-san, I have some gifts for the children."

"Yes. Noboru, Mayumi! Please come here. Granddad would like to give you something."

The two adolescents came back into the living room. Eizo passed his gifts around. Tamotsu, Akiko and two children all thanked Eizo, but in accordance with Japanese custom, they did not open their gifts. It was rude to open the gift in front of the giver. Eizo, accustomed to the Canadian tradition, felt a little out of place. He cautioned himself that he had better get used to Japanese customs again quickly.

Akiko, with the usual efficiency of a Japanese housewife, started bringing food out in a flurry, *tempura, sushi* and other dishes that jogged memories for Eizo. Everyone found a spot around the table.

"Help yourself, please. I cooked *tempura,* but ordered the *sushi* from the shop in front of the station. Their *sushi* is always fresh. First, how about a toast to your dad's homecoming?"

Everyone toasted to Eizo's return. Noboru and Mayumi joined with juice instead of *saké.* Eizo thought that he had tasted what an immediate family would be like and that how long ago he had experienced the warmth of life. He liked the sweet taste of *saké*, but now it tasted much sweeter. He felt the alcohol's effect quickly.

Now, I have it all.

"I thought about preparing everything at home, but I had to work. I'm sorry I had to have *sushi* delivered," Akiko apologized.

"No, it's very good, thank you. By the way, where do you work Akiko-san?"

"I work at the city hall. My husband's salary is enough to live on, but we want to build a home. We've bought a piece of property already."

"That's a great achievement."

"My husband is, of course, an architect and a field overseer of construction sites at work. So it wasn't too difficult for him to draft the blue prints for our home."

"You're doing well it appears."

Tamotsu's family seemed harmonious. Eizo had been worried that his sons might have turned out notorious criminals, but apparently that was not the case. He had lived on the other side of the globe, worried how his absence had affected his three sons, but was now relieved. *They were not in prison!*

Even after *saké*, Tamotsu was quiet.

What is he not telling me? He said that Kino and everybody were fine. What's wrong with him?

"I saw Canada on a television program a couple of times," said Akiko. "The Rocky Mountains seemed very mysterious and the Niagara Falls were magnificent. It's a pity that I can't see such a beautiful country with my own eyes."

Eizo looked up at her. To him the Rocky Mountains were not mysterious, but the real, rigorous, and ruthless place of the labour and concentration camps. But they talked about the scenery in Canada for a while because it appeared to be an easy subject for them to discuss. Eizo found it much easier to talk to Akiko than his own son. He felt that at some point she would ask why he did not return to Japan much earlier but she did not appear to want to probe into those issues that he was not ready to discuss.

Again, Eizo brought up Isoshichi's family, wondering how they were getting on. Tamotsu again descended into silence.

Akiko came to the rescue. "They're fine and have two boys. Do you know their names?"

"Yes, the older boy's name is Shoichi and the second one's name is … I'm sure it is Toshio," said Eizo.

"That's right. Shoichi-san is in his fourth year at university and living in a boarding house. He comes to our home occasionally for dinner. Toshio-san is in the last year of high school. He's the same age as our Noboru."

"Thank you for a dinner," Noboru said, about to leave the table.

"Studying for exams?" Eizo asked.

"Yes, I am," Noboru replied in a low voice, getting up and going to his room.

Mayumi followed him soon after.

"I'll go home by train tomorrow," Eizo said to the silent couple.

"What time is the train?" Tamotsu asked.

"I'd like to take the ten o'clock bullet train from Tokyo Station. Is that okay?"

"That's okay with us. I'll take you to the station," Tamotsu said.

"By the way, do you think your mother is home now?" Eizo asked, remembering.

Tamotsu and Akiko looked each other. Akiko's eyes were telling Tamotsu that he should answer that question.

"You'll be home tomorrow, anyway. Besides, she might have gone to bed already after her walk."

"Gone to bed after her walk?"

One would think that after all these years she would stay up to welcome me home. What is Kino thinking?

"When Mom comes back from a walk she always takes a nap immediately after."

"You said 'always'. Does she go on a walk every day?"

"Yes, I should say so." Tamotsu looked at Akiko for help, but she was sitting quietly and appeared to want nothing to do with the conversation. "In any case, you can see her tomorrow, so, you don't have to wake her up." Tamotsu seemed oddly bewildered with Eizo's persistence, the persistence of a man who had been away from his wife for decades.

"That could be true." Eizo surrendered to his son's suggestion. "I'm sorry, but I'm very tired. If you don't mind I'd like to go to bed, if it's okay with you."

"Oh, I'm so sorry, I didn't notice. Of course, you must be tired. Please sleep in Noboru's room tonight. We have only three rooms, unfortunately," said Tamotsu.

"How about taking a bath first? It'll be relaxing and will take some of the fatigue of your long journey away," Akiko suggested.

"Then, I'd better take a bath first."

Guided by Tamotsu, Eizo went to Noboru's room. His grandson went to the living room to study. Then, Tamotsu took Eizo to the bathroom.

*

Eizo showered and then plunged into the bathtub. The heat slowly drained the fatigue from his aching body. He stretched his arms and legs as much as he could and enjoyed the euphoria at being able to bathe in his son's home as if there had been no interruption in their lives, as if there had never been a Canada. The small steam from the bath swayed in front of him and evaporated into the air. *Saké* and the way Tamotsu's family welcomed him uplifted his mood. At one point, he tried to retrace his days in Canada but those memories were swiftly fading away like smoke rising from the fire.

Tomorrow, I'll be able to see Kino and Isoshichi. How is it possible that I'm suddenly so fortunate?

*

"Thank you. It was a good bath. I feel refreshed," Eizo said.

"Good. Before you get cold, please get into the *futon*," Akiko recommended.

While Eizo was taking a bath, she had set out a *futon* in Noboru's room.

"*Oyasumi-nasai.* Good night." She closed the door.

Climbing into the *futon* Eizo thought of how Tamotsu had grown up very decently and that Kozo and Isoshichi also appeared to have grown up as satisfactory members of society.

Ah, it was not a total waste to have been in Canada. But, Tamotsu was very quiet. Maybe that's Tamotsu. He was a sensitive, quiet boy and carries that trait even now.

Eizo could not pass judgement. He knew, though, it would be necessary to tell Kino and his sons about everything he had been through in Canada one day—the sooner, the better. If not, a chasm would remain in their relationship. He realized that he had not slept on a *futon* in a long time; it felt as if he were being drawn into the ground. Soon he fell asleep with the help of bath, *saké,* fatigue and the warmth of a dream that he had dreamt for so long.

13
Gifu Prefecture

The following morning Eizo woke to Akiko in the kitchen preparing breakfast, chopping something on a cutting board. The familiar smell of *miso* soup permeated the house with a sense of well-being. He could also hear the murmur of Noboru and Mayumi's voices from the same direction.

This would have been an ordinary morning for the average person, but for Eizo it was something extraordinarily precious and amazing: his first morning home. The solitary life in Canada was like a far-off nightmare: something like a mist that disappeared with the light of the morning.

"*Itte kimasu*! I'm leaving now!" Noboru and Mayumi called out as they left for school.

"*Itte rasshai*! Have a nice day!" Akiko called back.

Eizo revelled in the familiarity of his spoken mother tongue. He got up and pulled the clothes on that he had hung up neatly the night before and went to the kitchen to bid his son and daughter-in-law a good morning. Akiko, now preparing to leave for work, left to put her make-up on. The *futon* in the living room had already been cleared away.

"Did you sleep well last night?" Akiko asked, coming back into the living room.

"Yes, I did, thank you. A little *saké* and a warm bath helped me sleep well."

"That's good. I'm glad you had a nice rest," Akiko said.

Eizo, although happy to be in his son's home, still felt a little reserved. After all, they were perfect strangers. He smiled and thanked her again.

"I'm leaving for work. Your breakfast is ready on the table," Akiko said to Tamotsu and Eizo.

She put on a white coat, pulled the straps of a black handbag onto her shoulder, and stepped into the entranceway, looking very sharp and professional. She moved with the efficiency of experience and Eizo watched her in admiration.

Akiko turned as she opened the door. "I can't see you off at Tokyo Station, but please come again."

"Thank you." Eizo smiled back.

He and Tamotsu sat down at the kitchen table. Breakfast consisted of cooked rice, *miso* soup, seaweed, eggs, broiled fish, and Japanese pickled vegetables, all of which were neatly arranged on small dishes and platters. The two ate quietly keeping their thoughts to themselves. Soon after breakfast they left for Tokyo Station.

"Will you be late for work?" Eizo asked.

"No, it's okay. I told my supervisor I'd be late," Tamotsu answered, opening the car door for his father.

Tamotsu pulled onto the expressway and accelerated. The spring sunlight in April was soft and the promise of rebirth filled the air with hope. Eizo burned with questions about Tomotsu's mother but held back. There was little else of interest more important than Kino, so discussion between the two faltered. Eizo tried to spark a dialogue and asked about the building design of certain structures they saw on the way. Tamotsu described them briefly and then slipped back into silence.

When they arrived at Tokyo Station, Tamotsu carried Eizo's suitcase to the ticket counter and then went to park his car. Eizo bought his tickets while waves of people rushed back and forth: racing for trains, for businesses, for taxis, or sightseeing at the Imperial Palace. Tamotsu returned and bought a platform ticket for himself.

"Let's go," he said.

The train had not yet arrived. Tamotsu stopped briefly at a kiosk and came away with a box in a vinyl bag. Passengers began lining up behind Eizo as a bullet train slid into the station.

"I'm not supposed to get on the train," Tamotsu said, as if talking to himself. He climbed aboard with Eizo's luggage and helped him find his seat. "I have to get off."

"Thank you, Tamo …" Before Eizo had a chance to finish his words Tamotsu thrust the vinyl bag at Eizo.

"Please give this to Mom. She likes these. Whenever I go home, I take these for her. Please take care!" The expression on his face was mixed with sadness and pity.

Eizo shivered and tried to shake Tamotsu's hand, but he had already turned to leave. On the platform Tamotsu stopped. His face was like *Kojyo*, the Noh mask of sorrow, and when Eizo smiled at him, Tamotsu tried to smile back but failed. A siren blared across the platform. The doors hissed closed and the train began to glide away. Eizo smiled again and waved to his son. Tamotsu responded and then disappeared from sight.

Eizo watched the city fly by as the train built up speed, thinking of Tamotsu's pathetic look. When he thought of what had happened the previous day, there was nothing he could think of to account for Tamotsu's strange behaviour whenever Kino was mentioned. All seats in the car were occupied and in the seat next to him a businessman read a newspaper; he ignored Eizo. Now alone, he thought about the time he had just spent at his son's home.

Yes, Tamotsu came to the airport, offered me a wonderful dinner, and a refreshing bath. What more could I expect? But he did not call me 'Father' even once while I was there. What we need is more time to understand each other. Oh well, hopefully that day will come soon.

The shadow suddenly spoke up.

Do you think your wife's attitude toward you will be different from Tamotsu? Be my guest. I don't want to see you cry when you meet with your wife.

Eizo tried to elude the shadow's influence.

Get lost! I don't need your cynical comments and observations anymore. And I no longer need you—I'm in Japan with my family now. Go away and disappear quietly. I'm sure that she'll welcome me home.

However, he was not entirely certain of this. He tried to imagine how Kino would welcome him but failed. His only image of her was that from a picture taken before the war.

What would she be like now?

Eizo felt tired. He realized that he had to stop worrying about his wife, but his thoughts kept coming back to her.

*

Two hours later the train arrived at the Nagoya Station where he made the transfer to Minokamo City. At each stop the regional character of the passengers changed noticeably. A group of women were laughing with their mouths wide open, exchanging jokes, as if they were relaxing at home and not out in public. Some were eating lunches at their seats. People greeted each other and chatted in the provincial way, rather than ignoring each other as would be expected in Tokyo, or Toronto.

"Your daughter is pregnant, right?" the woman with no make-up by the window said.

"Where did you hear that from?" a woman about fifty-five asked.

"A little bird told me."

"Holy moly! You have long ears. I can't hide anything from you."

"Did you do something so wrong that you have to hide?" the third woman with yellow teeth said. They all laughed.

"Don't pull my leg. My daughter doesn't have money. She's pleased to say it's the fruit of love and couldn't help. She's a glib talker, you know. Youngsters nowadays! This will be her fifth kid. What can I say?"

"Tell her to buy a lottery ticket," the fourth woman said as she crossed her legs.

"But you never win."

"Did you buy a ticket? No? That's why you don't win. There is a right order for doing things, you dummy!" All laughed again.

Eizo had never noticed this in Canada. In Toronto, he had been surrounded by people from many different ethnic groups and although aware of them, had never connected in the way he did now. He felt as though he had just found something that he had lost, something that gave him a sense of place.

As the train neared his destination, Eizo watched for old acquaintances. At Mino-Ota Station, Eizo descended onto the platform. The old station had been re-built or refaced, he wasn't sure. He looked for anyone he might recognize. But there was no one, at least it appeared so. He followed the crowd towards the bridge. By now, he was already exhausted from worry. Carrying his suitcase, he climbed the bridge far behind the other passengers, breathing heavily and sweating.

Outside of the platform wicket, he saw several people standing and waiting, but could see neither Kino nor anyone that might look like Isoshichi. He again felt that terrible sensation; that dread at the airport just before Tamotsu found him.

It should be all right. Home is not far from here.

The area retained few traces of former days. Across from the station there was an open space, a tall hotel and multiple-storey buildings side by side. Eizo wondered if he had got off at the wrong stop. There was supposed to be bus services on the other side of the station, but he was not familiar with the schedule and wanted to see his wife without further delay. He took one of the taxis waiting at the curb.

The driver asked Eizo where he was from.

"Hoh! Forty years! In Canada!" the taxi driver exclaimed, capturing him in the car mirror.

Time had exerted change on the city; Eizo could not identify anything from memory; all sights were different than he remembered. According to the taxi driver, an expressway through a national park in the heart of the mountains beyond Eizo's town was under construction. People in the region were excited to see the modernization of the area. Many gas stations were open with over-the-top ads and signs which he did not see when he lived there before. Eizo soon started to give half-hearted replies to the driver as the landscape began to show its familiar face, being captivated by the scenery.

The mountains that I remember!

He looked around, searching for the life he had lost and was desperate to find again. Another ten minutes found them turning toward his hometown. When an old Buddhist temple appeared around a curve, Eizo felt his heart soar. This timeless structure was an integral part of the area and as familiar to him as an old friend. He knew it was only a short distance to his home.

I'm home at last. I've made it!

As the taxi was passing, he noticed an old, shabbily dressed woman sitting on the stone steps of the temple roughly a hundred metres away from the road. He only saw her profile.

No, that can't be Kino!

From the woman's dishevelled appearance, her sweater askew, hair scattered, mismatched baggy *monpe*, he could not imagine that she was his wife.

There must be many women in the town as old as that woman. The aged can be indistinguishable.

Eizo's anxiety grew. Turning the corner, his home appeared in front of him. The house seemed newly constructed, but looking closely, he could tell that a second story had been added to the first. He instinctively looked for his family, particularly Kino. The sliding doors of the entranceway were open. The laundry was hung out to dry, but there didn't seem to be anybody around. As the taxi slowly pulled up in front of the house three children ran toward Eizo, screaming with laughter.

"Mister! Which house are you going to?" a small girl asked as soon as Eizo got out.

"To this house," Eizo said nodding toward his house.

"This man is going to Osada-san's house," the girl, skipping behind him said in a high-pitched voice.

"Who are you, Mister?"

Eizo was astonished by the sudden interrogation from a boy waving his model gun around. Considering the boy's question more deeply than was intended, he found he had difficulty answering the question.

"Mister! Who are you?"

Eizo ignored him. Reaching the entranceway, "Kino, are you there? I'm home! I'm back!" he called.

There was no answer from the inside of the house. He became anxious and suspicious.

"Hey, Mister! Who are you? You said, 'I'm back.' Who are you?" The boy persisted.

Ignoring the boy again, he entered the house but saw no evidence that anyone was expecting his arrival. On the earth floor boots, shoes and *geta* had been cast off in disarray. He took his shoes off, stepped up onto the main floor, and shuffled into the house. In the living room a newspaper lay open on the floor beside the *irori*, the hearth.

"I'm back now. Kino, are you here?" Eizo called out again in a loud voice.

"She's out," one of the girls said.

Eizo turned and found the young girl looking up from the entranceway, while from behind him, a tall young man in a black school uniform came out from another room, scuffing his feet on the mat as he walked. When the children saw the young man they screamed and scampered away. Eizo shook his head and dismissed them. Turning to the young man, Eizo saw that the man in a school uniform looked a little uneasy.

"Oh, I'm Eizo."

"Ah, I'm Toshio."

"Oh, so, you're Toshio."

"Ah, yes …"

"Is Kino in? Or, did she go somewhere?"

"Grandma went for a walk."

"Went for a walk? Again?"

"Yes."

"What's the matter with her? At a time like this, went for a walk?"

167

Toshio stood there, obviously perplexed.

"She went for a walk last night too. Does she go walking often?"

"Yes, she does. I'll go bring her home." Toshio jumped into his shoes and dashed outside.

Eizo sat down by the hearth in the living room. There was no ember in the hearth and that told him that it had not been in use for some time. When he and his wife had moved into this house, it was brand-new. But now the sliding doors which partitioned the rooms were blackish and showing their age. He sat there for ten minutes, although it seemed like several hours, but Toshio did not return. His irritation grew into worry.

What a woman!

Eizo stood up deciding to go search for Kino himself. He might be a stranger but at least he knew the area. He put on his shoes and stepped outside. The children were no longer around. Then he noticed an old woman with baggy *monpe* and a cane walking slowly and unsteadily towards the house beside Toshio.

Kino ... It was Kino!

He was taken aback. The dishevelled woman of the Buddhist temple was indeed his wife.

"Kino!" Eizo sprang upright, rapidly approaching his wife, "Kino, I'm back now!"

Stunned at the sudden appearance of the old man from the house, the woman in *monpe* stared at him. Eizo stopped short; afraid of her blank expression.

Kino's face was a network of deep wrinkles. It was now narrow, bony and stained as if she had not washed for months. Long gone was the high-coloured face of her late twenties he remembered. Except for the frame of her face he barely recognized his wife. Most of her white hair was bundled in a ponytail with the rest of the tousled mess hanging in front of her face. Her eyes seemed to be filled with a pure innocence; he could not read any recognition in them.

"Kino, I, ah, I just, just arrived," Eizo stuttered. He wanted to find the words to apologize for his long absence, but before her gaze, he felt any words fall short.

Unexpectedly, a look of fear began to spread over Kino's face. She tightened her lips, her eyes opened wide, as the colour drained out of her face. She hid her eyes from him, moved quickly around him, and shuffled towards the house.

"Wha … hey! Kino! What's happening? I'm back now. Hey, Kino!"

Kino stopped, looked back at Eizo, her face now completely white. She began shaking. She looked as though a vengeful spirit pursued her.

"Hey, Kino, it's me, Eizo. Did you forget me? Your husband!"

Eizo quickly ran around in front of his wife and grabbed her hand holding the cane. Kino stared at him. Eizo shuddered. In his wife's eyes he saw nothing except abject fear and dread. They were the eyes of the insane. His wife was lost to this world.

Eizo was frozen, unable to speak. Everything around him suddenly lost its colour. He stood there blankly, in a place where a moment and an eternity became one. His ears rang and echoed with metallic sounds. Even sorrow and misery could not pierce his shock. Without a word Eizo reached out and took hold of Kino's other hand. As he drew his wife close to him, he saw his shadow take Kino by the shoulders, gaze into her face, and shake her violently in his illusions.

Kino. Forgive me. I should've come home much earlier.
I'm back now. Do you hear me? I'm back now. Let's live as
we did before, I beg you. Please, Kino, come back!

Eizo watched her helplessly as his shadow shouted and
shook his wife again.

I am sorry. Please forgive me. I didn't know.

A tortured sob erupted from the shadow as it took Kino
into a close embrace.

Eizo blinked in shock, while watching the shadow from
a distance, still embracing Kino tightly. The shadow
trembled, and timidly, very timidly, put his hand onto her
dishevelled hair and let her head gently rest on his chest,
weeping. His spirit, his very consciousness, was slipping
from his grasp. Eizo slowly released his hands from her
hands, being awakened from the illusions and regaining his
sense of reality in the process. His wife's body gave off an
acrid smell, the smell of fear and rot of her spirit.

Kino stepped away and began shuffling toward the
house. She walked as though she was about to fall over, but
her feet carried her forward quickly. She did not look back
at Eizo who was following her, unable to think anything else.
Arriving at the house, Kino sat down on the low veranda
outside the sliding glass doors off the drawing room and
glanced at him. The horror that was in her eyes several
minutes ago had already faded. Eizo had never seen such a
penetrating but vacant stare.

"Kino …" He gently called her name and reached over
to take her hand. But Kino pulled it away and slid down the
veranda with an unexpected nimbleness and stared at him.

"Kino!" He lost his self-control and tried to sit beside her
again.

"Ah, ah!" Kino gave a short cry, pulled both hands close
to her chest in defence and sprang to her feet.

Eizo felt completely lost. He did not understand what was happening to his wife. She sidled along a few metres away and sat down again. As soon as Eizo tried to speak the fear returned to her eyes. At a loss, Eizo buried his head between his hands and closed his eyes. Then he remembered the vinyl bag that Tamotsu had handed him at Tokyo Station. He stood slowly and retrieved the bag from his luggage.

Why the hell didn't Tamotsu explain this to me? He's a man with a social position and responsibility. Oh, damn! He must be extremely introverted. But who on God's earth tells a lifetime tragedy to someone, particularly to his father, who is almost a stranger? Probably hiding the truth was meant to be a kindness to me. True, such a man who tells tales on others can't be trusted.

Keeping his distance, Eizo handed Kino the bag. "This's from Tamotsu."

She appeared to have recognized her son's name, gingerly took the bag, removed the box and ripped it open. Inside were rows of small cakes. She picked up one of the cakes with her dirty hand and bit into it as if a ravenous animal tearing into a piece of meat. She devoured a handful of the cakes in short order. Eizo stood there dumbfounded. A feeling of deep pity came over him for her and, to a similar degree, for himself. He vacantly looked at the undulating ridge of mountains as if to call upon them to help him, but no answer came back.

Kino finished devouring, got up and walked around to the small garden in the front yard like that of a sleepwalker. She looked eastward, mumbling something first, and then called in a heartrending, straining voice, "My dearest, please come back to me quickly!"

Her pleading broke Eizo's heart.

Kino! Have you been calling for me all this time?

"My dearest, please come back to me!" Kino called again, straightening her back, as if the effort of all her body would carry her voice farther.

Eizo could no longer hold himself together. Great heaves shook his whole body. He grieved for the time he had lost with his beloved. Eizo burst into an open cry.

She's been waiting for my return for so long. How stupid was I not to know that. What a mistake I made!

Kino turned around and walked back to the veranda, nothing written in her expression. She barely glanced at Eizo and it did not seem that she cared about him. He wiped his tears with a handkerchief and watched his wife. Her tangled hair over her stained face and her pure but unfocused eyes moved him to cry again. Kino and the scenery looked distorted with the tears. The three children snuck up behind in the garden and peeped through the plants. As Eizo looked over without clearly seeing them, they dispersed, squealing as they went like a bunch of puppies.

Just then a small pickup truck, stencilled 'Agricultural Co-operative', pulled up to the house. Toshio stepped down from the truck, followed by a woman in *monpe* and a towel wrapped around her head. Then a sturdily built man in overalls, age about fifty-five, got out. Eizo knew immediately that it was Isoshichi, his eldest son. He had a square jaw, clean shaven chin with a pale complexion and broad shoulders, and a deep vertical wrinkle separated his thick eyebrows. That mischievous boy who skinned a snake and pumped air into a frog's stomach making it an ungainly shape had grown into an unapproachable man. What a metamorphosis!

"Dad, it's Grandpa," Toshio exclaimed.

Isoshichi ignored him.

"Isoshichi, I'm home," Eizo said, as gentle, humble and amicable as he could be.

The eldest son said nothing to him.

"You're back. I'm Fumi. How do you do?" the woman interjected, introducing herself and bowing politely. Close in age to her husband, she had a sunburnt face, droopy eyebrows, and a disproportionately long nose over a forced smile.

In the customary Japanese manner, Eizo responded with a deep bow and thanked her for looking after Kino and Isoshichi. Fumi, gratuitously bending her upper body in bow, invited him into the house.

"Grandma, please come into the house now," Fumi called back to Kino.

Kino stood up, like a doll that understood human language, and passed Eizo without even looking at him and shambled into the house.

Isoshichi now occupied the spot at the hearth where Eizo used to sit. Eizo, the former head of the family, sat where a guest would normally sit, a stranger in his own home. Everybody, including Kino, was at the hearth but nobody spoke. Eizo would normally have made an effort to start a conversation but refrained from talking. Kino's eyes were drifting as if she were a plastic doll. The silence was overwhelming.

Being unable to sit any longer, Toshio left the room mumbling something about homework. Fumi came into the living room with a tray and served tea, saying a few words to Eizo before going back to the kitchen.

"Looking back now, I've neglected my duties as a father and husband too long. I'm sorry," Eizo said, forcing himself to break the silence.

Isoshichi remained silent with his eyes fixed on the ashes in the hearth. Eizo knew that initiating a dialogue about his long absence so soon after arriving could backfire, but broached the subject anyway.

"There were times when I tried to come home, but …" Eizo hesitated and then pulled out Kino's last letter from his jacket pocket and laid it in front of Isoshichi. His son briefly cast his eyes over it, but ignored the letter, turning his face away. Eizo did not have enough courage to mention Kino's insanity and the fact that he did not know anything about it. Had he mentioned such a touchy issue at this early stage, he thought it would ruin the chance of reconciliation with his family.

After a while, Isoshichi stood up, turned the television on and stared glumly at the screen, his back to Eizo. Kino, too, absent-mindedly cast her eyes at the television. Shut out, Eizo was compelled to watch with them. He wondered if Isoshichi was waiting for him to continue the dialogue. Measuring the situation, he decided not to, understanding that there was no welcome for him and that further talk would fall on deaf ears.

The dinner served later was a normal fare. There was no *saké*, no toast, no *sushi,* no *tempura* and no celebration of Eizo's homecoming. This was his first dinner in his own home in forty-three years. To his family, it appeared that he simply did not exist. Tamotsu's kind reception to Isoshichi's cold shoulder was like night and day. While at dinner, Kino dropped her bowl, losing most of the rice on the floor. With the television off, other than Fumi asking Eizo if he wanted another serving of rice or *miso* soup, it was deathly silent. Eizo could not really believe what was actually happening to him in his eldest son's home.

"Does Shoichi go to one of the universities in Tokyo?" Eizo felt the silence unbearable and drew Fumi out with a question.

"Yes, he does." Fumi answered quickly, then became silent, killing the discussion before it started.

Eizo had many questions about what had unfolded in the family while he was away and particularly about the time Kino became ill. Although he had his suspicions, the current situation made it difficult to communicate even those basic things. When dinner was finished Isoshichi turned the television back on, an obvious sign that the silent drama was going to start all over again.

Eizo realized that he had not given out his gifts yet. He thought that there would be no problem with gifts to Isoshichi, Fumi, and Toshio, but under the circumstances, it seemed ludicrous giving the evening bag to Kino.

"Isoshichi. This's a gift from Canada."

Isoshichi reluctantly looked back at the neatly wrapped box offered, his facial expression tense. He appeared hesitant.

"I didn't know Kino was like this." Eizo finally brought up the subject he wanted to talk about but Isoshichi did not turn his face to his father. "I was very thoughtless."

Eizo looked over at Kino and their eyes met. He could not believe his intuition that he saw a gleam of recognition in her eyes. Or was it his imagination? He shivered, hoping … Then, it passed as quickly as it had come. Kino looked away with indifference.

"Thank you," Isoshichi said, barely audible over the television. He took the gift with one hand, set it down beside him, and turned his attention back to the television, abruptly severing this first, momentary exchange with his father. Eizo sensed he had lost the chance to talk about his wife.

Taking advantage of this opportunity to give Toshio a present, Eizo tried to talk to him but did not get the youthful, energetic responses he expected.

How will I get through to my family?

By the time Fumi finished working in the kitchen and had come back to sit down, Eizo felt drained. Toshio had left the living room as soon as he could. Kino was playing with a rip of her stained clothes, thrusting her finger into the hole, but seemingly tired of doing that, she disappeared into the back room without acknowledging anyone. Eizo wanted to follow his wife, but invisible restrictions held him in place: the bonds of a stranger and silence.

Eizo handed a gift to Fumi compelling her, out of courtesy, to ask questions about Canada. By now, he was too tired to talk about Canada and wanted instead to rest.

"I'm going to take a bath," Isoshichi said, standing up.

"Dear, don't you think the guest should bathe first?" Fumi said standing. "I mean let Father take a bath first," she quickly corrected.

Guest? Am I only a guest here?

Eizo was surprised that Fumi came to his defence, but at the same time disappointed. Intuition told him that his family had already determined how to treat him before he arrived. A verbal error often reveals one's true feelings. Fumi's thoughtlessness in her choice of words made this all the more evident.

"Father, please take a bath first," Fumi said.

Eizo did not resist.

The bathroom had been renovated sometime in the last forty years. Water service had been added along with a gas-fired water heater. He lowered himself into the hot bath and stared up at the ceiling. A bare electric bulb emitted a distressing orange light that wavered in the mist rising from

176

the bath. His mind drifted to Kino's mental state. He recalled her looking towards the east, the very direction of Canada, and shouting for him to come back quickly. No doubt his long absence and her overloaded responsibilities were the cause of her insanity. Eizo hated himself for that and thought hard about what to do next.

What on earth was the point of working so hard in Canada? Where is the Kino I used to know? Where are my family, my happiness, and the rewards of being deprived of a regular life?

Eizo climbed out of the bath, dressed, and went back into living room. Isoshichi and Fumi had not moved and his son did not even look away from the television. "It was a good bath. Thank you," Eizo said.

"I put down a *futon* in Mother's room for you. You must be tired. Please have a good night's sleep. I took your suitcase into your room also," Fumi said.

Kino's room was the same one Eizo shared with her before he had left for Canada. There were a couple of *futons* on the floor and Kino was sitting on one, staring at the wall. Eizo entered without any reaction from her.

He opened his suitcase, took out the evening bag and slowly brought it in front of her. Without looking at him, Kino quickly tore through the wrapping paper and pulled the evening bag out of the box with such force that Eizo was afraid she would damage it. As she held it in both her hands, a peaceful expression spread across her face as though miraculously relieved of her affliction. She repeatedly touched the patterns of the alligator skin with her fingertips. Eizo remembered the tall woman at the Eaton's Department Store where he had purchased the bag, a gorgeous llly in full bloom in the autumn of life. He saw such a vast difference between Kino and that woman.

Poor Kino ...

He came to realize how his new life in Japan diverged completely away from his former existence in Canada and the life that he had left a few short days before. While he was there living alone, he had lived in an illusive world but without any solid connections to ordinary life. He could not have imagined the vast differences in realities, between Japan and Canada. He could not find a point of contact within himself to anchor these two worlds.

"Kino, after you wrote that last letter to me I did not come back."

Kino raised her face, the peace already disappearing from her expression.

When Kino sent that last letter to me she must have been herself. What happened to her after that? She asked me to stay in Canada and keep sending money for the family's sake. Was her insanity the result of bearing all of the responsibilities of raising a family alone?

"Kino, I'm sorry I brought all of this on you," Eizo said, somehow knowing the words were not reaching through the veil of his wife's madness. They sat alone together in a world where words no longer had any meaning.

Kino eventually put the bag away under her pillow, slipped out of her day clothes, and sat back down on her *futon*. She had become very thin, a shadow of her younger days. She took out the evening bag and went back to touching the patterns.

"I'm glad you seem to like it." Unable to resist, Eizo reached out slowly to touch her hand. Not seeing any change in her expression he gently and tenderly began stroking the back of her hand, cold and thin with work and age. Kino had been a healthy, robust woman in her youth. Although a go-between had arranged their marriage, they once shared a bond of love.

I've ruined her life.

Eizo continued to stroke her hand tenderly, feeling that they were somehow connecting. Her cheeks started twitching. He was into touching her bony hand and did not perceive the fear creeping back into her face.

"Aah, ah, ah," Kino suddenly cried out, eyes wide open and filled with panic.

Eizo lost his head. All of muscles in his body immediately contracted. He shrank back. Kino abruptly stood up from her *futon* and backed against the wall. She cried out again like a stricken animal, bent over, grabbed at the evening bag that she had dropped and squatted back into the corner of the room. Eizo could not believe what he was seeing. Violent footsteps rushed across the upstairs floor toward the staircase.

"Mom, Grandma is ..." Toshio cried, his voice catching in his throat.

But there was no response from Fumi or Isoshichi. Everything was quiet outside his room. Eizo was utterly flustered, not knowing how to calm Kino's fear towards him.

It finally came to him that in order to calm her down he had to either leave the room or lie down with his back against her. He chose the latter. It took a while but Kino crawled back into her *futon*. After a few minutes, making sure she was unruffled, Eizo stood up and turned out the light, exhausted. But he was unable to sleep. The home and the life he had dreamt of for so long was no more than a mirage.

14
An Alligator Evening Bag

When Eizo got up next morning, Kino was already out of the *futon*. He slowly got dressed—feeling slaphappy with exhaustion—and went into the living room.

"Good morning," Eizo said.

"Ah, good morning." It was Fumi. Isoshichi and Toshio said nothing to him, and continued eating their breakfast.

Eizo cast a glance at Kino and was immediately taken aback. Kino had the alligator evening bag with her while she ate. How out of place! While the Isoshichi couple wore work clothes, Kino, a stained *monpe*, Toshio in a school uniform, the evening bag appeared unsuitably shinny and sophisticated. He assumed that Kino would keep her evening bag in a dresser, perhaps taking it out from time to time to appreciate it within her room. He never imagined that she would actually carry it around with her. She might even decide to carry it in the town. Soon the townspeople would gossip since people around here tended to be like that. He regretted the gift and felt guilty for having created another problem. *What an undiscerning man you are!* The shadow, who had laid low since he had arrived Japan, raised its head.

"Did you sleep well last night?" Fumi asked.

"Yes, I did," he said merely as a courtesy.

Isoshichi, who sat eating, had not changed from the day before. Toshio watched Eizo closely, reminding him of the previous night's incident with Kino.

Eizo went outside and washed his face. The sun had just risen and the air was fresh. He took a deep breath and immediately felt a little better. When he returned to the living room Kino sat alone by her tray. He could not help but conclude that his family intentionally wanted to avoid him. While he was having breakfast, Isoshichi and Toshio left the house quietly. He could hear the clink of dishes as Fumi cleaned up after her breakfast, but she too seemed withdrawn. Kino, moving her chopsticks with unsteady hands, again dropped most of the rice from her bowl on to the floor. While eating she occasionally reached down and touched the evening bag.

Eizo had his breakfast in a hasty manner, as if someone were chasing after him, cleaned up the dishes and then went out onto the veranda. In the warm and merciful morning sunlight his wife sat with her handbag on the veranda while his daughter-in-law hung the laundry up on the clothesline. The mountains were visible through a haze. It was a peaceful scene, but not one that Eizo felt he could share.

Before Fumi was able to leave, Eizo blurted out, "How is Murata-san doing?"

She stopped mid-pace. "Murata-san? You mean the Murata-san who lived in front of the school?"

"That's right. We worked together in Canada for a little while."

"He passed away."

"Passed away? Murata-san's dead? When?"

"Oh, about three years ago."

"Three years ago! What about Ryosaku-san and Hisashi-san?"

181

"Ryosaku-san, Hisashi-san who?"

"Both were volunteer firefighters in the town." Eizo recalled the two were eighteen or twenty years older than him.

"Ah, those Ryosaku-san and Hisashi-san. Both are dead. Long time ago now," Fumi said casually, as if she were telling him that a chicken had laid an egg.

"Long time ago, hah. How is Shoichi doing?" Eizo asked, throwing out another question to stop Fumi.

"Shoichi is okay."

"I didn't see him in Tokyo."

"He's doing fine."

"I wanted to see him. Is he coming back for summer recess?"

"I don't know. He does part-time work during the summer and sometimes doesn't always come home." Fumi stopped talking. He saw a flicker of guilt pass over her face.

"I'll come back by lunch. Could you take care of Grandma?" asked Fumi as she walked away to prepare to work in the fields.

Kino, holding the evening bag to her chest, stared blankly after Fumi.

Eizo sighed. *Was this how my life in Japan would be?* It was obvious that his son's family did not want him here.

What are you going to do?

His shadow turned up again. At that very moment, the idea of returning to Canada crossed his mind. He shivered with the idea.

... No, no. You shouldn't run away from this situation. How can you even think of such a cowardly thing?

Eizo denied the thoughts of leaving for Canada as quickly as he could. He was deeply ashamed of himself.

How can you leave Kino who has surely become insane because of you? Moreover, have you already forgotten about the hardships and loneliness you had faced in Canada?

Eizo watched Kino's movements silently, keeping a measured distance from her. She innocuously traced the patterns of the alligator evening bag. The fact that she was unresponsive when he spoke to her bothered him, although he understood this was not a reasonable reaction. Then all of a sudden Kino stood up and started walking down the street. Her cane and *geta* clacked as she went. She was about to fall down while walking but recovered her balance, swinging the new evening bag in one hand and a cane in other. She seemed unwilling to let her gift out of her sight.

"Hey, Kino. Where are you going? Why don't you leave the handbag? Hey, Kino!"

His wife ignored him. She worked her cane with one hand and gripped her evening bag with the other hand as she shuffled down the road at a brisk pace.

"Hey, Kino! Please leave your handbag at home!"

Left with little choice, Eizo followed a few steps behind. Kino did not look around, never minding how people in the town looked at her, single-mindedly moving her legs forward, sometimes staggering down the road.

Eventually they arrived at a place called *Mizusawa*, an undulation in the landscape amid a wide area of rice fields. A bank rose two metres above an irrigation canal, as wide as the width of a door. The channel was deep and had a good volume of water flowing through it. Kino sat down in the middle of the bank, which faced east and caught the warm morning light. A slightly depressed area was a perfect place for sitting, concealed from the road.

Eizo stood watching her. She seemed to have forgotten time and was completely absorbed in painstakingly tracing the patterns of the alligator bag. She did not look at him even once and did not appear to be aware of Eizo's existence. He had not recovered yet from the shock of his wife's insanity. The confusion that prevented him from collecting his thoughts left him feeling powerless.

After basking awhile in the spring sun, Kino started singing a well-known nursery song:

"Everyone hand in hand walking along the meadow path,
Everyone will become lovely little birdies,
Our shoes squeaking a tune, everyone singing,
Our shoes squeaking a tune, out in the sunny sky ..."

Her fragile voice was barely audible. She stared into the distance while pulling and tossing the withered grass around her, over and over again. She continued the tune without stumbling, giving Eizo the impression she had been singing the song over a long period of time.

Or does this mean that she still retains some memories in her heart? I wonder if there's a chance that she'll become herself again one day?

Eizo felt hope dawn inside of him, but he immediately repressed it. There was no use fabricating a dream. If the last few days had taught him anything, it was that the bigger the dream, the deeper the disappointment when things didn't work out.

Kino recited the song five or six times and smiled in an eerily sentimental way, as if someone else were sitting beside her. She seemed to exist elsewhere, looking into the distance without seeing. Her appearance reflected her mind: her skin stained, cheeks bony, white hair tousled, and her mouth hidden within her wrinkles. The flower of her youth had withered. Eizo thought about the life he would face with the wife who no longer recognised him. Never to walk together in the rice fields and live alongside each other as a couple should. He also thought of the cool reception from his family. They blamed him for Kino's condition in silence. He pondered how to live with them, muddled thoughts that depressed him. He raised his face and met his wife's gaze. For a moment her eyes, mounted in her thin face, had the gleam of saneness, transparent and infinitely deep; her eyes did not move. For the second time, Eizo believed that he saw Kino come back.

"Kino!"

The look was already gone.

Will Kino become herself again? When will that be?

However, he knew the danger in thinking that way. It could easily end up in fruitless delight or a new torment. He decided to go off and walk alone. His feet led him to the rice fields he still owned. Down the road from his own fields, he saw a middle-aged woman working in a field near the road. She bowed in greeting. Eizo returned the bow and continued walking. After about ten steps or so he looked back, sensing something: the woman was staring at him. She immediately turned and got back to work.

This town is definitely not Toronto. I'll have to re-adjust.

He was relieved when he finally saw his rice fields. The stubble of the rice plants from the previous year stood straight and looked healthy. Fumi must have cared for them properly. He looked around. The ridge of the mountains in the distance, the dykes separating the fields, the black soil, the stream of clean flowing water, and the bamboo grove, all embraced him like a mother cuddling her child. But this comfort immediately evaporated when his family situation came back to him. Eizo was tired, both from not enough sleep the night before as Kino cried out several times and

185

from the effects of jetlag. He felt weak and although he wanted to walk back to *Mizusawa* where Kino was supposed to be, he turned for home instead. There, he shuffled to his bedroom, laid down on the *futon,* and soon fell asleep.

*

He drifted in and out of consciousness and when he finally woke it was already three o'clock in the afternoon. Eizo got up and went into living room. Someone had left a dinner tray out for him. He sat down to a late lunch and then took the tray into the kitchen.

Eizo had not yet seen the whole house and decided to walk around. He started towards the storehouse built against the main dwelling. He stopped, surprised, when he saw Kino in front of the storehouse and hid himself behind the corner of the house. Her back was to him and so she did not notice him. She was artlessly piling dry branches from a mulberry tree on a large round, shallow bamboo basket used for silkworms. When she finished arranging the branches, she took them off the basket, set them aside, and repeated the procedure. Occasionally, she looked to one side and spoke as if someone was there. She laughed softly, a flattering laughter particular to a younger housewife. Now that she was old, her flirtatious laughter was unsettling and inappropriate to Eizo. He saw the evening bag near her, on the foundation of the storehouse. He felt awkward and went back to sit on the veranda. Kino had worked so hard before losing her sanity and probably thought that she was still performing the same tasks.

Poor Kino ...

Sensing someone approaching, he looked up and saw Kino at the corner of the house. He stood up to talk to her, but she suddenly bent over, grasping the cane, and tried to walk past him. He saw the evening bag clutched in her hand.

"Hey, Kino! Where are you going? Why don't you leave that darn handbag at home? Hey, Kino!" he shouted after her and then soon regretted it. How could he reproach her for not behaving as he expected?

If it makes her happy, let her carry it. Am I afraid of the rumours that will circulate? Maybe, I am ... very much so.

Eizo felt disgusted with himself that he would worry about the opinions of others to that extent. He followed after his wife, for lack of an alternative. She stopped at the Buddhist temple and as she had the previous day, sat down on the stone steps and looked away to the east. Eizo sat down too but, uncomfortable on the stone, stood up after a little while and started walking towards the main hall of the temple.

He looked up at the elaborate sculpture that lay under the soffit of the big structure. The noble, decorative doors were open to the hall. He climbed the steps and was able to watch two candle flames sway. Nobody was inside. He went into the building, as if being sucked in and inside, the tang of incense wafted around, a scent he remembered even after forty-three years of absence. *Butsu-tengai*, a sunshade for Buddha, hung from the top and the statue of Buddha, encrusted with gold lotus flowers and other altar paraphernalia, was in the back of the dark hall. *Kei*, a metal bell, and *mokugyo*, fish-shaped wooden drum, were set in front of the statue—those were the alter fittings he used to watch when he was young but had forgotten all about.

The temple was two centuries old and the time that had passed and the atmosphere of solemnity and stillness gave him the impression that he had missed something so terribly for so long: something for which he could not compensate with his pride derived from his long enduring labour in Canada and from the fulfillment of his financial responsibility towards his family. Far from bringing a peace of mind, those scenes aroused an elusive anxiety in him and it was spreading out like the film from a drop of oil radiating out over the surface of water. To make the matter worse, he did not know the way to cope with that disquiet. Eizo, who had been brought up in the Buddhist environment and later learned Christianity in the concentration camp, clasped his hands in prayer. Those feelings of satisfaction and pride were as meaningless as the wings of a chicken in the face of his family's rejection.

Dear Buddha, I'm deeply in trouble. The very meaning of my life for over seventy years is about to come into question. I've no idea what kind of troubles I'll face down the road and what my family decides for me. But I have to survive these difficulties. What am I going to pray for...? Pray for Buddha to give me an unpredictable smile of destiny? Oh shoot, I guess, at least I should pray for Kino's recovery?

He realized though, that Kino's condition was beyond the dimension of prayer and even the Buddha's ability to extend mercy to her. Eizo quickly offered a silent prayer, instead. Feeling helpless and restless, he looked back at Kino still on the stone steps in her stained clothes. Probably, the family gave up on the idea of putting clean clothes on her a long time ago, observing how Kino continuously made her clothes filthy.

That's my wife, the woman I've been dreaming of for more than forty years.

Seeking a diversion, Eizo went outside and walked across the yard to the bell tower, climbed the few stone steps, and saw a dedication stamp impressed into the *bonsho*, a big metal bell. The date showed that it was cast after the Second World War. He remembered hearing about the Imperial forces running short of bullets near the end of the war and stripping many temples of their bronze bells, and in some cases, even statues of Buddha, in order to manufacture bullets. While those religious symbols were disappearing in Japan, the Nikkei in Canada were being detained in the concentration camps. To live in peace with his family, he thought he had to talk about his experiences in Canada. He hoped he could talk to Isoshichi and Fumi that evening; if they were willing to listen.

When the sun was about to set, Kino cried out in the same way she had the previous evening, towards the sky in the east, in a low and hoarse voice. "My dearest, come back to me quickly!" She repeated the cry several times.

Later, when dinner was over and the clean-up complete, Fumi came out to sit by the hearth with her family. Even though Isoshichi and Toshio were watching television and Kino was playing with her evening bag, Eizo thought this was a good time to broach the subject of his long absence.

"Isoshichi. I have things to talk to you about."

Isoshichi only turned his head halfway, caught his father's eye, and saying nothing, turned back to the television. Toshio appeared uncomfortable, and looked back and forth between his father and this strange grandfather. Fumi looked strained and pretended not to see her father-in-law. But something in her stiff expression told him that she had already made a decision about some matters.

"At first I thought that I should tell everyone together about Canada, but I can tell Tamotsu and Kozo later." Eizo tried to continue.

189

Everyone was silent. The drama on television flashed scenes of a family laughing together in contrast to the real life drama unfolding in the Osada household.

"I think you've suffered enough since Kino became like this. Unfortunately, I didn't know. I wish you could've let me know long ago. I would've come back sooner."

Isoshichi shifted his position but showed no interest in his father's talk. Fumi cast a meaningful look at her husband.

"No, I'm not blaming you at all, not at all. I know very well I've no right to accuse others for my own faults. But, I didn't forget you while I was away. I rarely thought about anything else. I apologize for causing you so much trouble. But, please, I'd like to talk and for you to listen."

Isoshichi turned to Fumi, his expression severe, and said in a flat, emotionless voice, "Fumi, is the bath ready?"

"I'm going to check now," Fumi answered and she and Isoshichi stood up at the same time.

Eizo could hear Fumi cry out something from the bathroom. He could not catch what she said over the television.

"Since Grandma became sick, we've talked about moving out of the town. We've been a target for ridicule ever since," said Toshio before he dashed up the stairs.

Kino must be the laughingstock of the town. Face to face people will smile, but behind your back, they'll mercilessly cut you down. They're conformists and anyone different is a victim. My son didn't put her into a psychiatric hospital, but instead, looked after her at home. I have to thank him, but that decision made them targets.

Kino sat, a weird smile on her face, and kept tracing the patterns of the alligator evening bag.

15
You Must Have Met Someone Like *Otohime-sama*, Yeah?

The following morning after breakfast Eizo paid a visit to the immediate neighbours; it was the custom to bring gifts when someone returned from a place far away. Satoko, the woman in the house to the left was about Fumi's age. She invited him into the living room, and removed the napkin from a tea set, which was ready to serve in case anyone dropped by. While she prepared green tea using hot water from a thermos, she asked Eizo questions about Canada, which he was happy to relate.

"So, you were on Vancouver Island and it looks wild." Satoko said. "Where is it located?"

"The west side of the mainland of Canada. It's a big, big island. There were pods of killer whales in the Georgia Strait …"

"Where is the Georgia Strait?"

"Ah … it lies between the mainland and Vancouver Island. From the ferry, you could see the island was covered in thick forests stretching miles and miles. I was a logger there and the trees we had to cut were as big as six or seven people hand-to-hand around the trunks." While talking, Eizo stretched both hands. "Sword ferns were so big they came up to my chin and moss was so thick I sank up to my knees."

"Is that so? That big?" She listened to his talk admiringly.

Since the scenes of Canada seemed to be the only topic they could share, he talked for another quarter of an hour about his memories of Vancouver Island, its ancient landscapes, and life on the sidewalks in Toronto, the squirrels collecting nuts in parks and sights not common in Japan.

Although Eizo hesitated to ask his neighbour when Kino had become sick, encouraged by Satoko's pleasant reception, he yielded to temptation when an opportunity came. "Do you know when Kino became ill?"

"Have you discussed this with your family?" Frowning, Satoko filled his teacup again. "You'd better talk to Isoshichi-san. He'll tell you."

Eizo was surprised by her reluctance. At first, he had surmised she would tell him about it as a chat over tea but quickly chastised himself.

Her reaction is the rational one. I was in Canada far too long. When did I make any important family decisions? I seem to have lost the ability to judge my situation.

Humiliated, he excused himself and left hurriedly.

Watch out what you say. You're in your hometown. You should've known their social protocol.

He forced himself to the next house where the visit occurred more or less in the same way. The men were already in the fields and had left behind Misa, a woman several years older than Eizo. He remembered Misa, though now she was stooped from age, lacked most of her teeth, and was very hard of hearing. Today she sat on the veranda while her granddaughter hung out the laundry.

"What happened to Kentaro-san?" Eizo asked, almost shouting in her ear.

"Kentaro-san? You mean that Kentaro-san who was very sharp and clever?"

"Yes, that's right."

"Ah, he is confined to bed by palsy."

"By palsy? That's too bad. He was so smart."

"Being smart doesn't mean anything here. You gotta be healthy."

"Oh. How is Bunta-san, then?"

"Bunta? The boy that wasn't that bright when he was young?"

"Yes."

"Bunta made money to burn by investing into stocks and lives in a castle."

"Lives in a castle? That's good."

"People say life is not fair," Misa said, unsurely moving her mouth around its few teeth, "but I'd say life is fair." She spoke flatly and then continued, "You know Sada-san died a few years ago? The Sada-san, you know, your sister-in-law."

Eizo was startled. He thought it was fortunate that he did not visit his head family first.

If I had gone to my late brother's place without knowing his wife had passed away as well, it wouldn't only be embarrassing, but unacceptable! My family didn't even let me in on that. Maybe they thought me dead too—dead to them long all along.

On his return home Eizo could not find Kino.

He decided to go to the local graveyard alone and visit the family plot. Using a dipper, he poured water onto the tombstone so that the deceased would not be thirsty in the other world and clasped his hands in prayer.

"*Tō-san, Kā-san, Nii-san and Nē-san,* Father, Mother, Elder Brother and Sister-in-Law, I'm reporting to you that I'm safely back from Canada now. I've made a blunder and

193

been impolite to you all while I've been away. I'm deeply sorry about that. I entreat your forgiveness and pray for your happiness in the afterlife."

He then visited Murata's tombstone as well, to offer flowers in his honour.

*

That evening, Eizo decided that it was time to visit the family head, a hierarchy that would have had much less significance in Canada. When he was about to leave, Fumi warned him that his sister-in-law had died several years ago. Eizo appreciated that Fumi was considerate enough to inform him, but then realized that she acted as much out of self-preservation in order to save face.

Before Eizo set up his branch family, he had lived many years in the head family home with his parents, grandparents and elder brother. As the second son, by custom Eizo had to set up his own family home separately from the head family. Breaking away from the family home was never taken lightly and Eizo, for many reasons, felt much more attached to the old family home than he did to his own. The head family house he remembered had big reddish-black lacquered posts and large wooden sliding doors that were regularly polished to a shine with a bag containing rice bran. During the day the house was dark and in winter it was cold.

The old house had disappeared. In its place was a modern structure with large glass windows.

"*Konbanwa,*" Eizo called out.

"Good evening," greeted a woman with an inquisitive smile.

"I'm Eizo from the branch family," he said, differentiating the offshoot from the head family.

"Ah, Eizo-san, please come in." She was now showing a full smile. He assumed she was the wife of his nephew. She ushered Eizo into the Western-style living room, as though she had known him for a long time. Eizo, a little suspicious, was curious as to why she treated him so kindly.

"Ah, Uncle Eizo! You're finally back." A tall man, scruffy with two day's growth on his chin, walked into the room. His face looked as though it had been exposed to the elements for too many years. Although Eizo had not seen him for almost a lifetime, he guessed the man was Kin'ichi. Not just because he called Eizo 'uncle', but the contour of his face, and funnily enough, from the big moles on his arm and face. Kin'ichi was the eldest son of his late brother, only four or five years older than Isoshichi, although he appeared much older.

"How many years did you stay in Canada?" his nephew asked after they had settled in.

"Well, a little more than forty years."

"Such a long time?" Kin'ichi had a distant look, as though he were glancing back through the years.

"I'm sorry I was unable to attend your father's and mother's funerals. If I had come back by train and ship, it would've taken more than a half-month and I would've missed the funeral anyway. But, on behalf of me, Isoshichi …"

"Uncle, don't worry about that. At the time it was enough to get obituary gifts."

To this Eizo was surprised. He was aware of the obituary gift that Isoshichi had sent under Eizo's name for his parents' funerals, but knew nothing about anything sent for his brother and sister-in-law. Kin'ichi must be mistaken. Eizo's family never mentioned anything to him.

Maybe Isoshichi sent the gifts to the funeral in order to save face. There seems to be a lot that I don't know about my family ...

Regardless, Eizo could not ask Kin'ichi directly and expose his family's problems. He already went through this at his neighbour's house that morning.

"Today, I went to the graveyard to visit the family plot."

"Ah! Our area of the graveyard is a little rundown, isn't it?" He was clearly ashamed.

"Anyway, I'd like to make an offering to the deceased."

"Please, please," Kin'ichi encouraged Eizo, guiding him into the drawing room.

Photographs of his parents, his brother and his brother's wife were displayed in the household Buddhist altar. Eizo prayed silently in front of his nephew. He reported his safe return and asked for their eternal peace.

They returned to the living room where Kin'ichi's wife served tea. She asked Eizo a few questions about the weather in Toronto and his long trip to Japan and then left. Eizo looked around the room. There were two sofas and a chair, a wooden cabinet and on one side of the wall, a modern painting of scenery in a frame. Curtains were still open. He found nothing to affirm that he had once lived there.

"Uncle, your face has an expression that you might expect to see on a foreigner." Kin'ichi spoke in a deep voice thinned a little with uncertainty.

"I was in Canada for a long time," Eizo said, pausing. "When you're in a foreign country, time flies. First a year, then two and three, before you realize it, forty years have gone by just like that."

"Sounds like *Ima-Urashima.*" Kin'ichi referred to a fairy tale about Urashima, a young fisherman who had rescued a turtle and in return for his kind deed, was invited to the castle under the sea by *Otohime*, the princess of the ocean. Time stood still while Urashima was there. He was still a young man when he finally returned to his village, but the world had been utterly changed: he now knew no one. In despair, he opened the casket that *Otohime* had given and warned him never to open. It emitted a smoke that caused him to become old.

"That's right. When I came home the station, the town, and the people had all changed. Everything is new to me. In some ways I feel like a foreigner."

"Of course, things have to change over time. Since you stayed so long in Canada you must have met someone like *Otohime-sama*, yeah?" Kin'ichi was trying to draw the truth from Eizo in the guise of a joke.

"No, no. I'd never ..." Eizo denied, confused at Kin'ichi's subtle yet direct thrust.

"Yeah, time flies. You look even younger than I do," the nephew said.

"Eh? No, no, no. It was tough though! You don't understand their language so well and you struggle to fit in, meanwhile time slips away."

"Uncle, how is it that you were there forty years, but you don't understand English? Is that English?"

"Yes, it's English. No, it's not that I didn't understand their language completely. I was able to do everyday things in English, but when it came to more complicated subjects, I was usually lost."

"I thought you must have been fluent."

"Well, while I was working with other Japanese people, I didn't have any problems. But once I started working with white people, then my troubles began. To be honest with you, I played with *hakujin* kids on the weekends ... I helped take their toboggans to the top of the snow hills and slide down with them in order to learn English," Eizo said reluctantly, forced to disclose his weak point, but not the real motive: so that he was not completely alone and did not have to spend money on English classes. "The Nisei quite often helped the older Issei as interpreters. The Nisei played with other English speaking kids and went to English schools. That's how they learned and then they would teach English to their parents."

"The Nisei kids acted as interpreters for their parents?"

"You know, it was quite natural that Canadian-born Nisei were fluent in English. But for the Issei, having them around was great. We used to say, 'Hey, look at those guys. They speak as well as *hakujin* people.'"

"Hah! Then, the Nisei can speak both English and Japanese fluently."

"That's right. In Western Canada, at one point before the war, I heard that there were more than fifty Japanese language schools. The Nisei were Canadian citizens so they went to regular school first, as was expected, and then went to Japanese school in the afternoon."

"After school finished they went to another? Sounds like Japanese cram school."

"It was important for the Nisei to know Japanese. That is …" Eizo paused. He did not want to discuss certain things with Kin'ichi just for the sake of talking. Before the war it was difficult for the Nisei to get decent jobs due to the discrimination in the white society, even though they spoke English fluently. They had to be prepared to work at retail stores or saw mills that were owned or managed by Japanese people. Knowledge of their mother tongue was a necessity. Many of their parents intended to return to Japan after they had become rich in Canada. He could sense old, unpleasant feelings creeping back. "… At that time many of us planned to return home and those that had kids in Canada expected that they would leave too, so it was important that the Nisei learn Japanese."

"I see. How many Japanese schools are there in Canada now?"

"I'm not entirely sure, maybe around ten."

"Really? Why did the number decrease?" Kin'ichi probed.

Eizo did not think it important for his nephew to know about the concentration camps: it was a shame to Eizo to tell his nephew about it and why the Japanese language schools were dissolved. "There were many reasons, I think. But, I didn't have my kids with me, so I don't know much about that."

"Ah, of course, you're right."

Eizo was surprised by Kin'ichi's easy acceptance of his explanation. He began to realize how much he himself had changed while in Canada and how many social cues he had forgotten. He understood that Kin'ichi was just attempting not to cause bad feelings. His nephew had lived too long in a small, close-knit society where survival depended on maintaining the respect of the other community members. This was accomplished by not only obeying the law, but also longstanding social customs. Tacit approval of the community was necessary: never become *deru kugi wa utareru.*

Eizo suddenly felt his connection with Kin'ichi, of family and being Japanese, dissolve. He looked around the room. The walls were painted a traditional moss green; a décor mute and expressionless in a way that he could not seem to bear. Night drew its veil down and as the sky darkened, car lights cast their silhouettes on the window surface.

Kin'ichi noticed Eizo's appraisal and said, "The original house was so old that even during the day it was dark inside. About five or six years ago we built this place. Uncle, do you remember the room in the back? It was always musty and damp even in the summertime."

Eizo still felt a childhood attachment to the old place, despite its age. "This looks like a well-built house."

"This kind of house would be called 'modern' in English? Ho, ho, ho." Kin'ichi laughed.

Eizo believed his older brother's family should be the closest of his relatives, but instead they felt like total strangers. Again, he had that sinking feeling in the pit of his stomach. He pondered whether he should ask his nephew about Kino. He wanted to know the cause of Kino's lunacy, but didn't want to make the same mistake with Kin'ichi that he had made with his neighbour. He believed he knew the reason. The guilt tore at him; his absence was the cause.

"My mistake was not coming home sooner. I'd never have guessed that Kino was ill."

No sooner had Eizo started to speak than Kin'ichi's look changed. His face fell and his expression darkened. He clearly became uncomfortable and shifted awkwardly.

"I didn't know Kino's situation while I was away," Eizo said and waited for Kin'ichi to talk.

"Uncle, did Isoshichi-san not say anything to you about that?"

"I don't want to bring shame on my family, but to tell the truth, Isoshichi does not talk to me," Eizo said, his voice breaking.

There was a long silence.

"That ... still, Uncle that's your family matter, you know, I don't ... I don't really know why Aunty Kino became

200

sick," Kin'ichi said, averting his eyes. The earlier brightness left his face.

"I saw Kino pretending to feed silkworms. Even though she's sick, she still thinks she's working. What a pity."

Kin'ichi sat, speechless. He would not look Eizo in the eyes, choosing to stare at the glazed windows of the sliding doors. "Aunty Kino worked so hard, you know," he said flatly.

Eizo severely regretted speaking of Kino again. He did not want to stay at the head family any longer. He was badly embarrassed, asking a wrong question. "Well, thank you very much for your tea. I have to go. It was a nice meeting with you." Eizo stood up.

"You are home now and that must feel good."

"Well, I guess ..."

"Sumiko, Uncle Eizo is leaving." The nephew called his wife to come out from other room.

"Thank you for coming. I hope you've enjoyed your visit with my husband," Sumiko said, coming to the entrance with hasty steps.

"Yes, I did. Thank you."

Eizo opened the sliding door and deeply bowed to Kin'ichi and Sumiko. "*Sayonara*." The couple bowed back respectfully to him.

When Eizo returned home after his hour long visit to the head family, Isoshichi and Fumi were watching television.

"I went to visit the head family. Kin'ichi and Sumiko-san were there. I spoke to Kin'ichi, he was ..."

Isoshichi half-turned his face back, cast a sober glance at him, but still refused to speak.

Eizo sat at the hearth for ten minutes and seeing no opportunity to improve the situation went into Kino's bedroom. She held the evening bag like a child absorbed with a novel toy.

A shadow flitted across Eizo's face.

16
Alien Registration

The town offices had been partially renovated over the years but were still very much how Eizo remembered them. Storage lockers here and there gave the rooms an unkempt feeling, reinforced by the dim lighting and cooler temperature. The clerk at the front desk was a little confused as to why this old man, who spoke and wrote perfect Japanese, had to register as a foreigner, but processed him in the usual efficient way. Eizo left as quickly as he could, though being reminded that he did not possess Japanese nationality did not leave him feeling as depressed as it had before.

Instead of going straight home, Eizo climbed aboard the next bus heading for downtown Minokamo. Clothing he had sent ahead from Canada was now proving to be insufficient for his needs.

When he had taken the train a week earlier, changes to the buildings and streets in front of the station had left him feeling flustered. Now he saw that the whole city had undergone significant rebuilding. The buildings that had been modern forty-odd years ago were now old. A few decaying structures could still be found standing beside contemporary edifices.

His shopping complete, Eizo let his legs carry him into the central part of the city.

Tired, he finally went into a noodle shop. He placed an order for his favourite *Kitsune-udon,* a Japanese thick noodle soup with fried *tofu.* Deprived for the last four decades, Eizo savoured it to the last drop. Reluctantly he got up. He left a tip, paid his bill, and exited the shop. Before he had walked four or five shops farther down the street he heard someone calling behind him.

"*Okyaku-san*! *Okyaku-san*!"

Eizo turned. A young waitress with a white handkerchief tied over her hair ran towards him, her sandals pattering on the cement.

"Sir, you left this behind." She held out her hand with his tip in her palm.

"That's a tip for you," Eizo explained quietly as people passed by looking at them.

"A tip?"

"Yes, I left it for you. Please keep it."

"But, I don't need it, sir," the waitress replied, confused and hesitant to accept money this way.

"It's okay. I gave it to you," Eizo repeated, walking away. He chuckled to himself as he considered how difficult it would be to abandon some of the habits he had acquired in Canada. This brief joy gave way to thoughts of Isoshichi sitting by the hearth like a wooden statue, distress chiselled on his face, watching television and ignoring Eizo. As the initial reserve wore off, Eizo began to sense an unspoken resentment from Fumi and Toshio as well. He was not welcome amongst his family. He had once considered that if his family rejected him he would build his own small house nearby and live alone. He had dismissed the idea as absurd. Now he felt it was not too far off the mark. Kino's insanity had marked his family for segregation from the community. Now his sudden appearance after forty years' absence and asking neighbours about his wife's lunacy had possibly made him the target of ridicule as well, and perhaps they thought him as insane as his wife. There was little Eizo found he could do except endure and take care of his wife, making the best of his time with her. Even if his family rejected him, he could never bring himself to completely abandon Kino. She was his wife. Eizo looked at his watch. It was already past three o'clock. He turned and walked back to the bus. After twenty minutes waiting, he got on a bus.

Strangers!

Glancing around in the bus he did not see anybody he knew. A couple of seats ahead two schoolboys were playing with plastic models of some *anime* characters that Eizo didn't recognize. The bus ran smoothly, though it sometimes swayed over bumps in the road, but even so, he felt comfortable. For a while the bus passed through the shopping district. He watched people and their baskets, until the streets gave way to a more rural landscape. He saw the familiar ridge and the hazy sky close to the edge of mountains, scattered houses, fields and rice fields, under the mild April sun. The bus gradually emptied. The fresh breeze through the open windows pleasantly brushed his face, cheeks and hair. He saw several farmers at work in the rice fields. The nature of land offered moments of comfort and relief at how normal the day seemed.

The bus turned a corner and Eizo saw that his stop was approaching. Suddenly the two schoolboys started shouting and pointing outside the bus.

"Look! Look! That's the crazy old woman!" one of the boys cried.

"She's carrying that purse!" the other boy shouted.

Eizo cast around quickly. There was Kino, with the support of her cane, shuffling along the low dykes separating rice fields, with her new evening bag in hand. Some of the other passengers glanced out through the windows to see what had stirred the boys' interest.

"Hey! That's 'My dearest, come back to me quickly!' you know," snorted the boy next to the window.

"Yah! 'My dearest, come back to me quickly!'" the other boy laughed.

"My dad said her husband has recently come back from Canada," said the boy by the window.

"My dad said her husband is stupid. He must've bought her that purse. He doesn't know anything."

"My granny said the same thing. He's a donkey all right. What a dummy" The schoolboys laughed again, looking at each other.

Eizo could barely restrain himself. He now knew without a doubt what the townspeople were thinking and saying about his family. He boiled with rage at the injustice of it all. Who could he blame? Who could he confront? In the bus window, he saw a dark film of sadness and desolation wrapping his whole existence. He knew that there was only himself to blame.

Eizo stood up at his stop. All adult passengers seemed to be oblivious to what had just occurred. It seemed nothing novel to them. Only the schoolboys were still looking at Kino. As he walked towards home, their laughter echoed in his head. He couldn't shake his anger, until it dawned on him that Isoshichi and Fumi must have experienced this type of humiliation innumerable times. Toshio had told him a few nights before that Isoshichi had considered moving out of town. Now Eizo understood. His heart broke when he considered the whispers and gossip Isoshichi had to endure, particularly when he had to deliver fertilizer and other goods to people's homes. His eldest son had probably suffered the most.

I'm the cause of Kino's insanity and my family has suffered.

Isoshichi and Fumi had taken responsibility for Kino, acting as the head of the family in his absence.

How else could they have reacted towards me?

Eizo decided to try to better understand the distant wooden statue: his eldest son.

"Isoshichi, I'm very thankful to you and Fumi-san," Eizo said, breaking the silence that hung over the living room that evening.

Isoshichi stood up, turned the television on, and sat back down by the hearth. Pop music blared. Kino stared blankly at the busy screen where half a dozen dancers were kicking up their legs behind singers. Looking down Eizo saw that she still held her evening bag, as if she could not bear to be parted from it, even for a moment.

17
A Letter from Martin

The season for planting rice had come and gone. Swallows were seen flying and diving above the rice shoots, a sign that life was returning anew. Mechanization had swept into the agricultural field, even in this remote town, replacing the old way where farmers and their families stooped to plant by hand. Eizo did not have to get involved in it because of his age. Instead, he spent his time taking care of Kino—actually accompanying her everywhere she went—, but it was heartbreaking to see her so ill, and he was filled with remorse.

Isoshichi's family had not changed their attitude towards him except that Fumi and Toshio had now relaxed their guard a little. If he had not come back from Canada, the family would not have fallen into this dismal state of affairs. By not sending him a copy of his family registration they had all sent the message that he was not welcome, but driven by his long-cherished dream, Eizo had ignored the signs and returned anyway.

*

Late in June, Eizo went to Nagoya and acquired a permit to stay longer in Japan from the immigration office. He needed certainty as to whether or not he could live with his family.

Then a few days later, a letter arrived from Martin. The letter began by saying that the Satos hoped all was well and expected that Eizo was happily settling in with his family. Martin informed Eizo that he had been successfully placed in seniors' housing, but if he did not plan to return to Canada, then he should advise Martin as soon as possible. The letter was a great surprise to have arrived this early.

Eizo was torn. He had decided to stay with Kino and look after her, but in the face of such antagonism, his resolve was shaken. Against his will, he found himself vacillating between the duty to live with his wife and family and the desire to return to Canada. If he missed this chance, he thought, it would be impossible to return and apply to seniors' housing once again. The next surprise was that he might actually be considering going back to Canada, leaving his ill wife behind in Japan.

How could I do such a cold-hearted thing? That would be unpardonable on my part. That wouldn't be humane, leaving when the going gets tough.

However, he was not fully convinced that Isoshichi and Fumi would accept him under the same roof and some day show genial feelings toward him. They never said anything directly that rubbed Eizo the wrong way, but he could feel the waves of resentment.

One afternoon on a cloudy day, he followed Kino on the low dykes that separated the rice fields and listened to her sing a children's song.

She sings those words and calls out for me to come back quickly day after day. If I'm to be punished for leaving my family for so long, am I not punished enough to find my wife insane?

Eizo realized that it was time to meet with his three sons together to talk about why he had not returned sooner, and decided to visit Tamotsu and ask him to arrange a family meeting. He needed to determine whether his sons were prepared to accept him or not, in the face of Martin's letter. He was also worried about Kozo who had neither called nor written since he had arrived. Kozo was only two years old when Eizo had left for Canada, yet he needed to see how his youngest son had grown.

Later at home, Eizo called Tamotsu, hoping to stay with him in Tokyo. He furthermore asked Tamotsu to call Kozo to see if he was able to come and stay with the third son's family as well. Under the circumstances, Eizo felt it best for Tamotsu to ask Kozo, but still, he felt humiliated that he could not call his son and ask for himself. Once the details were set, Eizo came back to the evening hearth and told Isoshichi that he was going to stay with Tamotsu and Kozo for several days. Isoshichi did not take his eyes off the television, only grunted in response.

In the morning, when Isoshichi was about to go to work Eizo said, "Well, I'm going to Tokyo today. I'll be back in four or five days."

Lacing up his shoes, Isoshichi paused for a moment and then left without saying anything. Once he had gone, Fumi came into the room with some boxes of chocolates and cookies. "Father, Shoichi will also be at Tamotsu-san's this evening. Could you take these for him?"

Eizo was surprised to see that Fumi had arranged for his grandson to be there. He promised to take the gifts.

It was late in the afternoon before Eizo arrived at Tokyo Station. After the usual confusion in the crowded station he found Tamotsu who led him to the car. Once they were on the road he noticed that the tension that had gripped Tamotsu during his last visit had been replaced by a more relaxed, but still reserved countenance. Eizo did not blame Tamotsu for

210

not mentioning his mother's condition on the day they met at the airport. Nor did Tamotsu apologize. Eizo broke the silence to talk about the changes he had noticed in town and his visit to the head family and to the family graveyard, but restrained himself from speaking about his immediate family. Neither of them was too eager to break the fragile veneer that seemed to be holding their delicate relationship together.

Shoichi arrived just before dinner. He was twenty-three, a solidly built youth with broad shoulders, and had a long nose that took after Fumi. Shoichi gladly received the items Eizo brought from his mother. While polite towards his grandfather, over the course of the evening he spoke mostly to Noboru and Mayumi in a shaky Tokyo accent, like a country boy trying to acquire the rhythm of the big city. He appeared to have enjoyed his youth and left behind any bitter experiences of his hometown. But when the conversation was interrupted, Eizo noticed a gloomy shadow cross Shoichi's face. Eizo assumed the guilt, driven to feel that his absence had left an indelible imprint on the life of his grandson.

Shoichi left late into the evening. Noboru and Mayumi, too, retreated to their own rooms.

"Home has changed in almost every way," Eizo said to his son and daughter-in-law. "It was a great surprise for me." He tried to hold himself in but his voice resonated with his remorse.

Tamotsu stiffened and glanced over at Akiko.

"Yes, *Okā-san* is much different than she used to be," Akiko said hesitantly, obviously feeling great pity for her mother-in-law.

"To tell the truth, I was stunned to learn about Kino. Nobody told me. I had known nothing for so long." Eizo sighed, trying not to say anything that might upset them, but like the tide, was unable to hold it back.

Tamotsu shifted uncomfortably.

"I'm sorry. I'm not blaming anyone but me for your mother's condition. I should apologize."

"You apologize? No, y-you didn't ..." Tamotsu stuttered, leaning over to catch his father's every word.

Eizo did not let him finish. "It's because of me everyone is suffering."

"No, that's not ... you've got it all wrong," Tamotsu said and glanced at Akiko who refused to look at her husband.

"No, I don't think so. When I see your mother and your brother every day, no matter how hard I may apologize, it's not enough. Isoshichi is so angry. He doesn't talk to me." Eizo's voice fell away into a barely audible whisper again.

"He's distant to begin with. I don't think he's silent because he feels ill will towards you."

"How can you say that? I can see very well how angry he is with me. He has no problem getting on with everyone else. When your brother was a kid, he was not distant, not at all. He was mischievous and noisy, racing around all over the place. I can hardly imagine that mischievous kid in Isoshichi today."

Tamotsu was at loss for words and looked down at the *tatami* mats.

"About two months ago while I was on the bus, by chance I saw Kino out walking. She had never been to that area before. Two schoolboys on the bus made fun of her, mimicking her. I became so angry that I almost shouted at them. Isoshichi and Fumi-san have had such bitter experiences, probably every day. I can understand why they have a grudge against me."

Tamotsu looked at his wife who still remained silent but appeared uncomfortable.

"Kino doesn't recognize me. In the evening, she cries out in the direction of Canada and calls for me to come home. She doesn't know I'm sitting right beside her."

Akiko suddenly stood up and went into the kitchen. Tamotsu followed Akiko's departure with his eyes. Akiko poured the water into a kettle and put it down on the gas stove with a bang, and stayed in the kitchen, staring into the stove's flames.

When his gaze met with his father's, Tamotsu quickly looked down at the *tatami* mats again. He frowned, his mouth tight and downturned, and his expression cried out for someone to help him solve the unsolvable. He then stretched his right hand to his head and scratched it.

"When did Mom become like that?" Eizo asked. "I asked Isoshichi about it but he says nothing. Fumi-san said that it happened about twenty years ago, but she wasn't sure."

"Akiko, what year was it?" Tamotsu called to the kitchen.

"It was just before we got married, remember? It was the year Shoichi-san was born."

"The year Shoichi was born?" Eizo got a start.

"Yes, that's right. That was twenty-two or three years ago," Tamotsu said unsurely.

"Well then, it was twenty-three years ago, when the letter from Kino arrived," Eizo said with a strained face.

"What letter?" Tamotsu asked.

"Your mother's last letter. It arrived the year Shoichi was born. She said in the letter that the Japanese economy was not doing well and that there were no jobs here. She asked me to keep working in Canada and to continue sending money home."

213

Tamotsu's mouth dropped open, unable to hide his shock. He tried to say something, but the words would not come. Akiko stopped boiling the water in the kitchen, and stood still staring at them.

"Didn't you know anything about the letter?" Eizo asked.

"No, nothing!"

"If you don't know, then Isoshichi and Kozo probably knew nothing about it either."

"I was in Tokyo," Tamotsu said.

"I see."

"But, Isoshichi might know about it," suggested Tamotsu.

"Isoshichi knew?" Eizo pondered. He recalled that he attempted to show Kino's last letter to his eldest son when he saw him for the first time after his return but Isoshichi ignored it. However, there was a good possibility that Isoshichi might have known about it since he lived at home with Kino, yet still refused to see it.

But if he knew about it, he would not be able to take such a cruel attitude towards me. He couldn't know ...

"And where is the letter?" Tamotsu asked. Akiko now sat beside him and listened to the conversation intently.

"I have it here." Eizo opened his jacket to expose the inside pocket.

"May I see it?" Tamotsu pushed forward.

Encouraged at last, Eizo slid the old yellow envelope out of his pocket and handed it to Tamotsu. After carefully examining the envelope to confirm the sender and addressee, Tamotsu carefully pulled the letter out. Akiko leaned close to him, their eyes riveted to the lines of characters on the page and soon Eizo saw their eyes start moving along the lines of the letter. The living room became deathly still.

When Tamotsu tried to turn over the first page Akiko held his hand in place until she had finished reading. Tamotsu looked at her, his irritation evident, but as Akiko finished reading and turned the first page over, he was again absorbed by the letter, attention focused. Where they found parts difficult to read, their brows wrinkled and they brought their faces closer to the paper. Tamotsu's face was pale. Akiko had to turn the second page over for him.

When they finished reading the letter, they looked at each other. Eizo could not interpret their expressions, but it was evident to his eyes that they did not know that Kino's letter had ever existed. Tamotsu still held the letter near his face, but turned to Akiko.

"Tamotsu, I need to tell you about what happened to me in Canada, with Isoshichi and Kozo, everyone together. Can you arrange a meeting for me this weekend?"

"Where?" Tamotsu muttered numbly.

"At Isoshichi's home."

"I don't mind, but so soon? Kozo is a busy man."

"Of course, when I see Kozo, I will ask him too. But before that, can you ask Kozo to leave this weekend's schedule open?" Eizo deeply felt ashamed that he could not even call his own son directly. The years and blows to his psyche had left him timid and shy.

"All right," Tamotsu said, "but since you took so much trouble coming here, why don't you talk about it right now?" He looked at Akiko as if he were seeking her approval, or afraid of her real thoughts.

"Yes, but I'd like to have all three of you together. If you and Kozo are there, Isoshichi will listen. When I try talking to Isoshichi he turns on the television or walks away."

"He does that?"

215

"Yes. It hurts me. I'd like to have a conversation with all the family like the old days."

"What do you think, Akiko?" Tamotsu asked his wife.

She suddenly came to her senses, "… I think this's important. I think you need to go," Akiko said.

"Akiko-san, thank you," said Eizo.

Tamotsu closed the sliding door and went into the kitchen to the phone.

"Shall I make tea again for you?" Akiko asked Eizo, now somewhat recovering her normal expression.

"No, thank you. I'm fine," he said.

Eizo heard Tamotsu say in a low voice, "I haven't told him about that yet … then do it as a favour to me … I don't know." Tamotsu hung up the telephone, came back to the living room and sat down. "Kozo said he could come this Saturday."

"Thank you," Eizo said, with relief.

"Akiko, could you please make some tea?" Tamotsu said.

"Yes, of course," she said, getting up.

While the water was set to boil again the father and son sat silently with their eyes cast in different directions, immersed in their own thoughts. No sound came from Noboru's and Mayumi's rooms. Akiko came back to the living room with tea steaming in cups on the tray.

"Since I came back from Canada, I haven't managed to talk with Isoshichi. I can see what he's thinking. He doesn't want me here. Isoshichi bears a grudge against me and he's shunning me."

Akiko sat, served tea to Eizo and Tamotsu and one for herself and put the tray on a *tatami* mat beside her.

"I can hardly blame Isoshichi for that. When I think about how badly they've been treated by the townspeople, I can't blame him, but ..." Eizo paused, "I think it's my responsibility to look after Kino whatever Isoshichi's attitude might be towards me."

Tamotsu and Akiko looked at each other, their tea untouched.

"Considering the present situation, I don't think I can stay at home all the time. Well, it's rather a request to you than a consultation. If you don't mind, may I come to stay sometimes? Not to this company residence but to the house you are going to build?"

Before Eizo finished his speaking, Akiko deliberately stared at the side of Tamotsu's face without saying anything, grim determination set on her face. Tamotsu, however, refused to meet her gaze, instead keeping his silence.

"... Well, just if the house we build is big enough," Tamotsu said at last, his voice wavering.

Akiko unexpectedly turned her face away from him, stood up, and quickly shuffled off to the kitchen. Eizo was surprised by her sudden exit.

Tamotsu looked panic-stricken. "Well, to tell the truth, Akiko and I have already decided to build an extra room for Akiko's father to live with us. We made that promise long time ago. That's why Akiko has been working." He looked toward the kitchen.

Akiko was putting on rubber gloves to wash the dishes. Although her back was to her father-in-law and husband in the living room, she could still hear Tamotsu. She then started pulling the gloves off undecidedly.

Eizo understood. He was being told that there was no room for him. While disappointed, it was worth knowing their thoughts. Due to the entangled relationship with his sons' families, he hesitated mentioning to them that he had arranged for seniors' housing in Toronto. He decided not to at this juncture. Instead, he said, "Is that so? With Akiko-san's father? That's a good thing. Well then, I don't think you'll have space for me."

Akiko brought in a bowl of cookies and placed it on the table. "*Dōzo*," she said, indicating for Eizo to help himself. She sat down again. It seemed to Eizo that she had softened towards him, but Tamotsu still appeared troubled.

Eizo felt sorry for him. "I'm so glad that the three of you've grown up into fine men. It makes me happy more than anything."

His son did not reply and looked at his wife.

"That's right. Isoshichi-san and Kozo-san too," Akiko helped her husband out.

"There're many kids who don't turn out to be decent men even when they're brought up by both of their parents," Eizo said. "The three of you didn't let the hardships get to you."

Akiko stretched her hand to hold Tamotsu's but put it back halfway through, as she saw that Tamotsu did not respond. She changed the course of the conversation. "If you don't have anything particular scheduled for tomorrow, I'd like to take you around Tokyo."

"… Well, I think … I'd like that. Thank you," Eizo said, accepting Akiko's suggestion.

"Don't mention it. Oh, it's already twelve o'clock. Tamotsu-san, could you go lay out the *futons*," said Akiko.

Tamotsu automatically stood up to prepare the *futons* as though he were a puppet.

*

The following morning Akiko took Eizo, dressed in a polo shirt and khaki pants, on a customary tour of Tokyo by bus.

In Canada, where one would rarely see people running in the city, he saw pedestrians dash through crosswalks even after the traffic lights had turned green. Congestion was further confused by traffic abruptly crossing lanes. The pace of the city exhausted him and the tour guide droned on explaining historic sites and places of note with the precision of a machine. He could not simply follow the dynamism and speed of Tokyo.

When the bus stopped in front of the Imperial Palace, an incredibly peaceful place amid the tumult of Tokyo, Eizo recalled the stories of three soldiers who did not believe the leaflets that said that the Second World War had ended. Yokoi-san and Onoda-san had concealed themselves in the jungle for twenty-eight and nearly thirty years respectively, before finally returning to Japan. They were welcomed home as national heroes. Nakamura-san, a native Taiwanese who had served in the Imperial Japanese Army, was found in Indonesia in 1974, only four years back from when Eizo returned to Japan, speaking neither Chinese nor Japanese. It was reported that Yokoi-san felt shame at having returning alive—that was against the military code of the Japanese Imperial Army, 'Do not live as a captive to be subjected to humiliating treatment.' He had brought back the rifle he received from the Emperor and wanted to apologize for not serving His Majesty well enough. Emperor Hirohito, however, did not grant him an audience.

Did Yokoi-san not think that his life would've been different, better even, if there were no war? Yes, he must've become completely enraged.

As the tour continued, Eizo reflected on his own war. The dark and confused images of his life in Japan and Canada welled up from his heart to poison his mind. He could have returned to Japan on several occasions, and now believed that he had remained in Canada on the basis of a wrong judgement and, ultimately, procrastination. He could hear Akiko's voice as she talked about the buildings and their history, but Eizo was not listening to her anymore. He had issues to settle.

After sightseeing the two went to a local restaurant. Akiko talked for a while about the places they saw, and after that, broached the subject of Kozo's daughter's death, about ten years ago. Tamotsu had already mentioned this, but Akiko filled in some of the blanks on Kozo's family. It reminded Eizo that he should take a bouquet of flowers to Kozo's home that night.

On the train back to Tamotsu's home an idea flashed through his mind. Eizo was surprised and angry with himself for not having noticed it up until now. Kozo's daughter had died about ten years earlier, about the time when Fumi's letters had stopped arriving.

There must've been a correlation between the two incidents. Kozo has probably never felt love for me. He was not really given the chance. Isoshichi and Fumi intentionally kept me from knowing about the death of my granddaughter. They cut me off completely.

Eizo abruptly asked Akiko in a loud voice, "Akiko-san, please tell me if there was a meeting between my three sons after Kozo's daughter died. And can you tell me if they together decided not to contact me anymore?"

"There was no such thing," Akiko said in a suppressed tone, conscious of the other passengers on the train.

They were still in public so Eizo did not press her any further. But he could not wipe out the idea that his three sons had arrived at an agreement on how to deal with their absent father. The signs of such an accord seemed very real and obvious to him.

18
Confession of the Third Son

Eizo and Akiko got off the train near her house, but he was already too exhausted to retrieve his suitcase. Akiko telephoned her son, Noboru, to bring Eizo's suitcase to the station and accompany them to Kozo's house in Koganei City.

When the three arrived, Michiyo appeared at the door and glanced at Eizo before taking her apron off to exchange formal greetings with them. She had an oval face, thin cheeks and lips, a slim nose, and long, carefully combed hair. In a chic light blue dress, she seemed to Eizo to be a woman of taste, an affable person. There showed a clear contrast between Akiko, who acts and talks in an efficient, businesslike manner, and Michiyo, who gracefully glides through life.

"Michiyo-san, this is Father, from Canada," Akiko said introducing Eizo.

Eizo felt strange hearing the word 'father' from his daughter-in-law, as was the Japanese custom. He had never been called by that word by his own sons since he had returned.

"*Hajimemashit.* How do you do? I'm Michiyo, Kozo's wife. My husband's been busy and I'm sorry he hasn't had a chance to see you yet. Please, please come in."

221

The living room was neatly arranged with high quality, up-to-date electronics, including a colour television and a high-fidelity stereo system: they appeared to be well off. Visible from the living room, the kitchen sported a large fridge, microwave oven, electric can opener, a counter blender and other modern gadgetry.

This display of prosperity unsettled Eizo. He was glad to see that his son's family was doing well, but at the same time he reflected on his plain and frugal life in Toronto and all the years he had scrimped to send money home to support them. Only when it was impossible during the war and his early re-settlement years in Ontario, had he not sent money home. The luxury of their lifestyle took him somewhat aback.

At the very least I did my duty to provide for them.

Taking heart, Eizo presented Michiyo a bouquet of flowers he had purchased for her deceased child. She went to the kitchen, put the bouquet of flowers in a vase to offer them in front of the Buddhist mortuary tablet and picture of her daughter which were placed on the black altar in the next room. Eizo followed her to the room.

The plump-cheeked girl in the picture was probably a year old. She wore a bib and seemed to be staring at him from the photo. He looked at the picture for a while, offered incense sticks and then clasped his hands in prayer.

This stupid old man didn't know that you passed into the other world. Please pardon this pitiful grandpa ...

Akiko also offered incense sticks and prayers and then the three went back to the living room.

"*Kon'nichiwa*!" a girl wearing a flower-patterned, one-piece dress greeted them.

"This is my daughter, Chiaki. She's sixteen years old," Michiyo said.

"Oh, Chiaki, I'm Eizo."

No doubt taking after Michiyo, she had a well-shaped oval face that promised to evolve into a beautiful woman one day. The contrast between the Buddhist altar, dark with the image of the dead, and Chiaki rejoicing in her young life made him feel dizzy. He imagined how much Kozo and his wife must have suffered with the loss of their young daughter and so had grown to dote upon Chiaki.

Chiaki did not appear interested in her grandfather and disappeared into the back room with Noboru. He knew he was not in a position to be what was known as the "tender grandpa," one who gave their grandchildren pocket money or bought clothes for them from time to time. If Eizo existed in their thoughts as grandpa even once, it would be as a wonder, and for him to suddenly appear from the shadows probably made them uncomfortable and unsure how to act. For his part Eizo didn't really know how to treat his grandchildren. Again he felt the weight of lost time and his physical energy grew weak.

In the living room, Eizo sat down and Michiyo exchanged a few social graces with him. She then stood and went into the kitchen.

Akiko joined Michiyo in the kitchen and left Eizo alone in the living room. He thought about meeting Kozo with whom he had not had any emotional connection. That made him feel uneasy.

His youngest son came home while it was still light outside.

"It's rare for my husband to come home so early." Michiyo commented. Together with Akiko, she welcomed him at the entrance. Eizo stood behind them but he could not read any emotion in his son's expression and shrank back, taking a step backward instinctively. Kozo was a tall, thin man, as pale and smooth as a peeled onion, with a sharp look and deeply sunken cheeks. He wore a fine khaki topcoat and appeared fatigued but authoritative. The picture Fumi had sent once showed a healthy Kozo with puffy cheeks and a full friendly smile.

"*Anata*, dear, this is your father from Canada."

Met with the awkwardness of being introduced to his own father, Kozo smiled sardonically, sniffing his nose once. Maybe, that was his habit. Eizo did not see that friendly smile come back onto his son's face.

"Kozo, I'm late but I'm here now. Everybody appears well and that makes me glad," Eizo said what he had been planning to say.

"Ah, I'm Kozo," his son answered, standing with his left shoulder drawn back, not facing directly to his father. "You came far out of your way. I'm sorry." His voice was flat, as if he were giving instructions to subordinates at work.

When he bent over to take his shoes off, Eizo noticed that Kozo's hair was thinning on top. He did not feel the same surprise to see that his son was grown up as he had with the other two. Eizo knew from Kozo's cold reception that he had purposefully avoided seeing him before now. This foreshadowing did not give Eizo much confidence for the outcome of his visit.

"Please sit down and relax," Kozo bluntly said to his father as he proceeded to the living room. "Akiko-san, is my brother busy?" he asked as he pulled his topcoat off. Michiyo helped him and held his coat.

Eizo's heart sunk. He was hoping his son would speak to him from somewhere in his heart despite the time and distance that had separated them.

"My husband is busy? No such luck I'm afraid," Akiko answered, laughing.

"Really? Which construction site does he work at?"

"He's in Chiyoda Ward now."

"Is that so? You're perfectly welcome to stay and have a dinner with us. I suppose that should be okay with my brother?"

"Recently Mayumi's been helping in the kitchen. I asked her this morning to take care of dinner if I was to be late."

"Well then, stay as long as you like. Michiyo, is dinner ready?"

"Yes, it is," Michiyo said, taking Kozo's suit jacket and topcoat to other room.

Eizo felt that he was neglected by his family. For the reunion after a forty-three-year interval, their meeting was a non-event.

"Father and I took a bus tour in Tokyo today, so I'm little tired. I won't stay too late."

"Ah, I see. Thanks for your trouble," Kozo said, again as if talking to his subordinate.

From the flow of their conversation between them Eizo sensed that they were in touch frequently. They probably knew everything Eizo said and did since arriving home.

"Have a seat. I'm going to change," his son said and disappeared.

*

They began dinner with a half-hearted toast. Kozo, now wearing a cardigan over his shirt and no necktie, sat at the head of the table with his wife Michiyo opposite him. Eizo and Akiko sat facing each other, beside Chiaki and Noboru. The table was set with *sashimi*, beef teriyaki, *tempura* and pickled vegetables in individual plates for everyone, along with rice and clear soup. Eizo noted that his son did not drink

225

much beer. Nor did he relax his guard as people customarily do when they have a drink together.

"Kozo?" Eizo called his son's name nervously. "You were two when I left for Canada. Do you remember me at all?" Unable to bear it anymore, Eizo tried to break the ice by asking the question, half-jokingly.

"No, I don't. Even that genius Carl Jung wrote in his memoir that the first memory he had was from the age of two or three. I'm no Jung."

A chill held sway over the party. Eizo did not know who Carl Jung was and, on top of that, had not been looking for an accurate answer. He was looking for words of consideration, regardless of the truth. Present at this elaborate dinner where everyone else seemed to have been smacking their lips over the meal, Eizo could not eliminate the bitterness spreading in his mind. He had dreamed of this moment for so long, almost his lifetime, yet what he saw and felt was the mere formality of welcoming him. Of course, his son made a toast for him, and so did Michiyo, but he found that something was lacking, something very important when a family was reunited. There was no rejoicing or any real connection between his third son and himself.

Kozo ate silently, robotically bringing his chopsticks to his mouth without paying much attention to the conversation. Akiko, however, drank with relish and monopolized most of the conversation. She congratulated Kozo on getting a director's position and suggested that her husband was too gentle to elbow his way through to success. As the evening progressed Kozo perked up a bit and laughed with Michiyo as Akiko's stories became more humorous with each drink. Eizo ate dinner quietly among them not relating to the conversation. The discussion seemed irrelevant to what he thought they should be celebrating.

Akiko, looking sober after her big laugh, noticed that Eizo was out of the conversation. "Father, did you enjoy your tour today?"

"Yes, I did."

"What did you enjoy most?"

"Well, everything was new to me. But I enjoyed the Imperial Palace."

"The palace is big and majestic, isn't it? Tamotsu-san works near there."

Michiyo then asked Eizo a few questions about Canada in an attempt to include him. But before getting more than a few words out, Akiko, now fairly drunk and her tongue more smoothly waggling, overrode her father-in-law and began telling a story about a friend who went to Canada. Kozo and his wife seemed not to notice as they laughed together.

Why are they laughing? Life is a struggle. We live on the borders of hell, always looking at the inferno and the tortures within. That doesn't leave much room to laugh. How can they laugh?

An hour later, Noboru finally convinced his mother that it was time to go home so he could study.

"Well then, I guess we have to go, Michiyo-san, I'm sorry I can't help you in the kitchen." Akiko said. She bid her farewell reluctantly, obviously having enjoyed being the centre of attention and having a good laugh.

*

After Akiko and Noboru left, Chiaki retreated to her room. Michiyo began to clear the plates from the kitchen table.

"I'll help you," said Eizo, getting up.

"No, don't bother. I can manage. Really."

Kozo urged his father to move into the living room and sat down in a leather chair. Eizo sat in the love seat and looked around the room. Besides the colour television and hi-fi stereo, there was a solid oak cabinet decorated with three shelves of fine porcelain figurines. In the *tokonoma* was an *ikebana* and a scroll of a black-and-white painting. Two elegant room lamps beside Kozo lit his profile. Eizo thought of his bare apartment and austere life in Toronto and shook his head slightly to dismiss the image. Probably because of the angle of lighting, half of Kozo's face was shaded, making him look ruthless and vicious, like a man set in stone. He talked about his work while Michiyo served tea and finally joined them in the living room. Michiyo seemed to be a better listener than a talker.

Eizo began to speak. "Everything has changed. I suppose it's natural that everything changes. I never imagined your mother would be like this. I apologized to Isoshichi and Tamotsu, and I have to apologize to you too."

Kozo listened quietly while Michiyo nervously toyed with her sleeve.

"My original plan was to go to Canada, make some quick money, and then return home. But then the war started. As a foreign enemy I was put into a labour camp and then later sent to a concentration camp far away from the coast. Everything that I planned to do quickly went to pieces." Eizo paused briefly to see if his talk was eliciting any reaction.

Kozo's expression remained unchanged, as if he were listening to a report from his subordinate. Michiyo appeared to be edgy and was listening intently; she kept her back straight, tilting her legs slightly, and observed her husband closely.

"After the war," Eizo continued, "I sent a letter to your mother describing what happened during those years.

Perhaps you heard about that. I lost the chance to come home. I'm very glad to see you fine boys, all grown up," he said, trying to smooth the crease in his pants with his fingers and watching Kozo's face attentively, as if groping for a way to solve the issue. "I'd want nothing else, but to see your mother better again."

Kozo now looked intently at his father. The apathy that he displayed earlier was gone. "Mom," his eyes gripped Eizo. "It's sad that she's this way."

"I know." Eizo sighed. "But why did nobody let me know about her condition? I have you three, but nobody breathed even a word."

"If we had told you, would you have come back immediately?"

"Well, that ... that," Eizo was not prepared for Kozo's sharp retort and stuttered, "Of course ... I'd have been back. Of course! But the last letter from your mother asked me to stay. And, other things happened too. She said there were no jobs in Japan so staying in Canada to support you guys was the only choice. I wanted to come home!"

"Do you have that letter with you?" Kozo demanded.

"Yes."

"Can I see?"

Eizo handed the envelope to Kozo. His son almost grabbed it and pulled the well-worn letter out and began reading. As he finished the first page, he passed it to Michiyo, who was now seated close to him. His expression did not change in the way Tamotsu's did. Eizo had to surmise that the two brothers had already discussed the contents of the letter. Kozo's face, already tired and pale, greyed marginally.

"When I realized your mother was ill, it hit me pretty hard."

Kozo's face grew a little darker.

"Isoshichi doesn't talk to me at all. And your mother, in that condition …" Eizo paused. "When I'm at home I feel as if I were sitting on a mat of needles. In the evening, Kino stands in the front yard and calls out for me to come home quickly. She doesn't understand that I'm back."

Kozo flinched, clearly troubled by something. Nor could Michiyo hide her grim expression; the two looked at each other knowingly.

"I realize now I'm to blame. I so much wanted to know when your mom became sick. I asked Kin'ichi of the head family, stupidly enough, I even asked the neighbour. But, they told me nothing and said to talk to my family." Eizo snorted. "That's why I asked them, because your brother refused to speak. I asked Tamotsu but he didn't tell me anything either. When he came to see me at the airport he didn't say one word about Kino's illness! Doesn't anyone want to take responsibility? I finally found out yesterday that she became ill about twenty-three years ago, almost the same time she wrote that letter you have in your hands. Strange! She must've been all right when she wrote the last letter. But, why so suddenly did she become …?"

Eizo ran his right hand through his hair, not knowing what else he could say. He could hardly bare to hear what his son would say.

Kozo stared hard at his father. Eizo leaned back slightly in his chair.

"It's true," Kozo said, undoing the second button of his shirt.

Eizo held his teacup, unable to either put it down or take a sip. Kozo looked at Michiyo, and then glanced toward Chiaki's room. Michiyo got up and checked that her daughter's bedroom door was closed. "It's all right," she said in a whisper.

"About twenty-three years ago," Kozo continued quietly, without changing his tone, "Mom had an affair with a man."

A sudden thudding in Eizo's ears drowned out any sound. His heart contracted painfully. He struggled to breath and leaned over, clutching the side of the chair. He could see Kozo's face, distress in his eyes. "No!"

An affair!

It felt like a heavy metal bar had just hit him across the back of the head. Eizo could feel his faithful, shadowy friend waiting on the edge of his consciousness.

"It's regrettable," muttered his son.

"Kozo, who …?" Eizo could barely bring himself to ask not really wanting the answer.

"It was with an instructor of sericulture. He went around to farms that kept silkworms."

Eizo stared at Kozo; his words cut like razors. Once the full meaning sank in, he groaned slightly as he leaned forward into the palms of his hands. Eizo felt light-headed, his skin cold and clammy. He heard Kino calling out towards the eastern sky in his imagination. And, all of a sudden, the scene of his wife arranging mulberry twigs on the invisible silkworm plate with a flirtatious laughter in front of the storehouse crossed his mind.

"My mom had left home for a while, but in the end she was deserted by him. Mom finally came back home."

"She came home, deserted?" Eizo spat, suddenly feeling angry.

"When Mom came home, the townspeople talked about nothing else. Many talked as if they had seen Mom getting on the train with him hand in hand."

"What?" Eizo gaped, stunned at his wife's lack of discretion for her children.

"She didn't leave the house after that. And we didn't notice when she became ill. I was in Tokyo going to university at the time. When we noticed, it was too late."

"You say she was already insane? Did you have a doctor see her?" Eizo asked.

"Of course, we did."

"What did the doctor say?"

"The doctor in town wasn't a psychiatrist. And he wasn't sure what she was suffering from exactly. Physically she was all right. So, we took her to one of the city hospitals later and she was diagnosed with neurosis."

"Neurosis? Wasn't there any way to cure her, put her into a hospital maybe?"

"Mom was hospitalized for about three months. But when she came home from the hospital there was no change to her condition."

"No change?"

"After that, Isoshichi took Mom to a university hospital," his son carried on without looking at his father. "She was diagnosed with depression by a psychiatrist and stayed there for a while. Mom was hospitalized several times after that for several durations without success." Kozo paused, blinked a few times. "Isoshichi and Fumi-san bore the brunt of the backbiting by the locals. At first they didn't want Mom to go out, but they felt pity for her and eventually let her wander wherever she liked. Besides studying, I was working part-time. When I could, I sent money to Isoshichi to help Mom. Tamotsu did the same as well. We all loved Mom—we were desperate to save her."

Eizo, unable to contain himself, gave way to crying. His under lip quivered unstoppably. Michiyo quietly wiped her

232

cheek while Kozo reached for his wife's hand. Eizo thought of Isoshichi's gloom. Behind that wooden face was a deep love for his mother. Eizo was ashamed that he had not understood Isoshichi's position in the closed community.

"According to the psychiatrist," continued Kozo, "people typically show the symptoms of schizophrenia in their young adulthood, men in their twenties and women by early thirties … but not always. Mom got ill when she was forty-five or forty-six, which is quite late."

"… What are you trying to tell me by that?" Eizo asked dubiously, raising his head.

"Well, that's what her psychiatrist said."

"I don't understand what you mean," Eizo said.

Did I see the light of recognition in Kino's eyes when she looked at me?

"Then is Kino sane?" *Is there any hope for her?*

"That we don't know. According to Isoshichi, the psychiatrist said that Mom hadn't made sense and she had seen the images of the man repeatedly but it turned out that she'd thought she was seeing …"

"How can you take this so lightly? Didn't her psychiatrist have other treatment for her? Was there anything you guys could do for her?" Eizo said sharply, cutting into the son's talk.

Kozo gazed at his father with dark reproachful eyes, but the words out of his mouth were calm. "We did everything we could for Mom at the time. Mom was heavily medicated and hospitalized … do you think we should've committed her?"

"No, no." Eizo lowered his head to his hands.

What now? What has happened? What am I supposed to do?

A long suffocating silence dominated the living room. Eizo felt that he was falling into a dark abyss. The world around him was quietly decaying, giving off a foul stench; the same stench that Kino emits from her body.

Kino was trying to live out the prime of womanhood before it passed her by.

Eizo spoke into the void. "Were you guys aware that Kino sent a letter to me?"

"No, we didn't know."

"Did Isoshichi or Tamotsu know?"

"I suspect neither of them knew. Tamotsu was in Tokyo at that time and even during the times we talked about you, it never came up."

"You spoke about me?"

Silence.

"Well …"

Again silence.

Nothing good about me then.

"Where did they go … your mother and the man …?"

"Tokyo."

"Tokyo. Tokyo?"

Kino cries to the eastern evening sky …

"You said Tokyo? Then …" Eizo felt a deep breath leave his body. "Of course… Tokyo is in the east."

Kino has been calling out for her lover in Tokyo! Not for me!

"Was it after her affair when she started calling out at evening?"

"Yes, it was. She'd become quite depressed."

Eizo felt the will to speak leave him. The pieces of the puzzle were finally falling into place. Kino's flirtatious laughter at the storehouse was not for him but for the man whom she had eloped with to Tokyo. What was left of me in Kino?

Time passed.

The silence deepened further. He thought he had seen the image of Kino getting into the train with the man.

His eyes were heavy with dark rings under them. He took up the teacup but it was already cold and put it back on the coffee table.

"You never came back." Kozo's words cut through the stagnating air.

"You guys loved Kino a lot," Eizo whispered.

"I saw how Mom was intent on bringing us up as fine men. Long ago I swore to myself that I would never sink into vice and would live the best that I could." Now Kozo's voice trembled.

"I'm tired," Eizo said, unable to talk anymore.

"Michiyo, please lay a *futon* out for him."

Michiyo went into the room with the Buddhist altar and it took only a few minutes to prepare the bedding. Eizo stood up and left without saying goodnight.

Kino must've been deeply in love with this man to abandon her family for him. She killed what was between us by leaving as surely as if she had wielded a knife. No, no! We were not close anymore.

His shadow nudged him. *Why don't you go back to Canada? No one is close to you now.*

Unpardonable! Shame on you…

The only way to reconcile himself with his sons was to take over the burden of care for his wife. First, however, he needed to tell his story.

*

235

The next morning Eizo woke up with a terrible headache, as if he had a hangover, weak and nauseated. He got up before Kozo went to work and asked him to come home that weekend so he could speak with everyone together.

"Yes, I will. But it'd be easier if you spoke your mind tonight, here," Kozo said.

"I'd like to see everyone together at home, like in the old days. Besides, Isoshichi will listen if you and your brother are there."

Kozo seemed to understand.

*

Late that night, Kozo came back home blind drunk. He threw himself on the floor of the entrance and sat there, hardly able to hold his upper body straight. Michiyo and Eizo had to urge him to go to bed.

"How beastly drunk you are!" Michiyo held her husband's arm.

"Who is … to blame? Ah, Michiyo, tell me … who is … to blame?"

"Shh! Dear, you're awfully drunk." Michiyo said, now trying to support her husband's body on her shoulder, "Please go to bed."

Eizo saw Michiyo was about to cry and helped her carry Kozo to their bedroom. Kozo was heavy, like a dead body. Releasing his son from his shoulder, Eizo left the room without delay. Michiyo seemed to be helping her husband get undressed, her voice came from their bedroom intermittently. Until retiring himself, he sat alone in the living room, thinking that his returning home had caused a great deal of problems for his family and to himself and questioned whether his trip to Japan was worth it. Still he faintly hoped that there would be some solution, though he did not know what that would be, as there seemed to be no convincing answer to that.

Next morning, Kozo ate his breakfast with his family as if he had never touched liquor last night and had never been carried to bed. Even the movement of his chopsticks was steady, though his pale face and taciturnity showed that he was not completely over the effects of the previous night. He was unabashedly calm but avoided eye contact.

Before noon, Michiyo saw Eizo off at the train station. He remembered to buy the same cakes Tamotsu had bought for Kino. They seemed to make her happy, a bright patch in the dark shadow that had enveloped Eizo's hopes.

Part III - Eizo Tells His Story

19
Life Before the Second World War

The rain started falling on Saturday morning and was still falling by noon. Although the sky was grey, the leaves of the trees, the rice plants and undergrowth stood out in vivid moss green. Eizo knew the insects stayed close to the ground during the rain, and watched the swallows following them, flicking about the top of the rice plants.

By evening the showers showed no sign of letting up, and when Tamotsu and Kozo arrived at their brother's home from Tokyo, the rain seemed to increase in volume. Tamotsu brought a box of cakes for his mother, as was his custom. Even though her two sons had come home, Kino was as timid. However, she seemed to recognize them, nodding as they spoke to her. By contrast, Eizo noted she still gave no sign of recognition to him.

"Are you all right?"

"Have you been good?"

The questions her sons asked were simple enough, sparing disappointment. Eizo thought that if his sons had more complex questions he might have seen her react differently. He did notice that when he had given his wife the box of cakes, she had devoured them; this time she ignored them. Eizo, however, was so anxious that he did not dwell long on Kino's odd behaviour. He had planned the day's gathering and was now completely absorbed in how to stage this play.

Isoshichi was late for dinner. On the day Eizo returned from Tokyo, he had told Isoshichi that Tamotsu and Kozo would be home that weekend. Now his eldest son revealed a different side in his younger brother's presence, smiling slightly when they greeted him. It was the first time Eizo had seen him smile.

Isoshichi sat by the hearth and asked Tamotsu and Kozo about their families and work, like a big brother would do. Eizo watched how they talked with each other; it was easy to see the strong bonds between them. Even though his entire family was finally together, he struggled for a sense of the family he used to know, since everything was happening outside of him and the mood was strained.

Did that family ever exist?

After the three brothers had talked with each other awhile, Tamotsu, with a concern that they were ignoring their father, asked Eizo about the weather at this time of the year in Canada. Grateful for his acknowledgment, Eizo spoke about the vastness of Canada's geography; how each region had its own weather patterns and how, in Toronto, the temperatures could go down abruptly even in early June. And then, as he ran out of things to say about the weather, he fell silent. Isoshichi and Kozo did not appear to have any intention of speaking with their father and continued on with their conversation.

Kino dropped her rice bowl at a dinner time. Her rice bowl was almost empty but Kino picked up dropped rice with her fingers from the floor and shoved it in her mouth. Tamotsu looked at her, but no one else, including Eizo, paid any attention.

242

After dinner the family gathered again around the unlit hearth. Eizo waited for the right opportunity for his talk. Just when he was about to speak, his wife stood up to leave.

"Ah, Kino! Please don't leave," Eizo said hurriedly, attempting to get his wife to stay by the hearth. Although he thought she probably could not join the conversation, he hoped that she would stay and listen as she was the person that most needed to hear what he had to say.

Everybody at the hearth looked at him and then their mother as if they had prearranged this. Kino ignored Eizo and shuffled out of the room. Nobody inserted a word but his sons looked as though they had expected a confrontation. Sensing it was too late to begin gently, Eizo drew a deep breath and jumped straight in.

"I've long wanted to speak with you about my life in Canada. I think it's important for you to know. Tamotsu, Kozo, thank you for coming. Now that we are all together I'm going to tell the whole story."

"Fumi, why don't you come and sit down," Isoshichi said, calling his wife from the kitchen.

Fumi, wiping her hands with her apron, came in and sat down by the hearth. She leaned over and whispered quietly in Toshio's ear. Immediately, Toshio disappeared upstairs. Preparing for his talk was accomplished with few words and Eizo was amazed at how skilfully it was done. As in Canada, most of the time he missed the little signals between people. Years ago, he had been well-versed in the complex inner workings of his countrymen and small town society, but it was these subtleties that he had long forgotten.

"We have wanted to talk to you at some point too, so today is good chance for everyone," Tamotsu said, mediating the silence between Eizo and Isoshichi.

"Thank you," Eizo said and continued. "I know that no apology will ever make up for my long absence in your lives. I understand very well that I can't expect your feelings toward me to change now. I have left everything much too late. I only want you to know that I was always thinking about you people," Eizo stammered. He looked up from his feet; everyone stared away into space in complete silence. He was still worried that someone was going to snap at him, questioning why he had not come back years, even decades earlier, but there was no sign that his three sons or daughter-in-law would ask. As usual, Isoshichi had put a wall up with his customary gloominess. Tamotsu looked perplexed; Kozo hung his face down, pale and without expression. Fumi simply looked into the ashes of the hearth, waiting.

"I have much to regret, especially about your mother. When I came back and saw her I was heartbroken."

Still, silence.

"I was a fool. I put your mother and you all to a lot of trouble. Above all, I accepted too easily what she said in her letter to me."

The eldest son grimaced.

"No, no. I'm not blaming your mom for that letter," Eizo said quickly. "I showed Kino's letter to Tamotsu and Kozo when I went to Tokyo. Isoshichi, if you want to see the letter, I have it here." He put his hand on his chest to show where his wife's letter was.

"No, I don't have to see it. Don't want to see it," Isoshichi replied sharply with his scowling face.

Even Eizo could tell by the looks around the room, his son's abruptness surprised everyone.

"If you have something to say, please say it. Don't beat around the bush," Isoshichi said slightly mollified.

"Then, let's do that," agreed his father. "Before and after the Second World War, I kept in contact with your mother on a regular basis and let her know how I was doing in Canada. Of course, it was my first time to live and work in the foreign country and not knowing English it was much harder than I thought to earn money and send it home. Perhaps you heard from Murata-san about how things were after he came back from Canada? The working conditions for the Japanese in Canada before the war were hard enough, but during wartime and after the war, it was much worse and more painful."

"I remember he came to the house, but I don't recall what he said. I was too small. How about you Isoshichi?" asked Tamotsu.

"I forget."

"You were so young," Eizo said. "When your mom and I branched out from the head family I had been given ownership of a patchwork of rice and other fields, which were hardly big enough to scrape out a livelihood on, let alone raise a family. At the time, Murata-san had gone to Canada to work in a logging camp in British Columbia and was rumoured to be making a handsome wage and would soon return rich and successful. After corresponding with Murata-san, I decided to follow him and leave Kino and you boys behind to tend the family farm. That was the summer of 1935."

All was quiet in the room, except the tapping sound of hard raindrops, but for Eizo's voice, now gaining in strength and purpose. He told the story of his thirteen day voyage across the Pacific Ocean to Victoria, where he cleared immigration, and the following day the ship arrived at the Port of Vancouver. Eizo met Murata who was there to welcome him. When he told Murata that his fellow countryman's wife and children had been doing well in Japan, he did not overlook that Murata's eyes became moist.

"We went to 'Little Tokyo' on Powell Street in Vancouver. Murata-san showed me what items to purchase for work in a logging camp: two pairs of working boots, gloves, duffle bag, plus a thick sleeping bag, and other items. Murata-san said I'd need to stay warm in the mountain. Little Tokyo seemed to be a prosperous community with grocery stores, restaurants, public baths, bars, barber shops, Japanese book stores, drug stores, cobblers, clockmakers, rooming houses, the gambling hall and even Japanese public houses with hostesses, standing side by side on the street. To my surprise, they spoke Japanese in Little Tokyo. In Canada! I felt my fatigue of the long trip and anxiety fading into thin air.

"The following morning we caught a ferry that crossed the Strait of Georgia to the Nanaimo terminal on Vancouver Island. I heard Murata-san say *Nana-emon.* I asked Murata-san who that was, as it's a Japanese first name from the feudal age. But it turned out to be the early Issei's way of saying 'Nanaimo'. I later learned 'one handle yen' for 'one hundred dollars' and 'Os mata yu?' for 'What's the matter with you?' Not knowing my way around and hardly able to speak English, except a few greetings and words, I had to obediently follow Murata-san's lead. After we left Vancouver, we climbed up onto the deck of the ferry. It was windy, rather cool for a summer day and strikingly sunny, with cobalt blue sky that expanded over our heads. The views from the deck were pristine, vast and breathtaking. I had never seen that sort of scenery before."

Eizo stopped, silent for a moment, reliving his own story, standing again on that deck in the wind and sunlight. The grown men in the room saw their father's memory of

246

that day struggle for translation that even now, after all these years, still begging for the right words across oceans and decades. "And then there were the mountains … 'Are those the Rocky Mountains?' I asked Murata-san.

'No, those are the Coastal Range Mountains. The Rockies are beyond that, behind those guys. You can't see from here,' Murata-san told me.

"We arrived at a logging camp near Cumberland, a mining community located in the forest, roughly a hundred kilometres north of Nanaimo. Murata-san introduced me to our boss, Motozo.

'You arrived finally. Work hard, uh, and I give you money for that, understood? No fooling in my camp,' Motozo told me heedlessly. 'Go start working! Murata, tell this greenhorn what to do. Make him a darn good worker.'

"I took an immediate dislike to Motozo. The boss, however, was among the few who could speak English, compelling many of the Japanese loggers to move around from camp to camp with him, unable to navigate on our own. Our accommodations, temporary huts, were shabby, small, quickly built and easily demolished. Loggers were able to see the moonlight through the wall planks and the roof. Three or four workers lived in each hut; they slept on the floor, the cold night air blowing up through the gaps in the wooden floor. If we were lucky, we could hear the call of an owl. I was glad that I had bought a thick sleeping bag, my only consolation in the remote mountain site.

"On my first day, I started my job as a bucker," Eizo said to the perplexed faces around him. "Murata-san instructed me how to do a task and how to avoid accidents, the rudiments of logging. My job was to cut branches off the trees that the fallers had cut down. The forests were wild and thick with Douglas fir and cedar, enormous, in some cases

247

over twelve feet in diameter, and taller than any trees I had ever seen in my life. We cut those trees down one by one with two-man crosscut saws and double-bitted felling axes. Sometimes workers were killed, smashed under a tree that fell, with the huge trunk bouncing up or rolling over as they were dragged from where they fell. By this time, mechanized modern logging—the use of railway, trucks and heavy machinery—was underway, but still way ahead was the use of chainsaws to cut down trees. Clear-felling was the common practice in the British Columbia logging industry.

"'Timber' I heard one of the fallers yell, just before a tree started crashing down. They fell like thunder at a dreadful speed, pelting off chunks of branches and debris in every direction that sometimes rained down on us. The footing was slippery, even deadly, because of the continuous rainfall. It was an extremely dangerous job with little margin for error.

"On the night I arrived, about fifteen workers started gambling in *koi* and *oichokabu* with *hanafuda,* or two dice simply thrown from a tea cup onto the floor, betting on the odd or even numbers. I watched them play. The men had gambled continuously for hours. After Murata-san had lost badly in dice gambling, we left the hut.

'Murata-san, you lost a lot of money,' I said.

'Yeah, I lost today, but I might win tomorrow,' Murata-san said.

'But why do you gamble like that?'

'I wanna get rich quick and go home. My family will be glad.'

'I'm sure they'll be.'

'Besides, what else do you do in the camp like this, during the long, lonely night?' Murata-san spat on the ground as he talked, frustration and impatience obvious on his face.

'I thought you were tired after all that work.'

'It don't matter. Gambling brings you money, you know. I can be a rich man tomorrow night. Who knows?'

I did not say anything.

'But, I tell you, Eizo-san. Younger guys gamble to the last penny and lose all in a single night, an entire half year's wage, money they had earned risking their lives. You'll see. You'll be getting into it soon.'

'Murata-san, I don't know about that,' I said."

Now years later, by the hearth in the comfort of his Japanese home, Eizo rocked his hand gently on his knee, haunted by the clatter of dice and calls for luck. How could he explain logging camp life to his businessmen sons? How the *saké* and gambling provided the sole amusement, although workers were usually too tired to do much of anything else. Everybody was pretty rough-tempered and that often led to fights when they gambled.

"There was one woman in the logging camp. Her name was Nami," said Eizo. He saw their backs straighten, even Isoshichi snapped to closer attention. Satisfied, he continued the story.

"There were thirty odd men and Nami-san, the wife of a logger who worked at the camp where I was. Preparing meals for thirty hungry workers twice a day and making *onigiri* for everyone's lunch was hard enough. Add to that laundry and other miscellaneous jobs. She worked with clenched teeth and had tears in her eyes, day in and day out. Even if she had wanted to go back to Japan, it would be impossible to leave the camp without her husband. He kept their money. How could she escape from there?

"'You see,' Murata-san took me out of the group after the meal one evening. 'Our boss negotiates contracts with *hakujin* companies and we, stupid we, you know, are here to support him to be rich. When the job's done, the Canadian company pays to the boss, and God knows, the boss deducts a rake-off, you see, and other costs and pays out us what's left. Our wages after deductions are peanuts.'

'What are you telling me, Murata-san?'

'No, nothing, that's all I tell you. We are suckers, you see. We don't speak English good and here we are ... we are suckers.'

'Well, why ...?' I was about to ask, *Why didn't you tell me that in your letter before I came to Canada?*

'But you see, it is better than the wages of a gardener or a trackman here. When you send Canadian money to Japan, it's much better than the wages you get in Japan. Probably three or four times better, I'm telling you, I heard it's got something to do with the foreign exchange. Have you heard those words before? Oh, I don't know, anyway some such trick.'

"I listened to him quietly.

'The thing is, some Japanese bosses take advantage of their power and add false costs by making victims of us. I heard they even take kickbacks from Japanese grocery stores too, as they deliver food from one logging camp to another. Monopoly, good business, huh! But they deliver and mail letters and sometimes even do some banking. That sort of services is important here.'

"I remembered that Murata-san's mailing address was 'c/o Hinode Grocer Co.', one of the grocery stores on Powell Street, where Murata-san had to pay a fee for the mail service. Everybody in the camp used these services.

'I heard some of the bosses were vicious, parasites to us, even worse than that … rats, yes, that's right, rats! But the bosses bring food for us and our lives are in their hands, you see. Our boss seemed to be nicer than those vicious bosses. That counts … that counts.'

'How do you know all those things?' I asked.

'You see, we go to Vancouver for *inochi no sentaku* and to send money to Japan once a year or maybe once every two years. Depends. We meet with *kunimono*, talk about all those things and exchange news at a *nomiya* in Little Tokyo. Aha, once we start drinking, it's the end of the world. We treat each other until we get dead drunk, till we can no longer stand up and walk. Ho, ho, ho! It's a big expense but that's the way you treat others here in Vancouver. We have a strong bond with *kunimono* and the bosses like to hire those guys because they are usually the best workers, you know. We also call other Japanese *dōhō*, sharing spiritual bonds. You can go to Vancouver with us next time. And, and, we can go to some kind of house, you know what I'm talking about? Men all know those things.'

' … No, no thanks."'

The silence around the family hearth seemed to deepen with Eizo's pause. He looked toward the door of Kino's room where eerie silence dominated. "But there was another friendship I found."

The family heard how, after a week of work in the logging camp, Eizo saw a young Japanese man reading under a kerosene lamp. He knew that the young man kept himself aloof from the fellow workers and he did not gamble either.

"'You are reading an English book?' approaching the young man, I said.

251

'Yes,' the young logger looked up with an affable smile. 'This is a novel called *A Farewell to Arms* by Earnest Hemingway.' He spoke perfect Japanese with a slight accent.

"I immediately detected that this young man's English pronunciation was extraordinary for a Japanese. 'I don't know who that is, but ...'

'He is an American author and uses plain language, but actually he's good. I can really picture the scene, that's how good he is. He writes about a love story in the last world war.'

'I see. You enjoy reading books, that's good, noble.'

'He writes about the Japanese at one point in the book. He lets the hero of the story say the Japanese are "a wonderful little people". Sounds like he lives in a different world. You rarely see that kind of person here on the West Coast.'

'Isn't that something? Where are you from?'

'I'm from Vancouver.' The young lumberjack showed a bit of frustration, but continued, 'My parents are from Mie Prefecture, in the middle or slightly southern part of Japan, I believe. But I've never been to Japan. By the way, I'm Josh ... Joshua Hideki Doi, a Nisei.'

'Ah, I'm Eizo Osada. Mie is the next prefecture to where I'm from.'

'Is that so? My parents talk about their birthplace all the time.'

'I heard Mie is a beautiful place.'

'A lot more than that.'

'Oh?'

'They are deeply attached to Japan. They are Japanese to the marrow of their bones. My parents keep the *goshin'ei*, hanging on the wall as if it gives them inner strength, or spiritual backbone, and they bow to it in the morning as soon as they get up and wash their faces. They may miss their meal but never miss a bow.'

'Understandable. In Japan, everybody keeps the *Tenno*'s photo on the wall and worships him. The Emperor is God,' said I.

'When I was at a Japanese school back in Vancouver, we had the Emperor's photo as well. We made a bow to him every time we went to the school.'

'I see. It's the same in Japan. Students bow to the divine picture.'

'I bet they do. But I guess I'm a Canadian.'

'What do you mean by that?'

'Well.' Josh inserted a bookmark and put the book on his lap and said, 'I have to resolve my problem one day, Eizo-san. To me, it's a big problem and it's been hanging in front of my eyes for a long time. I like Japan and it must be a wonderful, beautiful country. My parents wanted to go back to Mie but I gather that they're debating about it now. They've lived in Canada too long to return to Japan. Moreover, my siblings have all been brought up here and have never been to Japan. They're almost afraid of Japan.'

'How many siblings do you have?'

'Two. I have a brother and a sister, both older than me. You seem to be interested in Canada, can I talk to you now?'

'Yes, of course.'

'All right. As you can see, the blood running in me is no doubt Japanese. But our problems, or, at least my problem is that I'm torn between Canada and Japan. I don't know the *Tenno* so much, only saw him in the *goshin'ei*.'

'Not many Japanese see *Tenno* directly. *Tenno* is a god and you're not supposed to see him with your eyes.'

'All right, I learned about *Tenno* at a Japanese school and mainly from my father. Our Japanese teachers were sent from Japan. Naturally they were the fanatics of the Emperor and they didn't even speak English. On the other hand, we were taught about the King and Queen of Great Britain and their glorious history at our public school. We also had to learn successive Kings' and Queens' names by heart.' Josh paused. 'But my parents and Japanese teachers told me what a divine and great country Japan is. The English school taught me more or less the same for Great Britain, except the divineness of the Royal family.'

'I see.'

'I was told we're going back to Japan one day to serve the country that I don't know nor have any attachment to. I was born and raised in Canada and, I guess, or I can even say clearly that I belong to Canada. I only know Japan from books, my Japanese school teachers and my parents.'

'So, you're torn apart?'

'Yes, that's right. When I look at the picture of *Tenno,* I feel a man there, only a man, not the divine god that my parents told me.'

'Shhh … shhh … Be careful what you say against the dignity of the Emperor! There's lese-majesty in Japan. Those guys here are fanatics. You'll be in a big trouble!'

'See? That's the attitude of the Japanese. I don't know whether I can live in Japan or not. Will the Japanese accept me? That, I really don't know.'

'I think they'll accept you … Of course, they will.'

'Really? … You sound like you're hesitating to say that. But you're a nice man, Eizo-san. I think the best way for me is to stay in Canada and live as a Canadian. I know for sure that the time I have to choose Canada or Japan will come one day. Ah, as you are older, you know very well life is not fair and nothing is perfect in this world, right?'

'Well, I'm afraid what you said didn't sound like that of a young man.'

'There's a good reason why I said that. You might not know, but we face a clear discrimination here.'

'But you speak good English, don't you?'

'Yes, I do. Probably perfect English, I'd say.'

'Why then can't you find a job in Vancouver or somewhere else? At a Canadian company, maybe?'

'Well, I'll tell you something …'

"Josh explained to me how discrimination was the norm of the day. Wages for the Japanese or their Canadian born children were much lower than those of the *hakujin* workers doing the same work. In British Columbia, the Nikkei, those Japanese holding Canadian citizenship and the Nisei who were born in Canada, were not given the franchise for the election of the provincial or municipal governments when they came of age. They were also barred from becoming a candidate to those institutions. Nor did they have the right to vote in federal elections because they were not on the provincial electoral lists. It was not clearly written, but the Nikkei were unable to engage in public works, such as road construction and river work projects. Either regulations or by-laws further prohibited the Nikkei from becoming certain public servants, school trustees, lawyers or pharmacists, to name a few. Generally speaking, Canadian companies did not employ the Nikkei. It was the time that, even the Japanese Canadians who had graduated from the University of British Columbia hardly landed on a job and a handful of graduates indulged in '*Nanking bakuchi*', Chinese gambling, and ruined themselves. Lucky ones got a job, but they could seldom rise in rank.

"Josh kept on. I didn't understand or worry about some of those things. It wasn't my plan to stay in Canada for long,"

Eizo said to his family. "Josh told me that *hakujin* Canadians resented the Japanese. They felt the Nikkei threatened their jobs and businesses. We were paid less. So, it was natural that the Japanese went into business for themselves, like fishing and logging. Being diligent, Japanese fishermen caught much more salmon and other fish than those of *hakujin*. When it comes to farming, the Nikkei harvested larger strawberries than that of the *hakujin* farmers, that resulted in more berries per acre. I heard that, in Fraser Valley, near Vancouver, eighty per cent of the strawberry shipment came from the Japanese farmers. The Japanese worked so hard and the result was that we were threatening the *hakujin* workers' jobs and businessmen's survival. Supposedly, it was our fault that white Canadians were out of work and out of business.

"So, the Canadian business community and labour organizations got politicians to pass laws and practices against Asian labour. This is one of the stories I heard from a *dōhō* in Little Tokyo; particularly after the Great Depression in 1929 when job openings were virtually nil and the unemployed flooded the streets and there were long line-ups of people for soup and bread. Hatred against the Japanese mounted, since the *hakujin* people believed that the Nikkei had taken away jobs from them because of our lower wages. On top of that, some *hakujin* employers even negotiated with the Japanese that their already-low wage should be further lowered. The Nikkei took great pains so as not to give the *hakujin* any excuse to drive us out from Canada." Eizo looked to his sons for understanding. Kozo still wore his business clothes, even on this weekend visit and remained unruffled. Tamotsu at least nodded in acknowledgment of the impossible dilemma.

"Josh explained to me that the more the Nikkei were discriminated against, the more they turned from Canadian society to Japan. Before the war, the Issei built and managed their own businesses in forestry, farming, fishing, retail, and other areas. The Nikkei they employed had to speak Japanese to communicate. So, it was vital for the Nisei to learn Japanese. They also learned reading, writing, grammar, calligraphy, social studies and Japanese history, including the mythology of the divine country, at the language schools.

'I was sent to a Japanese school on Alexander Street in Vancouver,' said Josh. 'But by the time I attended the school, they taught only Japanese language, no other subject. After the regular English school, I attended the Japanese school for two hours on weekdays and four hours on Saturday mornings.'

'That's quite a schedule.'

'Yes. We were taught how the divine gods of the *Tenno's* ancestors—*Izanagi no Mikoto* and *Izanami no Mikoto*—a male deity and female deity, created the archipelago of Japan by churning the sea with a *naginata* and therefore Japan and the *Tenno* were divine.' Before I could say anything, Josh grimaced, his face flushed, and continued, 'The *hakujin* were willing to import cheap labourers from the Orient before, but now, they don't want their jobs and the European culture and values were threatened by our presence. They also say that small businesses are threatened because of us. Hard to believe what they say. I might not get a job after my graduation, but I have to go to university and help to improve the status and living conditions of the Nikkei one day … one day. That's my dream,' Josh said, his eyes bright with ambition and enthusiasm.

257

"I was rather amazed at Josh's frankness. Though it was our first conversation, Josh had shared his past and thoughts, even his dreams with a total stranger.

'I can get a permanent job at one of the stores in Little Tokyo, but what about my dream? I can't see any future in that kind of job. Right now, I'm saving money for my education.'

'For university education?'

'Yes,' stated Josh firmly. 'Wages here are much better than working at a store in Little Tokyo.'

'That sounds good,' I said to him, but silently wondered why Murata-san had not told me about this before. Did Murata-san know about those things? Or did he care about it at all? I don't know.

"As the days passed, Josh and I had relaxed conversations quite often. We shared a comradeship amid a bunch of guys who had become hopelessly addicted to gambling.

"One night, I escaped from the noisy shack and walked towards the edge of the logging area, paying attention to my step. Huge trunks still lay on the ground. I came to the edge, stood there and watched a big golden harvest moon rise above the mountains and I was totally alone: the quiet around me was unreal. I thought I could hear your laughter from somewhere among the trees and could see you. I missed you guys so much. Then I thought perhaps that Kino and you boys might've been looking at the same full moon in Japan. I had the tears running on my cheeks … I had a pain in my chest," Eizo said to his three sons and Fumi who were seated at the hearth.

How can I ever explain how hard it was to be away, but that I believed it was the right thing to do? That idea was what kept me going.

"'Eizo-san, I'm so excited! I've got a letter from a friend of mine in Vancouver,' Josh said one day in early June, a year after I had arrived in Canada. 'He said in the letter that a Nisei group had formed the Japanese Canadian Citizens League. They had decided to send four delegates to Ottawa to ask for the franchise and equal rights for the Nikkei. Isn't it exciting? Isn't it?'

'I see.'

'It's a shame we don't have a right to vote. I'd better go back to Vancouver and go to university. But it's too late for this year.'

'I'd be lonely after you leave.'

'Oh, Eizo-san, I'm sorry. But I have to go one day.'

'No, that's okay … totally all right with me. I just … you have to do what you have to do.'

"In the days that followed, Josh's spirits lifted as he prepared to leave the logging camp. The gruelling routine continued until one morning in late July when the work was broken by a terrible call.

'Accident! Accident!'

'What happened?'

'Accident!'

'What accident?'

'Josh!'

'Josh! What?' I shouted.

'Accident! It's Josh!'

"I dashed off toward the direction to which everybody was running. It was like moving through a nightmare in slow motion over the fallen trunks, through deep gullies, missing my footing between the stabbing branches and slash, arms and legs slipping and sliding on the wet ground as I fought the uneven terrain.

'Call the boss! Call the boss!' someone yelled. The man's voice was breaking in desperation.

"I ran and ran frantically, like running in a muddy river, and reached the site at last, breathless.

"What a sickening scene! Josh, who wanted to work for the good of the Nikkei to improve their status in Canada, was crushed under the monster tree. His body was squashed, like a frog lying flat on the ground, his head tilted to the side, hands trying to seize the earth, bleeding at the mouth and his hat ripped off.

'Josh!' I shouted. No groan, no movement. I bent down and held his hand. It was still warm and his face was not totally discoloured yet.

'Crushed to death, instant death!' the worker who was beside Josh with his hand laid on the head of the deceased said.

'No! No!' I shouted again.

'Misjudged. Josh tried to escape. Slipped!' the man said.

'Cut the small trees! Use them to roll over the butt!' Murata-san yelled.

"I was frozen in shock, not knowing what to do.

"Other lumberjacks clambered to the site and they started cutting small trees to use as levers against the tree that had come down on Josh. They intended to pull him out from under the trunk.

"Soon the boss reached the site, out of breath, 'Get the God damn trunk off!' Motozo shouted. 'God damn it! God damn it!'

"More than a dozen loggers started levering the butt end over, but the branches of the huge tree were stuck. I helped Murata-san and other loggers push the trunk with every ounce of our strength.

'Anyone know where Josh's parents live? The Dois?' Motozo yelled.

'In Vancouver! Near Little Tokyo,' I gasped.

'No good! Exactly where? Otherwise we have to look for the Dois!' Motozo shouted.

'Maybe Nami knows,' the logger named Sadao said between his teeth, bared with effort.

'Go get Nami here! Hurry!'

"Another logger put his shoulder to the tree trunk while Sadao started racing towards the huts.

'*Yoisho! Yoisho!* Oof! Oof!' The loggers hollered repeatedly, trying to lever the butt end up and slide it. The footing was slippery and unstable with the rain that had fallen the day before. I pushed the trunk desperately. The tree's branches had speared into the underbrush like barbed hooks.

'Use the lever! Push it over, harder!' Motozo shouted to us. He added his own muscle against the trunk. '*Yoisho! Yoisho!*' The trunk did not move. '*Yoisho! Yoisho!*' '*Yoisho! Yoisho!*' We beat time and tried to move it. The huge trunk slowly started shaking. '*Yoisho! Yoisho!*'

"We rocked it until the trunk slid wide enough to pull the body out from under it. I laid Josh on his back on the ground. Josh's face was covered with blood and his eyes were wide open, staring at the sky and blood covered his chest as well. I involuntarily averted my eyes from my friend's terrible death. But I looked at him again and placed my hands together in prayer. I was numb, not even able to feel any sorrow. The whole world stopped breathing.

"Nami-san and Sadao ran to the site. As soon as Nami-san saw Josh, she crumbled.

'Do ya know where Josh's parents live?' Motozo asked her.

"She nodded, crying and wiping her grief-stricken face, 'Vancouver. Near Little Tokyo. I have their address.'

'Sadao, go tell the parents Josh's dead,' the boss ordered. 'Quick! It's summer time and we can't leave Josh's body for long.'

"Sadao and Nami-san started running.

'Wait, Sadao! The money, here.' Motozo took a thick bunch of folded bills from his sack belt and handed some of them to Sadao, 'Use this for everything. Go, come back quick! Go! Go now!' The boss turned to the loggers. 'Does anyone have a white *hachimaki*, something like a white headband?'

'Nami might.'

'Go get it!'

"The logger ran after Nami-san and brought back a white *hachimaki*. Instead of a *sankakukin,* the white triangular paper headband worn in Japan for a funeral, the boss tied the white *hachimaki* on his head and stood in front of Josh's body. Every worker, walking heavily, stood behind him, knowing what would unfold.

'*Gassho*!' Motozo said and the lumberjacks pressed their hands together in prayer. 'Josh worked hard. He was a good man. A very good worker. We're sorry for the loss. A peace for him.' The prayer was short. '*Gassho*!' he said once again at the end.

"A couple of hours later we resumed work, although great sorrow hung over us.

"For another three days, I paid my respects and prayed for Josh after work. On the fourth day, when I got back for supper, Josh's body was gone. Sadao who had gone to Vancouver to get his parents was eating at the table.

'Did Josh's parents come?' I asked.

262

'Yes,' Sadao said, nodding slightly. He did not want to talk.

"And … that was it. Nothing more happened than that. Nobody wanted to talk about Josh from that day on. I was suspicious as to whether or not they were respecting the peace and silence of the deceased—or if recalling him was bad luck, for fear of being in the grip of Death."

Some four decades later, the noble ambition of young Josh's life was honoured by the attentive stillness of the Osada family. No one could move or speak while Eizo prepared to tell the rest of the story, his life unknown to his three sons and Fumi.

20
Hastings Park Internment and the Yellowhead Highway Labour Camp

"A year later, the summer of 1937," Eizo continued, "Murata-san found work at one of the sawmills in Campbell River, where I was able to get a job as well.

'The hell with logging! Risking my life for forty cents an hour? Big, big deal! We're darn suckers. To hell with it!' Murata-san spat as if having contempt for his boss when we descended from the logging camp.

"We, the Japanese Canadians, called ourselves *denden-mushi*, snails; we literally had our houses on our backs. Murata-san and I, squeezing all our belongings into duffle bags, took a bus from Courtenay to Campbell River on a dusty, hot day. The bus ran between the farmlands where cows grazed in the surrounded meadows and both sides of the road were dotted with houses but mostly covered with forest. After a half hour ride north, we started seeing the Strait of Georgia. The ocean was smooth with small ripples. I was anxious about the new job and even the shining surface of the strait did not soothe my worries.

"There were several other Japanese working at the sawmill and our wages—I'm talking about the Japanese Canadians' wage—were lower than that of *hakujin* workers who did literally the same job. All of us lived together in an unpainted, shabby barrack not far from work. We sorted and stacked lumber into sizes, working ten to twelve-hour days, without relying on machines. Towards the end of the day, we were exhausted, our working shoes ate into our feet, and even the meagre dinners which we prepared in rotation tasted like *sukiyaki.* On top of that, there was no entertainment. Murata-san gave himself up to gambling there as well. I learned some English at the sawmill and expanded my vocabulary with mainly swearing words.

'Osada-san, I quit. No more Canada for me,' Murata-san abruptly said to me one day, two years later.

'What? What are you telling me?'

'I'm gonna back to Japan.'

'What? Why all of a sudden?'

''Cause, I'm fed up with all of this. Working too hard is taking a toll. I don't wanna put up with no more! I miss my family. And I've been shoved around too much here. I know I'm stupid and don't speak English good, but I know you gotta feel good about something to live a life, you know. We've nothing of that sort here. We're nothing in Canada, maggots, yes, we're maggots. Nothing more than that! Enough's enough. To hell with it!'

'But what are you going to do in Japan?'

'I'll find some job. Don't matter I get paid less. I hate it here and I'm gonna home, no matter what,' Murata-san said and meant it.

"He left Canada for Japan just before Germany invaded Poland. Many Issei that had arrived in Canada single were now married and had children, and some had brought their families with them. The Nisei had grown up in Canada and many Nikkei already ended up calling Canada their home, abandoning their original intentions of returning to Japan. Murata-san's return was a far cry from the dream that he had held of being rich and successful. I, however, chose to stay and, after Murata-san left for Japan, went back to the logging camp where my *kunimono* boss, Motozo, managed.

"I had you guys and Kino on my back to support. I've never forgotten about you," said Eizo to his silent sons by the hearth.

*

But then the world changed. On September 1st, 1939, war broke out in Europe, the dark harbinger of the Second World War. Canada, the oldest Dominion of the British Commonwealth, soon followed Great Britain in her declaration of war against Germany. Meanwhile Japan's aggression in China, the Second Sino-Japanese War, which started in July 1937, had intensified and the Tripartite Pact of Japan, Germany, and Italy was signed on the 27th of September 1940. Judging from the international developments, there was every sign that 'something will happen' between the aggressive great powers of the world and the sounds of invading heavy tanks and dashing military boots were almost heard in people's ear. That fall, the Federal Government of Canada implemented a citizen registration program as a part of their war efforts, and the following year imposed a re-registration for all persons of Japanese origin.

They were under obligation to carry their registration cards, which had their photo and thumb print, at all times. The registration cards were issued in three colours:

- Yellow for a Japanese national (the card Eizo was issued)
- Pink for naturalized Issei
- White card for Nisei and Sansei

Re-registration was not required of German and Italian descendants living in Canada. Prime Minister Mackenzie King appeared convinced that Japan would wage war upon the Allies and was apprehensive of the Nikkei; many Canadians believed the Japanese among them were spies and engaged in espionage.

As imperialism with its aggression and gunboat diplomacy reached a climax, every single move made by the World Powers received sensational news coverage, inspiring fear and fanning suspicion and anxiety internationally and domestically. Even the routine behaviour of the Japanese in Canada was suspect. Nikkei fishermen cruising the Pacific Coast in their boats were, as so many British Columbians accused, involved in fifth column activities: making charts for the Japanese Imperial Navy for their attacks on the West Coast. By the summer of 1941, Canada halted the export of strategic materials to Japan, such as steel and copper, and imposed a total ban of imports from Japan. Shipping services along the Pacific route were also sharply curtailed.

*

"Three days before the Japan's attack on Pearl Harbor in 1941, I was in Little Tokyo, staying at a rooming house, along with six other guests." Eizo went on in front of his family in the living room. "People were busy shopping and making preparations for Christmas and New Year. '*Irasshai! Irasshai!*—Walk up! Walk up!' I heard the young store staff calling to passers-by. Little Tokyo was booming and the Japanese were enjoying the festive mood before the holidays.

"Then, just before 7.50 a.m. on the 7th of December, the Empire of Japan carried out a huge-scale attack from the air at Pearl Harbor, Hawaii. It happened late morning Vancouver time. 'Ooooi, Pearl Harbor is burning. Huge black smoke is engulfing Pearl Harbor. Something horrible is going on!' I heard a Nisei shout. The serenity in Little Tokyo was broken. I had a premonition and went outside. The groups of shoppers and store staff were standing on Powell Street, talking about 'something horrible', without knowing what was really going on.

"By late afternoon, the cry changed to: 'War has broken out! It's war!'

'What? What war?' one of the guests cried, appalled.

"The rooming house was thrown into an uproar. A young man half-yelled, saying the U.S. Navy base at Pearl Harbor had been bombed by Japanese Imperial forces. He said that was the cause of the chaos reported earlier. The bombing destroyed the fleet at anchor and appeared to have caused many casualties. He was trembling. 'Christ! Japan attacked America!' the young Nisei said in a panic. 'A surprise attack!'

"'Japan attacked America!' Every face in the inn showed disbelief and stupor. I stood there in a daze and then took heart and tried to think about how this would affect my family and whether I could reunite with Kino and you. I was worried what might happen to the Japanese in Canada, although Japan and Canada were not at war yet.

"I was stunned and confused by the news and didn't know what to do at first," Eizo told his sons and Fumi. Tamotsu and Kozo kept looking at Isoshichi while the eldest son looked at his wife. It was as if they had lost the ability to talk.

"That day, Little Tokyo was filled with the faces of worry.

"Still reeling with the news, I went to a friend's room and talked awhile, but I was unable to dispel my fear. Later in a restaurant I overheard a man talking about Japan's bombing. It turned out that man was Mr. Mizuno of the local Japanese newspaper *The Tairiku Nippo* (*The Continental Daily News*). Eager to know the latest, I asked Mizuno if I could come to the office with him. The newspaper had only two writers, the owner-chief editor Mr. Yamazaki and the junior writer Mizuno; they also employed two compositors to set the type. Their circulation was a little more than two thousand.

"When we arrived, the chief editor was at his desk trying to contact the Japanese Consulate in Vancouver, though it was Sunday, to look for direction. He also wanted to ask correspondents nearby to contribute by handwriting extra and posting updates on billboards in their areas. These people were just ordinary subscribers, but contributed articles to the newspaper from time to time.

'What a terrifying thing to have happened!' Mizuno said.

'Horrifying,' the chief editor replied, shaking his head in disbelief. 'Four battleships were sunk to the bottom of the harbour and others badly damaged. Where were you at this crucial time?'

'I was at Yamato's, listening to the news. By the way, this is Mr. Osada. He left his family in Japan and he is worried about them.'

'Hello. I won't bother you,' I said to Yamazaki and bowed.

'Are you a subscriber?' Yamazaki looked up from the phone, casting a glance at me.

'No, I work at a logging camp. But I'm worried.'

'Everybody is.'

'May I stay because …?'

269

'Suit yourself,' the owner-editor cut in and then looked at Mizuno. 'You know what to do. Call the main contributors. Tell them what happened. If you can't get them, send telegraphs! Blast it! I can't get through to the consulate.'

"While still attempting to contact the Japanese Consulate, Yamazaki's call was cut off. He tried again, but the telephone appeared to no longer work—a dead sound. Yamazaki and Mizuno started discussing what to do next. So, I thanked them and left to have a quick supper, but soon I returned to the paper. Yamazaki had already gone back home and Mizuno was writing and eating a dinner of *katsudon* at the same time. Mizuno said that Yamazaki owned a shortwave radio at his house and they intended to listen to broadcasts from Japan for the latest news copy. I desperately pleaded with Mizuno to take me along, which he hesitated at first but finally agreed. On the way the junior editor bought a pack of cigarettes in preparation for a long night. Yamazaki nodded to my request reluctantly, so we sat down around the radio and listened to the news from Japan at Yamazaki's.

'Dictate the news as much as you possibly can!' Yamazaki ordered Mizuno.

"I watched them, my despair mounting. The broadcaster from Japan repeatedly announced the single message of war against the United States and Great Britain with their successful attack of Pearl Harbor and then Hong Kong.

'Now, it's Hong Kong bombarded by the Japanese Imperial forces,' the chief editor said.

'Just this October, just this past October! Two thousand Canadian soldiers sailed for Hong Kong from here to reinforce the British. Do you remember?' Mizuno responded.

'Of course, I remember. It was big news. What happened to them? Killed or captured?'

'The Japanese bombed the same as Pearl Harbor. So …'

'I have an ominous feeling and I hope the Canadian people won't turn their rage against us.' Yamazaki said, reflecting on his predicament.

'Hope not. Can't tell what'll happen. After the bombings at Pearl Harbor, who knows what?' the junior editor said.

"At around seven o'clock, the shortwave from Japan started broadcasting the Imperial rescript. Yamazaki and Mizuno were glued to the radio. The strained voice started coming out from the speaker and with due solemnity stated that the United States and Great Britain were furthering the turmoil in East Asia by supporting the government still in existence in China, and attempting to conquer the Orient under the pretence of peace. By reinforcing armaments around and tightening the economic pressures against Japan together with other countries, the United States and Great Britain were threatening the existence of Japan. If this situation should continue as is, Japan's long-standing efforts to stabilize East Asia would come to naught and her existence too would be endangered. Therefore, Japan was compelled to stand up for the sake of her self-defence and existence…

"Mizuno started drafting the article to get it out in the extra for the next morning while Yamazaki looked at his writing over junior editor's shoulders. An intense hour and half elapsed in a twinkling and at the end Yamazaki fell on the chair to rest.

"Then someone knocked on the door. Yamazaki stood up to open it.

'Hey, you watch out! Tamaki was just arrested by the RCMP,' the Japanese man said to him. I couldn't see his face well due to the Yamazaki's back, but noticed the man's voice trembling.

'Tamaki? The Tamaki… who used to import foodstuffs from Japan?'

'Yes, that Tamaki. Be careful! Okay!' The man left hurriedly.

'Gosh!' Mizuno exclaimed when Yamazaki turned his face to us.

'I might be the next. Who the hell knows?' Yamazaki was in a flurry. 'Let's issue the extra quickly!'

"Mizuno had to leave to the office promptly to prepare the articles for print.

"As if in place of the Japanese man, someone knocked on the front door again.

"Yamazaki looked at Mizuno with tense and fearful eyes and opened the door. 'Yes?'

'Sir, are you Mr. Yamazaki, the publisher of *The Tairiku Nippo*?' A man in a black overcoat and a black hat asked him and beside the man was a police officer in uniform. I stood up to see them well.

'Yes, I am.'

"The man in black overcoat flashed police identification at Yamazaki from his inside pocket without a word. 'We're the RCMP. You already know what happened at Pearl Harbor today?'

'Yes, I do, sir. I heard the news.' For an instant, Yamazaki suspected that the RCMP came to his door to arrest him. 'Did I do something wrong?'

'We're here to protect Canadians,' the police officer in uniform said.

The words irritated Yamazaki. 'You mean, protect from the Japanese? Sir, I'm a Canadian too, a naturalized Canadian. We didn't do anything wrong.'

The officer faltered slightly by Yamazaki's bristling attitude, but collected himself. 'Well, never mind it. We, the

RCMP, have to advise you that you're to close your newspaper immediately.'

'Close my newspaper? Why is that so? I don't understand. Is that an order, sir?'

'No, it's advice, sir, as a precautionary measure.' The officer in uniform was polite but resolute. 'You can communicate with your comrades in many ways through ...'

'No,' the man in black overcoat cut over the officer's talk. 'You don't need to mention that.'

'Our comrades?' Yamazaki repeated after the officer.

'No, never mind,' the man in overcoat and a black hat said to him and urged the officer. 'Carry on.'

'Yes sir,' said the officer. 'We strongly advise you to close the paper from this point on. Is that clear, sir?'

'Yes, I heard that, sir.' Yamazaki said, still trying to ask some questions.

'That's all we have to tell you. Well, good night.' The men did not wait for Yamazaki's response. They turned around and walked to the police car.

The chief editor was speechless.

'Surely, you're known to the RCMP. We must've been put under police surveillance. We're marked men,' Mizuno said to his boss.

'You're not kidding,' Yamazaki said in a tremulous voice.

"With the Canadian government moving quickly to restrict activities of the Japanese community, particularly key people of interest, Yamazaki decided to close his newspaper. I excused myself from the Yamazakis soon after the RCMP officer had left, bowing low and thanking them several times.

"On the way to the rooming house, I was confused, disconcerted and desperate like the sky overhead: dark,

273

unearthly and fathomless … The outbreak of the Pacific War was about to change my life completely, swallowing me up in the vortex of world history.

"That night the Federal Government of Canada swiftly moved to declare war on Japan, which was proclaimed the following day, and initiated the following policies against persons of Japanese origin:

- A total ban on fishing by the Nikkei
- No long-distance calls allowed
- The use of Japanese language prohibited on the telephone
- The closure of Japanese language schools.
  The government also introduced the provision to categorize Japanese nationals, naturalized Issei, and Nisei with Canadian citizenships as 'enemy aliens.'

News that the RCMP had arrested Japanese suspected of being a threat spread like wildfire through the communities.

"The day after the Pearl Harbor attack, I left Little Tokyo for Vancouver Island, worrying about being in a jam in Canada. When I arrived at the logging camp, the Japanese lumberjacks were hungry for the news. Although workers were on the job, they crowded around us to urge us to tell them what had happened. With the news of Japan's Pearl Harbor attack, they all were silenced.

"Five days after the bombing, the Canadian company who had closed the deal with my boss annulled the contract. We all lost our jobs. Many Canadian companies on the West Coast, large and small, began dismissing their Japanese employees after December 7th.

"I was totally lost," Eizo told his sons. "Upset and couldn't think logically. Canada was at war and there was no way to go home to Japan. All routes and possibilities were closed. We were afraid of what would happen to us next. Uncertainty is the worst enemy when you face a crisis. We felt entirely powerless and scared because of the uncertainty. The Canadian government imposed restrictions against us, one after another. The RCMP arrested many of those regarded as leaders. *Hakujins* who resented the Japanese before the war were seeing red, citizenship didn't matter.

"On the 10th of December, Britain's battleship the HMS *Prince of Wales*, known as the 'HMS Unsinkable,' and the HMS *Repulse* were sent to the bottom of the sea off the coast of Kuantan, Malaysia in fierce attacks initiated by the Imperial Japanese Navy. The news of the sinking of the unsinkable came as a disaster to Canadians. The next day, Germany and Italy declared war upon the United States. Once again, the world was engulfed by war. On the 11th, Reverend Ono, representing the Nikkei from Cumberland and its vicinity, carried the following statement in The Comox Argus—a local newspaper: 'We the Japanese residents of this district would like to reaffirm our loyalty to Canada and we will continue to the utmost to support this country's war effort. Nearly all the Japanese residents here are Canadian-born or are the parents of children born in Canada. This is our home and our future lies with the welfare of this country, and so on ...' But our plea did not reach the ears of the Federal Government of Canada in Ottawa.

"On the 15th of December, a U.S. Military source reported that the surprise attack on Pearl Harbor was the result of very effective fifth column work by the Japanese. The following day, the provision to categorize the Nikkei as 'enemy aliens' became law.

"Although I was unemployed, I was fortunate to room with the Akiyamas in Number 1 'Jap-Town' in Cumberland. Akiyama came from Gifu—the same prefecture as me—, and we got to know each other at a *hanami* held in Cumberland before the war. Akiyama had two children, twelve and eleven, both boys.

'Dad! Radio broadcast!' the younger boy said to Akiyama when he got back from school.

'What radio broadcast?'

'Clive told me that the radio had said the Japanese here were the spies of the Japanese Navy. He said, "You people are searching for just the place to attack Canada for the Japanese Navy."'

'What? Did your *hakujin* friend say that?'

'Oh yes! He said we were doing all kinds of sabotage along the Pacific coast.'

'Nonsense! We were muckers, just coal workers before. Tell him we've got nothing to do with the sabotage on the Pacific coast,' the dad told his son, while looking at me anxiously.

'And Gifford said that Japs smell from miles away.'

'Did he say that?'

'Yes, he did.'

'That kid is a nutcase.'

'No, Dad, he is the brightest in the class.'

'No, he isn't.'

'Yes, he is. … Dad, I was listening to the radio the other day. An American radio station. It said the Japanese Forces were going to invade the Pacific Coast and British Columbia soon.'

'What? Why didn't you tell me immediately?'

'I was scared!'

'Damn it! I'm totally shut off from the world,' Akiyama exclaimed. 'What's next?'

"West Coast *hakujin* people had long criticised the Nikkei that our spiritual attachments were oriented more for Japan than for Canada. Steady advances by the Japanese military, fears that the Nikkei were involved in the fifth column activities in Canada and the suspicion that we would be loyal to the Empire of Japan in the event of her invasion onto the West Coast, plus the perception that Canada's defence facilities in the West Coast were under-equipped, fueled the beliefs behind the urgency to have the Nikkei removed from the Pacific Coast.

"On Christmas day, after the fierce battle, the Allied Forces of the Great Britain and Canada surrendered to the Japanese Army in Hong Kong. The Japanese captured two thousand Canadian prisoners of war. Hatred and fear reached a peak. Public sentiment rallied sharply in support of the removal of the Nikkei, backed strongly by provincial and municipal politicians who pressured the Government of Canada to act.

"On the 14th of January 1942, a 100-mile strip from the Pacific Coast inland to the Cascade Mountains was designated the 'Protected Area'. The evacuation policy of Japanese male nationals between the ages of eighteen and forty-five to the road camps in northern British Columbia—a partial evacuation—was made public. The government also banned Japanese nationals from having cameras and shortwave radios and banned the Nikkei from handling gasoline and explosives in the Protected Area until the war ended. However, one month later, on February 26, pressured by the mounting public outcry, the Federal Government of Canada changed the 'partial evacuation' program to the 'total evacuation' policy of all Nikkei who lived in the Protected Area.

"While cities were blacked-out at night to ward off a feared invasion from the air, not a single Japanese warplane emblazoned with the sun on its wings and body ever appeared in the skies over British Columbia; only the seagulls circled and called to each other over the Pacific Ocean."

*

"'We're the RCMP. Are you Mr. Akiyama?' On the 14th of April 1942, an officer in uniform stood in front of the Akiyamas' door.

'Yes sir,' Akiyama answered.

'You … your … and … children here. Is that corre …?'

'One moment please. Ichiro, come here,' Akiyama called his elder son for help. It was a Tuesday afternoon and the son was already home from the school.

'Sir, can I help you?' Ichiro asked the officer.

'Are you Mr. Akiyama's son?'

'Yes, sir.'

'Mr. Akiyama, his wife and two children live here. Is that correct?'

'Yes, that's correct, sir. And Mr. Osada.'

'Mr. Osada? Who is he?'

'A Japanese. He is staying with us temporarily.'

'A Japanese! All right,' the officer recorded it on a note. 'All of you have to evacuate to Vancouver tomorrow. Your family and Mr. Osada must come to the front of this Number 1 Mine town before seven o'clock tomorrow morning. There'll be several Vancouver Island Coach Lines buses waiting. Then, you're to board a ship in Union Bay at eight o'clock.'

"Ichiro translated what the RCMP officer said to his dad and me.

'Tomorrow?' Akiyama asked his son.

'Yes, that's what the officer said.'

'Ask the officer again if it's really tomorrow.'

But the answer was the same.

'God damn it! We don't have much time left. Ask the RCMP where we're really going to be sent?' The elder son asked the officer.

'We don't have that information, yet. You'll be notified later.'

'Don't know where to …?' Akiyama said and looked up at me. I read an ominous fear on his face. Probably he read the same on my face.

'You're allowed to carry the maximum of 1,000 pounds per family. That'd be roughly two suitcases and a duffle bag for an adult. One suitcase and one duffle bag per child. You mustn't take big belongings with you. If you've a pedal sewing machine, blankets, mattresses and a small cooking stove, take them with you.' Then the officer added, 'Oh yes, take a few days' food supplies too. That'd be helpful for you.'"

Now years later, Eizo translated to his own family how the evacuation for the Akiyamas began, as it did for the rest of the Japanese.

"The Nikkei were only able to pack up some kitchen ware, albums, valuable articles, clothes and food for several days. That was all. We lost our heads and didn't know what to take. I later heard in the concentration camp that some Nikkei were given only a few hours to prepare for the move. Some who had a little time before the evacuations sold their household goods and cars at unduly low prices because the buyers took advantage of our helpless situation. Most of the Nikkei had to leave their belongings and property behind, unguarded.

"When the students at the Cumberland Elementary returned to school after April 15th, they found one third of the entire student population was gone. When they asked where and why those Japanese students had suddenly disappeared, a teacher said, 'They had to go far away. Those students were the children of Canada's enemy in this war. Yesterday, they were your friends. Today, they are your enemies. It's sad, isn't it?' At the time Cumberland and its vicinity recorded the largest Nikkei population on Vancouver Island, including a Japanese language school, Buddhist temple, community hall, and two grocery stores.

"The 15th of April was the day of 'a leaden sky with a biting south east wind.' Under the supervision of the RCMP and the Provincial Police, the Nikkei from Cumberland and the surrounding area were taken fifteen kilometres south to Union Bay to board the S. S. Prince George for the Hastings Park detention centre in Vancouver. There were eight buses in all from different areas, the total of more than five hundred eighty evacuees. Some of them had already gone aboard the ship long before we arrived. We trudged up the gangplank like livestock. Those evacuees already on board looked as if they were at a deathwatch, overwhelmed with despair and horror. Some of them, old Issei and women with children, went to the cabins below the deck. Some were seated on their trunks and some were standing with shoulders and hands drooped, their eyes filled with fear. They were not talking. Some children were held by their mothers, still on the deck. No smiles. They stared at the new embarkations. My knees were shaking as I descended from the gangplank to the deck.

"Then, our ship sailed into the Georgia Strait at ten after ten. Several Canadians gathered on the wharf and wished us good-bye. I still remember the sound of the foghorn which echoed in the bay like someone had beaten a gong at a funeral. It still resonates in my ear even today. Nobody talked and the mood of the boat was dreadful. Behind us, Vancouver Island floated on the surface of the sea in eternal stillness. There was no way I could believe that we were in wartime and that I was being shipped to the detention centre. We were in an unreal environment. I thought Nature never lied but it lied that day. How could it be that serene while there was a war going on and we were gathered on the ship like cattle being taken to a slaughterhouse?"

Eizo paused, caught between the stillness of a remembered world and the one he now faced.

"I didn't lose anything materially, like other Japanese did, but I lost my future, the freedom to live where I wanted, the money that I was going to earn otherwise and that was to be sent to you guys. The anxiety of an unknown future … I couldn't stand that more than anything else. I didn't know what would happen to me or even where my final destination was."

Eizo raised his eyes from the floor to his sons, who had been avoiding looking at him.

"Together with the Akiyamas, I was put into temporary facilities surrounded by barbed wire on the grounds of the Pacific National Exhibition at Hastings Park. About two thousand Nikkei detainees were already being held inside. The structures were originally built for livestock exhibitions and the Nikkei evacuees were housed in revamped stalls with the stench of animals filling the air. Moreover, men and women were segregated by sex and age into different stalls. Inside the men's facility, tiered seats for auctions bordered all four sides; bare industrial lights hung from the ceiling and a big wall clock had been installed. The beds were set in rows and the mattresses stuffed with straw. Rumors circulated between the detainees: we would be kept in the detention centre forever. Amid the rumors, some sought comfort in religion and some were stupefied with despair while others paralyzed with fear, succumbed to severe mental stress. The aged and the women with small babies were extremely miserable as their milk did not flow due to the severe distress and the diapers that they had brought with them were not enough for their daily needs.

"I was still young at the time, so I could rise again. But for the elderly Issei, it was a death sentence," Eizo told his sons. "Their fishing boats were confiscated. They had to leave their businesses, houses and all their belongings, behind. Some old Issei talked to me about their difficulties, but I couldn't find even a word to console them. Can you imagine how those parents were feeling for their babies and children? They had to raise their children in the detention centre with the *hakujin's* hatred outside the barbed wire. I know how they suffered seeing their children sink into silence and inactivation and many cursed their doom. My heart clenched whenever I looked at the children's faces. They had forgotten how to play while in the detention centre. Some Nisei lost hope for their future in Canada. Mentally and spiritually speaking, Hastings Park was a slaughterhouse for us.

"The War Measures Act vested the Cabinet with enormous power to deal with all kinds of matters: evacuation, detainment, moving us to the East and the repatriation of the Nikkei to Japan. The British Columbia Security Commission was set up by the Federal Government to evacuate the Nikkei as efficiently and smoothly as possible."

Eizo struggled for the words to explain how this trauma had overwhelmed him and so many others. The Nikkei were deprived of their fundamental civil rights as Canadians and they could not bring their case to trial or demand public hearings. The people of Japanese origin, particularly the Issei, were resigned to their fate, because it was *okami no meirei,* an order from the authority or heaven. One of the most fundamental values of Confucianism was loyalty to one's ruler. This belief combined with reverence for the Emperor, a nurtured sense of awe for authority, seemed to have played a key role in Japanese compliance with the order from the Federal Government of Canada. The Buddhist sense of resignation and passivity, the belief in reincarnation and therefore, emancipation from worldly happenings or particularly sufferings, further influenced the Nikkei to accept the evacuation without resistance. The Nikkei had no precedent, or model to follow, no one to stand up for their cause. Powerful systems of belief and profound cultural ethics, piled on top of the normalcy of discrimination and suppression by the Canadian *hakujin*, created an inescapable mortar that ground their morale to powder.

*

"'Osada-kun, the British Columbia Security Commission wants you to go to a road camp,' one of Morii's men told me, a week after I had arrived at Hastings Park. Etsuji Morii was a judo master and ran *Kokuryu-kai*, a club with enigmatic purposes, and *The Showa Club*, a gambling house, the notorious 'gambling king' of Little Tokyo before the war. He was the figure most feared in the Japanese community and had formed the Wartime Security Committee, a private organization that gave a helping hand to the British Columbia Security Commission and the RCMP for the evacuation of the Nikkei. Up until this time, the RCMP had investigated Morii for a couple of charges, manslaughter and smuggling, and for a time had doubted his loyalty to Canada.

'Me?' I asked the big-boned Japanese man who was possibly a judo expert. Not many Japanese wanted to go to the road camp of their own accord.

'Yes, you, Osada-kun! You don't have your wife or children here. Go to a road camp for the sake of other Japanese. We need those good-hearted Japanese. The British Columbia Security Commission is scratching their heads as to how to carry out the evacuations and it's good if we show them our co-operation at this stage. Our Chairman Morii says, "Do them a favour now and wait and see what that brings us later." Go to a road camp, all right, go!' The judo man stood up and threatened me. 'Our Chairman Morii understands the position of the Japanese in Canada very well and knows how the world works. No excuses for you! Go!' Nobody knew for sure what was behind the Morii's intent to cooperate with the RCMP and to send the Japanese to the road camps. He was the man being active out of sight of the troubled Nikkei, his compatriots, and was a controversial figure."

All was quiet around the hearth. Eizo grimaced. "I couldn't say 'No' to him, or to Morii, for that matter, because of my moral obligation to those Japanese with families. Other Issei did the same thing and went to the road camps. I was already deeply disheartened at being uprooted, outraged by what had happened to us and suffered from not being able to work or live freely anymore. In addition to that, there was war and everyone experienced fear. The whole situation

284

demoralized us to the verge of suicide, but again, those government policies came down as the *okami no meirei*," Eizo said. No one in the living room spoke.

"A total of twenty-six road camps had been planned by the Federal Government. We, including six Nisei, were sent to one of the road camps in the wilderness between Jasper National Park in Alberta and Blue River, British Columbia, to build the interprovincial Yellowhead Highway. Before we departed, we were worried as to whether or not the northern interior was much colder than the southern West Coast and had to prepare for the cold climate accordingly. But as we arrived, we found it was sunny and dry and that weather continued most of the spring and summer. At the construction site, we saw mountain pine and brush, rivers, streams and lakes waiting for us. I noticed that I could see none of the familiar big trees that fell in the Vancouver Island logging camps. The village of white tents for the Nikkei labourers emerged, as if a bunch of white flowers had burst into full blossom in the wilderness.

"The whole thing was unfair and nonsensical to us and there was no incentive to work at the road camp.

'Hey, look!' one worker yelled, 'There is a fox looking at us!'

'Where? No, that's a coyote,' another said. The road camp workers spent some time arguing about who was right. They later witnessed all kinds of animals, including bears, elk, moose, deer, wolf and beaver.

"The Nikkei workers were not given any machinery to build the highway, so, the project made but slow progress. Looking at the landscape horizons, I pondered how many decades it would take to finish the highway and how long I would be forced to live in the camp. Maybe, the war would not last that long. Or it might last for many years. What the hell would happen in the end?

'How quiet it's here. I can't believe Japan and the Allies are at war,' one worker said.

'God damn it! Are you a dupe? Be optimistic. It's free of charge. You'll be sorry later, if you're not,' another responded.

'No, I just can't imagine there's a war going on right now.'

"On one occasion a *hakujin* supervisor came and said, 'You guys didn't do anything wrong in Canada, did you? Come on, I mean, why are you guys here at this insane project with no machinery? Now listen, you don't have to work hard, okay.'

The Japanese workers did not know what to say.

"But remember this—you have to show how hard you're working when the inspector from headquarters comes here. Otherwise, it's up to you guys how hard you work,' the supervisor said.

"While working, or supposed to be working, Senkichi-san, two other workers and I replanted young pines that had a good branch shape, resembling those of *bonsai*, and other miniature trees with large leaves and created a small but elaborate Japanese garden behind the highway construction site. The result was masterly workmanship. Looking at the garden, one worker said that what he needed was *saké* and *sushi*. Other workers did not think that was funny. It was a reserved way of showing our resistance, besides slowing down the work schedule.

'When do you think this futile road camp ends?' I asked Senkichi-san one day.

'It might take twenty or thirty years. Who knows? But, it will probably never end as long as the government needs us for this stupid project.'

'Ridiculous! There's no single Caterpillar here. This project is going nowhere. The goddamn government thinks it's one day's job to flatten the mountains with only shovels and pickaxes?'

'Don't think about it. It's too depressing. I've no idea when we'll be back to our families. Maybe we're trapped here for good,' Senkichi-san moaned.

"In the late spring of 1942, elderly Nikkei who were not sent to the road camps were evacuated to the five ghost towns—abandoned mining towns—located in the southern interior of British Columbia. The young Nisei were sent to six new concentration camps, beside the already existing ghost town camps, to build houses for the evacuees.

"Senkichi-san and I were called to build the housing facilities at the newly-created Tashme camp—formerly farmland, situated in the rugged mountains near Hope, in southern British Columbia. The camp was named by taking the first two letters of the surnames of the commissioners of the British Columbia Security Commission, Taylor, Shirras and Mead, and combined them into one. There was only one trail connecting the camp to the outside world. The houses we built were partitioned in half by a sheet of thin lumber; detainees had to share one kitchen with the other family in the unit. We built houses, row after row, where there was no electricity at first. The evacuees had to use kerosene lamps and candles for light.

"Early October 1942, six trucks with triangular hoods and open load-carrying platforms arrived at the Tashme camp. Loaded in the open boxes in the back were Nikkei evacuees, mainly women, children and the elderly Issei.

Senkichi-san, along with other workers, ran to see if their families were in the vehicles. Newly-arrived evacuees looked around to see if their husbands or fathers were in the crowd. Every evacuee appeared frightened and exhausted. At the end of one platform, Matsu-san stood holding Martin's hand.

'Matsu! Martin! Here, here!' Senkichi-san called out. His wife and son looked back at him. As they got off the truck with his help, the wife and husband took each other's hand in joy, reunited again. Then Senkichi-san held Martin in his arms and had a good look at the boy.

'Sorry Martin, Daddy wasn't at home with you. Were you lonely?' Senkichi-san asked. His son only nodded without looking at him.

'How have you been? You look well to me,' Matsu-san said to Senkichi-san.

'Well, let's put it this way—I survived. At least we were fed.'

'That's okay, then. The trip here was long and tiring.'

'I bet it was.'

'Martin is well.'

'That's our one bright spot.'

'How huge this camp is!'

'Who the hell planned this kind of camp? We're going to stay in a hut in the fifth row.'

'Don't be surprised, Little Tokyo is desolate. No *hakujin* customers came, except Germans and Italians. The Nikkei businesses were almost bankrupt.'

'I'd suspected that would happen.'

'Some stores closed, like the Onami's.'

'The Onami's was closed? How is our house?'

'You know, you weren't there, so I couldn't do anything. I locked the doors and windows and … that was all. We left everything in the house. The Custodian is going to look after it, I hope,' Matsu-san said. She believed, as most of the Nikkei did, the Custodian of Enemy Alien Property would take care of their properties while they were evacuated.

'I see. Oh, this is Osada-san. We were at the road camp together.'

"I exchanged a greeting with Matsu-san. She was well dressed, so was Martin. They did not look like they were coming to a concentration camp. No way! It was like two butterflies descended onto the garbage dump.

'To which camp did the Dois go?' Senkichi-san asked his wife.

'They went to Kaslo, in the Rockies. Mainly those people who belong to the United Church moved there.'

'I see. Are they okay?'

'They've gone there well ahead of us, so I don't know.'

"Later, I asked Senkichi-san if the Doi family they were talking about was the same family I knew at the logging camp.

'There was only one Doi's around Little Tokyo, so they must be it,' said Senkichi-san.

'The name of the youngest one was Josh Hideki.'

'That's it. His name was Josh, a dreamy boy. I don't know why, but he wanted to be called Josh rather than Hideki. A very good-natured boy.'

'What a strange fate. We were in the same logging camp.'

'Mere coincidence! We were very close to the Dois. A very nice family. I'm sorry for what happened to Josh.'

'Josh was my good pal.'

"Thus, the Doi family tragedy bonded me to Senkichi-san and his family,"

"By the end of October 1942, the government's 'total evacuation' for the Nikkei was completed: more than 20,800 Nikkei were uprooted, evacuated and detained in the concentration camps.

Although the German and Italian Canadians were interned, unlike the case of the Japanese Canadians, no 'total evacuation' was imposed on them. What is more, compared to the sheer number of the Nikkei internees, about 600 Italian and 870 German Canadians—much smaller figure—and only those who were suspected dangerous to the security of Canada were detained and some of them were released later as their charges were cleared. They were treated as a human, but we were not. The Nikkei who had lived within the 'Protected Area' were all removed forcibly." Eizo said.

He noticed Tamotsu's face changed to a set expression at his talk but those of anyone else at the hearth stayed unaffected. He continued;

"In December 1942, most of the road camps that had opened earlier that spring with 2,200 detainees were closed because of their inefficient progress and proximity to strategic infrastructure, such as the transcontinental railroads.

"The Nikkei families were allowed to live together in small barracks, but I was taken into the wooden facility provided for single males. Beds for about fifty detainees were arranged along the walls. Two rectangle tables with long plank benches were set at the centre of the building; the two stoves were oil drums cut in half. Many single males gambled there, too, but I stayed away from it.

"Barracks crouched on both sides of the 'streets' and 'avenues' in Tashme. We, the detainees, had already named the streets between the barracks 'Avenue' and 'Boulevard', and First Street to Tenth Street, as if trying to curb the heartless winds of the world we lived.

"We had eventually gravelled the main street using trucks we borrowed from the British Columbia Security Commission. It seemed to Matsu-san and Senkichi-san that the elaborate main street appeared a dreadful contrast to the shabby barracks, all in vain.

'I don't know how to get along with Ayano-san,' Matsu-san complained to Senkichi-san when they went out to fetch firewood for their cooking stove. It was already winter and the barracks were buried by the deep snow. They told me about this when I visited them later in Toronto.

'Why can't you? We live under the same roof.'

'We've got one kitchen. That's the problem. You know we take turns, but Ayano-san is so slow. Martin and you are hungry, aren't you? She looks blank and stands in the kitchen for a long time, thinking and thinking. What is she thinking? The good old days? Never mind about it. Then she slowly starts cooking. Why can't she think some other time and fry whatever quickly? Job's done. I wait hours for my turn.'

'Everybody is not like you, Matsu.'

'But, why can't she think about other people?'

'Ayano-san family is running out of money. They were talking in whispers but I overheard them talking in their room. You can't hide anything here. No privacy. She's worried about their life and money.'

'Worried about their life? What about our life? I see life here is extremely hard, but she has to think about other people, too. Don't you think?'

'You have to understand her. We're in the same sinking boat.' Senkichi-san patted her back.

291

'Why can't she try it for once in her whole life? She must be suffering from something, but she lacks consideration for others.'

'Take it easy.'

'You say so because you don't cook. Why are we here in this camp in the first place, facing this kind of care and injustice? Why do we have to go through this hell? This is hell here, you know.'

'Don't think about the things that we don't have any answer and control to.'

'You are no help. By the way, you know Kaji-san's wife gave a birth to a baby girl a few days ago. Kaji-san, from the house on the Third Avenue.'

"It was more convenient for us to identify the people by the street names and also easier for the mail service.

'Why at this terrible time?'

'That's life. Some people are born and some die, even in the terrible time. But imagine! Mr. and Mrs. Kaji have to raise the baby under this kind of circumstances, in this slaughterhouse.'

'I don't have to imagine. I know that.'

'I don't think that the Kajis had expected any of this would happen.'

'Obviously not. Nobody had ...'

'Poor girl! What kind of childhood is that baby girl going to have? There's nothing in the camp but misery and unhappiness and sad stories and cold. It's the end of the world.'

"Senkichi-san did not say anything to his wife."

*

"It snowed insanely in the camp that winter." Saying so, Eizo gave a start at his careless use of the word 'insanely', considering the situation he and his family were in. He looked in the direction of Kino and then Isoshichi, but his son did not show any change of emotion. He then carefully restarted his talk.

"The temperature fell more than 30 degrees below zero. The lumber we used to build the barracks was covered only by tarpaper. No way was that enough to keep the inside warm. I put all my clothes on myself in bed, even the duffle bag, too." Unconsciously, Eizo pulled his arms in close to his body, now remembering the ice on his bedding. "I heard from Matsu-san she had to keep the kitchen stove going all night. The firewood was greenwood and it made their barrack very smoky. When the fire died out, the condensation froze, just like sugar all over the walls. It was Matsu-san's job to get up and feed the kitchen stove, and she spent every day trying to dry the wet blankets and straw beds. Martin was four years old. Tamotsu was almost the same age when I left Japan. Fortunately, I guess, Martin didn't realize how hard Senkichi-san and Matsu-san were trying to hide the reality from him and he seemed to have had a jolly good time with other kids in the camp. He was at that age. I asked him later how much he remembered about those days and, surprisingly, he said he had remembered it quite well."

Eizo looked at his daughter-in-law. "Fumi-san, I received a letter from Martin in Canada about ten days ago. He is a kind man and now fully grown. When he was a little boy, I used to play with him, showing him *origami* made with old newspapers. I folded *origami* cranes, airplanes, ships, pigs, that sort of things. He reminded me of you guys."

Tamotsu quickly looked at his father, only to lower his eyes a moment later.

Eizo continued his story.

"In January 1943, the Government of Canada ordered The Custodian of Enemy Alien Property to liquidate the properties and assets of the Nikkei. Until then, many Nikkei believed that the 100-mile 'Protected Area' would become meaningless when the war ended—if it ever ended—, and they'd be able to go back and run their businesses and farms as they did before."

*

'What a thing! The Custodian decided to sell our house,' Matsu-san said to her husband outside their barrack. The grey cloud was hanging low and the chill was felt deep under the skin.

'The Custodian was going to keep our house 'in trust' until the war ends. Isn't that right?' Senkichi-san said.

'That's what I understood. But now, they've decided to sell. When we bought that house six years ago, we paid all in cash. It was not easy for us, remember?'

'Jesus! Who can we trust? I've never forgotten how hard it was to buy that house. I can't forget!'

'What should we do?'

'I've no idea, whatsoever. Nothing has been working for us. Luck gave up on us a long time ago.'

"In the spring of that year, Senkichi-san received a document from The Custodian of Enemy Alien Property, saying that their house was sold at $1,850 and asking them to assent to the sales in return.

'Bloody hell! This can't be the sales price! It's way too low, much less than we paid.' Senkichi-san growled.

'Dirt cheap! But how is it possible for the Custodian to have sold our house? We didn't give them consent to sell.' Matsu-san said.

'What do they think we are? Livestock or worm? Remember how happy we were when we bought that small beauty?' While his anger surged within him, helplessness and his distrust of the Federal Government grew fiercer.

'Yes, we were very happy. We had to pinch and scrape to buy that.'

'On top of that, the Custodian is going to deduct our living costs from the proceeds and send money every month to the British Columbia Security Commission to support us in the camp?'

'Crazy, crazy, crazy! They can't do that.'

'We didn't ask them to confine us into this camp. And we're paying our cost to live here, in the camp! The devil.'

'I don't know what to do.'

'We're in a room with no exit.' Senkichi-san said.

'How are you going to respond to them? You have to say something to them?'

'Okay, I'll just say, 'I acknowledge I received the document.' I'm not going to say I agree to the sale or the price, or anything about the contents of the document. If I say something, it'll be considered that I've agreed with the sale of our property.'

'We should've gone back to Japan.'

'It's too late now ... but think this way. The people in Japan might be in a much worse situation.' Senkichi-san tried to console his wife, as she wiped the tears with the back of her hand. Matsu-san seemed to be giving in to despair.

"The British Columbia Security Commission created jobs in camp, but the food allowance was deducted from the detainee's wages. The detainees were given the difference,

295

if any. Food allowances were given to the Nikkei who had already spent their savings: the savings that were to provide for their old age and their future events, to buy businesses, farmland, fishing boats and their houses and cars.

"I got a job as a fire warden in the camp, because I was a volunteer firefighter before I left Japan," said Eizo. "The camp was huge and there was a fire lookout inside. They paid me twenty-five cents an hour. Sometimes we went out of the camp to help extinguish the forest fires. Those were monstrous fires, licking up the forest in seconds and burning for weeks. Never mind risking our lives, the wage was still twenty-five cents.

"Before I was shipped to the camp and had some money, I sent it to you. It was just before the war broke out, I was about to send money from Vancouver, but banks were already closed for the day. That cash helped me while I was in the camp. I'm sorry you were waiting for the money," Eizo said softly, and they quietly listened to him.

"One day in the spring of 1943, an Issei evacuee named Gentaro said to me, 'Hey, Osada-san. Japan is gonna win the war. You'll be released from the camp,' The Battle of Midway was considered the battle to have changed the fate of the Pacific War and had already taken place early June, 1942, with the decisive victory for the United States.

'Do you think so?'

'Oh, yeah. Look, we're in the camp, detained. But the Japanese Imperial Navy's gonna liberate us from here soon.'

'Soon?'

'Oh, yeah! Remember, what happened in Pearl Harbor? Japan's gonna win.'

'But, that was more than a year ago.'

'Are you saying Japan's gonna lose?' Gentaro spoke high-handedly.

'No, no. I don't mean that. Some Nisei say the Allies are winning, taking good offensives against the Japanese military.'

'Where did they buy that crap? They know nothing! A bunch of greens.'

'They read English newspapers, though.'

'English newspapers tell downright lies! You know that.'

I kept quiet.

'Hey, never believe those guys. They're traitors! We have to knock them down. Badly, you know. We have to teach them a lesson.'

"On April 25th of that year, the Satos and I celebrated Martin's birthday. There was no birthday cake, so Matsu-san bought him a small *manjyu*, a bean-jam bun, from one of the Issei in the camp who had owned a confectionery shop in Vancouver before the war. Martin enjoyed the *manjyu*, chewing it quickly.

'Martin is five years old now. I don't know if he knows the true story of the camp. I don't want to talk about it with him,' Matsu-san said to Senkichi-san.

'We'd better not talk about it. Not yet. He is too small to understand. And there might be a deep negative effect on him, if you talk about it right now.'

'As long as he doesn't ask, it's okay. But if he starts asking me, what should I tell him?'

'Hope he doesn't. I really hope not.'

'You don't have any answer, do you?'

'Well, no, you're right.'

'You're no help.'

"At one point, there were 2,600 evacuees in Tashme camp, all frightened of the future and isolated from the world's current events. The irony was that the Nikkei were

297

able to have 'leisure' for the first time in Canada; they had worked so hard before the war and had not taken any time to relax. There was entertainment in the camps too: plays and Japanese dancing, young Nisei girls danced in *kimono*, amateurs sang popular tunes or the folk songs of their hometowns. Since they had plenty of time to rehearse, the performers polished their talent to a semi-professional level. The Nikkei detainees, old and young, men and women, could not wait until the next performance.

'Hey, the next production is *Okaru/Kanpei*,' Takeji said.

'Really?' Shiro said. 'That *Okaru/Kanpei* who were in love with each other and *Samurai* Kanpei killed Okaru's father—or thought that he had killed him, and then he committed suicide? And Okaru was sold to a red-light district in the old days?'

'Quite right. I saw the play once before at a travelling theater in my village in Japan. I remember I cried.'

'Who's gonna play?'

'The youth group is.'

'This is what we call *Jigoku de hotoke,* meeting the Buddha in a hell.'

'Quite right. I've never seen a real *Kabuki*. So, I'm looking forward to it. What else is possible to do here in the camp, eh?' Takeji was about to cry.

"Also, the Japanese evacuees built the shack to teach Judo to their children. They brought 80 *tatami* mats from Vancouver and laid them on the floor of the shack. It is said that anywhere between 110 and 300 children, depending on the season and year, practiced judo.

"They made *miso* and soy sauce in the camp too and sent the surplus to the *dōhō* living in the ghost towns and in the east of the Rockies.

"I started learning English for the first time since I had arrived in Canada, some eight years ago; I knew neither the basic grammar nor the conjugations of verbs, so my progress was slower than snail's speed. I began by trying to read English newspapers with the help of a dictionary I brought from Japan but had never opened before. What really surprised me to my bone were headlines about the Allies' victory after victory, everywhere in the battle. Those headlines really shook me up.

Is this true? Am I interpreting the English newspaper correctly? Maybe, I'm wrong?

"At the same time, a Japanese newspaper from Denver in USA, *The Rocky Shinpo,* kept reporting Japanese victories on many fronts in the Pacific. Some Issei translated and mimeographed the articles of *The Rocky Shinpo* which reported that the Japanese Imperial Army had *tenshin shita*, changed the directions of their offensives, the expression the Japanese Army coined to camouflage their defeats. As most of the Japanese in Japan believed their victories in the battles as the Army reported, so did many Nikkei in the camp in Canada. Copies that were secretly distributed among the Issei encouraged them to believe the day of Japan's victory was imminent and their liberation was around the corner. The real story was this.

"Some Issei had secretly brought a shortwave radio into the camp, an item forbidden to the Nikkei, and set up two antennas in such a skilful way that no officers from the Commission were able to detect them. Detainees listened to the broadcasts from the Military Headquarters of the Japanese Imperial forces, who concealed the news of their defeats at the frontlines, and distributed the news. Misled Issei were jubilant with the victorious news from Japan.

"I was totally confused by the contradictory news about the war and did not know whom to believe. Isolated in the heart of mountains, I was intellectually blindfolded. The Canadian Postal Censor examined every single piece of mail received and sent by the detainees, whether in English or Japanese and crossed out the lines that were not suitable. Rumours spread swiftly in the closed-up camp and since detainees had a plenty of time, they talked about anything, whether it was true or not. Sometimes an untruth sounded truer than the truth. In one case, a person in the other camp who was rumoured dead turned out to be alive. The worst rumours were ones about the Federal Government's policies that the detainees interpreted or misinterpreted, and spread unintentionally, mainly out of fear.

"With the long, internal and emotional battles about my fate and family, I badly needed something to hang on to and joined a Bible study group, looking for a salvation that I could believe in from the bottom of my heart. I had never picked up a Bible before but now started studying the New Testament in search for salvation. An elderly Japanese, a staunch Christian who had long belonged to a church in Vancouver, led our group and recommended me to study the New Testament which teaches forgiveness. I was influenced by the teaching of forgiveness in the time of my unhappiness, desperation and calamity.

"The education of the Nikkei who were of compulsory school age came under the jurisdiction of the Commission, but they did not have a responsibility to provide kindergarten or high school instruction. Virtuously enough, though, volunteers from the United, the Catholic and the Episcopal Churches, including ones who had been previously assigned as priests in Japan, taught these students in the Tashme camp. They did not charge for their services."

21
Tashme Concentration Camp and the Forced Relocation East

"Newspapers in Canada started reporting the bombings on Japan in the summer of 1944.

"In late November, I saw the photo and read the headlines that Allied forces had bombed Tokyo. At first, I could not believe it. If it were true, the tide of the war was obvious. There were huge discrepancies between the shortwave radio broadcasts from the Military Headquarters of the Japanese Imperial forces in Japan and what the Canadian newspapers reported. Some Nisei believed that the Japanese forces had been defeated in many major fronts and were retreating towards their homeland. While some Issei continued to believe the radio reports, others had doubts the war would end in Japan's victory: Senkichi-san was one of them.

"In April 1944, the Cabinet War Committee of Prime Minister Mackenzie King approved the Loyalty Survey of the Nikkei as a part of 'The final solution of the Japanese problem.' The RCMP conducted the Survey and handled 'Voluntary Repatriation' applications to all Nikkei evacuees age 16 and over. In essence they asked:

1.   Will you go to Japan after the war and 'Declare your desire to relinquish your British nationality?'

2.   Will you relocate east of the Rockies?

"It was quite an odd standard of judgement the government employed to determine loyalty to Canada." Eizo told his family. "If an evacuee said that they wanted to remain in Canada, they were 'loyal' and had to provide an immediate plan to move out of British Columbia; if an evacuee chose Japan or failed to move to the east of the Rocky Mountains, he or she was deemed to be 'disloyal' to Canada. Regardless of the Nikkei's choice, the Canadian government intended to either deport evacuees to Japan or disperse them across the country away from British Columbia."

*

"The Loyalty Survey began in the Tashme camp on Friday, April 13th, 1945. A young RCMP officer and a man in a grey suit were seated at a table to conduct the survey.

'Please identify yourself,' the RCPM officer said to a young Nisei, sitting across the table.

'I am Derek Naruo Kubota.'

'Your birth date?'

'February 14th, 1927.'

'So, you are … how old?'

'I'm eighteen years old, sir.'

'Good. Your nationality is?'

'I've a dual citizenship, Canadian and Japanese.'

"I was listening to their conversation, waiting my turn." Eizo said in the living room, wiping his forehead with his fingers.

'Do you have a job?' the officer said.

'No, I don't.' Derek Naruo said.

'All right. Do you want to return to Japan or stay in Canada? If you want to stay in Canada, you have to move east of the Rockies.'

'Jesus Christ! What do you mean by "Return to Japan," sir? I'm a Canadian citizen. This is my home. My country.' The young Nisei raised his voice. 'The Canadian government and you people are deporting me from Canada where I was born and brought up! You want us to disappear from your sight.'

'Don't swear in front of the officers! Understood? All right. Return to Japan or stay in Canada?' The RCMP officer ignored the young Nisei's protests.

'I was born here. In Canada! There is no other place for me to 'return' to.' The young man spoke as if he were angry, but pleading for his life at the same time. 'This is the country where I pledged my loyalty, not Japan.'

"I could see only the back of the young Nisei's head, whose voice was breaking.

'We're doing our duty. This is the policy that our government in Ottawa decided to pursue. If you pledged your loyalty to Canada, then, there's only one answer for you.'

'Yes, I'm going to stay in Canada, stay in Canada! This is our home country, nowhere else'

'Well then, you have to relocate east of the Rockies.'

'Do I have to?'

'It's your decision. But not in British Columbia. Remember, this is the loyalty question.'

'Okay, okay, sir. I'll go east. There's not much choice, is there, sir?'

'To which province?'

'To which province?' The young Nisei thought about it for a moment. 'I don't know.'

'Think hard and fast.'

'Okay… I'll go to Ontario.'

'All right. To Ontario.' The RCMP officer nodded and recorded his answer. 'Now, you should see the relocation officer from the Labour Department.' He waved his hand to indicate the man in grey suit who was seated beside him. 'And this gentleman can tell you about the job opportunities in Ontario.'

'I'm entirely worthless here, just like a dead mouse. Or less than that. A dead mouse is more worthy than us. At least it's dead and won't bother you anymore.'

'Do not swear in front of the officers, okay?'

"The next interviewee was an Issei who had to use an interpreter.

'My son is in Ontario, at a sugar beets farm.'

'A sugar beets farm in Ontario?'

'Yes, sir. He went there with the sugar beets project.'

'All right.'

'I have to talk to my son before I decide the matter.'

'Don't worry. You son will be looked after by the RCMP in Ontario.'

'But, I'd like to talk to him before I decide. Otherwise, we might end up living in Canada and Japan, separately.'

'Then report your decision to us by five o'clock at the end of this month.'

'Sir, there isn't enough time to think about it and send a letter to him and then receive his response.'

'That's too bad.'

'But … and I have a twelve-year-old daughter and I can't leave her alone in Canada. What would you think I should do?'

'I'm not in a position to give you any advice.'

'I don't know what you're saying, but I'm in a deep trouble, sir.'

"The RCMP officer ended the interview.

"My turn came next. I used an interpreter as well to avoid any mistakes.

'You're a Japanese national?' the RCMP officer asked.

'Yes, I am, sir.'

'Did you read the two notices from the Labour Department recently posted in the camp?'

'Yes, sir. I read the translated version into Japanese.'

'Then what's your intention? Are you going to return to Japan, or stay in Canada?'

'Do you know what's really going on in the war, sir?' I managed to ask before giving my answer.

'That's not my duty to tell you about that. Are you going to return to Japan or stay in Canada?'

'I don't really know the situation about the war, sir. We're so isolated and cut off here. I ought to know more before I decide.'

'If you're unable to answer right now, report your decision to us by five o'clock at the end of the month, Monday, the week after next. All right. Next.'

"That was the end of my interview."

*

Eizo continued speaking to his sons and Fumi. "It was a terrible time then. Everybody in the camp was desperate, particularly those who had already signed the repatriation papers. We didn't know what was really going on in the war and what was happening in Japan. I debated for about ten days, wondering if the Canadian newspapers had been reporting the truth about the war and whether I should stay

305

in Canada to keep sending money to you. Or, were they misleading us? That was possible, very possible, indeed. But I saw newspaper photographs of big B-29 bombers in formation with vapor trails over the land of Japan. It was a large formation of bombers, and I was worried about Tokyo, lying in ruins. It was painful to imagine that. I had to make a hard decision. I finally decided to stay in Canada for the sake of the money to send home to you. Some Issei held on to the idea of Japan's victory until the end of the war. But after I told the RCMP of my decision, the newspapers reported the sudden surrender of Germany. The headline was so big—I felt dizzy at the news."

Eizo told of the upheaval and confusion of the event. Most of the Issei were getting old. It was simply too much for them to start their life from scratch all over again, either in Canada or Japan, especially in the unknown eastern provinces, and no doubt under discriminatory circumstances. Many of them could not take it any longer and decided to go back to Japan, unwillingly.

In most of the cases, the youngest Nisei son or daughter of the family, who may have wished to stay in Canada, had to sign the repatriation paper in order to accompany their aged parents deported back to Japan, while their elder siblings in the east decided to stay in Canada. There were a lot of sad stories around that time, explained Eizo in the living room.

"After Germany's surrender, I had suffered from mental agony for about three months. Thinking about the Germany's surrender and the bombing of Tokyo by the Americans, I felt very depressed. Other Issei were still talking about Japan's victory. All kinds of rumors spread. I was confused. There was no one to talk about my true feelings. Irritated, I was aggravated even looking at the quiet and lonesome view of the camp that was seen from the fire lookout. It was unbelievably still. And then one morning, I read the newspaper headlines that reported the A-bombs dropped on Hiroshima. Three days later at Nagasaki. I didn't know what it meant to Japan until one Nisei told me.

"Soon after that, a rumor circulated among some Nisei that Japan had accepted the Potsdam Declaration and made overtures to accept her surrender to the U. S. Government. But the bombings on Japan by the Americans were still being carried on. And after that, the war all of a sudden, all of a sudden, came to an end.

"I still clearly remember the day I heard the news: the siren went on at dawn in the camp. I got up and looked outside but not a single thing was happening. I talked to my *dōhō* in the barrack but he didn't know anything about the siren either. We went back to bed. But a little later, from nowhere, a Nisei jumped out onto the main street of the camp, opened his both arms and ran through the street, repeatedly shouting, 'Japan surrendered! The war's over! Japan surrendered!' Then evacuees dashed out onto the main street, throwing up what they were doing.

"I went out, too, quite unprepared. The leaves of the trees were trembling with the breeze as usual, but I saw several Issei lose their heads, void of any expression. Soon one Issei started crying, clasping his hands almost in the gesture of prayer. Another Issei sank down weakly to the ground. Those were the ones who had believed in Japan's victory. Somewhere in my mind, I had expected the war would come to an end one day. Even so, it was so sudden, as if the time had stopped moving. I remember all the strength left my body, my spirit collapsed flat, and I felt as if I were vanishing into the sky. After that, I could hear and see nothing for a while, as if the world were dead. To me, the world was a

307

desert, all in yellow, totally perished, dead. Later, I heard that, in Lethbridge, Alberta, the Canadian people gathered to a public square with the news and burnt the effigies of *Tenno*, Hitler and Mussolini with the shouts of joy…" Eizo told his sons and Fumi.

That moment in the living room, only raindrops on the roof were heard. Nobody said anything, except Eizo who now seemed to have gained the complete control of the room. He thought that he had appealed his difficulties to his three sons and Fumi sufficient enough and that the purpose of the meeting was nearly accomplished in his favour.

Eizo breathed once and looked around at everyone casting their eyes at the ashes. He then carried on.

"I heard that the War Measures Act was good until the end of 1945 and that the government had introduced another bill that had the same effect and had somehow made it a law. We, the Nikkei, took legal action against the federal government. I know that there suddenly emerged enormous protests from every corner of the Canadian society: church groups, universities, newspapers and civil organizations as well as the Nikkei. The previous perception the Canadians had had about the repatriation of the Japanese changed course quickly. That had something to do with universal civil rights. In a nutshell, what it meant was, I guess, if the government could do anything under that law, other Canadians in general, in the future, could be affected in the same way as the Nikkei had been affected. Canadians supported us this time. Probably, for the first time ever!"

Eizo's eyes grew moist as he spoke, while his three sons and Fumi listened in silence.

"Although the Nikkei didn't have much money, we raised funds to challenge the bill. I don't know every detail, and all those details probably don't matter to you guys, one way or another, anyway. There were a lot of legal and political fights in Canada and I later heard the appeal was even brought to the Privy Council in London, Great Britain, for the final decision and that in turn Great Britain supported the position of the Canadian government. But, all I can say is that the church groups were very helpful throughout the concentration camps, fights against the repatriation of the Nikkei and finding us jobs and housing in Canada, all the way through.

"After the end of the war, many Nikkei who decided to go back to Japan had second thoughts about returning to the war-torn and devastated Japan and had made requests to annul their repatriation declaration. As of November 21st, 1945, about 6,900 Nikkei were involved in the repatriation documentations, and when children were included, the number swelled to 10,300, about half of the total Nikkei population in Canada. Of that figure, more than 4,300 were the Issei.

"Prime Minister King had been in contact with General Douglas MacArthur, the Supreme Commander of the Allied Forces in occupied Japan, on the timing to repatriate the Nikkei. It was unlikely that MacArthur would accept repatriates within the year 1945 because he knew that there was already enough starvation and unemployment in the burnt ruins of Japan.

"In the middle of May the following year, four buses arrived at the camp. The buses were to take the repatriates to the Hope Station, then to the Port of Vancouver by rail. There were more than one hundred desperate Nikkei waiting for the buses. I don't know how the Nisei could've afforded to travel from Ontario and Quebec to the camp, but they came to see their parents and young siblings off—it might've been the last time to see them. They helped their parents load their trunks and other belongings into the buses and hugged and kissed them. Most of them were crying openly. It was heart-rending to watch families split up again. Most of them followed their families to the Hope Station, some even to the Port of Vancouver, and were loath to part from their parents and siblings again. Tashme camp became the assembly base for the repatriates to be shipped to Japan. There was nothing I could do but watch those agonizing farewells. I cried every time when I saw them parting from each other." Eizo stopped for a moment, struggling, and wiped his cheeks under the eyes with his fingers. "The Nisei were worried how their elderly parents would physically and financially cope in Japan and their younger siblings were apprehensive as to how they could survive where their language skills were limited and in a country they had never seen.

"On May 22nd, 1946, having acquired the assent from General MacArthur, the Government of Canada shipped the first 800 Nikkei to Japan by ship from the Port of Vancouver.

"In July 1946, I, with my fellow detainees, were crammed into a freight car filled with the strong stench of animals. We were shipped out of the concentration camp to one of the hostels in Summerville, Ontario, where the Federal Government provided temporary shelter. As the placement officer in the camp arranged, I started my job at a farm, together with several other Nikkei. After having lived in Canada for eleven years, mostly in Japanese speaking environments—the logging camp and concentration camp—, I was thrown into the world where Japanese was no longer the language to communicate. My struggles in language and daily life continued." Eizo took a deep breath again.

"The owner of the farm provided a garage for us to live in. Ontario is much colder than British Columbia in winter.

Sometimes the temperature went down to minus forty. I harvested sugar beet, pulling them out from the ground, cutting the leaves and loading them on the trucks. The next season, I thinned the sugar beet in the fields with a hoe for long hours every day and that reminded me of my work here in Gifu and you guys. Although I had decided to stay in Canada in the interview with the RCMP, I started preparing for coming back home, saving every surplus penny from my basic living needs again. My wage was thirty-five cents an hour—mere chicken feed but a tad higher than I was paid in the concentration camp—while the white workers were paid double or even more. The Japanese were cheap labourers, enduring the poor living conditions and doing the job more conscientiously. Nobody thought it was injustice in those days. One day, I was walking in the town nearby the farm and saw a woman peeping at me from behind a curtain. The moment when our eyes met, she hid. It was a very rural area and probably she had never seen an Oriental before," Eizo said, allowing a small grin.

"After a while, I quit my job and went to Toronto, a big city, to earn more money. I had to find a place to live, and walking along a street, I saw a 'Room to Let' sign. I knocked on the door of the house, and as soon as the owner saw me, he slammed the door in my face. I was shocked. I eventually found a room, paying a much higher rent to the owner. Some Nikkei who had landed city jobs were laid off when the owner found out they were Japanese. We sought invisibility. We didn't want to stand out and we lived like shadows. We knew from the past experience that being conspicuous in Canada is a bad thing. We always sat in the corner seats of bus, streetcars, and restaurants."

Eizo looked towards his wife's room. "I was so glad when I received a reply letter from your mom for the first

311

time since the war ended and read that all of you were well. But the life in Japan seemed to have been still very difficult, filled with poverty, and I thought that I had made the right decision."

He explained to his sons how he had followed the newspapers that were reporting on the legal fight between the Nikkei and the federal government both in Canada and in Great Britain concerning the legality of the deportation. Opposition by Canadian society to the deportation of their own citizens was growing stronger. The repatriations were finally suspended. On January 24th, 1947, Prime Minister King rescinded the repatriation order to the Nikkei, but by then almost 4,000 Nikkei had been shipped to Japan.

The year 1947 also witnessed the increment of claims by the Nikkei for the losses caused by compulsory property disposition during the war: namely, the difference between the low sale prices and the 'fair market value' of their properties.

"Senkichi-san was one of the claimants. The Japanese Property Claims Commission was created to examine and handle the cases. Senkichi-san did not say the exact number, but he did say that what his family had received as compensation was a far cry from what the fair market price would have been at the time of the sale. All the while, I was a *denden-mushi,* moving from one job to another with my all belongings on my back. I was affected the least."

After having been 'dispersed' east of the Rockies, Eizo said the Nikkei did not form their own ghetto like Little Tokyo but scattered in Toronto and other cities and lived quietly. They did not use Japanese in daily conversation and tried hard to assimilate into the *hakujin* society. Some even concealed their Japanese identity, unwilling to be visited by the *dōhō,* and in an extreme case, one man changed his

312

surname to an English one. They became unobtrusive beings within Canadian society and lived a scared life worrying if and when their properties would be dispossessed by the government again.

"After having worked as a gardener, cleaner, popcorn maker at a movie theatre and swamper to a truck driver, I finally found steady work at a soft drink company located in a suburb of Toronto." Eizo told his family.

"I had been very worried about how to send money to you guys until I found a job at the Hi-Lite Soft Drink Company, so I was very happy. But the noise of factory machinery was unbearable and the work was monotonous. I was always feeling ill. How could I afford to become sick? When I thought about Kino and you guys, I fought against it. I don't know how many times I thought about coming back to Japan and I should've come back regardless of my situation in Canada …

"The Issei and Nisei did not tell the Sansei about the hardships they suffered during the war, the terribly excessive punishments that had been committed against the Nikkei by the Canadian government. They did not want to extinguish the light of hope for the Sansei's future in Canada by telling them what had happened to their parents and grandparents. The bitter irony was that this silence earned only criticism by the Sansei. The younger generation insisted they had a right to know and those who had been stripped of their fundamental civil rights, for no reason other than race, should have told them the story.

"However, the Nikkei's excruciating memories were that they had to start all over again and move towards a new destination. Willingly or unwillingly, that was all they could do for tomorrow and have a new hope within the landscape of the Canadian society. To move on! To take one step forward into the new environment and the future!"

That was the story Eizo told his sons and Fumi at his home in Gifu.

22
If My Wife Just Disappeared ...

Everyone sitting around the hearth was quiet as Eizo had been talking about his experience. It was only Tamotsu who contributed to Eizo's talk, and he asked a few questions. He cast pitiful looks at his father whenever Eizo spoke of the difficulties he had faced. Isoshichi kept gazing at the ashes like a bronze statue, although he hid his antipathy against his father and his long enduring years of pain that came from Kino's behaviour. His face was tense and no word of comfort to his father was spoken. Kozo appeared to be considering something intently, crossing and uncrossing his arms, but kept his expression neutral. It seemed that he neither had an attachment to, nor cared about, his father.

If Eizo had missed something during his talk, those were Isoshichi's and Kozo's attitudes toward him. Fumi kept looking down most of the time and moved the fire tongs through the ashes as though writing something in them. Judging from what she was doing, Eizo was again forced to think that he had no blood relationship between her and him and that he had failed to establish a rapport and trust with her. But Eizo had a purpose. Tamotsu's few questions also supported him to carry through on.

"Twenty-three years ago I wrote a letter to your mom and told her that I wanted to come home." Eizo stopped his story there, hoping that his wife might be listening from the next room. He thought perhaps Kino was crouching in the darkness listening and thinking.

Listening and thinking? She's insane. What could she possibly be thinking? But, why is it so quiet there? She is usually fidgeting. Has she been listening to me all along? No, no, that's impossible.

"Soon after that, I received a reply. She said there were no jobs due to the impact of the war and that I ought to stay in Canada and keep sending money home. When I was in the camps, some Nisei showed me newspaper photos of Hiroshima's destruction—the photo that showed the miles of destruction that had been wiped out by the A-bomb. So I believed staying in Canada was the best thing to do under the circumstances."

Eizo paused. "I've already shown the letter to Tamotsu and Kozo. That was the last time that I heard from your mom."

Kozo looked at Eizo suspiciously and appeared to be assessing what his father might say next. His eyes were that of a shrewd businessman who was considering the possible answers to any questions the counterpart might ask him in a business deal. He seemed to be ready to challenge his father.

Eizo reflected on his wife's affair and troubled over how he would broach the subject. He had already talked with Tamotsu and Kozo about it, but had to seize an opportunity to talk to Isoshichi and Fumi. They knew little about the contents of the letter, or so Eizo had thought. Isoshichi had shown little surprise and no interest in its existence before. But Eizo would not have been surprised if perhaps one of his other sons had already brought it to attention of the eldest son.

It might not be impossible that Isoshichi had known of the letter. No, no ... if he had known about its contents before,

316

then his attitude towards me now is his way of saying there can be no reconciliation.

"Isoshichi …" Eizo said softly, no longer being able to contain the question. "Did you know about the letter your mom sent to me before she became sick?"

" … No, I didn't know," Isoshichi said, still staring into the ashes in the hearth.

Eizo couldn't tell if his son spoke the truth or not and thought himself a miserable old man to suspect any of his sons of lying. He realized there was no choice but to accept this as the truth.

Kozo had said that Isoshichi had let Kino do whatever she liked when she came home from the hospital after the affair. She must've told Isoshichi that she wanted me to stay away. But then … the only the time she could've spoken about the letter was after she came home completely dejected. No, no, she wouldn't have then. Had Isoshichi known of her intrigue before she committed to it? Shouldn't that make his attitude toward me more conciliatory?

"If you want to see it, I have it here with me."

No response from Isoshichi.

"When I received that letter from your mom, I was ready to come home but shortly after that, I lent my money to one of my colleagues. But that man never repaid it. He died with some renal disease. When I think of it now, it was a stupid mistake." Eizo did not see any response from his sons. He continued, "Realistically speaking, there wouldn't have been any work in Japan for me, anyway. I was getting too old to find the type of work I'd need to feed you guys. It would've been foolish to try. Of course, I checked fares at the shipping companies and airlines but they were very expensive, and after that letter, I couldn't simply come home." Eizo waited, hoping for some reaction from Isoshichi.

317

There was only silence.

The humidity had become oppressive. Their clothing was sticking uncomfortably to their skin. Rain began drumming loudly on the roof.

"I never forgot about you, never gave up the hope that I'd come home. Please understand at least that point," Eizo said, gasping for air. A deep, unbearable fatigue came over him.

" … As I listened, you had made a conscious choice not to come home earlier. Did you know Mom had become so ill?" Those were Kozo's first words.

"No, I didn't know. No one told me. How many letters did I send and received no response? I wish you had told me," Eizo responded quickly.

How can I be blamed for not knowing such an important family matter?

He looked at his three sons in turn and then remembered that his intent was not to confront them. But still, he hoped that they would at least try to understand what he had been through, even if they didn't feel compelled to welcome him home.

"I am the youngest, but I saw how Mom, Isoshichi and Tamotsu struggled through their life. Being a small child, I realized how Mom was exhausted at the end of the day and sat at this hearth alone with a heavy heart. Looking at Mom, I sometimes called to her and she forced a smile and patted me on the head and gently said to go to bed."

Listening to that, Eizo could not look straight at his third son.

Kozo inhaled deeply, raising his shoulders and casting a quick glance at his father, and continued, "Mom had to bring us up. Mom shouldered the heavy burden of raising us, supporting us, cultivating the fields, managing the family finances, preparing meals, laundry, raising silkworms and keeping up appearances in the town. Mom did all those by herself. Isoshichi and Tamotsu struggled through their life when they were young. Mom didn't have anybody she could rely on. When the instructor of sericulture came to her, there was no way she could resist him. Who can blame her? Mom must've felt saved by his appearance. And the contempt and ridicule of the townspeople followed … for years. The most affected were Isoshichi and Fumi-san. You don't understand how it was a sad, lonesome, painful, miserable, pathetic and unrewarding battle for us. Never think Mom had been unfaithful to you! Mom raised us with love. We love Mom." Kozo said those words without a hitch as if upbraiding his subordinate and again breathed deeply. Eizo's name was not mentioned even once.

Isoshichi's face was softened with his eyes slightly moist, a rare moment for the man who had never shown his emotions. Tamotsu, taken by surprise, stared at his younger brother. Fumi was tense, looking at the ashes of the hearth with her shoulders dropped. Eizo instinctively shrunk up and hung his head. He was terribly ashamed of having selfishly told his story and not paying attention to the story of his family. He blamed this on his solitary existence in a foreign country, only making decisions for himself. He lost his sense of balance. *Hang it all!*

"Did you ever think about us seriously? You haven't told us why you didn't come back after you settled in Toronto. You became a Canadian citizen. Seems to me like you had forgotten us." Kozo stated brusquely.

"Yes … yes, of course," Eizo said, screwing up his face, now painfully comprehending the true feelings of his sons. He was forced to understand that his sons had lived in an entirely different world, and so still lived in this world where their blame towards him underlay everything. He felt his effort having been all for naught. "You were in my thoughts every day. But, as you say, the reasons I have given you …" His voice trailed off, struggling to answer Kozo's question. He might have been able to explain away his absence up to the end of the war, but the thirty-some years after that was more difficult to excuse. The contents of Kino's last letter now appeared a minor reason. His negligence and inability to grasp the passing of time could not be made clear—it was as if he had been holding fine sand in his cupped hands, and it had slipped through his fingers little by little, until finally he had realized the sand was almost all gone.

"I wonder if you had your own woman in Canada," Kozo snapped.

Given the incident of Kino's elopement, Eizo thought it was not unnatural that Kozo was suspicious about this in Canada.

Why else would one stay for so long? It is only normal for them to suspect me. Their mother's infidelity was their only example.

"No, no. I didn't have anyone like that. I've been alone, from the beginning to the end of my stay in Canada," said Eizo, shifting his body slightly to face Kozo more directly.

Only Tamotsu's face showed a small measure of relief. Eizo could not see any change in the expression on Isoshichi and Kozo. The sound of rain dominated the living room. He suddenly felt a more profound sadness and helplessness.

Eizo knew that he had put all his energy into what he had believed was right, though his life in Canada was not what he wanted or sought. To his chagrin, it was now clear that his three sons could not comprehend this and did not recognize any value in the hard life that he had lived.

Where did I do wrong, except to do my duty?

But Eizo was torn between his own defence and defending his sons.

For the family's sake it should be the father's duty to come back home.

If his sons accused him of not returning earlier, Eizo did not have a legitimate answer that they could understand or accept. He had already told them what had happened to him in Canada and there was nothing else he could do. He momentarily drifted into thoughts of Senkichi and of Martin. He recalled the care and respect they had shown him.

Leaving Kino like this? I have an obligation to look after her. She is my wife!

"Will you be getting a pension from Canada?" Kozo asked, interrupting his father's thoughts.

"Yes … well, it's not much, but I'm getting one."

The relief was evident in his sons' faces.

"What is this all about?" Eizo asked.

"No, nothing," Kozo said, averting his gaze.

Eizo had wanted to ask if he could live with them, but now he could not. His attempt to gain his sons' understanding turned out to be a complete failure, so did his hope to live with them. The burden resting on Isoshichi because of his insane mother was too heavy to clear away by only telling them his experience. But he struggled with a growing resentment toward his sons for not showing even a flicker of compassion. He felt a particular bitterness toward Tamotsu, who appeared to care but failed to support him when he needed it most. The deeper Eizo put his trust in his second son, the deeper the hurt. He was fatigued and he felt that time had flown far, far away from him while at the same time stretching infinitely in front of him.

"My dearest! Please come back to me quickly," suddenly, Kino called in other room.

Everyone jerked. Eizo saw the torment on Isoshichi's face and turned his face from his son. His existence was denied by his wife, and feeling beaten, Eizo closed his eyes. The memory of Kino and her cry to call her lover on his first day home flitted through his mind with bitterness. At that time, there was a stark disappointment and upset but sheer hope as well for him, since he did not know the outcome of his return. But now, that hope was melting like an ice cube under the burning sun.

Isoshichi fixed his gaze on his father. He was flushed, his eyes red, anger naked on his face. But, he still kept his silence and straightened his back as if restraining himself. Fumi looked at Eizo nervously. She glanced at Tamotsu and Kozo then looked at her husband.

When Tamotsu's eyes met Eizo's he turned away. After that he kept his face toward his mother's room. Kozo's face was pale, his emotions wiped away. He turned his sharp eyes upon everyone in the room. The clock ticked interminably in the background. A grim mood ruled the room.

Eizo finally broke the silence. "I think … having you gather here today … was pointless. I understand now what you have been thinking about me all these years. I guess I had expected unreal things, like a grateful and understanding family. I'd … rather go back to Canada … if it were not for my obligation to your mother."

His sons looked up at him like they had been slapped. They looked around at each other as if trying to search for an answer on each other's faces.

They had already reached their conclusions before my talk started, for sure. Can I spend my last days here? Am I ready to accept Isoshichi's resentful silence and live with the wife who still reveres the memories of another man? It would be a hell.

But his family had endured the derisions of the community while taking care of their mother.

Would I have the same courage to face such scorn in my old age? I don't know.

The home he had long dreamt of had vanished; perhaps it had never existed. His sons remained mute. He understood well that his presence was undesired and that he would be a burden. He was a trespasser, an obstacle in their already difficult lives. Their father, indeed, was only a father by blood, and they refused to grant the honour of calling him *Otō-san*. Eizo had hoped for some warm words from his family. Now he was looking for any words, even reproach. "Please say something! You must have something to say to your father." He knew his plea did not tug at their heartstrings. His eyes gradually filled with tears.

"… What do you want us to do for you?" Tamotsu asked timidly, as if being unable to combat his guilt any longer, and looked at his brothers for support.

Kozo caught Tamotsu with the corner of his eye, but Isoshichi was still staring into the ashes of the hearth. Only the rain and the clock answered the heavy silence.

Eizo had already lost direction in his thinking and struggled to answer the most important question his sons had posed for him. "I don't know anymore," he mumbled, overwhelmed by fatigue. "I don't know anymore." With that, he slowly rose to his feet and left the room.

When Eizo staggered into the bedroom, he found that his wife was lying in her *futon* with her back to him. Her dishevelled white hair stuck out from under the *futon*; pieces of straw were entangled here and there. Her frame barely visible in the shape of the blanket revealed how small she truly was; Eizo wouldn't have known she was there except for her hair. He closed the sliding door to the bedroom and held it tightly, resisting the dizziness and the desire to collapse onto the *futon*. Turning to look down at Kino's back, Eizo recalled his second night back in Japan. She had been sitting here with an unfocussed gaze, a rot pungent smell in the room. Eizo remembered giving her the evening bag, watching her tear the package apart and how she had taken the bag in both hands and stroked the alligator skin artlessly with her dirty fingers. *Shit!* No longer able to stand, Eizo turned, made his own bed and lay down.

Was there any love between this woman and me? Did I ever love her?

He remembered their wedding, their three children, and life as a family.

Perhaps the love I felt was only for the children. Did I really love her to the point that... I could not live without her?

Fatigue finally drew the last of his strength. Reality wore on his body heavily, its dark, wide mouth about to swallow him as he began to slip into the embrace of unconsciousness. Time did not seem to proceed in a linear direction anymore; it whirled around in a vortex coming back on itself. His existence was limited to the confines of his own gauntness. Yet sleep did not come. The smell of decay in the room attacked his senses. He couldn't remember how long he had been on the *futon*. Eizo looked over at his wife; he could not hear her breathing. Suddenly he stiffened, captured by the idea of his wife no longer here.

If I didn't feel obliged to look after Kino and she disappeared, I could retire quietly to Canada. My dilemma would be resolved.

Beside him, his wife was almost as half the size she was when she was healthy. He thought of their world of sorrow.

Why do I have to face these difficulties?

No answer.

He wanted to turn off the light. Everything felt like it had sunk a little, softened, like his pain. He tried to stand, but couldn't. He ordered himself to move, but his body would not react. His arms wobbled. Finally, with the slowness of one trying to escape a dream, he rose to turn off the light and fell back down onto the *futon* again. The discussion with his sons intruded into his thoughts. And the hoarse voice crying out to her lover still rang in his ears. Next to him Kino was perfectly still.

If my wife just disappeared ...

Eizo's body flinched and his breathing suddenly became laboured. He tried to push the horrible thought away. To relieve the pain, he rubbed his chest and felt its miserable boniness: thoughts of the frailty of human life prevented him from dropping right off to sleep.

23
An Investigation

"Whaa ... a body was found? What do you mean it looks like my mother?"

Eizo sluggishly woke to Isoshichi's muffled, but loud voice.

Two plain-clothes detectives stood in front of Eizo's house. It was around seven thirty in the morning. Fumi ran to Isoshichi's side from the kitchen, her slippers slapping on the floor as she crossed to the front door. "Isn't she here? *Okā-san* ... Toshio, check on your granny!"

Toshio ran to his grandmother's room and slid open the door with a crash. Eizo sat up slowly and looked at the *futon* beside him. "What's going on?"

"Grandma!" Toshio yelled, ignoring his grandfather as he lifted the half-turned top *futon* of his grandmother's bed. Her evening bag was on the floor.

"Grandma's not here!" Toshio yelled out to the living room.

"What happened?" Tamotsu and Kozo called as they rushed into the living room.

"... In the irrigation river in Mizusawa," Isoshichi repeated dumbly after the detective.

"What?" Eizo asked Toshio again, slowly getting up.

"Grandma's dead!"

"Whaa ... dead?"

"The police said Grandma was found dead in a river."

"Dead in a river? Aa … where?"

"In Mizusawa."

"Mizusawa?" repeated Eizo.

"Yes! Grandpa, didn't you take off your clothes last night?"

Eizo looked down at himself. He did not answer his grandson's question as they made their way into the living room. Two detectives, both wearing beige-coloured raincoats, were just outside the entrance. Eizo bowed deeply to them.

"I'm Detective Bito and this is Detective Hoshino."

Detective Bito was stocky, looked like an intimidating judo player, with his lips tightened, cropped hair and square jaw. Hoshino was tall and thin and seemed rather nervous, jiggling his left foot, shooting quick glances at Eizo.

"We must go to the Prefectural Police headquarters to identify the body. Will you come?" Tamotsu asked Eizo, dismay written on his face.

"Ah … y-yes, I will, but … how …" Eizo stuttered, seemingly confused about what had transpired so early in the morning.

Everyone was discussing who should go with Eizo. Isoshichi settled the matter suggesting he and Tamotsu should accompany him.

"Fumi, tell the head house, but don't tell anybody else about this yet," Isoshichi said firmly before leaving.

"I understand," Fumi said with clarity despite being shaken by the situation.

Eizo slipped on his shoes and went out of the entrance. Detective Bito patted Eizo on the shoulder as if urging him to come to the police headquarters.

The rain that had been pouring down the previous night had ceased; the air felt fresh. Isoshichi expeditiously climbed in behind the steering wheel. Tamotsu and Eizo sat in the passenger seat. They followed closely behind the detectives' car.

"How do the police know it is Mom?" Tamotsu asked as they pulled out of the drive.

"They didn't say. Maybe someone went to check the water levels in the rice fields and found Mom and called the police."

"Did the police say anything else?"

"No, nothing," Isoshichi answered bluntly without taking his eyes off the car in front of them.

On the way to the station the detectives made a detour, passing through Mizusawa. Eizo and his sons peered from the car windows to see if they could find any trace of Kino. Instead, they saw two police cars parked on the roadside and two policemen guarding the area cordoned off with police tape fluttering in the breeze and looking at the two cars driving away.

"I hate to think what everyone in the town will say about this," Isoshichi growled under his breath.

"Don't think about that right now," Tamotsu said trying to calm his elder brother.

"You say that so easily."

Tamotsu said nothing.

"You don't know what it's like here because you live in Tokyo."

"I know that, brother. Calm down," Tamotsu said.

Eizo could not say anything and just stared out the window in front of him. It was Sunday morning; the traffic was light.

Half an hour later they arrived at the Prefectural Police department, a tall reinforced concrete building with an extended radio antenna on the top, giving it a cold but dignified appearance. Entering the building, the three were guided by the two detectives to an elevator and then through the hallways to one of the rooms in the back, passing uniformed policemen along the way.

As they entered the chamber, they saw the body lying on a table wrapped with a white cover. One of the detectives lifted the cover to the chest of the body and asked Eizo to look at her.

The face of the female body was grey with fewer wrinkles, swollen from submersion in water. It was Kino. Her hair was a little muddy and still wet, clinging to her head and face. Eizo saw an eternal stillness in her lifeless features.

He choked on a sob and then broke down and cried openly. Tamotsu held Eizo's arm to support him.

Eizo stuttered finally, "Yes, this is my wife …"

"What is your wife's name?"

"Kino."

"I'm asking you your wife's full name," Detective Bito said to Eizo.

"Kino, Kino Osada."

Hoshino wrote it down to his notebook with a black cover.

Detective Bito placed the white cover over Kino's upper body, and the two detectives asked the three men to follow them. They came to an interrogation room where Eizo was motioned to go in first.

"Please follow Detective Hoshino," said the stocky detective as he blocked the doorway indicating Isoshichi and Tamotsu to follow him to another area down the hall.

The room provided a table and four chairs. The detective showed Eizo a chair and sat down across the table from him.

"What's your name and relationship to the deceased?" Detective Bito asked abruptly and without formality, already knowing the answer.

Eizo answered slowly, still feeling uneasy.

Detective Hoshino came into the room silently and sat down off to the side. He cleared his throat loudly, as if intimidating Eizo, without covering his mouth.

"What time did you last see your wife?" Detective Bito asked.

"I don't know exactly ... probably at around two o'clock last night."

"Around two? Late at night. What were you doing?"

"I was lying down trying to sleep but I couldn't fall asleep."

"Why? What were you worried about?"

"... I was worried about my wife." Eizo placed both hands on his thighs.

"Worried about your wife? So, where were you last night? Until six o'clock this morning?"

"At home."

"Did you go outside at all?"

"No, I didn't."

Detective Bito stared at Eizo for a minute. "Were you lying down with your wife in the same room?"

Eizo explained that they slept on separate *futons* in the same room. He blurted out that Kino had been insane for the last twenty-three years and that he had recently returned from a long absence in Canada. After his talk, he felt uneasy, though he had not said anything wrong. He added that they were not in a conjugal relationship. This was more than the detective asked, but Eizo somehow could not help himself.

"You wife was insane. Was that why you were not sleeping with your wife?"

"She didn't want me near her."

Detective Bito gazed at Eizo, "What did you think about that?"

"… I thought there was nothing I could do about it."

"Do you resent her for that?"

"Ah no, I didn't, of course not."

"Did you detest her because of her insanity?"

"No. I felt pity for her."

"Pity? Why did you feel pity for her?"

"She had been working hard, alone, and raised three sons while I was away. And then to lose her sanity … Yes, I felt pity."

"Did you want to do something for her? Because of her insanity?"

"Yes, I wanted to make up for my long absence."

"You felt pity for your wife and wanted to do something? What did you do?" asked Bito. Detective Hoshino stared at Eizo.

"I took care of her."

"You took care of her? How?"

"When she went out, I followed her everywhere she went. I didn't want her to get involved in trouble."

"Did you take care of her more than that?"

"No."

The two detectives looked at each other and then Detective Bito changed the direction of the questioning. "Didn't you notice when your wife left the room last night?"

"No, I didn't."

The two detectives watched Eizo's every twitch.

"Did she leave anything, like a will, for you or for your family?"

"…I woke when you came this morning. We left immediately so I didn't look around. My son would know more about it. Besides, my wife having been like that, I couldn't talk to her about that kind of thing."

"Like what?"

"Kino was insane! I doubt very much if she had prepared a will."

"Hmm … do you remember this rope?" asked Bito, showing Eizo a rope roughly three metres long.

"No, I don't."

"Try harder. It's for your good to recall." The detective was gradually probing into his behaviour of last night.

"No, I can't. I've never seen that rope before. What is that for?"

The two detectives glanced at each other again, but did not answer his question.

"You don't know anything about the rope?"

"No, I don't."

"Was there anything unusual about her last night?"

Eizo awkwardly began to explain the family meeting held the previous night and what they had talked about. But he did not mention Kino's affair.

"So, there was an important family meeting last night at your home. Where was your wife when you were talking?"

"Kino was in other room."

"Do you think she was listening?"

"… Well, again, I don't think she was aware, so, no, I don't think she was listening to the conversation. I doubt it."

"Did anyone tell you how she became ill?"

"Yes, my third son told me she suffered from severe neurosis. Then her condition worsened."

Detective Bito considered something Eizo said and made quiet comment to his partner.

"She suffered from neurosis and finally went insane? I've never heard that happening before."

"But ..."

"I understand neurosis and dementia, which is what I think you mean, are different categories of mental illness. Usually, you don't become insane even when you're suffering severe neurosis."

Eizo realized that he had to mention his wife's affair and her self-confinement after the affair ended. In as few words as possible he related his wife's past indiscretions. His face flushed deeply with shame about the matter.

"So ... your wife left you for this other man, though you weren't in Japan. She was then deserted by him, and then became insane?" the detective said, clearly in disbelief. "Was she hospitalized?"

"Yes."

"Which hospital?"

"Hospitals in the City of Minokamo ... and a university hospital, I don't know exactly."

"Even if she was insane as you say, did you still love your wife?"

"Yes, I did. She was ... my wife ... after all," Eizo stuttered as tears started to run.

"Was it possible for you and your wife to communicate with each other?"

"No, not really. We haven't been able to talk to each other since I came back. I'm not sure she recognized me."

"I see," Bito said softly. After a pause he continued, "What is puzzling to us right now is, if your wife was insane, how she was able to make the decision to commit suicide. It involves some sort of thinking, planning, and finally, decision-making ability. From my experience, that can only be done by a person who is mentally capable."

Eizo sat in stunned silence. He could not say anything to the detectives.

"Well, that's all for now. Thank you. We're going to conduct an autopsy on your wife. We'll contact you again very soon."

After the interrogation, Eizo was taken out into the hall where Isoshichi and Tamotsu were waiting for him. Isoshichi went in next, followed by Tamotsu a while later. The detectives asked the two brothers which hospitals Kino had been in, among other questions.

After Tamotsu came out they were finally permitted to leave the police headquarters. In the truck no one wanted to talk; silence dominated the small space. Eizo's eyes were wet with tears, but he suppressed the grief that threatened to overcome him. When they arrived home, not knowing what else to think about and do, Eizo decided to go to Mizusawa and lay flowers and offer incense sticks. The family discussed whether or not this was an appropriate thing to do at this particular time, but decided to let him go. Fumi handed a lighter to Tamotsu as a way to say that he should take his father.

Tamotsu drove his father to a store in town to buy flowers and incense sticks and then drove over to Mizusawa where the police cars were still parked on the shoulder of the road. He parked the car far away from the police cars. The river had risen overnight because of the rain; the water was red with mud. The current was swirling at the point where the rapid stream was stagnant, blocked by the sluices. They walked slowly on the low dykes separating the rice fields until they came to a point where the policemen were standing a hundred metres away. Eizo bent down and laid the flowers on the ground. Piling up a little soil he then lit several sticks of incense and stuck the ends in the pile he had created.

Tamotsu crouched down beside him and Eizo mumbled a half-remembered Buddhist prayer. The policemen did not ask them any questions.

Shortly after Eizo and Tamotsu came home from Mizusawa, the detectives returned with a forensic team.

"Do you have a search warrant?" Kozo asked Detective Bito.

"We can get it very quickly, if that pleases you." The detective treated Kozo with near contempt. "Let's get cracking!" He raised his hand and gave an order to his squad, ignoring the third son's claim.

The forensic team took soil samples from the soles of Eizo's shoes and inspected his wife's bedroom and other rooms in the house, including the bathroom. They bagged the evening bag for later examination and dusted the lock on the front door for fingerprints, as well as the stick used for locking the *amado*, wooden sliding door.

Meanwhile, Kozo, Fumi, and Toshio provided their statements to the detectives separately. After speaking with Toshio, Detective Hoshino asked Fumi to show him the garbage dump, returning half an hour later.

Bito then informed Eizo, "You have to come back to our headquarters for further questions," but he did not pat Eizo's shoulder this time.

*

In the examination room Detective Bito calmly started grilling Eizo. "Last night, you didn't take off your clothes when you slept. Why?"

Eizo immediately knew that the investigators had managed to draw even the smallest detail from Toshio. "I was exhausted. I had just finished telling my family about

335

my forty-three years in Canada. I could barely move to turn out the light and finally fell asleep without noticing I still had my clothes on." He carefully chose the words to answer.

"Why did you need to explain your time in Canada? Didn't they already know about it?"

"No. Judging from their reaction to me, I'm not sure they cared much."

"They didn't care much?"

"No, I don't think so."

"Do they have negative feelings toward you?"

"Yes, regrettably, they do."

"Why is that?"

"They think I've neglected them, even though I sent money to them for all those years. And … they blame me for my wife's insanity, because of that."

"Oh, wait a minute," scoffed the detective. "There's a leap in logic. Your negligence of the family caused your wife's insanity? How do you connect the negligence of your family with your wife's insanity? Where do you get the idea that they think you are the cause of your wife's illness?"

"As I said this morning, my wife left me for another man during my absence."

Eizo explained his knowledge of his wife's indiscretions in greater detail. How her lover eventually deserted her, the processes of her insanity, how his family had become a laughing stock in their own town, her cries every evening for her lover to return, and the deep discord between his family and himself. "My family thinks I neglected Kino and caused her insanity. They won't accept me, though I tried my best. I'm a nuisance to them. I'd leave if not for my obligation to my wife."

"Why did your wife scream at you the first night you returned?" the detective asked.

Someone in my family told that to the police. "I wanted to embrace her because I felt so sorry for her. I loved her."

"You *loved* her? Not anymore?"

"My wife is dead now. And I didn't know at that time she had another man on her mind."

"On her mind? Hmm, did you try to embrace her again?"

"Yes … no, no. I was afraid that she'd scream again if I tried to."

"The two layers of sliding doors at the entrance of your house appeared to have been unlocked from inside last night. Who do you think unlocked them? You?"

"No, no, I don't know. I was asleep."

Bito was silent for a moment, looking down at his documents. Detective Hoshino kept glaring suspiciously at Eizo.

"Last night, you told your family that you'd rather go back to Canada, if your obligation to your wife was no longer the case." Detective Bito now looked up at Eizo. "Today, she was found dead quite conveniently. Suitably, indeed. And this morning, you said you felt pity for your wife and wanted to do something for her. Something smells here …," the detective said, leading Eizo to draw out the information he needed.

"No, yes, but it was an expression of my obligation. I did nothing wrong."

"Everybody says so at first," Detective Bito said, carefully watching him. "Isn't it true that your wife was an obstacle to you returning to Canada?"

Eizo stared at the detective incredulously, not quite believing what he had heard.

"What were you thinking while lying awake until two o'clock?"

"… I was thinking whether or not I should return to Canada again … and Kino's plea."

"What plea?"

"Kino said, 'My dearest, please come back to me…' and she disappeared."

"Disappeared?" The detective almost jumped up from the chair with his taut cheeks, "To where? To where?" He showered questions on Eizo.

"To … her room."

"Most criminals return to the crime scenes within several days. You went to Mizusawa this morning, very quickly after your wife's body was found dead. Why?"

Eizo knew that the policemen guarding Mizusawa had already reported his visit to the detective.

"… I felt obliged to dedicate a prayer and incense sticks for her. She was my wife."

"She was your wife …?" Detective Bito gazed at him.

Then all of a sudden, he shot out bluntly, "Did you kill your wife?" He and Detective Hoshino observed Eizo closely so as not to miss even the slightest flicker of guilt that might flit across his face.

"No, no, no, I didn't kill her!" It was if an electric current had jerked Eizo. The shock pushed him backwards in the chair. He looked Detective Bito in the eyes. "I didn't kill her. I felt so sorry for Kino. But I didn't kill her," Eizo cried, now waving his arms frantically.

"You have to be faithful to the truth at least once in your life, and this is the time."

"I've been faithful to the truth all my life, all the time."

"This world holds together, because truth is there. And humans are honourable, because we act out of duty for the truth. Did you kill her?"

"No, no, no."

"You can't establish your alibi. You have a motive to act." Detective Bito thrust the words to Eizo. "Tell us exactly what happened last night or early this morning."

"I told you everything I know already."

"This is a murder case dressed up as a suicide. Come clean, now! You'll feel relieved."

"I didn't kill her."

The interrogation extended well over an hour, the two detectives repeatedly asking the question: did you kill your wife? Eizo, however, denied any responsibility for his wife's death.

He was finally taken home.

*

Kin'ichi stopped in to offer his condolences. He spoke quietly for a while with Isoshichi and his wife about the incident and then left. Tamotsu and Kozo had called home to relate the news and say that their return would be delayed. They told their families to begin preparing for the funeral, though they were not certain about the direction of the police investigation and when Kino's body would be returned home.

A reporter and a camera crew from a local TV station came to cover the incident. Tamotsu eventually relented to the TV station's request for an interview in front of the house. The news that evening indicated that the police were still investigating the 'suspicious' death of Kino. However, the program only showed a long shot of the house and the

Mizusawa area, but not the interview with Tamotsu. When the broadcast was finished Isoshichi spat, "Dang it! Just what we need. Rumours are going to start flying again!" He got up and stomped out of the living room.

Fumi went back into the kitchen and Toshio quietly went upstairs. Tamotsu and Kozo spoke in low voices, ignoring their father. Eizo could no longer stand the looks Kozo was giving him and went into the bedroom. He knew he was not welcome and although the father would normally be the bedrock amid a crisis, he held no such position in this household.

He was bothered by the sense that somehow his family had betrayed him. He knew either Fumi or Toshio had told the detectives about Kino's scream the first night he had returned home and the fact that he had not taken off his clothes the previous night, also that someone had told the detectives that he would rather be back to Canada if Kino were no longer his responsibility. He knew that it was ethically and legally right for his family to tell the police about those things but what bothered him was not a problem of ethics and legal obligation, it was the lack of loyalty and family bond that broke his heart.

*

Eizo was tense as he waited for the outcome of the investigation. His wife had died an unnatural and suspicious death, and as a matter of course, was subject to police scrutiny. Little of the evidence, however, found a compelling motive in the family, except that of Eizo. Kino had nothing of worth, no savings, and her life insurance had been cancelled a long time ago when Eizo was put into the concentration camp in Canada and could not send money to

340

the family anymore. Although Kino's hands had been tied behind her, the rope had only been wrapped, not knotted. She was weighted down with stones in her clothes, but this she could have done herself. And there was no trace of a struggle either at the house or on the banks of the river; at least the police could not identify it. None of the usual signs of assault were found on the body, except a few bruises, which might have been caused by the stones that she had used as weights. Too weak to use as evidence. As well, the local police knew Kino and it was common knowledge that she wasn't well, mentally and this was further confirmed after interviewing her neighbours. No one had noticed anything the previous evening, although the rain may have drowned out any noise.

The laboratory compared the quality of the earth from Eizo's shoes and the earth from the scene. The samples showed similarities but were not identical. By then, the police guarding the scene informed the detectives that Eizo and another middle-aged man had come to lay flowers and burnt incense sticks. Despite the mud, when Detective Bito patted Eizo's shoulder, his clothes showed no sign of having been out in the night's weather, nor was there evidence of him hiding any other clothes. Finally, the autopsy was inconclusive; Kino was assumed to have drowned between 3:00 a.m. and 4:00 a.m. Her lungs were filled with water which most likely meant that she had come to the scene of a crime or accident alive—but the coroner in charge of the incident was unable to substantiate that the bruises on her chest were the results of a struggle.

With all the information they had gathered and with no material evidence other than the body, the detectives and the forensic team could not avoid drawing the conclusion that there was no foul play involved. The case was brought to a close concluding that Kino Osada had committed suicide, that she was sane to the extent that she was capable of deciding her own fate.

One more time, the interrogation of Eizo ended without apology, as if it had never happened.

*

Soon after the investigation was over, Kino's body was released to undergo funerary rituals. Isoshichi phoned an undertaker in the city to take Kino's body home from the police headquarters. After her body arrived, the workers from the undertaker set up a temporary Buddhist altar in the *zashiki*, the drawing room, at Isoshichi's. Kino's body was enshrined in front of it on a new *futon*, with her head facing north. The custom derived from the historical fact that Buddha laid his head towards the north when he died. A worker from the funeral home placed four bags of dry ice around Kino's body. A bowl of fruit was decorated to the right and of cookies to the left on the altar. Eizo knelt by his wife and then broke down. He shed tears over his wife's misfortune and his own bizarre fate but, more than anything, over his guilty conscience. No one made any attempt to console or even speak to him.

The family began preparing for her funeral. Tamotsu and Kozo informed Eizo that he had to act as the *moshu*, the chief mourner, for the funeral. Eizo hesitated to accept the role, citing his lack of Japanese funeral customs and knowledge. But his two sons pressured him, saying all he needed to do was to greet people who came to offer their condolences.

That afternoon, Isoshichi took Eizo to the temple nearby to discuss preparations for Kino's funeral with a priest but all the way in the car the two barely talked. Eizo decided to pay all her funeral costs but kept it to himself for the time

342

being. He thought it was a little too early to talk about it. The priest told them that he had another engagement on that evening and night and, therefore, would come to their home the following day. He also offered some advice about Kino's *hōmyō,* a posthumous Buddhist name. It is a customary practice to pay a *fusé,* an offering, for obtaining a *hōmyō* and their services. As to a *hōmyō,* if the deceased gets nine characters and certain combination of them, it will cost a great deal of money. The *hōmyō* Kino would receive consisted of only five characters and would cost less to the family. In order to commence the harsh training of Buddhist teachings after death, the deceased is given a *hōmyō* to cut off one's connections to this world and to keep observing the religious precepts so that one could finally connect to Buddha himself in the next world.

Fumi and Tamotsu began to put the house in order. Kozo was asked to go to the town hall to obtain the cremation permit and take Kino's picture to a photography studio to have it enlarged so that they could use it to decorate on the altar.

Kin'ichi came to the aid of the family. He had recently held his parent's funeral and, being familiar with the Buddhist customs, efficiently gave detailed advice on what should be done and what should not. Tamotsu concealed the *kamidana*, Shinto altar, with white paper to maintain its mystical purity and attached a notice of 忌中, *kichū*, characters for mourning, to the entrance along with a black and white curtain for the traditional *tsuya*, vigil.

In the late afternoon, Akiko, Michiyo, their three children, and Shoichi arrived from Tokyo. With everyone in the small house, the atmosphere became suddenly very busy. But the activity swirled effortlessly around Eizo, as if he were a rock in a stream. Nobody consulted him about

343

decisions or customs that should be adhered to, so he was kept out of the loop.

That evening, although Kino's body was to be washed, since it had been through the autopsy, the family ceremoniously wiped her forehead and legs instead. A piece of white cloth covered her face and a razor was placed on her chest as an amulet. Two candles were lit to guide the dead to the Pure Land, irradiating her step, and not to let anyone, particularly animals, attack her body. Incense sticks were kept burning to remove the putrid smell of a corpse— although the undertaker provided the bags of dry ice—, it was the custom to keep the incense sticks burning on the altar, as well as candles, until the formal *tsuya* was held.

After cleaning up the dinner dishes with the help of Akiko and Michiyo, Fumi sat down near the hearth. By custom the whole family was to reminisce about the deceased. No one felt like talking.

Fumi was quiet. She had worked alongside a healthy Kino for only a handful of years; the twenty-three years that followed were painful memories of caring for her ill mother-in-law. She talked briefly about those few good years, barely alluding to the difficulties that followed.

Isoshichi, though, glanced at his wife, his eyes lit with adoration, knowing her life had been difficult. This was the second time Eizo had seen any look other than a scowl on the eldest son's face. When Tamotsu and Kozo expressed their thanks to Isoshichi and Fumi for their dedication to their mother, Isoshichi's eyes misted over. Through simple acts like these, it was easy to see the strong bond between these three brothers.

Everybody in the living room seemed to be carefully avoiding Eizo and any mention of him. When their conversation came close to something related to him, the room fell quickly silent. When Eizo could no longer bear the pain of their unspoken scorn, he went to his bedroom. He looked at Kino's old *futon* on the floor. He tried to imagine Kino's shape, her unkempt hair sticking out from under those blankets. Then the doubt as to why Kino had gone to Mizusawa, especially that night, entered his head.

Why Mizusawa?

Suddenly the image of his wife's eerily amorous smile at the storehouse struck him. Right, Mizusawa must have been the place where Kino and her lover had had their secret rendezvous. It was warm and hidden from the street, an ideal spot for their assignations. They must have planned their elopement there, holding each other's hands, and staring into each other's eyes. Still, he had to realize all this could not go beyond his suspicions.

Besides, when she unlocked the front door, she must have paid particular attention so as not to make any noise ... Wait, paid attention? If she were truly insane, she wouldn't have cared about that. If, and it's a big if, Kino was not insane, then she overheard my talk on Saturday night. Had she also heard my desire to go back to Canada?

Eizo considered as to whether Kino had committed suicide because life with him would have been a misery and she wanted to harbour her memories of love for the man she had eloped with.

Why, then, would she behave like a mad woman? Did Kino have to sham madness in order to survive in the town? Was it easier for her to be accepted that way than to spend life as an object of contempt? Her life must've been a hell. Kino, what was your life after all? And, at the end, did she sacrifice herself so that I could go back to Canada? No, no, it can't be! No ... no!

Eizo knew that his questions would remain unanswered. Kino had taken her secrets with her.

That night the informal *tsuya* took place without a priest. Most of the family stayed up all night so that the deceased would not feel lonely on her last day.

*

The next morning the funeral services company delivered two flower baskets which each carried the Tamotsus and the Kozos names and arranged them around the alter. They also delivered three wreaths dedicated by Kino's nephew, Fumi's brother and Kin'ichi and put them in front of the entrance.

That afternoon the Buddhist priest in a formal robe came on a motorcycle and the Osada family received an *ihai,* a mortuary tablet, with her *hōmyō* on it. Eizo placed it on the altar. The priest chanted the *makura-gyo*, a sutra by the pillow of the deceased.

On the third day, the rite to place Kino's body into the coffin was held. Everyone dressed in black except the children who wore dark-coloured clothing. The priest chanted a sutra while several incense burners were circulated among the attendants who sat behind him in the *zashiki*. After the priest's chanting, the new coffin was carried into the *zashiki,* the piece of white cloth over Kino's face and the bags of dry ice were removed. Her cheeks were hollower than when she lay at the police headquarters, her closed eyes were sunken and mouth slightly open. Her face looked tragic as though she were saying it was too much to endure the life that she had gone through.

Eizo blamed himself for being unable to be with her and hesitantly put his hand on her forehead to say a final good-bye. Her forehead was icy cold, but he did not remove his

346

hand. Time came to a halt altogether in front of her cadaverous face.

Her mask was telling him something; a fire was out, time melted into thin air, language did not have any meaning, and her being did not exist. *What is it all about?* He could not understand her mask's message. He was frozen. Wraithlike chilling air ran throughout his body, without a sound and without being noticed or seen. *Is Kino's death true and real? Is the reality in this world a mere semblance?* He came to understand that what she was revealing was the transitoriness of human life. *What is the truth? Kino's death—this can't be real.* He was being frozen by the feelings that all the reality in this world was vain and meaningless—the sense of emptiness and nothingness. *Pitiless!* He pulled his hand from her forehead and started groaning. His shoulders trembled slightly first and then whole body shook terribly. Tamotsu stepped forward and moved Eizo to the side.

Soon after that, the family placed Kino's body into the coffin. The mourners offered flowers in turn, carefully avoiding her face. They laid her favourite belongings beside her body and six ten-yen coins she would need to cross the *sanzu-no-kawa*, the River Styx, as a fare to go to the other world.

That evening, the formal *tsuya* was conducted and the Buddhist priest chanted a sutra. Again several incense burners were circulated among the mourners, praying for Kino with *jyuzu*, the beads of rosary, in their hands. The mourners bowed toward her body once, pinched a smidgen of incense with their fingers, took it to their forehead and prayed and then sprinkled on the embers smouldering in the incense burners.

347

After the ceremony, Eizo's family served food, pre-ordered dishes delivered by a restaurant in the city, to the attendants.

The next morning—it was a clear day—, the funeral was held. Tamotsu went to the temple to pick up the Buddhist priest. Arriving, the priest in a dark green robe sat on the *tatami* floor front and centre of the altar. The family and guests sat behind the priest. He began chanting the *San butsu ge*, praises of the Buddha—a sutra.

" …

光顔巍巍, Your face shines in great splendour, 威神無極, boundless divine dignity,

如是炎明, such the greatness of your light, 無与等者, beyond all comparison.

…

如来容顔, Tathagata's countenance, 超世無倫, transcends all comparison,

正覚大音, the great voice of awakening, 響流十方, resounds through the ten quarters.

戒聞精進, Your precepts, learning, effort, 三昧智慧, meditation, wisdom are,

威徳無侶, virtues beyond all compare, 殊勝稀有, ultimate supreme and rare.

深諦善念, Your deep meditation, 諸仏法海, ocean of Buddha's dharma,

窮深尽奥, has brought full understanding, 究其涯底, limitless comprehension.

…

南無阿弥陀仏, NA MAN DA BU, 南無阿弥, NA MAN DA BU…

願以比功徳, May these virtues be shared, 平等施一切, equally by all.

348

同発菩提心, May all awaken Bodhi mind, 往生安楽国, attaining the Land of Bliss."

When the priest had completed the formal ceremony, he shifted his position to the side of the altar and sat staring straight across the room, indicating that the family and other mourners could pay their respects.

Eizo proceeded to the altar. He held his hands in front of him in prayer, the *jyuzu* hanging from his left hand. While keeping his left hand in the position of prayer, he reached with his right hand to take a pinch of incense, which he lifted to his forehead and then put it on the embers in a bowl on the altar. Then he brought his hands back together to pray. A framed picture of Kino sat on the altar behind the bowl. Eizo stared at his wife, trying to understand that the life of Kino, which he had known for only a little less than ten years. They had lived happily together as a young couple, but it felt to have been extremely short, condensed into a mere moment. And so was his life, he thought. He felt an infinite emptiness.

The family put the lid on the coffin and everyone hammered the single nail into it three times with a small stone, taking their turns. The stone is thought that it came from the *sanzu-no-kawa* and the hope that she will cross the Styx without any incident.

At the end of the ceremony Kino's coffin was lifted and carried outside, not through the entrance but crossing the veranda, the legs' side first, and placed into a hearse. The family watched, particularly Fumi and Michiyo with tears. Before leaving to the crematorium, Isoshichi broke the rice bowl Kino had been using so that the soul of the deceased would not come back to the house.

At the crematorium the priest chanted a sutra again and the family went into an anteroom to wait. Fumi's elder

349

brother was seated on wooden chairs in one corner of the room. He spoke briefly with Isoshichi, but ignored Eizo, as if he were someone of no importance. Urged by Tamotsu, Eizo approached and exchanged greetings with him as a chief mourner and thanked him for attending the funeral. The reaction of Fumi's brother was pitifully polite but Eizo read coldness in his eyes. Then he thanked Kino's nephews who returned an extremely polite but chilling greeting. Facing those pathetic receptions, Eizo thought that they were blaming him for his neglect and reprimanded himself again. Akiko and Michiyo spoke quietly to each other. The grandchildren sat en masse, fidgeting. Tamotsu, Kozo and Shoichi sat near Akiko, but were silent. Eizo found it difficult to be in the room, so he went outside where he felt able to breathe.

When the family was to gather Kino's ashes, three nearest relatives stood on both sides of Kino, a total of six, and picked up her bones and each time handed them over to another person with chopsticks, repeating it three times. Then other mourners followed. The bones were set into the box, legs first and then her skulls at the end. The number of attendants at the ceremony, including the family, was just over twenty; it was a small funeral.

Coming back home, Eizo and his family enshrined the box of Kino's ashes on the *chuin-dan*—the undertaker took the previous wooden altar away and now set up a new temporary cardboard altar covered with a white cloth until the memorial service would be held forty-nine days after her death.

*

That night Eizo brought up the topic of property inheritance to his sons who were sitting around the hearth with their wives. Eizo suggested that the cost of the funeral must be paid first, and since he was not entirely familiar with the law governing the division of property, he asked his sons to discuss the best way to distribute their mother's property, although it was still registered under his name. Privately, Eizo felt that Isoshichi should inherit everything since he took responsibility for the household and his mother, although there wasn't much of great value. However, he remained silent on the issue. He did not have the nerve or the authority to force them to follow his preference. At this point, he had almost decided to go back to Canada but he did not say anything to his family yet.

The group was surprised with Eizo's sudden suggestion and looked at each other for a way to respond. The most surprised was Isoshichi who looked as though he had had enough of this stranger meddling in their family affairs. But he relented; it seemed the reasonable thing to do with everyone already present.

"Tamotsu, Kozo, please tell me what you think," Isoshichi said without enthusiasm. His expression was coloured with fatigue. Everybody's eyes fixed on Tamotsu. He appeared uncomfortable, looked at his wife first and then at Isoshichi who was anxiously waiting.

"Elder brother and Fumi-san had been looking after Mom, so I think they should assume all the property," Tamotsu said without looking back at his wife.

"I agree with Tamotsu," Kozo said, in a quiet but firm voice and added, "We did little to help Mom. Fumi-san had taken the greatest responsibility for her care."

"Up to now, I don't know? So ..." Fumi mumbled, confusing everyone as to what she meant.

351

"We couldn't do anything to assist Mom. We weren't simply here to help. I don't think we have a claim on the house and fields," Tamotsu said, looking at Akiko in such a way as to warn her against complaining later. Rather than Akiko, Eizo felt ashamed again. Tamotsu's words made the father conscious of his long absence.

"Thank you, we appreciate your sentiment," Isoshichi said, relieved.

"Truly … that is really true, you know," Fumi said unintelligibly.

"Ah," Isoshichi paused, looking strangely at his brothers, and then continued, "we'll send you the documents later."

Eizo stayed by the hearth with his family. No one was particularly talkative just after the funeral. But he perceived a new coldness towards him. He did not share the nuances of the language and customs and it was exceptionally hard for him to express himself well. Those qualities he might be able to acquire and eventually reconcile the differences, but Eizo was painfully aware that this was not likely. He thought of the time that he could have spent with his family … his family may have ended up poor had he stayed in Japan, but then he might not have lost them altogether. Seeing the inheritance matter being settled, he stood up to leave the room.

"Fumi!" Isoshichi nodded toward the bedroom.

"Yes, Mother's *futon*." Fumi agreed instantly, standing.

Wanting to stay out of the way Eizo went into the drawing room where the *chuin-dan* altar was laid out and offered incense sticks he lit and prayed. He considered Kino's troubled life and whether he had ever provided any meaning for her. *There must've been … otherwise her life had been entirely meaningless.* But he could not avoid thinking how abnormal it was that he had spent his life separated from his family for so long. He finally realized that he needed to take a different path other than that of his family. He needed to let them go.

Eizo went back into his bedroom after Fumi was finished. The room looked bare.

She may have been insane and bedraggled, but her image sustained me all these years. Now, she's no longer here. She'll never cry out to the sky nor walk on the low dykes in the rice fields again.

He recalled the custom of passing the personal effects of the deceased, *katami-wake,* on to close relatives. He pulled out one of Kino's drawers and took it into the living room. He asked his sons to fetch the rest.

He did not know why, but the bedroom with only one dresser reminded him of his apartment in Toronto. He sat down on the floor under the orange electric bulb and looked about the room as though he were back in Canada. Memories of the Sato family, particularly Martin, crept into his mind. He longed for them as if they were his real family, his real son. *Martin!* The people in the next room were heartless and resentful, though they were related by blood. He knew that they would never pardon him for his long absence and therefore, never try to close their distance and difference from him.

He had been unable to make the decision to remain in Japan or return to Canada while Kino was alive. Now that she was gone there was nothing to keep him here in Japan. He had acquired a new kind of freedom, but felt his destiny lay in the whims of the wind and not his own will. He needed to find something or someone to bond to, something social and private. He needed a solid footing, but was not able to think of any. His thinking was muddled by Kino's death.

Then an old familiarity tickled the back of his neck, tenderly, very tenderly.

I'm still here with you, my friend!

24
Sayonara

The family ate quietly. On the dining tray were fried eggs, dry seaweed and pickles, as well as rice and *miso* soup. Although they lifted their *hashi,* chopsticks, with the same regular rhythm, breakfast the morning after the funeral was a cool affair. After the meal, Tamotsu and Kozo's families made preparations for the departure to Tokyo. Shoichi decided to accompany his uncles' family. The sky was dark, heavy with clouds that released their moisture around mid-morning. Isoshichi described the shower as a 'rain of tears'.

They had to call two taxis to get everyone to the station. Eizo's four grandchildren started bickering; usual things like, "Don't push me so much!" and "It's too tight!" as though leaving for a long road trip. Eizo sat in the passenger seat of Isoshichi's truck with Toshio beside him. They followed the taxis to the station. Eizo barely managed to recognize the beauty of the mountains and the familiar scenery did not incite any emotion in him.

While they were waiting for the train to arrive, Eizo watched his five grandchildren enjoying one another without any tension. He found it difficult to believe the children were his descendants and he imagined sitting in a field covered in spring flowers as they played around him. To these young lives their grandmother's death was a remote event; so too was their grandfather's existence. They lived in a different

355

world; one that Eizo knew would soon drift further and further away from him, as they aged.

He turned his eyes to his sons and their wives. Compared to his grandchildren, they appeared to be living in shades of grey, conformists, fully immersed in the thick of worldly problems and demands; it seemed to Eizo that, without forgiveness, their hatred toward him would fester and poison their souls.

Tamotsu and Kozo's families, along with Shoichi, all shuffled onto the train and waved to Isoshichi and Toshio, who then walked away together on the platform, paying no attention to Eizo. He followed well behind them, after acknowledging the formality of a polite wave from the train towards him.

When they got home Fumi handed a bundle of letters to Eizo. They were his letters to Kino, mailed after she had become ill. He did not see any bundle of his mail in her drawers when he and his sons took them to the living room for *katami-wake*.

"Fumi-san, have you kept the letters that I had sent to Kino before she became ill?"

"Oh, I don't know where those letters are. Mom used to keep them somewhere else," Fumi replied.

"Somewhere else … where? There was nothing in any of the cupboards or drawers."

"We've never seen any," she now said. "There were no letters in the drawers we looked in."

"Was there somewhere Kino kept important things?"

"I don't know. I don't think so," Fumi answered.

Eizo thanked her and went back to the living room. The thought that his wife would have disposed of all his letters before her affair had crossed his mind.

Kino was in love with him, and wanted to forget me. She had probably burned them before she eloped, so that she could fling off me totally. She must've prepared for their elopement carefully.

Sadness crept over him.

What was I to her?

He knew that world events and time robbed them of their lives altogether. In his absence, Kino's affection for another man metamorphosed into a thirst for love as a woman. In desire, she willingly accepted her lover, so the pledge between Kino and Eizo had been broken. In Canada, he had become nothing more than a shadow to her.

At lunch and dinner Kino's dining tray was conspicuously absent. She was truly gone. So too, was any connection to his eldest son and his grandson. At least when Kino was alive, he felt he had a place to occupy in his own home. But now that the funeral was over and everything had settled down, the atmosphere in the house had delicately changed.

After dinner, Eizo sat by the hearth and waited for the chance to talk to them. Soon, Fumi went back into the kitchen. Toshio left the hearth and went upstairs. Eizo and Isoshichi sat without speaking. Isoshichi finally stood up and went to the bath in the back of the house leaving Eizo alone. He listened to the clink of dishes from the kitchen. This was his house, yet it no longer felt like his home. It belonged to strangers who had made up their minds to condemn him.

After his bath, Isoshichi shuffled slowly into the room with the altar, rang the bell for his mother, then went to his room and shut the sliding door leaving Eizo cut off from everyone. Fumi and Toshio did not come out again. Eizo sat in the living room and could not stand the thought of living this life. The hearth was illuminated by a dim electric light

357

bulb hanging from the beam. He looked around the deserted room and came to grasp the true nature of his solitude: it was the condition of being alive alone in this world and he felt his existence like steam that would evaporate before long. Not knowing what else to do, he looked at his gnarled and tobacco stained fingers, the years of hard labour in Canada. What was it for? Yet there was no answer. He dragged his feet to the drawing room, offered lit incense sticks at the altar, rang the bell, and went to bed.

*

The tension in the house did not ease as the days wore on. Isoshichi, Fumi, and Toshio seemed to be purposely keeping him at arm's length. When watching television they did not speak to Eizo, only amongst themselves. Certainly, Eizo was unfamiliar to them and did not know enough about local politics to contribute, but he wished he were included as a member of the family. When everyone finished dinner, the three usually disappeared into the back room or upstairs. Eizo could only guess that they had agreed to make him feel like an outsider.

He considered the daily social minefield in town. New rumours about Kino's death must abound, but unlike the family, Eizo did not yet have to go out and face those problems. He could not help feeling concern as a father, but was powerless to offer any help or defence.

After the first seven-day mourning period and its memorial service were over, Isoshichi went back to work at the Agricultural Co-operative Association and Fumi returned to the fields. The house regained its routines. With nowhere to go, Eizo watched the news and melodramas on television, none of which really appealed to him. The *tsuyu*, the long spell of wet weather in early summer, began and the soft rain continued for over twenty days on end. This is the season that leftover food moulds very quickly and skin sticks to underwear.

When the showers finally stopped Eizo decided it was time to go out for a walk. When he passed people on the road, they bowed deeply to each other. But when Eizo looked back he saw their cold stares as if they were accusing him. He detested this façade of polite silence, in himself as well, for breeding an environment of distrust. Although his hometown, it was no longer his home. The residents were as unwelcoming as his son. Sometimes he met an old acquaintance, but they were not the same people Eizo once knew and the din behind closed curtains about the affairs of Eizo's family would have been deafening.

They've no understanding of my heart, my life! They've never tried to understand and probably wouldn't bother to listen. Why listen to me? There's nothing left for me here. Canada ... maybe that's my home!

As soon as this thought crossed his mind, Eizo ran from it.

Leave your family again!

Eizo agonised for several days about the thought. He was afraid of pushing himself to make a decision; he had rarely done so in the past. Current circumstances, however, left him with only one choice. So he wrote:

July 15, 1978

Dear Martin,

How have you and your parents been? I imagine everyone is fine.

I am sorry I have not written to you since I returned to Japan. I regret to say my wife recently passed away. The house without her is a lonely place. I have put some serious thought into coming home to Canada, permanently.

May I ask you again for your assistance? I would appreciate it if you could speak to the people responsible for the seniors' housing and ask them for an extension on the apartment reservation for another three months or so? There is nothing left for me here.

Please send my best regards to your parents and take care of yourself.

Eizo Osada.

Eizo looked back on the days when Kino had walked the roads and dikes between the rice fields with her evening bag in one hand and her cane in the other. He had often wished she would quit that once and for all, but no matter how crazy, she had filled a void in him. He now felt nobody was there to reach out and hold his hands. Freedom from obligation to his wife had now become his solitary confinement. The only time he found tranquility was when he rang the prayer bell, a connection with Kino through the sound, and prayed for her peaceful rest. Or, when he conjured up an image of Martin and his parents.

Eizo now seldom left the house, except to visit the grave—though Kino's ashes were not buried yet, there was a small section in the town cemetery for the Osada branch family and the family tomb had been erected some time ago, a detail Isoshichi arranged in the past. Although he had been observing the rituals of mourning, he did not want to be on view to fuel local chatter and he felt the importunate eyes of the community on him. As he had spent a good portion of his life in Toronto, where many ethnic groups spoke their own languages in public places, it seemed to him that Torontonians tended to have more tolerance towards others; they seemed to respect the need for privacy. Compared to Toronto, one would find a deeply rooted conservativeness in this town. He remembered the looks of contempt after he had given his wife the purse. He almost decided not to go out again after that.

*

Three weeks after mailing Martin's letter, Eizo received a response. Martin expressed his condolences to Eizo and then went on to say that he had contacted the city for an extension on the housing reservation. Martin also wanted to know when Eizo would arrive at the airport and his flight number. The letter brought an indescribable relief and he quietly thanked Martin.

Eizo offered to purchase a new *butsudan*, a Buddhist altar, as a memorial for Kino so that Isoshichi and his family could have it in the corner of the *zashiki*. He had already paid the expenses of Kino's funeral. Behind this was his deep regret and need to atone for her barren life. Since he had almost decided on a return to Canada, he wanted to do whatever he could to help, and hopefully, avoid further regret. If he let Isoshichi pay, Eizo felt that his dignity as a father and as a person would become worthless.

The period of mourning ended after forty-nine days according to Buddhist tradition. The same people who attended the funeral, except Tamotsu's and Kozo's children, gathered again for her memorial service. On the way to cemetery Eizo held the cinerary urn of his wife. In Isoshichi's truck he let his eyes drift over the passing landscape; farms, houses, stores, rice fields, cars, gas stations, people and trees flew by and he felt dizzy. Although holding the cinerary urn, he could not convince himself that the person holding it was actually him and he could not seem to understand just what he was doing. One thing for sure was that people would bury Kino's ashes today. The priest in a robe arrived at the cemetery and recited a sutra which took only ten minutes. After setting the urn in the hole provided, Eizo threw the first red-coloured earth onto the box. He did not cry; rather he felt empty and realized that a part of him was lost with Kino's death. When the last of the dirt was pushed over the urn, Eizo thanked everyone and bowed, hiding behind custom. The surroundings and the people around him appeared to be dry, colourless and far away. Their politeness seemed to be a mere sham. The only thing left to him was to pray for tranquillity.

Inheritance and property transfers from Eizo's to Isoshichi's name had been completed. Spring passed into the end of summer and the hot sun shone without mercy for days making the humidity even more unbearable. Species of cicadas competed for singing time during the daylight hours, certain kind of cicadas into evening, and even when they stopped after dusk, Eizo's ears still rang with their crazy din. The summer in the countryside caused him to reminisce and yearn for his youth and its innocence. But he was the only one in the family who indulged in reverie. His family lived with the day-to-day reminder that the town despised them.

They had little reason and room for nostalgia. His presence made that all the more difficult for the family. Eizo came to accept that he could never overcome the past no matter what he did in repentance except perhaps leave their home, sadly forever.

*

One hot summer night and tired of quietly sitting at home, Eizo, without any definite purpose, went to visit the head family. Despite the fact that Kin'ichi politely received him and offered cool sliced watermelon, he could feel the coldness and annoyance emanate from him and his wife in their language and behaviour. They gave him the same look the townspeople gave him, with politeness covering over the surface.

Or was it contempt?

They tried to hide behind an air of civility, but paradoxically, it only helped Eizo to perceive their true feelings. He left without staying long.

There is nothing left for me here.

Eizo finally confirmed his resolve to leave. Isoshichi and Fumi would hardly notice his preparations. Most of what he came with was still packed in boxes. He mailed another letter to Martin confirming his decision.

*

One day before Eizo was to dispatch his belongings he informed Isoshichi and Fumi that he was leaving.

"Why don't you stay here as you have been?" Isoshichi cried. "Mom just died and now you want to leave for Canada?"

"We've now finished with the mourning period," Eizo answered, surprised by their reaction to his news.

"You know, your decision endangers our honour here."

Your honour? You don't have any honour in this town to begin with!

"My duty as your father is already over."

"But think again. It wouldn't be respectable for you to leave."

"That's right, Father. Please stay with us. Your leaving would damage our reputation further. We don't need that, do we?" Fumi supported her husband's decision.

This unexpected turn of events confused Eizo. He had resolved to go to Canada but wavered considering his son's and daughter-in-law's persuasion. Yet he knew that if their words had come from a sincere desire for their father to stay that would be one thing, but the real reason they were concerned was how his leaving would look to the townspeople. Eizo knew that his son would continue to blame him and that their differences would never be resolved; their relationship would remain awkward whether he stayed or not. The words 'wouldn't be respectable' and 'damage our reputation' said it all. He felt something he had thought crucial for the past 43 years in Canada collapsing quietly inside him and could hardly look into the gaping abyss of his past that represented the vast ruins now for fear. What underlay the Osadas were deep suspicions, the lack of sympathy, and iciness which would leave no place for reconciliation, while there was a definitive bond of love between Senkichi, Matsu and Martin.

The following day Eizo finished packing and shipped his belongings to Canada while Isoshichi and Fumi were at work. He continued to question the decision to leave, but knew it was the right one. He called Tamotsu and Kozo and let them know. They too, tried to persuade him to stay for reasons unknown, but when he told them that he had already sent his baggage, the other end of the line suddenly became quiet, with an air of abandonment.

Eizo visited the graves of his wife, parents, and elder brother. He paid one last visit to Kin'ichi and his wife to bid farewell. His nephew was surprised with Eizo's decision, but did not try to change his mind. The last place he went to was Mizusawa, where he dedicated flowers at the spot of his wife's death. When he looked at the concave where he believed Kino and her lover had had their secret rendezvous, grief overcame him once again. But the tears did not cleanse him; they left him with a deep bitterness.

The day before his departure, Eizo phoned his two younger sons to say good-bye. Tamotsu insisted on meeting him at Tokyo Station to take him on to Hakozaki Bus Terminal where Eizo could catch a bus for the newly built Narita International Airport. Eizo hesitated but then accepted Tamotsu's kindness. After he hung up the phone he told Isoshichi and Fumi that he would leave the following day.

After some consideration Isoshichi offered, "If you become sick in Canada, feel free to come home anytime." This expression of sympathy moved Eizo and tears came into his eyes.

Why does Isoshichi talk at cross-purposes? I'm leaving tomorrow and I'll never return.

But Eizo politely thanked Isoshichi for his words. For him, it was too little too late.

The next day dawned crisp and clear and the already warm temperature suggested a hot afternoon to come. Isoshichi offered Eizo a lift to the station. Fumi and Toshio stayed home and said their good-byes to Eizo at the entrance to the house.

Four decades ago, it had been a clear day as well. Isoshichi, Tamotsu and, particularly, Kozo had been just little boys. Even now Eizo could picture that Kino held Kozo in her arms while Isoshichi and Tamotsu stood beside her and the youngest boy had his thumb in his mouth. When Eizo said *sayonara, tasshadena*—stay healthy—, Kino held Kozo's hand and waved it to say good-bye. Isoshichi and Tamotsu waved their hands as well without knowing what that parting meant. Eizo remembered his tremendous anxiety, jumping out into a new world, and the pain of wrenching his young family apart. Kino forced a smile but was unable to stop her tears running down and turned her face away. Still, he thought Kino was beautiful. While in Canada, he regretted that he had not said 'Please, don't cry' to her at the time. His mind was too preoccupied with his own emotions to be attentive to such a small but important detail.

This day, however, played out in contrast to the past. Kino was gone and dry-eyed Isoshichi was fifty-one years old and ready to send him off at the station. Eizo himself was resigned to his fate. He felt sad, mixed with anxiousness and strangely enough some relief—but no regret—, and could no longer feel resentment towards his sons.

At the station Isoshichi insisted on coming onto the platform with him. Eizo let him do what he wanted. They walked quietly together onto the platform. The rail lines stretched off in either direction, vanishing into the urban landscape. Father and son stood without speaking. Eizo was afraid that if he spoke to Isoshichi now the quiet balance of emotion might break with unexpected results. As the moment of their parting approached, Eizo could hear the palpitations of his heart.

What would I say if Isoshichi had asked me not to leave? But, to stay and spend the rest of my life with them would be

... but what if ... when the train comes into the platform he asks?

Eizo could not restrain himself and cast a furtive glance at Isoshichi's profile. He saw the tension on his son's shadowy expression. Isoshichi stood beside his father's suitcase biting his lower lip and watching for the train.

When I'm about to leave ... if Isoshichi asks me to stay, what do I say? If he asks me, should I cancel my plans?

Eizo's head spun.

The train suddenly appeared. As it got closer and closer, his heart felt as if someone was bashing it with an iron hammer.

What on earth will I do in Canada? Tell me! Now!

Eizo blacked out momentarily. A loud thumping and screeching vibrated through the platform. A whirlwind moved up his body. He opened his eyes and saw the massive metal cars rolling in front of him, like the stream of time passing before him. But the train finally did come to a halt. A few passengers got off before others on the platform boarded.

"Your suitcase," Isoshichi said, lifting his father's suitcase.

"*Arigatō,*" Eizo thanked, looking at his son.

Isoshichi stood without looking at Eizo. A signal sounded to indicate the train was about to depart.

"Isoshichi ..." Eizo said his son's name, a thousand thoughts coursing through his mind. His mouth hung there. He did not know what to say. His son's eyes were still dry and cold; Eizo knew that the hope in his heart was only an illusion. "Well then, *tasshadena,* stay healthy."

"Please be well," Isoshichi said in a low voice, almost drowned out by the noise of the station.

Once he was on the train Eizo found a window seat on the platform side. He heard an announcement blare across the station. The train started moving slowly. Eizo leaned his upper body towards the window. Isoshichi stood still, his face shadowed—no indication of whether he was sad or relieved—, but the tension was no longer etched into his features. The eldest son simply watched the train as it pulled away.

*

Eizo arrived at Tokyo Station in the early afternoon. As he trudged along the platform with his suitcase he found Shoichi anxiously scanning the crowd. Tamotsu was waiting at another part of the station. He finally saw them and came over. Eizo glanced around for Kozo, almost as a reflex, but could not find him.

Without talking, the three rode in the car for Hakozaki Bus Terminal. Tamotsu's company helmet was on the back seat, a reminder that he was taking time away from work. The afternoon traffic in downtown Tokyo was heavy and they had to wait through several traffic lights to get through some of the intersections. Eizo tried to think amid the constant engine roar thick with exhaust fumes from the open window. The racket would not let Eizo's thoughts settle in any one place and the Tokyo streets seemed to reflect his state of mind. Many things had happened to him in a short period of time. He felt a strange disconnect, as if those experiences had existed outside of himself.

They arrived at the Hakozaki Bus Terminal. Eizo again looked furtively about the terminal to see if he could catch glimpse of Kozo but to no avail.

For Kozo, am I still only a shadow? If so, should I have made a greater effort to get to know him? Everything is too late now.

"Is Kozo all right?" Eizo could no longer hold back from asking about his third son, knowing that it was embarrassing for him to ask why Kozo did not come.

"Yes, he is away on a business trip." Tamotsu replied.

"I see. … On a business trip, huh? No wonder he couldn't come." But he was not able to determine whether it was a quirk of fate or Kozo would not have come anyway, even if he had been available.

Eizo finished at the check-in counter with the help of Tamotsu and Shoichi. He thanked them and bowed deeply. Then, he realized that he was being overly formal. Yet his second son and grandson were indeed foreign. They were his descendants, however, only a tenuous symbolic bond held them together.

I have been a bad father and grandpa. I've done little for you. Pardon me. I love you both so much. Tamotsu, I loved … loved your mother. Be in good health. Don't worry about me. I only wanted your happiness. You have no idea how fearful and desperate I was in the concentration camp and how much I was worried about you then. You knew nothing of my difficulties. I wish there had been no war, no concentration camp ever. I don't want to part from you. Please ask me to stay. I'll stay without hesitation.

"Please take care of yourself," Tamotsu said with tearful eyes and stretched his hand out to Eizo.

Eizo, tears also in his eyes, gripped Tamotsu's hand tightly. He then suddenly embraced his son tightly. Tamotsu was surprised by this public show of affection and patted his father on the back a couple of times, unsure what else to do.

Eizo slowly released him and then shook his grandson's hand.

Why must I leave? Why? Tamotsu, please tell me to stay. I'll stay. I'll be here.

"Tamotsu … I …" Eizo stuttered, unable to shape his thoughts.

Tamotsu looked perplexed, but did not say anything. Eizo did not hear the words that he longed for; his son maintained his silence.

"Thank you very much," Eizo then had to say and said repeatedly as he again bowed deeply and started walking towards the bus.

And that was that.

It was as if he were witnessing someone else's life. Parting with Tamotsu was too casual, as if they were to meet again the next day. After ten steps or so, Eizo looked back. Tamotsu and Shoichi saw Eizo turn around. They waved. Eizo knew this meant farewell. He then recalled the scene where Tamotsu had waved his hand to him when he had left for Canada some four decades ago. Everything around him slowly turned grey. The noise stilled. Eizo lifted his arm mechanically, returned the polite wave, and shuffled slowly to the bus.

*

Later that evening a passenger jet lifted off from Narita International Airport en route for Canada. Not long after take-off, the aircraft bustled with activity as stewardesses moved about. Beside a window near the wing sat the crumpled figure of an old man wiping tears from his eyes with a handkerchief, taking one long last look at the landscape of his home, the land where he was born, as it disappeared slowly beneath the haze below.

Isoshichi, Tamotsu, Kozo, Japan, I'll never see you again. Sayonara ... SAYONARA!

25
Cherry Blossoms

As Eizo had come back to Canada, Martin helped him to move into the seniors' housing complex in the suburb of Toronto. First, Eizo was happy to be able to see Martin and receive his help.

But Eizo's happiness did not last long. For several days in his new home, he made efforts to go down to the sitting room on the first floor to try to escape from Kino's memory and open a new window into this new life. However, those seniors were not Donald McCord or Gus—Eizo contacted neither of them out of shame after having come back to Canada—and it soon became clear that he had little in common with the other residents. He quickly withdrew into his room and hid behind the door. It was unbearable for him to be asked about his past life. He had finally disposed of his belongings which had the scent of his family, including Kino's last letter, save the sepia family photo taken in Minokamo-City. Yet, the image of Kino still haunted him.

Two years wore on and one glaringly hot summer day Matsu suddenly passed away. Despite his depression, Eizo attended the funeral held at a downtown church. The obsequies reminded him of his wife's death. Again he started dreaming of Kino's horror-stricken eyes. When the nightmares were dire, he jumped out of bed and sat by the window, watching the dark night dotted with lights of houses that looked like the stars that had fallen to the ground, until the first streaks of dawn drifted across the sky. On leaving Japan, he had expected the shadow to stand by his side, but on the contrary, he now had to face the fierce struggles against the shadow that constantly tormented and reprehended him for his past.

Do you remember Kino's frightened face? She was listening to your story in the darkness. What do you think she was thinking?

"I don't want to recall. Hell no!" Eizo cried.

You can't drive me away ... I'm your conscience. Kino's life was disastrous. Are you not taking any responsibility for her death? The shadow became torment incarnate. The state of deep regret conquered Eizo and he fell into an utter confusion and could no longer tell who he was—his real self or the shadow.

One autumn night, Eizo finished his supper, the time of day he detested most. He carried his plates to the sink and heard children running happily in the hall. He listened to the cheers behind the door and assumed that the children were visiting their elderly relatives. Next moment, the realization of being all alone pressed him hard. He had had the same feelings in his tiny apartment before he headed for Japan. That called back his past: the concentration camp, his unsettled life after that, a solitary life in his apartment, the failed family reunion, Kino's elopement and particularly her death, his sons' neglect and reproach, contemptuous looks of the townspeople and his regret and remorse.

He had failed in every field and any attempt in his life. He had received a fatal blow and the wound infected his soul and his health and was now suppurating. *Can I expect anything good to happen tomorrow?* The suppuration was becoming worse one every day. *Are you going to drag your shame around for another ten years? You have both qualities of sinfulness and stupidity within. Now, how do you redeem yourself?* The shadow and even his real self were reprimanding him. He yielded to self-disgust; hated everything about himself, and was in despair about his past, this universe, and the worst of all, every single sense of values and hope of humanity. He could not but soak himself in the pathetic sense of nothingness in life, and suffered from the loss of his objective of living and of his desire to live. No end was seen.

Enough!

Fetching a piece of paper and pen, he sat at a kitchen table and began a letter to his sons:

November 17, 1980

My Dear Sons,

I have spent the last while in Canada considering my life: the time that has passed, the things that I have missed, and the pain I have caused. With foresight perhaps I could have prevented this but that can no longer be helped.

I never felt that I had abandoned you. I believed that I was doing my duty. But I realize how wrong I was; a fool to think that I could be a husband and father from so far away. I held onto the image of your mom holding Kozo's hand and calling for me, again and again, to return home soon and that you would all be waiting for me.

For the last two years I have been haunted by the guilt that it was I who drove your mother to her death. I see only shame in my future and guilt in my past. I realize now and deeply regret that I have been but a shadow in your lives. I have wandered through time like a puppet, controlled by the

*strings of others with no will of my own. Those threads are
now about to snap.*

*You have all grown up into fine men. In the past couple
of months, your mother has appeared in my dreams, calling
my name. Finally, I will be with Kino. I am deciding my own
path. I am going home.*

Please forgive me.

Your Father

He left his suicide note on the kitchen table, trusting that
Martin would mail for him.

Eizo climbed into a bathtub full of warm water and
applied a sharp knife to his wrists. His black blood started
trickling down into the water. Soon the water mixed with
blood turning a dusky red. The colour reminded him of
autumn in Japan, the red and yellow leaves that covered the
mountains near his hometown like a carpet of nature that had
always sustained him. He pictured himself playing with his
grandchildren in the forests of endlessly falling leaves. The
image gradually changed to the field full of flowers in spring,
sounds of his descendant's laughter filling the air.

Eizo was patient looking at the blood flow out from his
wrist into the water. As time went on, he was steadily getting
tired and felt his body empty. The halo encircling the sun
was becoming thicker in his vision and now he felt his body
emptier. When he closed his eyes, he noticed the weak throbs
of his heart beating unreliably. He knew his life was ending
soon. Then his grandchildren, particularly Mayumi, Noboru
and Chiaki, reappeared into his fading mind—they were still
laughing and talking, saying something to him. He closed his
eyes, yet his consciousness was still roaming about on this

375

side of the world. He then recalled his first encounter with the new blood line of his offspring in Japan—Mayumi. She was looking down at him from the second floor of Tamotsu's residence.

That sensational emotion when he had met Mayumi struck him again. She now started waving and calling at him. She was calling something. But he could not hear. She called at him again. He pricked up his ears. Then without thinking, he lifted his left hand from inside the water and opened his eyes. He saw the blood oozing out from the open cut of his wrist. Red blood! Red bloody bath! *No, this isn't what I wanted.* Suddenly overcome by the will to live, Eizo crawled out of the bath, bound his wrists to stem the flow, and called an ambulance. He listened to his real self this time, not motivated by his shadow.

*

"Are you all right?" Senkichi said as soon as he entered the hospital room. "What a pity!"

Eizo lay on the bed in an unwrinkled white hospital gown, his wrist wrapped by a bandage. His eyes were lethargic, complexion poor, and cheeks emaciated.

"A person like you … I couldn't imagine this'd happened to you," Senkichi said as he sat in the chair while Martin stood by him.

Eizo began to describe what and why he had done in a faltering voice. At the end of his talk, he bowed slightly in bed to them.

"You don't need to apologize, for goodness' sake! You properly and honourably discharged your duty for your family." Senkishi took Eizo's right hand.

"I'm very sorry, Eizo-san. What do you think … shall I contact your sons?" Martin asked.

"Please don't," Eizo responded flatly with a frown. He looked disgusted with the question.

Martin recalled how Eizo had suffered from the blow of his family's refusal and tried to find words to comfort him. But he knew that no words would provide solace to him who had gone through such anguish. "Then, do you need anything?"

"No, nothing. But … you look like my son," said Eizo, the topic totally disconnected from what they were talking.

"Do I? I'm glad you think so."

Senkichi looked up at his son but kept his thoughts to himself.

"You're a hope … paragon and future of the Nikkei." The man in bed spoke to Martin hesitantly.

"No, I can't be. I don't merit that title."

Eizo deeply breathed out and looked to the other side. There was a short silence then Eizo set eyes on Martin again and he murmured as if he had attained enlightenment, "If there is some fear that we the human beings harbour, it is that it lies in our being alive, not in our death."

Martin was taken aback. As long as he remembered, Eizo had never spoken about his philosophy of life, mostly talked about his family, concentration camp and Japan, but the phrase sounded so thoroughly true as to what Eizo had undergone.

*

Eizo left the hospital after a week with a prescription for anti-depressants and an appointment with a psychiatrist. Through therapy, he learned that the shadow had been nothing but a

377

torment and eventually became free of its influence. He took a long time to comprehend that, but eventually he realized that the heavy load he had been carrying on his back for so many years was being lifted away.

He met occasionally with Martin and Senkichi, but the hard memories of the war and life in the camps that had simmered for years, no longer fired his conversation.

In the beginning of May, 1988, Eizo gazed at cherry blossoms in full bloom through the window of his room. He enjoyed seeing the flowers, sitting beside the window all day long. In the night, the cherry blossoms shone white, reflecting the lights from the houses behind the cherry tree. Japan and what had happened to him there now seemed to be far, far away like a scene in a fairy tale. Four days later, he watched the cherry blossoms fall as a rain of petals blown by the wind. He did not hear any remorse from his shadow and took it that he was disentangled from him.

In early August, Eizo became extremely exhausted—a fatigue that lasted for several weeks—and he found himself spending more and more time in bed, dozing and waking briefly to glance out the bedside window. The scenery looked hazy to him. Feeling chilly and shaky, despite the muggy weather, he covered himself with a bed sheet and closed his eyes. The image of the Coastal Range Mountains he had watched while crossing the Strait of Georgia to Vancouver Island, under a strikingly blue sky, upon arrival to Canada, came to his mind but that memory faded away quickly. His mouth was dry and his sight grew dim. Eizo held his sweaty hands in front of him and saw both hands shake like nothing could stop them. Then, next moment, he knew nothing.

The next day, Eizo's life ebbed away at age eighty-one.

According to Eizo's wishes, Martin and Senkichi cremated the body and took his ashes to the small Japanese cemetery on the hilltop overlooking the Village of Cumberland on Vancouver Island. Nearby was where Eizo had left his first footprints as a lumberjack in the mountain close to the village when he first had a hope for a good life in Canada.

Martin and Senkichi, after burying the ashes of Eizo and watching the tombstone erected to mark the site, began the long drive back to Vancouver. To pass the time they turned on the radio. In the news program, they heard that the Federal Government of Canada had formally apologized for the mistreatment of the Nikkei during the Second World War.

Epilogue

The Canadian Federal Government issued a formal apology to the Nikkei on September 22, 1988. The government offered $21,000 to each survivor of the camps, $12 million to the National Association of Japanese Canadians as a community fund, and Canadian Citizenship to be re-instated for those who were deported. Further to these symbolic redresses, $24 million created the Canadian Race Relations Foundation to avoid repeating the racially motivated discriminatory acts that had occurred. Financial compensation for internment and property confiscation was only awarded to living survivors, not heirs of those who had been affected. Seventy years later, the province of British Columbia made a formal apology on May 7, 2012, and seventy-one years later on September 25, 2013, so did the Vancouver City Council.

Works Consulted

Ken Adachi   *The Enemy That Never Was, A History of the Japanese Canadians*   (Toronto, McClelland and Stewart Limited, 1976)

Mitsuru Sinpo   *Ishi o Mote Owaruru Gotoku (Just as Driven Away with Stones, A History of the Japanese Canadians)*   (Toronto, Tairiku Jiho sha, The Continental Times, 1975)

Forrest E. La Violette   *The Canadian Japanese and World War II*   (Toronto, University of Toronto Press, 1948)

Ann Gomer Sunahara   *The Politics of Racism*   (Toronto, James Lorimer & Company Ltd., 1981)

E. D. Isenor, E. G. Stephens, D. E. Watson   *One Hundred Spirited Years, A History of Cumberland*   (British Columbia, Ptarmigan Press, 1988)

Ken Drushka   *Working in the Woods, A History of Logging on the West Coast*   (British Columbia, Harbour Publishing, 1992)

Richard Somerset Mackie   *Island Timber, A Social History of the Comox Logging Company, Vancouver Island* (British Columbia, Sono Nis Press, 2000)
Stephen Hume   *The Honour and Absurdity*   (British Columbia, The Vancouver Sun, November 9, 1990)

Eric Jamieson   *Photos recall life in Cumberland* (British Columbia, Islander Magazine, April 16, 1989)

Shigeru Hayashi   *Nippon no rekishi, Volume 25, Taiheiyo Senso, (A History of Japan, The Pacific War)*   (Tokyo, Chuokoron sha, 1979)

Cumberland Museum   Periodicals   Cumberland, British Columbia

Jodo Shinshu Honganji-ha   *San butsu ge (Praises of the Buddha)*

CBC News, September 22nd, 1988

The Federal Government of Canada   *Redress for Japanese Canadians, Eligibility and Application Information,* 1988

Unreleased interview tapes of the Issei and Nisei compiled by Maya Koizumi

Courtenay Museum   The Comox Argus   December 11, 1941/ April 16, 1942   Courtenay, British Columbia

Judy Hagen   *The sad removal of the Comox Valley's Japanese families*   The Comox Valley Echo   February 24, 2017